BEACH HOUSE CONFESSIONS

BEACH HOUSE
HOUSE
Confessions

KARA GORSKI

CONTENTS

Dedicated to beach chairs, bottomless flutes of Veuve Clicquot, and book-loving hearts everywhere—and to every woman who's dared to rewrite her story.

Seaside Secrets Beach Read Series

Welcome to Cape Henlopen—a vibrant small town on the Delaware shore where everyone knows one another, and no one knows quite everything.

The *Seaside Secrets Beach Read Series* follows exceptional women navigating friendship, family, love, and second chances, often while carrying truths they're not quite ready to reveal. While the books in this series share a setting—and several familiar faces—each story champions new heroines and stands on its own.

Start anywhere. Readers who love returning to the same town may enjoy reading the books in publication order for added depth, but every book is designed to be enjoyed independently.

Here, the next chapter is always waiting.

Other Books in the Series
Christmas Confessions

The life you have led doesn't need to be the only life you have.

-ANNA QUINDLEN

Prologue: April

Chapter 1

Bel Air Hills, Los Angeles

MEAGHAN IS THREE CHAMPAGNE GLASSES DEEP AND pulsing with adrenaline when she misses the first sign that her secret's been discovered. She's dedicated the last six months to meticulously planning every aspect of tonight—the grand ballroom at the Beverly Hills Hilton, DJ Calvin Harris on the decks, an unreleased Drake track, plates of Thai curried mussels and spicy sweet chili chicken wings served by Wolfgang Puck himself—not his staff, but the man in person—and the crème de la crème of Hollywood. Each element has been painstakingly selected to make this evening the ultimate Hollywood party as hundreds congregate to celebrate her daughter Bella's nineteenth birthday.

She mingles with a few guests and cozies up to the Vice President of Paramount Pictures, Lassiter Greene, a glass of champagne in each of her hands. She offers him one, "Time to celebrate." Hours before, she called Lassiter not only to extend a last-minute invitation for this evening's celebration but also to accept his offer for the lead role in his next film. One he assures her will be the studio's biggest blockbuster ever. *Naturally.*

"Your compensation demands are a little hard to swallow, Meaghan Jones," Lassiter remarks, knowing full well that as Hollywood's highest-paid actress for the past decade, her fee is set in stone. He takes a sip of his champagne.

"Looks like you can swallow just fine." She smiles and tips her glass in his direction. Lassiter's posse of studio executives encircles them, awkwardly joining their private party in the way stuffy corporate men always do. *Too many suits.* She scans the room behind them, watching her celebration play on like a flawlessly conducted symphony with Bella's sweet laughter as its chorus. Bella stands beneath the crystal chandelier, smiling among her friends and the A-lister guests who all spent months embarrassingly hustling for tonight's invitation.

Everyone's here. She smiles. Everyone, except Duncan. Her big-shot director husband is a no-show despite his incessant promises that he would attend. He called last week to explain that sandstorms had pushed the production schedule of his shoot in Morocco. *When will he ever get a handle on his schedule?* She shakes off the thought. *Does Bella even miss her father? I haven't thought of him once this evening until right now.*

She turns her focus back to the party when her phone buzzes in her pocket. She retrieves it, glancing at Duncan's name flashing across the screen. Heart racing, she opens his message:

"Wish I was there. Send my love to Bella." Another predictable letdown. *Does he even care?* Her fingers hover above the screen, tempted to type a reply. Filled with exasperation, she refrains.

"Who are you thinking of to play your leading man?" One of the suits brazenly asks. "Clooney? Bradley Cooper?" She listens to the men around her debate her options when Thorne

Cassidy catches her eye. He walks right behind Lassiter, looks Meaghan square on, and whispers, "We are screwed."

Is that what he said? She stares at Thorne, whom she's met only once previously, when he picked up his daughter from their house after a sleepover, a job he typically relegates to his ex-wife. He exudes a nervous energy as he crosses the room and lands at the bar, his eyes finally losing their lock on hers. She pauses to consider Thorne and his words but instantly forgets both when she's abruptly overrun by kids sprinting onto the dance floor enticed by Ed Sheeran's "Bad Habits."

And just like that, she misses it.

IT'S FAR TOO EARLY THE NEXT MORNING WHEN MEAGHAN is jolted awake. Her eyes flutter open to the soft morning light, but an uneasy feeling washes over her like a cold wave. The sensation isn't completely new; five years ago, she grappled with whether to close her once-celebrated restaurant, now buried under embarrassment and disappointment. *What if this morning brings another wave of disaster?* Her stomach knots at the thought. She reaches for her phone on the nightstand, instinctively scrolling through her Instagram feed to drown out the nagging anxiety.

The screen, far too bright for dawn, fills with fake friends tagging her in their posts, each one exquisitely documenting her party success. Her Hollywood acquaintances pretend to be her friends, but their relationships are empty. Will TMZ cover the highlights? *Of course they will.* Last night's success will be retold countless times today by national headlines and local gossips alike.

"Definitely not screwed," she says aloud to absolutely no one. But the celebration feels overshadowed; Duncan has yet again pulled a disappearing act.

Determined to shake off the weight of her unease, she rolls out of bed and slips into the edgy black camo lounge set she designed—a piece meant for the empowered woman she presents to the world. She grabs the *Moonlight Magnolias* script from her desk, whispering her lines as she glides down the hall. Bella sleeps soundly in her room, blissfully unaware of the storm brewing.

Meaghan heads downstairs and into the depths of the kitchen. Setting the script on the counter, she grabs a mug and puts the Nespresso on to brew. While she waits for her first steaming hot mug to fill, Meaghan stands at the pristine white quartz kitchen counter, her left hand twirling her hair through her fingers and brushing its ends against the side of her cheek, while she practices Belle Dixon's southern accent. "I find it amusing. Men are suppose' to be made out of steel or something." She repeats the line over and over, each time testing a new intonation, still unable to find the right one.

The sprinklers go off outside beyond the pool, jolting her from the Deep South back to her L.A. reality. She opens the fridge and pulls out a coconut LaCroix with one hand, places the script under her arm, grabs the coffee mug, and heads to the patio for her private morning read-through. The movie begins filming in three weeks.

As she opens the sliding glass door with her tush, a pit grows in her stomach. Duncan's shoes, jacket, messenger bag, and keys have been discarded onto the floor in a perfect trail leading to the couch. A plate with dried pasta sauce and half-eaten baguette sits on the large leather coffee table beside an empty stemless red wine glass. Chaos. He must have taken the last flight from Morocco yesterday. He's been on set, though it seems they must have wrapped early. She wonders if he stayed in a guest room last night to avoid waking her, or if he succumbed to a comfortable distraction in the arms of a younger woman again. *Don't go there,* she chastises herself, pushing the thought away.

She nestles into the pool-side chaise with her coffee and her script, choosing to forget Dunc and get to work instead. Which she does, uninterrupted for three hours straight. Line after line, recited over and over, until they're unforgettable. A successful morning for any overachiever. Promptly at 9 a.m., her cell rings. She knows exactly who is on the other end.

Meaghan picks up. "Good morning!"

"Buenos días, hot stuff."

Holly Fisher is Meaghan's agent, publicist, and right hand. More than two decades ago, Meaghan went from struggling starlet to star in a hot Hollywood minute, avoiding the dreaded casting couch known to occasionally launch a woman's career and almost always ruin her life. Holly discovered Meaghan when she attended an audition for a new sitcom, *Parker Street,* in an attempt to swoon the casting director to negotiate a movie deal for another actor. Three months earlier, Meaghan skipped out on the spring of her high school senior year in Cottonwood Falls, Kansas bound for Hollywood. So instantly impressed by her unavoidably noticeable talent, Holly secured her a spot as an extra on the show, which revolved around four twenty-something women starting their lives in New York City and sharing a one-bedroom studio in Greenwich Village on Parker Street. When one of the female leads ended up in rehab two days before shooting the pilot, Holly sweet-talked that director into casting Meaghan in her role for the pilot. The other actor's movie deal never got negotiated. The show became an overnight success and Meaghan became America's sweetheart. Holly has been calling her at nine every morning since, except Sundays.

"Have you heard any talk about last night?" Meaghan asks. She knows the party was a smash. But she craves hearing what a great time everyone had and, subsequently, how very much they love her. It's her oxygen.

Holly delivers the Page Six headline as if reading a script. "It may have been the dangling crystal chandeliers that lit up the dance floor, but Meaghan Jones lit up all of Beverly Hills last evening." She shrieks. Then Holly redirects their conversation to upcoming events. "I'm calling to let you know the promo shoot for *Moonlight Magnolias* will be next week in between your on-set read throughs. Wednesday at 11 a.m."

"Got it." She puts Holly on speaker so she can put the appointment into her work calendar on her phone. "We start shooting in three weeks. One problem, however. I cannot get Ms. Dixon's accent right. I keep trying, but still nothing."

"It will come."

She sets her script on the table beside her pool chaise. "Hey, did you speak to Thorne Cassidy last night?"

"Who is Thorne Cassidy?"

"He's the guy who looked like he walked right out of the 1980s. White double-breasted jacket and matching pants with a mint-green tee underneath. No socks with his loafers."

"Right, I saw him," Holly says.

"He's the dad of a girl who graduated with Bella last spring. I think he's a coach somewhere local. Anyway, he whispered something mysterious to me last night, when he passed me. Very strange." She sips the last of her coconut LaCroix. "I wondered if maybe you met him? What you thought of him?"

"What did he say?"

"Well, he didn't say. But he whispered, 'We are screwed,'" she says.

"Hmm. Well, I avoided him all night. Probably because of that outfit. The poor suit selection is burned into my brain like a male celebrity's unfortunate penis pic on his Instagram story … how could someone knowingly put it out there?"

Meaghan spews LaCroix like a sprinkler. This is what makes Holly truly invaluable. She delivers brutal honesty every time. "Jesus, Holly!"

"What?"

"Okay, well, I'm sure Thorne Cassidy is just trying to get my attention." *And he has for some reason.* She hears a knock. "I've got to go. Someone's at the front door."

The knocking quickly becomes heavy pounding. The person on the other side successfully navigated past the front gate guards, indicating they must be friendly, despite the fact that their now incessant banging is not. *Please do not wake up Bella!* She screams her plea in her head. She peers through the small peephole. Stunned, she swings open the massive wooden French doors.

The knocking ceases abruptly. Staring at Meaghan are six beefy men in black sunglasses and navy-blue jackets, the initials *FBI* printed in bright yellow across their chests. The man at the center of their pack flashes his badge.

"Agent Hendrix. FBI. Is Mr. Duncan Jones home?"

She takes a step back. "Um, yes. Well, I think he is home. I haven't actually seen him, but I am pretty sure he is here." Her nervousness grabs hold of her tongue and doesn't let go. "Let's go with yes. Duncan Jones is home." Her eyes scan the agents. "Is there a problem … Agent … Hendrix?

Agent Hendrix ignores her question. "May we come in?" he asks as the agents push their way through the front door.

"I … guess so?" The men enter in single file and make their way into the large open foyer of the sprawling home.

"Can you please get Mr. Jones?" Agent Hendrix asks politely. Then he leans down to meet her at eye level and says, "Assuming he is in fact home."

She takes another step backwards when something behind her catches her attention. Duncan stands at the top of the staircase that leads down into the foyer. Instead of his usual morning running shorts and tee, Duncan wears khaki pants, a gray quarter-zip with a button-down shirt underneath, and Veja sneakers. He smiles and confidently descends the massive staircase while slipping his wallet into his back pocket and lands at the bottom next to the agents and Meaghan. *He's ready to go.*

"Mr. Jones." Agent Hendrix pulls a folded piece of paper from his jacket pocket. "We have a warrant for your arrest for conspiracy to commit bribery and fraud and a second warrant to search the premises." He hands the papers to Duncan. The other agents disperse. In search of what, she has no idea.

"Whaaat?" She scowls in disbelief. Three agents pass by Duncan and head up the stairs. She wants to grab them each by their elbows, pull them to the couch, sit them down, and interrogate them herself.

Instead, she runs in front of them and tries to stop them with a verbal warning. "My daughter is sleeping up there."

"Mrs. Jones, you'll need to step back and let them do their job," Agent Hendrix says.

"What job? What is their job?" He offers no explanation.

She turns to Duncan. "What the hell is going on, Dunc?"

Duncan says nothing. He shrugs his shoulders and his eyes circle back to the front door, avoiding her gaze.

"Please turn around," Agent Hendrix tells Duncan, who hands the warrants to her and obliges.

"It's going to be okay," Duncan finally says.

"You're putting him in cuffs?" She shouts her disbelief.

Bella, blurry-eyed, confused, and in rumpled hot-pink pajamas, runs down the stairs in time to see her father, his wrists shackled behind his back like a common criminal, escorted from their home and into an unmarked black Chevy Tahoe. Meaghan wants to vomit as she watches Bella dissolve into tears.

"Daddy? I thought you were in Morocco. What is happening?" Bella runs toward him. She catches Bella's wrist and reels her into her arms, holding her tightly to shield her from what transpires before them.

Duncan finally looks Meaghan in the eyes. "I'm so sorry, Meggie. Bella," he catches her staring at him, "I love you, honey." The door to the Tahoe closes. The sincerity in his voice pierces through the chaos all around them.

"For what?" She has no clue.

Agent Hendrix stays behind with the men at the house.

"Can anyone tell me what is going on?" she asks, standing in the living room now as men swarm every inch of their home, weaving from the kitchen through the bedrooms, to the basement and theatre viewing room.

"Your husband is charged with conspiracy to bribe College representatives to secure your daughter's placement at the Southern California College," Agent Hendrix says, catching Bella's attention with his words.

She freezes. She can't take her eyes off Agent Hendrix as she processes his words. A sick feeling grows in the bottom of her stomach.

"Okay, that is ridiculous," Bella interjects. "I got into SouthCal myself. Dad had nothing to do with it." Bella speaks directly to Agent Hendrix, stepping right in front of him and getting in his face. "I took the exams. I did all the extracurriculars and volunteer work, I submitted my own written essays, and I earned a 4.2 GPA in STEM! My father did nothing. Honestly, what else was there for him to even do?" Meaghan knows that Bella isn't boastful or spoiled. She is wicked smart. Bella started fixing her friends' skinned knees as a toddler and has wanted to be a doctor ever since. So, in seventh grade, Bella figured out how to fast track herself into a pre-med college program by taking certain AP high school classes. But right now might not be the appropriate time for Bella to relay those details to Agent Hendrix.

"Of course you did, honey. We know you did!" She takes Bella by the arm and leads her to sit down on the sofa.

"I can't tell you any more details at the moment," Agent Hendrix explains, brushing off Bella's teenage confrontation.

"I'm calling Mack," she tells Bella. Mack Harper is her personal attorney. His Midwestern upbringing won her over in her search for a talent lawyer years ago. Mack keeps his salt-of-the-earthiness sufficiently submerged below the tough-talking, shrewd exterior he exudes nearly 24-7. Mack's cunning legal maneuverings catapulted him to the top of L.A.'s best lawyer list, fifteen years running. But once he opened a door to her, Mack became Bella's Uncle Mack, uniting quite possibly the only Midwesterners in L.A. as family.

Her face unlocks her phone, and she presses Mack's name. "Morning, Meaghan! I'm surprised to hear from you so early!

Look, I know you want to go over the *Moonlight Magnolias* contract, but we can do that tomorrow. I mean, we had such a great time last night! You guys recovering?"

"We're not. That's why I'm calling," she says, stroking Bella's long blonde hair. Bella sits bent forward on the couch, elbow on knees, scrolling through her phone. Meaghan stops and turns her back to Bella, taking a few steps away in order to speak more privately with Mack. "Listen, I've got a problem. Any chance you can come over right away?"

"I can get there in a few hours. What's going on?"

"There are six FBI agents swarming the house and grounds. They've arrested Dunc. Something about bribing College officials at SouthCal? I don't know any more than that." *If I keep saying that out loud will it be true?*

Mack's voice grows tense on the other end of the phone. "Change of plans. I'll be there in thirty." He starts to hang up, but his lawyering takes over. "Meaghan, do not say anything to them."

"I wouldn't know what to say even if I wanted to."

The agents dig through drawers, closets, kitchen cabinets. They check the main house, the pool house, the garage that houses Duncan's Lamborghinis. Nothing is untouched. But as far as she can see, everything is put back where it belongs. The agents are respectful of her home. This isn't the movies. Plus, they know she'll sue them otherwise.

Mack arrives in thirty minutes as promised. He always does what he says, a quality she feels most people lack these days, which makes her appreciate him even more. He speaks with Agent Hendrix first. He won't reveal any details other than those he has already told her, except one. Duncan's current location. He will be arraigned today in federal court. Mack sets up his command post off the kitchen in the living room, where Duncan's pasta plate still sits on the leather coffee table, a reminder of his entitled sloppiness. Meaghan, who already gave the housekeeper the day off post-party, picks up Dunc's mess and loads everything into the dishwasher.

Two hours later, the FBI agents announce their departure. They leave with everyone's laptops, iPads, and phones, all of the files and papers from Duncan's office, and the messenger bag he left lying on the floor last night. She watches them pile their loot into boxes and put the boxes in the back of the FBI van. She counts the devices and Mack writes down the inventory of every single electronic device they've taken.

An hour after that, Holly arrives with new cell phones for everyone. She joins Mack at his command post and the two work to discern the details of the morning's events. Holly, who plays a double role as her publicist, feels out the media, and Mack focuses on getting any information he can from his contacts within the local police and the FBI. His partner JB Donahue, the lead criminal defense attorney at Mack's firm, is working his connections as well, from home. Bella retreats to her room with her new cell. Meaghan, impatient for information, sits with Holly and Mack, constantly refreshing her X and Instagram.

Somehow, the news has yet to break. But it will and soon.

AT SIX IN THE EVENING, DUNCAN SLINKS THROUGH THE front door, wordless. Meaghan, Mack, and Holly stare at him like he's forgotten his next line. They wait for him to say anything. Finally, he does.

"Waverly posted my bail." Waverly Shepard is Mack's attorney. In Hollywood, everyone has their own.

"How did he get it posted so quickly?" Mack asks the obvious legal question, and Meaghan wonders the exact same thing.

"He just did." Duncan spouts mistruths like a dolphin spouts water, in regular intervals to keep breathing. Another indication that Dunc, and Waverly too, were prepared for the FBI this morning.

"Okay, Dunc, you need to explain what is going on," she presses, her voice trembling with urgency. "Why were you dressed and ready this morning? Were you expecting the FBI?" She twirls her hair, her nerves manifesting in anxious gestures. "We need to know everything you know. We need the truth, not whatever half-truths you and Waverly are cooking up."

Mack slides in between her and Duncan. "Actually, let's not do that yet." She understands Mack's job is to protect her. She instantly realizes that Mack isn't sure what Duncan will say, only that whatever he says could potentially put her at risk.

As Duncan opens his mouth to either answer or evade Mack's instructions, Bella flies down the staircase and into the kitchen where everyone is gathered. Her face red and puffy from tears, anger, and embarrassment. "I'll tell you what happened. You two bribed my way into SouthCal." Bella clenches her fists, punching them toward the ground for emphasis while screaming at them both. "Why would you do that? It may not be on the internet yet, but all my friends are talking about it. I'm trending on Snapchat!"

Mack and Holly take their cue and exit onto the back patio by the pool.

"They are calling me a fraud. Everyone doubts me because of you." Bella's words hit her like a slap across the face. "Do you even think I'm capable on my own? I've put in so much work to be successful on my own. Now I'll only be known as 'Duncan Jones's daughter ... a total cheat.'"

Meaghan glances at Duncan, desperate. "Wait a minute. I'm not sure what your father has done. But I can guarantee you that I played no part in your father's choices. I'm right here, fighting to help you!" She walks toward her daughter, who takes a step back.

"Seems like a weak fight," Bella shoots back, wiping away fresh tears with her sleeve. "You think I'm not good enough? You don't believe I can make it without your help?" Her voice cracks as she steps back, shaking her head in disbelief. "I'm a disgrace now, and it's all because you needed your egos stroked!"

"Bella!" Meaghan's heart fractures. She reaches out again toward Bella; this time, her hands shake. Bella pulls her shoulder back, escaping her touch. "You could never be a disappointment! We love you so much. You must know that."

"Love?" Bella laughs bitterly. "What does love mean when you're out here paying off people to take my college entrance exams? You think that earns my respect? Look at my notifications. 'Your family's a mess,' 'you've never earned anything,' 'you'll never be anything but a spoiled kid!'"

Meaghan's chest tightens. The weight of Bella's loathing is so thick in the air, she struggles to breathe. She can't find the right words. Nothing she says dissuades Bella's disdain. "Honey, I've never seen you so angry." *With me. I have never seen you so angry with me.* "You're scaring me." She shoots a glance toward Duncan. "Dunc, please tell our daughter I had nothing to do with this."

"Your mother's right. She did nothing," Dunc confirms. And then, as if he can't help himself, he adds, "Well, almost nothing."

"See? You can't even own up to it, Mom!" Bella turns on her father, eyes blazing. "You two did this to me. I can't stand being here!"

Holly runs back into the room, Mack trailing behind her. She waves her hand in the air to silence everyone and grab their attention while staring down at her phone. "You guys. Holy shit. Sorry, Bella." Meaghan doesn't mind the profanity; the situation warrants it. "They arrested twenty-three parents this morning at the exact same time. All charged with participating in this conspiracy. Ten parents in California. The rest are scattered across the country. The press is calling the scandal 'Sinful Admissions.' It's just breaking."

"Sinful Admissions." Meaghan repeats the crime out loud. She should be worried about the immediate impact on her career, but the only thing she cares about is how Bella will react.

"It's kinda catchy," Mack says, trying to lighten the mood. Meaghan and Holly exchange an eye roll. Meaghan lands a shoulder punch.

"Not helpful," Holly says.

"This is going to ruin me, Dunc! What have you done? Twenty-three parents," Meaghan muses. As she does, Thorne's words light up in her mind. "Who?" she asks Holly. "Who else did they arrest. Do they mention names?"

"No names yet, which is great, because no one knows about Dunc." Duncan glares at her, and Holly brushes him off. Duncan Jones is no match for Holly; he never has been. Meaghan will listen to Holly over Duncan every day of the week and twice on Sundays.

She turns on her heels and throws a dagger stare at Duncan. "Dunc, do you know Thorne Cassidy?"

"He's Lassie Cassidy's dad," Bella says. "I invited Lassie to my birthday party, and he brought her and hung out for a while, which was pretty weird. What does Lassie Cassidy's dad have to do with anything?" Bella asks.

Duncan lifts his head, and Meaghan turns to him.

"You know Thorne," she says. "Was he arrested this morning?"

He bites his lower lip. "Probably."

Bella tilts her head as she realizes the implications for Lassie, too. "You both are totally not getting it. This isn't a game. This is my life!" Bella explodes, her frustration boiling over. "This is going to ruin me! I'll be the spoiled girl who fell from grace. The world is already turning against me!" She grits her teeth, trying to hold onto control as her voice trembles. "What did you think would happen?"

As her phone buzzes, Bella checks her notifications again, her expression shifting sharply from anger to despair. "Look! Another direct message!" She shows it to her mother and Mack. "They're saying I must be thankful for your money since it bought my future for me!"

"Don't read those!" Meaghan pleads. "They're not true. You know the kind of person you are inside."

"No, I don't. Do I really know who I am when I only got here because of your mistakes?" Bella hurls back, the tears flowing freely now. "I can't take this! I'm out of here," she says. "I don't want anything to do with you two. I can't stand to be with you right now. I'm going back to the dorms."

"Wait, you can't leave, Bella. We're in the middle of this thing," Meaghan pleads. "We need to figure this out together." She feels ill again. What if her daughter leaves now and she never comes back? *I can't be left again.*

Mack appeals to her, too. "Bella, come on, stay while we get a better handle on things. We have no idea what is waiting for you out there."

"I need to think." Bella's voice wavers. "I can't stay here. I need my own space, free from any guilt trips." Bella points to her parents. "You have destroyed my life. I am a total joke now. Everything I have worked for, you two have ruined!" She walks over to the door and picks up her bag. "I don't want to see you ever again!"

"Bella, please don't do this!" Meaghan panics. Fear engulfs her. She rushes to the front door where Bella stands. "We're a family! We need to stick together! We only have each other. You can't walk out like this."

"Count me out of this family. I'm ashamed to be connected to you." Bella picks up her bag, flings the door open, and glares back one last time.

"Bella!" Meaghan reaches for her. Bella is her greatest love. She will break wide open if she leaves. Bella jerks her arm away, stepping outside. The door slams shut, sending reverberations through Meaghan's heart.

Meaghan stands paralyzed, disbelief settling over her.

"Shit." Holly walks over to Meaghan and puts her arm around her.

After a heartbeat, Meaghan's sorrow explodes into anger. She storms toward Duncan, her voice rising. "Look what you've done!"

Duncan sinks against the kitchen island, the weight of reality settling in.

She wants to hit him until he feels as bad as she does. Instead, she collapses into a white slipcovered club chair. Mack and Holly resume their seats on the couch across from her.

"I'll keep my eye on her," Mack reassures her. She nods her gratitude.

Duncan scoots his bar stool back from the kitchen island and stands up. "I need to make a couple of calls."

"Of course you do." She shoots an icy glare in his direction. "What did you mean I did 'almost nothing'?"

Dunc walks toward the staircase. When he reaches it, he turns around to her and says, "You'll figure it out, Meggie ..."

Meaghan's heart races at the implication; the donation check flashes in her mind. *Everyone makes donations to colleges, and no one gets arrested for making them. They're completely legal. How can any of this be illegal?*

Mack interrupts, "We are skipping this conversation for now." He turns back to her, "I need to dig deeper first; then you guys can talk."

"Fine," she agrees reluctantly, her hands still trembling. Duncan heads upstairs to his office.

She scans her phone in search of the story. It takes thirty minutes for the outlets to begin revealing the names of those arrested. Soon after, the TMZ headlines include Duncan's name and Meaghan's. Every other headline in town carries the same story. "Hollywood Power Couple Meaghan & Duncan Jones Caught in Sinful Admissions." The world now knows their family drama.

Tomorrow, Sinful Admissions will dominate front pages across the country, a topic for every dinner table.

Thorne was right. They are screwed.

Meaghan closes her newsfeed and dials the only person not on her payroll who always answers her calls. Palmer answers immediately.

Chapter 2

Alexandria, Virginia

PALMER'S DISAGREEMENT WITH HER HUSBAND, MILES, has gone on long enough. It's time to do what she always does. Apologize.

She spends the morning whipping up Miles's favorite meal, Blissed Out Chocolate Cake. She invites him to come home early that afternoon to talk, something they haven't been doing in nearly a month. Instead, they've been dodging each other—not even midday texts or lunch break phone calls. Their disagreement over their eldest son's future has ballooned with each passing day.

She keeps their quarrel to herself, embarrassed their marriage could falter, if even a little. She hasn't even told Meaghan, although since Duncan's arrest three weeks ago, they've discussed little else besides the ensuing chaos.

Miles shows up right at three o'clock at the back porch kitchen door, soaking wet from riding his bike home from his office. It's literally raining buckets outside, but Miles made it home, torrential downpour be damned. He throws back the hood of his jacket, shaking off the water it carries, as he walks up the steps of their covered porch.

Palmer takes a long look at her husband through the window. *Damn it. He's hot even when I'm mad at him.* His wavy flaxen hair, deep-brown eyes, and golden skin make her quiver. She's spent weeks being furious at Miles for his selfishness splitting their family apart. For his inability to see beyond his own ego, pushing their son away and making her wonder if she truly wanted to be married to this Miles. He's made her question everything she knew about their lives together over the past twenty years. *Until last night.* Now only guilt consumes her.

The door creaks as Miles opens it. She hears him hang his jacket on the hook in the mud room and kick off his shoes. When he enters the kitchen, she hands him a towel and then steps back, fidgeting with the corner of her white apron. A large streak of chocolate cake batter runs down its front. Her stomach spins like she's arrived at the top of the roller coaster and sits peering down in anticipation of the very steep fall that's coming. She's about to go over the edge. Will he catch her?

"Thanks," he says, smiling softly at her. A simple smile can be a powerful drug. It's the one he wore when he asked her to marry him. The one he wore when each of their boys was born. The one she's seen ever since they met at Princeton in the fall of her freshman year. Except she's been deprived of that smile for weeks.

She throws her hands up in the air, "Miles, this is so stupid." She reaches for him. The tough, rigid exterior he's put on for nearly a month melts the moment she touches his arm.

"It really is." He pulls her closer, wraps his arms around her. The distance between them dissolves like salt into a pot of boiling water, quickly gone. Miles kisses her, softly at first and then, after a few moments, very deeply.

She reciprocates. It feels amazing to have their mouths intertwined again. After a few moments, she pulls back. *How much should I explain?*

"I love you, Miles. I am so sorry. This is all my fault." She knows this isn't entirely true and wonders if Miles knows it, too. But after last night, she is willing to shoulder the blame if it means getting her life back with Miles. Miles places a single finger over Palmer's lips, and she stops talking. He kisses her again. Every cell in her body lights up like a sparkler struck inside her. Miles takes her face in his hand, leans into her, and kisses the edges of her mouth. She can feel how hard he's grown. When he stops, she comes back up for air, interrupting the moment again.

"Aiden wants to earn his own stripes. It is no reflection on you or how much he loves you and looks up to you."

"I know," Miles says, avoiding her attempt at discussion. He gently turns her head to one side in his hand and kisses down her neck. Miles doesn't want to talk about Aiden, and she knows why. Talking about your kids will always render a hot and steamy kitchen utterly frigid. But she can't help herself. She needs to clear the air. She couldn't risk losing him … forever. She puts both of her hands on Miles's chest and pushes him gently.

"We have to talk about this first," she says.

Miles's hands drop to his side. He adjusts his pants, which remain perfectly tented. He sits down at a bar stool at the kitchen bar. "Okay," he says reluctantly. "You go."

Palmer pulls out the bar stool beside him and sits down beside him.

"Aiden worked hard for this opportunity. I want him to feel he not only has our permission, but our encouragement to take it."

This feels monumental. Six weeks ago, Aiden informed them that his super-famous architecture professor at the University of Virginia, Professor Ellison Abernathy, had selected him to be his summer intern at his private design firm. A prize coveted among all residential architecture students and a particular honor for Aiden because he is the youngest student to ever be selected.

She couldn't have been prouder of Aiden. The experience could launch Aiden's career far past anything his father has accomplished, which is wild success. Miles couldn't have been more offended. He could not understand why Aiden would want anything other than to continue working with him at his firm.

Miles grabs her hands. "Aiden will do what Aiden will do. It's his choice. It's a good choice."

Whoa. Too easy? The ease feels unsettling, How can weeks of endless standoff be reconciled so effortlessly?

He glances at the chocolate cake sitting on a marble cake plate in the center of the kitchen island. "Is that what I think it is?"

She grins slyly. "Maybe." If there's one thing that can seduce Miles, bringing him to his knees with desire, besides her standing naked in front of him, which she predicts will be happening very soon, it's her legendary blissed out chocolate cake, with its layers of pillowy chocolate between an espresso buttercream icing.

"You really are sorry, Dr. Harding." No one outside a courtroom or her office refers to Palmer as Dr. Harding, Ph.D.

Except for Miles when he wants to woo her and Meaghan when showing her off to Hollywood.

She slips her arms underneath his, stands on her toes, and leans into him. "Yes, I am really sorry," she whispers in his ear and then bites it tenderly. A fire stirs within her. Being in Miles's arms makes her entire body ache for him, even after all these years.

"Me, too," Miles says, slowly unbuttoning her blouse. He fills his hands with her bare breasts. Goosebumps erupt where his fingers graze her skin. Sparks shoot through her body. The anticipation alone is lustful.

"Miles," she moans.

He stops. "No," she cries instinctively. She aches for more of him. Every kiss ignites a longing she thought had dimmed, awakening desires that had been buried in frustration.

"I need you," he tells her and finishes undressing Palmer with ravenous haste. "I can't live without you." She tugs at his belt buckle until it's unfastened. He lays her over the kitchen table. They cannot control their desire. Too many weeks have passed. She lets out an ethereal moan, and Miles follows as the two become one again. Heat replacing the cold tension that had consumed them. Pure rapture.

They fall to the hardwood kitchen floor, sweaty and consumed, backs leaning against the kitchen island.

"Oh my God," she says catching her breath. "I think that's the best sex we've ever had."

Laughing softly, he puts his arm around her, and she nestles onto his chest. "We should not speak to each other for another month. It could be worth it," he says.

"Not an option," she responds.

He looks around the kitchen. "We need some of that cake." She rises and returns with two slices of chocolate cake perfectly served on their silver-banded wedding china. They inhale both slices.

He says, "I know it's the same blissed out chocolate cake you always make, but somehow it's the very best one."

"Moist, creamy, and coffee-laced." She smiles coyly. She sets her plate down and nuzzles her head on his chest, again. She wants to stay here forever.

Miles has other plans for her. He stands up bare naked, grabs her hand, and pulls her into their bedroom.

They spend the rainy spring evening making love in their master suite with tapered candles dripping onto the dresser and nightstands and Van Morison playing on Alexa, this time tenderly reacquainting themselves with every inch of one another and falling asleep in each other's arms. For weeks, she's worried that this disagreement could be the end of their marriage. Now, Palmer is certain of two things. She will never tell Miles about what happened last night with Sanford Banks in her office. And Miles is never, ever leaving.

AT SEVEN THE NEXT MORNING, SHE WAKES TO A BUZZing alarm clock and the heavenly scent of fresh-brewed French roast coffee. When she opens her eyes, she spies her favorite mug filled to the brim with a splash of half-and-half sitting on her nightstand.

God, I love him, she thinks as she picks up the mug. Then she shuffles across the hardwoods and into their en suite bath. She showers, drains the mug, dresses for work, and makes her way to the kitchen.

"Good morning," she says softly to Miles, who already sits at the breakfast nook in the kitchen with his coffee and the *Washington Post*. She kisses him once and then makes her way to the kitchen island.

"A very good morning, indeed, Dr. Harding." He raises a mischievous eyebrow. Flashes of yesterday afternoon rush through Palmer's mind.

Miles is dressed for work in a navy suit with his lucky sunshine yellow tie and a pair of white kicks, which are his usual attire to bike to his office in Old Town, the historic neighborhood of Alexandria where the cobblestone streets are the very ones George Washington once traversed. He discards the *Post*, downs the last gulp of coffee left in his mug, stands up, and moves toward Palmer, who begins to prepare breakfast, gathering cereal, milk, bread, and butter from the cupboards and refrigerator.

She glows a smile at him. "You ready for today?" He meets with Robert Duvall at 4 p.m. to present the plans he's designed to renovate Mr. Duvall's guest home at his 362-acre estate, Byrnley, in The Plains, Virginia, an hour west of town. Miles has designed and built homes for celebrities, politicians, and local Alexandria families for the past two decades, making him one of the most sought-after residential architects on the Eastern Seaboard. His greatest masterpiece, however, is their beloved beach cottage on the Delaware coast in Cape Henlopen. The Hyacinth, their name for the cottage, is so impressive that *Architectural Digest* featured the home as a companion piece when Miles was first ranked one of the top forty architects under forty.

"After last night, I am ready for anything." He approaches her from behind at the counter and nuzzles his lips into the softness of her neck. He sweeps her hair to the side, kissing her neck, and she feels the heat in her body rise again.

"I'm glad we're back," he whispers in her ear. "I really missed you."

She turns around and kisses him. Their bodies pull toward each other like magnets. They kiss long and slow for several minutes. She understands where he's trying to take this, but she's got too much work on her mind this morning. She's spending the day preparing with her client for trial testimony in two weeks.

"Me too. I missed you more than you can imagine." She wraps her arms around his neck and kisses him sweetly. "Can I get a continuance? I have to get to the office."

Miles plants one last insatiable kiss. "Okay. Continuance granted. But only until tonight."

She gathers herself. "Great, we will reconvene this evening. Although I do have a five o'clock FaceTime happy hour with Meaghan, but I'm guessing it may not be too happy given everything that's going on." She gently slaps his tush, causing him to jump back to his seat at the table. She notices an odd grin on his face as he sits down.

"What?" she asks.

"Nothing."

"Miles, there's something wrong. I can see it on your face."

"It's nothing," he says and picks up the *Washington Post*, placing it squarely in front of him. "There's nothing on my face."

Bewildered, Palmer skips nagging him in an effort to keep their renewed rhythm going. She slathers two slices of toast with raspberry preserves and places them neatly on a plate in front of Miles, who has poured another cup of coffee alongside his morning paper.

"Tonight, we can celebrate what I'm certain will be your success this afternoon with Mr. Duvall by ordering fried oyster po'boys and onion rings from Northside 10," Palmer says.

"Sounds … perfect," he says with a slight hesitation that catches her attention, again.

"Miles," she says. The aching pit in her stomach is gone, but something between them still doesn't feel quite right. *Does he know?*

His eyes remain glued to the newspaper despite her standing at his side. "Honey, there's something I should tell you."

"Morning, guys." Quinn, their fair-haired younger son, inexplicably taller than anyone in the family, walks into the kitchen with his school backpack, baseball duffle bag, and an empty bowl that Palmer assumes previously held last night's blissed out chocolate cake topped with ice cream.

She turns around. "Hi, Quinnie," she says greeting him with an embrace. "I thought I heard you come in around eleven last night. You were so late getting home!" Quinn hugs his mother. "Sorry I didn't get up. I was nearly sleeping."

"Morning, Quinn. How was practice yesterday?" Miles asks. Quinn pitches for his high school baseball team, and Miles is an assistant coach. He's coached Quinn and his teammates since little league. Yesterday, he let the head coach know he was going to have to work late that evening and miss practice.

"Practice was fine. Sorry you had to work late, Dad." Quinn joins his father at the breakfast nook. "It's going around. I met Liam after practice to wrap up a joint presentation we're doing in Personal Finance class. It's due next week. Obviously, we just started."

Palmer rolls her eyes. Despite her best intentions, she's raised two of the world's best procrastinators. "Let me know if you two need any help. You know, I'm pretty good at these things."

Quinn takes a turn rolling his eyes. "I might have heard that somewhere."

Palmer kisses the top of his head and hands him a bowl of Cheerios with sliced bananas and honey. "Have you talked with Aiden?"

She notices Miles flinch when Aiden's name is mentioned, although only slightly. *An open wound still a bit too raw.*

"He texted me last night. I guess crew is pretty intense this season with the new coach at UVA."

Palmer marvels at what good friends her sons turned out to be. She spent years thinking they might never speak to each other after the wrestling matches she witnessed between them. But somehow they ended up sharing friends and being friends. Although Aiden is two years older than Quinn and in college, the boys talk daily, and sometimes more than that.

"He said his classes are a breeze," Quinn adds. "I'm so jealous."

Miles stands up to leave. "I've gotta head out. I'm going to be late!" He stuffs the last bite of toast into his mouth, then tousles Quinn's hair. "See you at practice later this afternoon, buddy."

She places her hand on his. "What do you need to tell me?"

"It can wait." He places his mug and empty plate in the sink and grabs her with one arm around her waist, sweeping her into one last embrace. "And I'll see you tonight." He kisses her sweetly and throws her a wink.

Quinn looks away and shakes his head, "You guuuuys!" He cringes at the flagrant romance between his parents. Did he detect their romance has been MIA these past few weeks? Unlikely. Quinn is so busy with school and baseball, he's hardly ever home. Now, the romance has returned. Her world is right again.

"Have a good day! Love you guys." Miles climbs onto his bike and rides out the driveway with sun beaming above him. The storm has passed.

PALMER SITS IN THE HOT SEAT OF A MOCK TRIAL, HER heart pumping as Sanford Banks, a managing partner at the law firm of Banks, Brighton & Smith, drills her with questions that the opposing side will ask next week in court. He has hired her as their star economic expert witness in the largest false advertising case he has ever tried. Failure is not an option. The room buzzes with tension; five associate lawyers hunch over their notes, their eyes fixed on Palmer as she struggles to hold her focus.

She remembers their first meeting fifteen years ago at an American Bar Association mixer at the Willard Hotel lobby bar in Washington, D.C. She instantly knew Sanford and Miles would hit it off, their personalities were similar despite their professions being different. So she invited Sanford and his wife, Cinnamon, to join them for dinner out. The two couples have been having dinner once a month since. Until five months ago, when Cinnamon told Sanford she had fallen in love with their landscaper, someone she claims spends more time at their house each week than Sanford spends in an entire year. Sanford responded as he always does when his personal life hits a bump, by burying his head in his work.

But this afternoon, the weight of unresolved emotions floods the air; heavier than the high-stakes queries flying at her.

Two nights ago, after wrapping up a long prep session accompanied by take-out Mongolian beef and dumplings from Mie Wah in the West End, Sanford kissed Palmer in her office. The kiss felt amazing. And then it didn't. Everything she had spent weeks questioning—if she really knew who Miles was anymore and whether their relationship could endure or even if it should—came into crystal-clear focus. That's the moment she decided she needed to apologize and end her argument with Miles.

As Sanford propels forward with pointed questions, Palmer's phone buzzes, shattering her concentration. "Sorry about that," she murmurs, fumbling to silence her ringer. But a wave of dread washes over her when she sees the name "Frances Lindemann" flash across her screen. Frances is Liam's mom and has been Miles's executive assistant for the past thirteen years. She never calls during the day. A sick feeling punches her in the gut. *Are the kids safe?*

She looks up at the room full of lawyers who are paying her 650 dollars an hour. "I'm so sorry. I need to take this." Flushed and uneasy around Sanford anyway today, she excuses herself into the hallway. She grabs the corner of her suit blazer, running its edge through her fingers, and answers her cell. "Hello?"

"Palmer? It's Frances." Palmer hears the trembling in Frances's voice. "You need to come to the office immediately. Something's wrong with Miles."

Palmer feels the earth shift underneath her in slow motion. "What do you mean something's wrong?" Frances sobs loudly on the other end. "Frances, what happened?"

"He collapsed!" Frances mutters through her tears. "He's not conscious, Palmer. We can't wake him up."

Her heart races. The adrenaline kicks her into autopilot. "I'm leaving right now." She hangs up. She returns to the room where

Sanford and his army of associates wait. "I'm so sorry, I have to go." She looks down at the materials she's gathering, avoiding eye contact with Sanford. "Something is wrong with my husband."

A stunned silence envelops the room. "Of course," Sanford replies.

She nods and leaves the room. Sanford follows her into the hallway. "Palmer, wait." His eyes search hers. "Is Miles okay?"

Palmer hesitates, guilt and vulnerability battling within her. "I don't know. He collapsed at his office. He's not conscious. I need to go."

"Go. I'll handle everything here. I ... Let me know ..." Sanford stumbles all over himself in a way that he never does. She doesn't have the time or the desire to deal with him.

IT TAKES PALMER FIFTEEN MINUTES IN AN UBER TO NAVI-gate through the one-way streets of D.C. to reach Miles's office in Old Town, Alexandria. Frances meets her at the door, her eyes puffy and wet.

"He was in the conference room with two junior architects, going over the Duvall presentation for this afternoon. They said he stopped writing mid-sentence. He couldn't move his right arm anymore. His words slurred into a jumbled mess. Then he slumped over in his big leather chair."

"Oh my God." Palmer nearly drowns in panic. "Where is he now?"

"Still in the conference room. The paramedics arrived a minute ago." Frances takes Palmer to the back of the office. Everyone is gathered outside the conference room, where Miles lies on the floor tethered to blinking machines making obnoxious noises, surrounded by four rescue workers speaking in code. A gurney and several black bags filled with medical equipment are strewn about the room, transforming the meeting place into an emergency medical unit.

She rushes toward Miles, breaking through the crowd of familiar faces. A paramedic catches her and keeps her at bay. "Hold on, ma'am."

"That is my husband!" she screams. She sees Miles up close, and it's terrifying. He's not simply lethargic; he's completely inanimate, his face expressionless as stone. Tears spring to her eyes for the first time. *Can he hear me?*

"The medics need room to work, ma'am. I'm sorry," one man tells her as the other three men pound Miles's chest, lift his nose and throat to clear his airway, and breath into his mouth. They place a mask over his face and begin to pump air into his lungs. She watches them lift Miles onto the stretcher. His arms are heavy and lifeless. They place one hand on his chest and then another.

Once Miles has been strapped onto the stretcher, the paramedic releases her. She rushes to his side, clasping his hand between both of hers. It's cool. She squeezes it to let him know she is there. He doesn't squeeze back.

"Miles," she says sternly as if that will get him to answer. "Miles! Can you hear me?" Her voice softens upon knowing he does not. "Hold on, honey. Hold on." One paramedic sits on top of him pumping air into his mouth as everyone loads into the ambulance. The sirens blare. The monitor beeps faintly.

"What is wrong with him?" She begs for answers, clinging to his hand as two paramedics continue their work while the other whisks them through the city to the hospital. "Please, what has happened?"

"The doctors will assess at the ER," the lead paramedic says gently. "But we believe he has suffered a stroke."

Palmer doubles over onto Miles, binding herself to him as if trying to give him life through her own.

"Miles Harding. You hang on. You cannot leave me. Do you hear me? You do not leave me!"

The ambulance pulls into the emergency bay. The doors fling open, and three emergency doctors pull Miles out of the ambulance and into the hospital. The paramedic escorts her to the waiting area. The second she walks through the emergency room sliding doors, the distinctive hospital smell hits her, causing her stomach to churn and evoking memories Palmer has spent years quietly suppressing. She pushes them away once again and fills her mind only with Miles.

"A doctor will be with you in a moment," the paramedic says and motions for her to sit on the bench. "You can wait there."

She nods. Fear consumes her ability to speak.

Thirty minutes later, Dr. David Laskins, a tall cardiologist perhaps in his mid-fifties, locates Palmer. "Mrs. Harding?"

"Yes," she says, but she doesn't want to be Mrs. Harding right now. She doesn't want any of this to be happening and can't even believe it is happening. Twenty-four hours ago, she and Miles were feverishly making love in their kitchen. It seems so long ago now.

"Mrs. Harding, your husband suffered a massive stroke," Dr. Laskins tells her.

Palmer clasps her mouth with both hands and crumbles into the waiting room chair behind her. "I didn't want to believe it."

The doctor takes the seat next to her. "A blood vessel in his brain ruptured. It deprived his brain of oxygen for too long of a time. When that happens, brain cells immediately begin to die. The part of his brain that was deprived of oxygen the longest controlled his heart muscle, causing it to stop beating."

Palmer buries her face in her hands in disbelief. "His heart stopped beating?"

Dr. Laskins puts a hand on Palmer's back. "Yes, his heart stopped. I'm so sorry, Mrs. Harding. There was nothing we could do. He's gone."

She feels her hands begin to quiver. "He can't be gone. He was here this morning. We made dinner plans. I watched him walk out the door. He biked to work. He was completely fine."

"I understand. I really do." Dr. Laskins explains, "His blood pressure was extremely elevated. A person can function normally like that for a while. Do you know if he suffered from high blood pressure?"

"No. We always get our annual physicals. He had some cholesterol issues, but never high blood pressure."

"Do you know when he saw a doctor last?"

"Late last spring, I think."

"So, it had been a while and he was probably due for his exam. From what we can tell, his high blood pressure may have caused the hemorrhage in his brain. Sometimes things like this happen unexpectedly."

"Oh God," Palmer whispers as a familiar guilty feeling courses through her. "Would an unusual amount of stress cause his blood pressure to rise?"

"Yes, it could, for certain. But so many things could also. It is hard to isolate just one." He looks at her for a moment, as if telling her with his eyes that he truly does understand. Dr. Laskins is good at his job; he's not new to delivering bad news. "I'm very sorry for your loss, Mrs. Harding."

"Thank you." But she doesn't mean it. She doesn't mean it at all.

Dr. Laskins stands up and walks away, slipping through the emergency room doors. She sits surrounded by empty chairs in the middle of the waiting room.

"I did this," she tells herself. "I did this."

THE HOURS AND DAYS THAT FOLLOW BLUR TOGETHER. Palmer calls Aiden and Quinn from the hospital waiting room. When everyone arrives at the house, she holds her boys in her arms and delivers the news. Their father is gone.

"I'm so sorry," echoes from her lips for days amid uncontrollable sobbing episodes. Palmer's sorrow is greatest for her children. She knows intimately how they feel; losing a parent as a child is something they now share. The missed birthdays, graduations, and weddings will pile on top of each other year after year, cruel and heavy.

Even worse, how would they feel if they ever knew what I did? Stupidly arguing with their father for weeks on end. Causing him extra stress that shot his blood pressure through the roof, triggering his stroke. Kissing Sanford! *If the boys found out any of this, they would never speak to me again. I would lose them forever.*

Palmer buries the past weeks in the back of her mind where she keeps her most grievous memories. She tells no one. Not even Meaghan.

Days later, the First Presbyterian Church in Alexandria fills beyond capacity as people offering sincere but futile condolences stand in the back of the church, spill out into the corridors and down the long hallways. Robert Duvall sends the largest arrangement of flowers she's ever seen and makes a generous donation to the newly established Miles Harding Scholarship Fund for Architectural Study, which she and the boys started. Bradley Heartfield, who drove four hours from the Cape to say goodbye to his best friend, sits in the pew behind her and the boys, attempting to stifle his sobbing. When she stands to leave, she notices Sanford and Cinnamon seeming to hide out in the back pew, oddly together, and avoids them. Afterwards, invited guests gather at the Harding residence for a reception. An urn filled with Miles's ashes sits prominently in the center of the foyer table, surrounded by flowers, as if Miles himself greets each guest upon their arrival. She walks through today completely numb. It's the only way she can survive.

By four, only a handful of people remain gathered in her den: her boys and their friends. They watch Marvel's newest Spiderman movie, a much-needed distraction, and devour the last of the catered Best Buns roast beef and horseradish sandwiches. Palmer picks up remaining coffee mugs and tidies the foyer. She carries Miles's urn to the kitchen, sets it on the island, and pours herself a coffee. The mug warms her hands as she stares at the urn. Remorse washes over her.

Her cell phone rings, breaking the trance.

"Hello," she answers in whisper because it's all the energy she has left.

"It's me," Meaghan whispers back on the other end.

"I wish you were here," she says. "No one should have to endure their husband's funeral without their best friend at their side." She wanders into the pantry, grabs a stepstool, and climbs up to look through the items on the top shelf.

"Not many have a best friend who is embroiled in a criminal scandal," Meaghan says.

In the weeks before Miles's stroke, Palmer watched Meaghan's life burn, spreading across the tabloids as wildly as the California fires that burn every summer now, the limits of their reach unknown. Meaghan's career and family are both gone. Duncan moved into a condo while he awaits trial, and Bella won't return Meaghan's calls. When Miles died, Palmer and Meaghan agreed that Meaghan could not attend the funeral. Too much paparazzi. Too much of a scene.

"I watched the memorial service livestream. I don't have an unemptied Kleenex box left in the house," Meaghan says. "How are you?"

Palmer locates what she's looking for—a white bread box from Crate and Barrel that's never been used. She grabs the box and steps down off the stool, considering Meaghan's question.

"Lost," she whispers. "Overwhelmed by the constant feeling that the world will never be right again. I can't sleep. Every time I close my eyes, I see him smiling back at me." She sets the bread box on the island and pours herself an ice water to go with her coffee. She sits down at the kitchen table. "And also, so you know, I hate that question—how are you? You can assume I'm not well. Instead, you can ask me, 'Is today a medium day or a horrible day?'"

"Got it," Meaghan says. "Is today a medium day or a horrible day?"

"Horrible. They are all horrible. I need to get away," she admits. "I can't stay here. Miles is everywhere." She returns to the island, flashes of their lovemaking days ago popping into her head. She opens the bread box and sets the urn inside, as if doing so might keep her pain concealed. She wants to flee not only her kitchen, but their entire lives in Alexandria. "I'm focused on making sure the boys are happy. They both say they want to keep their summer plans. So that's what we'll do. Aiden is going back to Charlottesville. Quinn has that gig as a camp counselor through July at Camp Horizons. I can't stay here alone this summer."

"I'll go with you," Meaghan invites herself into Palmer's escape plan. "Where should we go? Name your place, Dr. Harding."

Palmer expects this reaction. Meaghan is a runner; she always has been. "Are you fleeing L.A., Mrs. Jones?"

"Damn straight. Everyone here hates me right now. It's killing me. I can't go anywhere. No one will be seen with me. No one will even talk to me. Everyone thinks I'm guilty of whatever crimes Dunc has committed. Even Bella! I could stand a change of scenery."

"And with someone who loves you?" Palmer boasts. "No matter what."

"You're the only one," Meaghan confesses. "It will be like old times. Just the two of us again."

The idea is an intriguing one, and Palmer takes a few seconds to consider it. She and Meaghan haven't spent a summer together since the one before their senior year in high school. Those days were small-town heaven on repeat. They slept till late morning without any responsibilities. Spent the afternoon at the city pool, rubbing their skin with a mix of baby oil and iodine, reading magazines, and munching Doritos, Twizzlers, and Laffy Taffy from the snack stand while gossiping about who started or stopped dating whom. They spent the evenings at the baseball fields, cheering on the high school boys' team. After the games, they dragged Main Street until midnight, shouting at friends through their open windows and occasionally stopping to get out of their cars, sit on top of them, and flirt with boys.

We were inseparable.

But not even a year later—right before their graduation—Meaghan abandoned her, heading straight to L.A. and never looking back. Meaghan's disappearance and her obvious but flimsy excuse of wanting to "jumpstart her acting career" never felt right to Palmer. Couldn't Meaghan have waited to spend the most important three months of their lives together? Or at least, those months seemed like the most important at the time.

The sun setting outside the kitchen window slips to an angle that hits Palmer right in the eye. She asks Meaghan, "Where should we go?"

"I've already thought of that. Costa Rica. I know a great secluded beach nestled alongside the jungle where no one will find us. Very private." Palmer can feel Meaghan reveling in the notion of completely vanishing from Hollywood for the summer. Meaghan's excitement permeates the phone line.

"Don't be ridiculous," she tells her. "You know I can't be that far from the boys. Plus, I'm pretty sure no one is letting you leave the country right now."

She can feel Meaghan's eyes roll on the other end of the phone. She is always Meaghan's mirror, reflecting her reality. But the thought of sun, sand, and water lapping at her feet calms her instantly. The healing powers of ocean waves and salty air draws her in.

"Okay. Where, then?" Meaghan asks. There's a long pause as both women consider a summer safe harbor.

"Let's spend the entire summer at our beach cottage."

A short silence. "I thought of that, but won't Miles be there, too?"

Nestled on the north shore of Cape Henlopen, a stone's throw from the bustling boardwalk of Rehoboth Village, the Hyacinth was Miles and Palmer's first baby. It was their passion project; something they created together that will undoubtedly be their legacy for their children. The Hyacinth is full of warm summer memories. The Hardings are somewhere in between locals and vacationers; they are summer people.

"Yes. I suppose he will be," she says. She looks around the kitchen and considers that any change of venue will curb the guilty feelings torturing her. "But much less than here, I think." She wants to explain herself to Meaghan, to tell her what she's done, but she's promised herself no one will ever know. "Are you coming?"

"Absolutely."

Blissed Out Chocolate Cake

Cake

Ingredients

- 2 cups bread flour
- 2 cups sugar
- ¾ cup cocoa powder
- 2 teaspoons baking soda
- 2 teaspoons baking powder
- 1 cup buttermilk
- ½ cup canola oil
- 2 eggs
- 1 ¼ cup Starbucks Italian Roast Instant Via Coffee
- 1 ½ teaspoons Kahlua

Preheat oven to 350 degrees.

In a stand mixer, combine buttermilk, oil, eggs and vanilla. Add flour, sugar, cocoa powder, baking soda and baking powder. Mix on slow speed until well combined. Add the coffee and Kahlua.

Grease 2 8-inch cake pans. Pour batter equally into each. Bake 40 minutes, testing with a toothpick until it comes out clean. Cool in the pans for 20 minutes, then remove onto wire rack and cool completely.

Cakes can be frozen and stored until ready to frost, or frosted when completely cooled.

Frosting

Ingredients

- 8 ounces semisweet chocolate, chopped
- 2 sticks unsalted butter
- 1 large egg yolk
- 1 teaspoon vanilla
- 1 ¼ cup powdered sugar
- 1 tablespoon Starbucks Italian Roast Instant Via Coffee Powder
- 1 teaspoon Kahlua

Place the chocolate in a glass bowl over a pot of boiling water to melt. Keep stirring until creamy and completely melted. Set aside to cool.

Dissolve the coffee powder in 2 teaspoons of very hot water. Add 1 teaspoon Kahlua. Set aside.

In a stand mixer, beat the butter until softened, light and creamy. It is best if butter is at room temperature. Add the egg yolk and vanilla and beat for a few more minutes. Add the powdered sugar on low speed. Add the chocolate and coffee mixture until blended completely.

Spread on top of each cake layer and assemble cake.

Additional Notes

Perfect for apologies of any kind. Often induces make-up sex.

June

Chapter 3

Cape Henlopen, Delaware

PALMER JOGS HER WAY ALONG THE WATER'S EDGE, breathing in the Village as she begins her day. She passes surfers at Rehoboth Beach, riding their perfect wave until its crest disappears onto the shore, and early morning bikers, winding their way along sand dunes around Gordon's Pond. She breathes in the crisp air filled with the sweet scents of pillowy donuts fresh from the ovens at Rise Up, and taffy pulled by hand at Dolly's ready for today's beachgoers. Summer has arrived in full splendor. But the salt air she'd hoped would be an immediate antidote to her ailments appears powerless. Before leaving Alexandria, Palmer's doctor diagnosed her waves of nausea to be the result of increased stress and anxiety, combined with the sudden onset of migraines, all of which seem fitting since losing Miles. The doctor prescribed a therapist, copious amounts of ginger tea, and salt air. She's still waiting for their cure.

A few blocks off the boardwalk, past the quaint streets lined with popcorn shops, ice cream parlors, and T-shirt stores, Palmer swings open the doors of Big Fish Market. She is greeted by a brisk wave of air-conditioning, which settles her queasiness on contact despite the scent of snapper. The relief may be temporary, but she'll take it. Palmer heads straight to the icy trays filled with fresh oysters, clams, scallops, crabs, and fish fresh off the boats early this morning.

Duncan's sentencing hearing is scheduled for eleven this morning in Los Angeles and will be televised live across most cable news networks. Three weeks ago, Duncan's trial ended with the jury finding him guilty on all counts of the bribery and conspiracy charges. No one can get enough of Sinful Admissions. CNN, Fox News, MSNBC, and more will all put the spectacle front and center because ratings, of course. The one thing Palmer knows will help Meaghan navigate the day's events is food. Meaghan loves to eat, something her size two figure discreetly conceals, but she's completely lost in the kitchen. Palmer plans to prepare a mouthwatering lunch, which they will enjoy on the deck overlooking The Hyacinth's beach while streaming the courtroom drama. If you have to watch your convicted husband be sentenced along with the rest of the world, you might as well do it beachfront.

Since informing her partners that she would be taking a leave of absence for the summer and withdrawing herself as Sanford's star expert, leaving him in a complete lurch, Palmer spends her time cooking up a storm in The Hyacinth's kitchen. It's a wonderful distraction. She cooks and Meaghan eats, because Palmer's unable to stomach much food even with the ginger tea. So far, the arrangement couldn't be more perfect.

She stands in the middle of the aisle, soaking in the air-conditioning and poring over the scallops, when she feels a tap on her shoulder. She snaps around expecting to discover the paparazzi in search of Meaghan. Instead, standing before her in plaid shorts and a pink polo, sunglasses dangling around his neck and curly blond hair waving in all directions, is a beautifully tanned Bradley Heartfield.

Palmer clutches her chest. "Bradley, you scared me!"

"Well, I didn't mean to." Bradley opens his arms and she falls into them, bursting into tears. He gives her a squeeze and kisses the top of her head. The last time she saw him, at Miles's funeral, he held her boys just as tight.

She gathers herself a bit. "I didn't realize how much I needed to see you," she says in between sniffles.

He holds her like any guy would hold his best friend's wife when that best friend has unexpectedly died.

"It's going to get easier," he whispers quietly to avoid a scene. "I miss him too. So much. But it has got to get easier." He puts both hands squarely on her shoulders and looks her straight in the eyes. "I mean, Jesus, it can't get worse, right?"

She cracks a smile. "Right." She uses the back of her hands to wipe the tears from her cheeks. "It absolutely cannot get worse." She finishes putting herself back together. "What are you doing here so early this morning?"

"Ah, I'm hand-picking the freshest seafood, just brought in by those fine fishermen." He points to the back of the market where six men in rubber overalls are filling their coffee mugs. "I'm creating tonight's menu at The Oyster House."

Bradley launched The Henlopen Oyster House twenty-two years ago; it's a family staple and a magnet for vacationing celebrities in the Village. It's often frequented by President Biden and his family, who spend weeks at their summer beach estate down the road from The Hyacinth on the north shores of the Cape. The Oyster House is a local favorite, much like

Bradley himself is a favorite in the Harding household. More than a favorite, really. He's family.

"And what seafood have you decided on?" she asks, always inspired by his menus.

"We're focusing on fresh oysters and rockfish tonight, but I'm leaving the dish selection up to Chef Antonio. He'll know what to do." Bradley smiles. He writes down his order and hands the paper to a man in a white apron. "Here you go, Chuck. Thanks, man."

Bradley turns back to Palmer, who places a final sea scallop into her bag. He puts his arm around her shoulder as they walk toward the produce area. "Okay, we know by the looks of you that you are not doing so great," he says. She rolls her eyes at Bradley and elbows his ribs, despite remaining acutely aware that she's wearing constant heartache and sorrow on her face. She does own a mirror, after all.

"I'm doing okay," she argues. "I'm washing my hair. I'm not eating or sleeping, but my hair is clean."

"Clean hair is a start." She steers him back toward the fresh mussels. "How is our Meaghan?" As the words leave his lips, Bradley spots Chuck waving at him and heads back toward the counter to answer a question about his order. "Hold on a sec."

"Go ahead." She shoos him toward the counter and pretends to peruse the mussels. *Our Meaghan!*

The first time Bradley met Meaghan, almost twenty years ago, Palmer's sure she caught them making out like a couple of teenagers. Meaghan had come to visit Palmer's newly renovated summer cottage for a few days. She and Miles decided to throw a dinner party and introduce The Hyacinth to the neighborhood. Bradley showed up straight from The Oyster House for what would become his regular Sunday summer supper, sans the rest of the invited guests. She noticed Meaghan and Bradley spent hours huddled around a wood fire blazing on the beach as night fell, laughing and swapping stories, so entranced with each other. Later, while she and Miles served coffee and dessert, she brought some out to the bonfire and caught them lip locked. Though she's pretty sure neither spotted her.

When the weekend ended, Meaghan went back to L.A. Six months later, she and Meaghan both found themselves pregnant. Meaghan had been dating Duncan for four months, after he directed her in his latest film. The press dubbed them the new Hollywood "power couple." That fall, Meaghan and Duncan had Bella, and their fans went wild, everyone trying to get a glimpse of America's sweetheart's new baby girl. Six weeks later, on the other coast, Palmer delivered Aiden with Miles at her side and little other fanfare except for the giant six-foot stuffed panda Meaghan sent from FAO Schwarz. When Bella was two, Meaghan and Duncan tied the knot. But every time Meaghan comes out to the Cape, often with Bella, Bradley shows up more often than usual.

"Sorry about that." Bradley brings her attention back to the fish market. "I guess they ran out of oysters. We have some, but not as many as I wanted. We'll adjust."

"I have no doubt."

"So, has Meaghan arrived?"

"Four days ago." Palmer smiles. "She's at The Hyacinth, sleeping in. West Coast time, you know."

"Good to hear she's made it safely. Any sign the paparazzi are onto her yet?"

"Not yet. Duncan's sentencing is today, and the press appears entertained by that circus. I'm planning a delicious lunch to help her stomach the scene unfolding across the news." *And keep my mind off Miles.*

"Something's got to. Dunc sure got himself in a mess this time," Bradley says with a touch of hostility. "What are you serving?"

"I'm trying a French twist on a classic seafood salad," she answers. "Shrimp, scallops, and lump crab meat, but no mayonnaise. Instead, an oil-and-herb dressing with a splash of lemon."

"You'll save me a bite to try? Could wind up at the top of The Oyster House menu this summer."

"Absolutely." She smiles at him. "How's it going this summer at the restaurant anyway?"

"Record season. We are booked every night for the next six weeks solid. I'm guessing by week's end, we will have the summer reservation list filled. Chef Antonio spent two months this winter in the Seychelles and is incorporating some exceptional grilled seafood curries onto the tasting menu. Hey, listen, I'm taking Serenity out tomorrow for a few hours. Why don't you and Meaghan join me? You can get some fresh air and bring that leftover seafood salad, assuming there is any?"

Serenity is Bradley's first love: a fifty-seven-foot Boston Whaler. The term "boat" does not do justice to Serenity. She is equal parts luxury and sport fishing. You could stay on Serenity for weeks at a time, navigating to the destination of your choice, while preparing meals in the marble kitchen, soaking in the hot tub off the back deck, or napping in one of her four estate rooms. Palmer, Miles, Meaghan, Bradley, and all the kids have vacationed together on Serenity twice, taking her all the way to the Florida Keys and back both times— once for a New Year's Eve celebration and another for the kids' spring break. Dunc was away on set both trips.

"Oh, that sounds …" Palmer pauses because she isn't sure how it sounds. A day on the water drenched in sunlight should sound cathartic, but the work of getting there sounds a little daunting. Plus, she's not sure how her stomach will fare.

"Come on, I won't keep you two out at sea for too long." Bradley's phone rings in his hand and they both glance down. The name "Bridgette" flashes on the screen. Bradley hits the phone's side button silencing it and sending Bridgette to voicemail purgatory.

"Sounds like heaven. We'll go," she says graciously.

"Wonderful. I'll pick you up at 11 a.m. tomorrow morning?" His cell buzzes a second time in his hand. Bridgette is persistent. *Does Bradley have a new girl?*

They move into the checkout line, where the attendant begins to ring up Palmer. "Hey, any suggestions for a simple but sophisticated birthday dinner? Meaghan's birthday is in a couple weeks."

Bradley turns to her, a little dumfounded. "How did I not remember that?" She wonders the same thing. "Nothing. You make nothing. Come to the restaurant and we will celebrate together. I'll put Chef Antonio on it."

"I thought you are totally booked?"

"We are. But I know a guy who can get you in." Bradley winks at her.

"That's very sweet of you. But I don't think Meaghan wants to alert anyone that she is in town. She wants to keep her location a secret for as long as possible. A night at the restaurant might ruin that."

"Understandable. Think about it. Tomorrow we'll enjoy Serenity for an afternoon."

BACK AT THE HYACINTH, PALMER SPENDS THE LATE MORN-ing soaking up the deep-blue ocean through the kitchen's wall of glass doors expertly designed by Miles. She prepares her soon-to-be classic, French seafood salad, while sipping a ginger tea. On the kitchen counter, in the far corner, sits the Crate and Barrel bread box. Beside it a host of family photos line the counter, including one of the day Meaghan and Duncan married. She's never questioned Meaghan about her decision to marry Dunc, but she's always wondered whether Meaghan would have been happier without him, even if that meant never achieving Hollywood "power couple" status.

Her mind wanders back to that day. She and Meaghan were alone in the bride's room, slipping Meaghan into a billowy princess Vera Wang gown, when Meaghan suddenly broke down into tears. "When I came back from St. Thomas, I knew exactly what I wanted," Meaghan sobbed. *When did Meaghan go to St. Thomas?* "Bella needs her father. More than anything in this world, I want Bella to feel loved in a way I never did." Meaghan's father dropped her at kindergarten one day and never came home. *Bella has been loved. Has Meaghan?*

Palmer pulls together a fresh berry and rhubarb tart from her haul from Garner's farm stand. While the tart bakes, she grabs her laptop, goes out to the deck above The Hyacinth's beach, and settles into a chaise lounge chair. She scrolls through the morning headlines and then checks her Instagram feed. Halfway down, she comes across Cinnamon's late-night post. It's an usie, or a group selfie, with her girlfriends dancing the night away. The location tagged is The Hamilton, a local bar two blocks from the White House, always filled with Capitol Hill staffers, lobbyists, and celebrities. She zooms in on the picture. She can't believe her eyes.

Igor Overlauder, the Capital hockey team's greatest player, possibly of all time, stands in the middle of the women. He's got one arm around Cinnamon and one hand raising his glass to the camera. Cinnamon's caption reads "An Ovi Usie 🏒 💚."

"Unbelievable," she says out loud. *Maybe the landscaper is out of the picture?* Where was Sanford last night when Cinnamon snapped this pic? He was probably slaving away at the office, which was always part of their problem. She can feel Sanford's kiss on her lips. Her good friend. Her work husband. Pangs of guilt pelt her. Self-loathing courses through her veins, leaving her squeamish again.

The last time Palmer felt this way—constantly uneasy, tired all the time, unable to even look at food—was during chemotherapy. Ten years ago, Palmer discovered a lump in her breast, brushing her hand up against something hard when changing her clothes. She immediately knew the small marble underneath her skin was cancer because her mother, Linda, died from the same disease. Palmer's suspicions were confirmed twelve days later when her biopsy pathology revealed the most aggressive form of breast cancer, triple negative, and her genetic test confirmed she carried the BRCA1 breast cancer gene mutation, no doubt inherited from Linda.

Palmer closes her Instagram feed and opens Google. She hadn't even discussed cancer with the doctor she'd seen before leaving Alexandria, only listed it in her history. It seemed so long ago. She types symptoms of breast cancer recurrence. She's got the headache, nausea, fatigue, and loss of appetite. *Why are symptoms basically the same for everything?*

"Shit." She stares at the page, frustrated and fearing her worst fear may be coming true. Well, what she thought was her worst fear; the past few weeks have provided strong evidence that she may need to reconsider. She watched her mother die from this disease, and even though she was only seven at the time, she will never forget the inevitable cruelty it imposes. She's absconded with ten beautiful years of living with her boys since her first diagnosis. Those years seem too good to be true, which means they probably are.

My cancer might be back. Maybe it's precisely the punishment I deserve.

Chapter 4

MEAGHAN DEVOURS HER ENTIRE PLATE OF FRENCH SEA-food salad, accompanied by a tall glass of iced ginger-peach sun tea, and decides to save the berry tart to eat during the hearing. Comfort food will be required.

"How's the lunch?" Palmer asks.

"Five stars!"

She sits cross-legged at the teak dining table on the deck. "You're not eating. Is something wrong?"

"You mean besides Miles is in the Crate and Barrel bread box in the kitchen?" Palmer asks dryly, a lump forming in her throat.

"About that, honey," she says, "I think we need to move him somewhere more … restful … for the summer."

"Not the kitchen counter?"

"Perhaps the master bedroom closet."

Palmer nods. "Definitely, more restful. Noted."

"Now, is today a medium day or a horrible day?"

Palmer pulls her sunglasses off, staring down the beach at kids tossing a football. "Today is a medium day. My jog helped. I was exhausted beforehand, but I got through it, and that feels like an accomplishment." She exudes a hint of pride in herself. "I also ran into Bradley in the Village at Big Fish Market, which definitely helped."

Meaghan feels a small spark at the mention of his name. "Bradley," she says slowly, dragging out each consonant. "Now there's a man I haven't thought about in too long. How is Bradley?" Palmer's eyes grow wide. "Besides the fact that his best friend is in the Crate and Barrel bread box in the kitchen," she clarifies.

"Besides that, he's exactly the same. Which means I am pretty sure he still has that crush on you." Palmer raises a curious eyebrow.

"Oh please." She waves her hand in the air as if to wipe away the notion. "We had a … small spark … years ago. Before the kids were born! Plus, I'm married." Remembering this little fact brings renewed disappointment. She sets her glass on the table, "Not to mention my life is a train wreck. My husband is a criminal and my daughter refuses to speak to me. I guarantee Bradley wants nothing to do with me."

Palmer rolls her eyes at her. "Well, he asked us out on Serenity tomorrow. I think we should go. We've spent almost a week only at the house. We can't really go anywhere else. A day of sunshine on the water will be good for us both. Saltwater cures everything …."

Meaghan sets her fork down on her empty plate, imaging a warm, sunny day swimming in the deep-blue water. "That does sound lovely. Surely no paparazzi will be in the middle of the Atlantic. I'm in." She points at the screen sitting perched between them on the table. "Oh! It's starting." She slides the still-warm tart in front of her.

On Palmer's laptop, Judge John Strickland enters the L.A. courtroom. Nervous energy rushes through Meaghan's entire body. Palmer turns the volume up and the two friends listen intently, waves crashing onto the shore in the background.

The prosecutors stand to address the court. One of them, a young guy in a knock-off Armani suit sitting second chair, says, "Should it please the Court. The prosecution is prepared to give its sentencing recommendation today. Before doing so, however, we have discovered new evidence that we believe is pertinent to Mr. Jones's guilty conviction. This evidence will impact his sentencing."

Meaghan stops mid-bite. She and Palmer exchange confused looks. In the courtroom, Waverly immediately objects. His objection is overruled by Judge Strickland because the defense delayed their own document production. The prosecution presents their new evidence.

"Your Honor," the female lead prosecutor who is dressed in an actual Armani suit takes over. "This evidence came into our possession just last evening." She moves forward to hand a copy to the bailiff, who then presents a document to Judge Strickland and then another copy to Duncan's entire team of lawyers, including Waverly and three associates.

Duncan's face looks blank. Meaghan cannot read him, although she wonders if she ever has been able to. Dunc has been lying to her for at least the past year, and quite likely longer than that. *Maybe I shouldn't have turned a deaf ear to rumors about those other actresses.* One lie is enough to question all the truth.

"This is a falsified curriculum vitae for Bella Jones," the prosecutor continues. "It details her equestrian riding achievements. Specifically, the CV falsely claims that she placed ninth at the California Interscholastic Equestrian Association Championships in 2019 and fifth in 2020. These fake achievements allowed Bella Jones's name to be placed on the women's equestrian team roster at Southern California College, subsequently guaranteeing her admission."

Meaghan's eyes widen and her mouth falls open. "Bella has been horseback riding only a handful of times with friends and once on vacation in Hawaii." Palmer reaches for her hand.

"Next, I have a sworn affidavit from the Southern California College's head women's equestrian coach, Dede Drummond from Pleasant Farms, who confirms Bella Jones's name was initially listed to be part of the incoming equestrian team, but once the year began her name was removed."

"Who would put Bella on an equestrian team and then withdraw her?" Meaghan asks.

The prosecutor forges on. "She never attended a single practice or a competition. Not in college as part of the Intercollegiate Horse Show Association; not in high school. Instead, her fake CV is another act of fraud perpetrated to ensure her entrance into the college as an athletic recruit. This new evidence demonstrates that the fraud perpetrated on her behalf was done with intent and went far beyond the initial bribe that paid for another individual to take the SAT on her behalf."

Meaghan slumps into her chair in disbelief. She weaves her long blond hair through her fingers, repeatedly. *Did Duncan know about this?* She's refused to answer any of his calls since the trial started, partly on Mack's recommendation but mostly because, once Mack finally allowed them into a room together, Dunc blamed Bella. Before they talked, there was a small piece of her that could understand why Dunc did what he did. Societal pressure. Maintaining status. But once Duncan blamed Bella, all she's felt is rage.

"As such," the prosecutor says as she delivers her final zinger, "we recommend Duncan Jones's sentencing should be the maximum."

Her jaw drops. "She means jail time. Doesn't she?"

"Yes, the maximum sentence will send Dunc to jail," Palmer confirms.

"I didn't think he would actually go to jail! A fine, yes, absolutely. Community service, very likely. But this? Bella will be mortified."

Meaghan picks up her phone and dials Bella's number. *Is she watching this?* She needs to hear her daughter's voice and know she's okay. Surely Bella will pick up now. She stands up and paces back and forth on the deck. Without ringing once, Bella's phone goes directly to voicemail.

"Bella, it's Mom. I'm not sure if you are watching Dad's …" she hesitates to even say the words, "… sentencing. It seems there's some sort of new evidence, something about a false CV … honey, they're saying it's … *yours*. I am calling to check on you." She pauses; her words feel futile. "I'm so sorry that all of this is happening. I want you to know I am going to get to the bottom of this. I have *no* idea what is going on. I'm going to call Uncle Mack right now and find …" The voicemail recording ends with a loud beep and cuts her off mid-sentence.

"Shit." Palmer says what she thinks.

Meaghan sits down. She tosses her phone on the table and buries her face in her hands. She looks up at Palmer. "What has Duncan done? What if the college decides to kick her out now? So far, they have let these kids keep attending. But this …" Meaghan waves her hand in a circular motion in front of the court room shown on Palmer's laptop. "… this may change the college's stance."

"It may have to," Palmer agrees reluctantly. "Unless Mack can get to the bottom of this equestrian team thing." Judge Strickland grants an hour recess to consider the new evidence and its impact on Duncan's sentencing.

"I going to call Mack," she says.

"Of course." Palmer stacks the plates on top of each other and sets their lunch dishes on the wicker tray.

Meaghan retreats to her room. The moment she collapses onto her bed, her phone rings. Her heart races. Bella is returning her call! When she turns her phone face upwards, Mack's name flashes back at her instead.

She answers. "Hey, Mack. I was about to call you. We saw the hearing. What is going on?"

"Glad you're watching. I got this new evidence this morning right about the time Judge Strickland got it in his courtroom … unearthed yesterday from Chip Sullivan's massive trove of papers. The authorship of the document appears unknown. No digital signatures on the file, completely wiped."

"Do you know if Dunc was aware of it?"

"Whether or not Duncan knew, is irrelevant," Mack explains. "Because for all legal intents and purposes, the bribe paid for the fake CV in addition to the other individual taking the SAT in her name."

She purses her lips. Mack continues. "I spoke with Bella first thing this morning when we received the document. She was floored, of course, but at least she had a heads up before it was splashed across the TV in real time." Meaghan lets out a sigh of relief. Although Bella will not speak with her or Duncan, she has been talking with Uncle Mack since Sinful Admissions broke wide open. "I tried reaching you too, but your cell went straight to voicemail."

"I had my phone off earlier." She'd been attempting a quiet morning before the hearing began. "Besides, I'm not worried about me. I'm worried about Bella."

"I know you are. She's doing okay, all things considered. You have raised a smart young woman who has learned how to handle the press her entire life. She knows what she's doing. Do we wish she wasn't having to go through this? Of course. But she's okay, Meaghan. You know I'll never let anything happen to her."

"Thank you," she offers sincerely.

"I have some other news. News I haven't told Bella because I wanted to talk to you first." She feels Mack begin to tread lightly.

Oh God, what now? "What is it?"

"It's not good," Mack says. "The FBI wants to depose you again. I don't know how else to tell you." He pauses. "The FBI is going to bring additional charges. Completely unrelated to the equestrian team issue."

"What additional charges? Against whom?"

"An additional charge of money laundering against Duncan, which will land him back in court again and extend whatever sentence they give him today." Mack takes in a deep breath and exhales. "And very likely a single, new charge of money laundering against you."

Meaghan says nothing. A pit grows in her stomach. She breaks into a sweat. *They know.*

Mack continues. "The FBI claims they have evidence that you paid the bribe, Meaghan. Duncan made a first payment, and you made the second."

"I made a donation!" She blurts out what she's told no one else. She lowers her voice to a whisper and says, "A donation, Mack."

"To whom?" Mack asks, his voice authoritative, bordering on accusatory.

"Mack ..." Her tone tells him to back down.

"Sorry, Meaghan. But you didn't think to tell me about your ... *donation* until now? Come on. I can't effectively represent you if you hide things from me. You must tell me *everything*. Who did you donate to?"

Silence permeates the line. Meaghan runs over that day again and again in her mind. She can't remember.

Mack asks, "The SCC Farms?"

"Yes. That's it!" she says and then again, more quietly as the gravity of the connection sets in on her, "The SCC Farms. Dunc asked me to write a donation to the college, specifically to that foundation. I thought it seemed a little odd at the time and I remember asking him about it. He told me that the college had sent a list of affiliated organizations to which donations could be made, and this one was at the top of their list. As good as any, he said. I mean, who doesn't love a farm?"

"That's the charity Sullivan set up to funnel his proceeds," Mack explains. "Listen, they will allow you to give a second deposition remotely via teleconference so that you don't have to come back to L.A. for the time being. But I can guarantee that they will present you with the check you wrote as evidence."

"Mack?" She hesitates. "There's more."

"Yeah? What?"

She cringes. "I wrote the check from Awaken's bank account."

Mack lets out a deep breath as the world comes into focus. "Jesus, Meaghan! That explains why the charge is money laundering," Mack says. "Why did you donate on behalf of Awaken?"

"Well, it's a fully deductible expense for one. And I thought that the donation could make more young women aware of Awaken. I thought it would be good for the brand."

Mack exhales. "Well, it's not going to be good for the brand. Sullivan says you and Dunc *both* knew and participated in the bribe. On paper it certainly looks like you did. We need *actual* evidence to support your version of events. Can you think of any?"

Meaghan has run the series of events over those weeks through her head a million times since Dunc was hauled off in handcuffs. Was her donation a bribe? Does it even matter? The lines are fuzzier than watching an entire 3D movie without the glasses. "Nothing," Meaghan says. "Set up a time to talk to the FBI."

"Okay. They asked for three weeks from today. Early July before the Fourth holiday."

"Fine."

"I won't mention anything to Bella. Let's see how this second deposition goes. I will let you know if I hear anything from her. Anything at all." Mack pauses for a moment. "Meaghan?"

"Yes?"

"Is there *anything* else you haven't told me? No more surprises."

She hesitates. "No. Nothing else."

"Okay, then. We will keep working on things here."

Mack hangs up. Judge Strickland will be finished deliberating in ten minutes. She heads back up to the deck, where Palmer's eyes are glued to her laptop. Meaghan can see Palmer toggle between the constant stream of an empty courtroom and her Chrome browser displaying a very long article.

"Whatcha reading?" she asks playing cool. *Should I tell her? Would she make me leave?*

Palmer glances down at the article and back at her, handing her the laptop.

She sits down at the teak table and scrolls the article. "Why are you reading this? Are you really worried about this?"

"I have a number of those symptoms," Palmer admits.

"I can't say I haven't noticed. You're not eating, you're not sleeping, and you look like hell." She winces a bit as the words come out, realizing their unintended sting.

"You can't reign in that brutal honesty a little bit?" Palmer instinctively touches the puffy circles under her eyes with both hands and then points to the laptop. "Do you think my cancer has come back?"

She reaches for Palmer's hands and gives them a squeeze. There are things much worse in this world than Sinful Admissions. Like cancer.

"You know I love you. Look, these symptoms you're feeling could all simply be exactly what the doctor in Alexandria told you. Migraines and an uneasy stomach all the result of the anxiety and the stress of dealing with Miles's death, not cancer seeking vengeance for your kicking its ass once before."

Palmer shakes her head. "It's more than that. I can feel it in my core. It's been ten years since my diagnosis. Two awful years of treatment and surgeries, eight years getting back to living my life." Palmer lays her head back and raises her face toward the sun. "I don't want to end up like Linda."

"You are not going to end up like Linda! Medicine is different now. You are different. You caught your cancer before it spread anywhere. Linda didn't." Her eyes meet Palmer's, "Plus, I simply won't let it happen."

"I don't think it's up to you," Palmer says.

Meaghan glances down at the screen again. The internet always makes it sound like one is dying. "You know what we really need? An expert. Let's call my mom!"

Meaghan's mom, Victoria Blessing, has been a nurse for thirty-five years at the hospital in Cottonwood Falls, Kansas, and has treated every kind of patient with every kind of illness—even Palmer's mother during her final days.

"No way. Leave her alone." Palmer fondles her watch. "Does she love retirement, by the way?"

"She does. She decided to go to Paris for the summer. Get out of town a bit. She knows how to handle gossip about her daughter, but Sinful Admissions has taken everything to a whole other level. I'll give her credit though; she remains unfazed. She rented a flat near the Louvre for three months and a villa in Saint-Tropez for the weekends."

Palmer watches her run her hair through her fingers. "Someday you're going to pull all your hair out by doing that."

She stops abruptly. Her hands collapse onto Palmer's shoulders. Exasperated, she says, "Okay, if you won't let me call Victoria, please go for a checkup with Dr. Harlow. Let's clear your mind from this worrying about this, at least. You've got enough other kinds of worry to fill your head these days."

Dr. Elizabeth Harlow has been Palmer's beach doctor since the summer she was first diagnosed with breast cancer. Although Dr. Harlow's primary practice is in Wilmington, she has a second office location on the Cape and splits her time equally each week. All of which makes getting on her schedule difficult.

"I'm sure I can't get an appointment anytime soon," Palmer says and Meaghan's eyes roll. "Fine. I don't want to see

Dr. Harlow. I can't bear being at a doctor's office or a hospital right now."

She shakes her head right back. "Nope. Sorry. I mean, I get it. But you are going. Case closed."

A jolt of activity sparks inside the courtroom and Palmer's laptop blares the sound of a gavel banging. The drama draws them in again. "Turn it up," Palmer says reaching for the laptop as Judge Strickland returns to the courtroom. "They're going to start."

"I can't watch." She lowers her head to rest on the table. Palmer grabs the laptop and cranks up the volume herself. Palmer can't take her eyes away.

Judge Strickland gets straight to the point. Duncan has committed fraud, been found guilty of conspiracy and bribery, and now demonstrates broad intent. He sentences Duncan to the maximum penalty under the law.

Six months in jail.

Five hundred thousand dollars in fines.

Two hundred and fifty hours of community service.

Two hundred and fifty hours of supervised release.

"Unbelievable," Meaghan declares. She buries her head in her hands. Through her fingers the sand glistens in the sun. A glimmer of light, as only summer can offer, in the middle of darkness. More charges will come. Maybe she should tell Palmer about the donation. But what if it risks their friendship? What if Palmer leaves her, too? Only one other time was Meaghan too terrified to tell Palmer something she knew; she buried that knowledge deep inside her, so deep that Meaghan barely recalls it herself.

Meaghan can't bring herself to think about that now. She's too consumed with her current predicament. *Will I go to jail?*

Will she and Dunc go from being the Hollywood "It Couple" to losing everything and living behind bars? A light breeze blows her hair.

So many questions. Only one answer reverberates in Meaghan's mind.

"I'm never going to get Bella back," she says.

THE WARM SUN BLANKETS SERENITY'S DECK AS MEAGHAN leans against the polished wood railing. She was hesitant to come out today, for so many reasons, but the gentle rock of the waves beneath her feels like a soothing balm. The salty breeze pulls thoughts away from the chaos she fled in L.A. to the simplicity of the moment. A cool drink rests in her hand as she turns to find Palmer arranging the spread of fresh fruit and gourmet cheeses on the table.

"Do we have everything?" Palmer asks, glancing at the cooler stocked with drinks and more snacks than they can eat in a day.

"Looks perfect to me," Meaghan replies, her voice brightening. She hopes today offers a chance to relax, far removed from cameras and gossip columns, and her tangled thoughts of Duncan.

"Eat or swim first?" Palmer asks.

She catches herself glancing at the boat's stern in hopes of spotting him. "Um, eat. Definitely, eat."

And then, as if the universe has conspired to summon him, Bradley emerges from below deck. Sunlight glints off his well-defined features. He looks like he's stepped out from her fondest memories.

"Looks like you're starting the party without me?" he teases.

"Never. We're simply preparing for our Captain!" Palmer exclaims, and Meaghan feels her heart quicken ever so slightly at the glimmer in Bradley's eyes.

"Glad to have you both back on Serenity. Ready to escape reality?" His gaze settles on her, no longer the fleeting half-smiles they've shared during summers past. This feels more charged. More real.

"Ready as ever," Meaghan replies. Nothing can change the fact that she remains married to Duncan and consumed by scandal—a fact that weighs on her more heavily than the world knows.

They eat and recount stories of summers spent on Serenity with Bella, Aiden, Quinn, and of course Miles. They try to keep it light, but unsaid tensions linger. She catches Bradley watching her as she sips her Sancerre. There is an intimacy in his gaze that reminds her of their secret past—the stolen moments that once made her heart race with possibility—a time before Hollywood ensnared her in its glare.

Palmer excuses herself to the restroom below deck leaving Meaghan alone with Bradley, who stands next to her, elbows on the railing, looking out over the sparkling waters. "Thinking about going overboard?" he asks, interrupting her daydreaming, and she meets his steady gaze.

"More like contemplating how to escape the chaos of my life," she admits, a hint of frustration slipping through her carefully curated facade. The shadows of her marriage loom over her even on the open sea.

"I can't imagine what it's like." He breathes, sitting down beside her in a way that feels almost languid. "Duncan's the type who draws you into his world and leaves debris behind for you to clean up. You've spent too much time moving through his shadows."

A flicker of surprise registers on Meaghan's face. "You don't know the half of it."

"That's true. Sadly, I only know what I read in tabloids. Still, I would have never guessed all this—this situation you're stuck in." He sighs. "I wish I had. I would have been a better friend."

Emotions flicker between them. His frustration is palpable, and she fights to decipher his feelings—his hurt from the past mingling with the surprising, undeniable spark that brings them together once more. It feels impossibly fragile.

"Is that what we are?" she asks. "Friends?"

"After all these years, I hope we can at least be friends."

He means St. Thomas.

TWENTY YEARS AGO, SHE HADN'T PLANNED ON FINDING love at a seaside dinner party on the opposite coast. She'd worn her green dress—the one that made her feel invincible—and practiced her laugh, the one that sounded carefree even when she was calculating every move.

Then he walked into The Hyacinth.

Bradley stood in the doorway, removing his work tie and jacket, preparing to head out onto the beach. There was something refreshingly genuine about him—no practiced smile, no careful scanning of the room for the most important person to approach. When Palmer introduced them, his eyes met hers with an intelligence and warmth that made her rehearsed responses fall away. A spark ignited, immediate and undeniable. Later, as guests mingled with coffee and cordials, they found themselves alone on The Hyacinth's beach.

"I've never believed in instant connections," she confessed, filtering the sand between her fingertips, not looking at him. "But tonight feels..."

"Different," he finished.

Seven days later, they were stepping off a seaplane onto St. Thomas—a reckless, exhilarating escape from their carefully constructed lives, having told no one, not even Palmer and Miles, that they were going, together. For the first time since arriving in Hollywood, Meaghan felt herself breathing without the weight of her own expectation.

The island transformed her. With Bradley, she rediscovered parts of herself she'd tucked away in her pursuit of fame— her unfiltered laugh, her tendency to cry at beautiful sunsets, her ability to lie completely still and count stars until dawn. Bradley listened when she talked about growing up without a father, about the hollow ache that had driven her ambition.

"I want more than just being seen," she confessed one night as they lay on the beach. "I want to be known. I want people to fall in love with Meaghan Jones."

"I see you," he whispered against her hair. "I know you."

On their last night, they stood barefoot at the water's edge, the moon casting silver ribbons across the waves.

"When my filming wraps next month," she whispered, "I'll tell everyone about us. No more hiding."

Bradley kissed her temple. "I'll start looking for places in L.A."

"Promise me something," she said, suddenly desperate to anchor this feeling to something tangible. "Promise we'll come back here—the last weekend of September, every year. No matter what."

"I promise," he said, and they both believed him.

Then reality intervened.

The texts grew sporadic as her filming schedule intensified. The calls, once nightly, dwindled to weekly, then occasionally. "Duncan Jones is directing. It's ... complicated," she told him.

"Complicated how?" Bradley asked, but she offered no other explanation.

The entertainment headlines appeared days later: *"Rising Star Meaghan Jones Captivates Acclaimed Director—Hollywood's New Power Couple?"* Accompanying photos showed them leaving a restaurant, her head inclined toward Duncan as he opened her car door.

"It's just publicity," she insisted over the phone. "The studio wants buzz for the film."

"When should I come out?" Bradley asked.

Silence stretched between them. "Not yet," she finally said. "I can't announce us yet." She told herself it was only until the film wrapped. But as Duncan's interest became genuine and the studio's expectations grew, her own ambition illuminated the obvious path before her; she couldn't step off it.

At the movie's premiere, Duncan's hand at the small of her back, cameras flashing, she had the sudden, intoxicating realization: They were looking at her. Really looking. Not through her or past her, they were looking at the next Hollywood star.

That night, she wrote to Bradley: "I'm sorry." The complexity of her betrayal reduced to two words. She had no others.

They didn't speak for months. When they finally did, it was through late-night emails—raw, honest exchanges about their lives, their regrets. For three years, these digital confessions sustained a connection neither could fully sever, until the day Duncan found her emails. The morning that Duncan confronted her, his face white with hurt and anger, was the day she sealed away that part of her heart for good.

"This has to be goodbye," she wrote to Bradley.

The years transformed her exterior—polished, acclaimed, controlled. She collected accolades like talismans against doubt. She built a beautiful life with Duncan and their daughter. She convinced herself that contentment was a reasonable substitute for joy.

Their occasional meetings at Palmer and Miles's home became exercises in careful restraint, never letting on about their shared past to their friends. She perfected the art of the cordial greeting, the appropriate question about his business ventures, the polite laugh that revealed nothing of the thunder in her chest when their eyes met across the room.

Sometimes, in unguarded moments during the lull in conversation, she caught him looking at her with a flash of recognition—not of the actress everyone knows, but the woman who once counted stars with him until dawn.

They've never mentioned St. Thomas. Never acknowledged the promised last weekend in September. But she imagines that somewhere between the lives they've built and the people they've become, St. Thomas might still exist.

MEAGHAN TRACES THE EDGE OF HER WEDDING BAND. "Everything feels complicated with Duncan," she muses quietly, confessing a vulnerability she has long kept under wraps. "He's Bella's father—and yet, all I feel is—"

"Trapped?" Bradley finishes for her, his eyes searching hers, as though offering her a release from the weight of her own truth. "I'd feel trapped, anyway. You deserve better. You always have," he says softly.

The air thickens with the unresolved feelings she's buried for so many years. They surround her like the ocean mist, making her head spin. She finds herself wondering what would happen if they gave in to the tension dancing between them; if they dared to rekindle their connection. But she's married, with a daughter.

"I wish things were different," she whispers.

"Me too," Bradley replies, stepping away from the railing. The warmth of the moment lingers in the air.

Palmer returns from the head. "Ready for a swim?" she asks, shattering the intimacy between them.

"Let's go," Meaghan says, but she can't deny that part of her wants to remain anchored to Bradley a little while longer.

As they all plunge into the sparkling blue below, Meaghan feels herself caught between two worlds—what's left of the life she has built with Duncan and the deep pull of what could have been with Bradley.

Chapter 5

PALMER STALLS NEARLY TWO WEEKS BEFORE HER APPOINT-
ment with Dr. Harlow. This morning, she walks through the
beachy-white front doors of the clinic early, because she believes that early is on time and on time is late, and she sits
down in the bright-blue waiting area on the leather couch
with time to spare. She digs her ringing cell from the depths of
her purse to answer and sees she's missed a call while driving.
Her cell in do-not-disturb-while-driving mode sent the caller
straight to voicemail.

She looks closely at the missed number: Sanford Banks.
Her entire body tenses. She hasn't spoken with Sanford since
the day that Miles died. She avoided him and Cinnamon at the
funeral, and afterward, she let him know by email that she was
withdrawing as the economic expert from the EnviroClean
case.

What could he possibly want now?

Her ringtone grows louder, reminding her to answer.
"Hello, Aiden?" Her voice strains to seem normal, but she's
flustered by Sanford's missed call.

"Hi, Mom," Aiden says. "How's the beach?"

"Beautiful. Absolutely beautiful. But not the same without all my boys."

Silence follows, and her heart sinks. All her boys always included Miles. This is the first summer the entire Harding family hasn't spent together at the beach.

"How are you, sweetheart?" She puts herself on mute so Aiden doesn't hear the elevator pinging in the background. He fills his mother in on the details of his life in Charlottesville. *Summer in a college town agrees with Aiden.*

"I turned down Professor Abernathy's internship," Aiden blurts out his news.

"What? Aiden!" She looks around the waiting room to see numerous eyes scolding her for being too loud. "Why on earth would you do that?" she whispers.

"Because I didn't want the internship."

"Aiden, that internship will pave your way to a brilliant architecture career."

"Maybe."

"It bears repeating that you're the youngest student to ever be offered the coveted opportunity. Why would you give it up?"

"I decided to wait tables at The Ivy."

She clenches her fists. Her eyes close. Aiden has given up on the thing she and Miles argued about for weeks. She wants to scream at him. He's made a terrible mistake, and now Miles died for nothing. Doesn't he realize that?

No, Aiden has no idea. She plans to keep it that way.

Palmer breathes deeply before speaking, which settles her tongue. "Oh, Aiden. Honey, this simply isn't what we agreed you would do. Your decision is … frivolous."

Aiden cuts her off with well-rehearsed explanations. "The internship will interfere with Varsity Crew practice. If they keep our practice and training schedule this summer, we've got a real shot at winning the National Regatta in Florida next May."

"But Aiden…"

"Crew will open all kinds of doors too, Mom. Especially when the National Regatta is broadcast across ESPN. The Ivy is flexible."

Finally, Palmer interjects, "Aiden, is this because of Dad?"

"No. What does Dad have to do with anything?" Aiden asks so loudly that the entire waiting room turns again to stare at Palmer.

"Okay, I'm sorry. I thought maybe …" Her best option with Aiden is to proceed as if life is normal; even though absolutely nothing is normal. "Thanks for letting me know about your plans, Aiden. Call me tomorrow? After Crew and your first shift at The Ivy? You can tell me how it all went."

"Sure, Mom. Talk tomorrow," Aiden says.

"I love you, A."

"Love you, too, Mom."

She tosses her cell into her purse, thinking back to the foggy days after Miles's stroke. She can't remember seeing Aiden cry. She can't remember hearing him yell. She can't remember him consoling his brother. Was she so depleted by her own guilt and sadness that she completely missed Aiden's non-reaction? *I'd poll the jury, but it's so obvious. He's in complete denial.*

She wishes Meaghan was here right now so they could discuss Aiden's summer career change, but they agreed Meaghan shouldn't come with her today. Yesterday afternoon, Darby Shaw, who owns Powdered Temptation, Rehoboth Village's creperie, and holds the reigning title of town gossip, called Palmer to put her on alert that the paparazzi and major news crews are hovering about the Cape. President Biden and his family are in town through the weekend, and they always bring a gaggle of press. Meaghan so far has kept her presence concealed. So instead of outing herself in Dr. Harlow's waiting room, Palmer booked Meaghan a private salon appointment. Since spending the day on Serenity with Bradley, Meaghan claims she is in desperate need of a buff and puff.

"Palmer Harding." A nurse at the front desk calls her name.

She stands up and approaches. "Yes, I'm Mrs. Harding."

"Good morning. I just need you to review your information sheet to make sure nothing has changed."

She scans the paper. Her eyes land at the bottom. "My emergency contact has changed."

The nurse looks at Palmer's form. "He's no longer your husband?"

"No. I'm … a widow." The words sting. Her stomach churns saying them for the first time.

"I'm so sorry." The nurse looks embarrassed.

"It's fine. I'm fine. Thank you."

"We still need an emergency contact," the nurse says apologetically. She remembers HIPPA and writes down Meaghan's name and phone number.

The nurse leads her back to a room for bloodwork and a physical exam followed by an MRI, prescheduled by Dr. Harlow, if only to calm Palmer's own fears. By four that afternoon, she sits alone waiting in the doctor's office suite, which overlooks the Atlantic. She endures five painstaking minutes before breaking down sobbing. The last time she was here, Miles sat beside her and life was sweet.

Miles's architectural firm had been named one of the top ten on the East Coast. The exposé on his firm in *Architectural*

Digest featured his renovation of Duncan and Meaghan's Bel Air mansion, garnering prominence among the East and West Coast elite. Palmer had secured a headline-grabbing win for her largest client yet, Apple, in a major patent lawsuit spanning ten countries, making her the top billing partner at her firm five years in a row. Quinn and Aiden were excelling in school and sports, and soon both would be out of the house. They were on the verge of becoming empty nesters, teasing each other with tantalizing threats of roaming the house naked and making love at noon on the living room floor. The icing on their cake was when Dr. Harlow announced that her cancer continued to be in remission. *You are going to be all right,* she'd said.

That evening, she and Miles celebrated her good health and the life they'd built together over the last nineteen years. That time went by so quickly, even though some days seemed to never end, they admitted. They drank a bottle of Veuve Clicquot on a blanket spread out onto the sand on The Hyacinth's private beach, eventually slipping their clothes off and skinny dipping in the ocean with the dolphins under the moonlit stars.

She shakes her head. How wrong they had been. Absolutely nothing turned out to be all right.

Dr. Harlow embraces Palmer at first sight, offering in-person condolences and relegating Palmer's sobbing to sniffles. She sits down next to her, both on the edge of their seats.

"Something is very wrong," Palmer says between nose wipes. "I was diagnosed with anxiety and stress before coming out to the Cape, because of everything with Miles, but I've been reading the internet. I have all the symptoms of cancer recurrence." Dr. Harlow gives her a disappointed look. "I know I'm not supposed to google. I can't help myself. You know this is exactly what happened to my mother."

"Palmer." Dr. Harlow says her name like a mother attempting to focus her child's attention, and hands her a Kleenex. "Your MRI is clean. No evidence of cancer. Anywhere."

She stops crying. Her head tilts. "Really?"

"Really."

She sits back into her chair. "I can't believe it. I was so certain."

"I know," Dr. Harlow says. "But your blood test identified a certain hormone level is extremely elevated."

"Oh my God. I knew it. I could tell. It's estrogen, isn't it?!" Palmer's breast cancer was positive for estrogen. This meant that her cancer fed off the estrogen hormones in her body. If her estrogen level spiked, her cancer must be growing ... somewhere, even if too small to show up on an MRI.

"No. It isn't estrogen. There's no cancer in your body. None. Zero."

"What is it then?"

"Your hCG levels are through the roof." Dr. Harlow pauses. Palmer's mouth drops open. She's been here before, too. "Palmer, you're pregnant."

MEAGHAN SLIDES THE BLACK JEEP WRANGLER THAT HOLLY rented for her into the only empty parking spot, which happens to be right in front of Beach Waves, Ashley Brimmer's salon. She peers through the Jeep's tinted windows. The streets bustle with vacationers straggling in from the beach to grab a sandwich from Surfside Gusto and an ice cream from Coastal

Creamery. Surf boards, coolers, and umbrellas spill from their hands. Meaghan gathers her purse, wraps her hair in a scarf, and puts on her sunglasses. Not a single beachgoer looks at her twice during the eight steps it takes to get to the Beach Wave's front door and step inside.

Heads layered with foil stacks turn and all eyes land on her. Three women getting their nails shellacked flash a quick smile. Everyone returns to perusing their magazine and phones. *Is one of them tweeting out my location at this very moment?* When the salon swiftly returns to buzzing with activity, she relaxes and the thought vanishes. No one recognizes her as she announces that she has a 3 p.m. appointment and is whisked off to the salon owner's private studio.

Ashley has spoken with her personal stylist in L.A., and the two agreed on a salty summer style, complete with beach waves, of course. One cappuccino, two flutes of champagne, and three stacks of magazines later, Ashley turns Meaghan around to face the mirror for a final reveal. Balayage combined with subtle blonde highlights stream through her luxuriously curled locks, cascading down the middle of her back.

"Ashley!" she exclaims. "This hair is stunning. I look amazing. Thank you."

She heads back to the receptionist to settle her bill and leave Ashley the biggest tip of her styling career. Feeling so pampered by her fresh color and style, she forgets that her scarf and sunglasses remain stuffed in her Jerome Dreyfuss Pedro tote. When she arrives back at the front desk, the woman paying turns around with a smile that instantly fades to a glare. *Oh, no.*

"You know, my daughter applied to SCC this year," the woman says.

"Oh." Her hand searches the bottom of her tote, confirming her disguise's whereabouts.

"She didn't get in."

"I'm sorry to hear that. I hope she got in somewhere else she wanted to attend," she says. "These kids all have their reach schools, their favorite schools, and the back-up schools."

"In fact, two of my friends here today …" The woman nods toward two customers sitting with their heads under the dryers. "Their daughters also applied to SCC. They were all hoping to experience college and California together." The woman leans in. "*None* of them got in."

Meaghan would do anything to switch spots right now with Marissa Mabry, who has been her movie body double for the past decade. She wants to escape this terrible scene.

"They all earned a 4.5 GPA in high school … so many AP classes. Volunteer and service hours exceeding school requirements. Two were cheerleaders. All played on the varsity tennis team, which won state three years in a row. They were members of the National Honor Society. On Student Council. I mean, they did it all. They sacrificed every step of the way. Four years of non-stop, over-the-top hard work. Early mornings, late evenings, weekends filled … the whole thing. They got into every other college they applied to. Except their top choice, SCC."

She stands paralyzed. In California, dagger glares were often thrown her way after Dunc's arrest, but no one dared to confront her directly. But on the East Coast, Hollywood is worlds away.

"I'm sorry," she finally says. "It's so hard when our kids don't get what they want … and deserve." But her apology is too little too late.

The woman bursts into incredulous laughter. "You're kidding me, right? Yes, it is 'hard' when our kids don't get what they want. But it is downright cruel when they work so hard and earn that recognition everywhere except where they are truly meant to be, because someone else with an egocentric God complex simply pays for the spot that should have been theirs."

Shit.

"What you did … you and your husband … you changed the course of young lives forever. If it weren't for your money and your privilege, lives would be different."

The woman's words cut deep. She's right. Lives would be different. The system is unfair. Kids get turned away all the time. Donations or bribes, whatever way you look at it, the system is rotten.

"Listen, I am very sorry for what your daughters … all of them … have experienced." She turns around to address the woman's two friends as well. "And I do realize that 'sorry' is not sufficient for the impact this …" Meaghan tries to think of the right word but resigns to calling it what it is, "… scandal has meant in their lives …" She wants to apologize more, but she cannot go any further. *The equestrian team?* "It's just Duncan did things I wasn't aware of … "

Everyone in the salon is now focused on her.

"Are you defending yourself in this mess you've created?" the woman asks. "Are you continuing to lie about the situation? Everyone knows you and Duncan Jones bribed college officials. You'll soon be sharing a jail cell with your felonious husband, I bet. Honestly, no one understands why you aren't yet." The woman spews words while collecting her phone, keys, and purse off the receptionist's counter. She slips on her sunglasses and inches right up to Meaghan, nose to nose. "You're not Hollywood royalty. You're Hollywood trash. The dirtiest, sneakiest kind." The woman turns around, walks out, and slams the door behind her. She watches the woman get into her car and drive off. Every woman at Beach Waves stares at Meaghan.

"How much do I owe you?" she asks the receptionist, who has witnessed the entire exchange with her eyes and mouth wide open.

"Four hundred dollars."

She throws down six hundred dollars in cash and leaves without saying another word.

She barely gets the door of the Jeep Wrangler closed before bursting into tears. Her hands shake so much she can hardly hold onto the steering wheel. *People hate me.* On the West Coast. On the East Coast. Everywhere.

Chapter 6

MEAGHAN CRIES THE ENTIRE DRIVE BACK TO THE Hyacinth. She arrives and heads straight to the wine refrigerator, pulls out a Stag Leap Cabernet, and pours herself a large glass. She downs it and pours herself another. Then she grabs the near-emptied bottle and pulls another full one from the wine fridge, scooping them in her arm while carrying her wine glass in the other hand. She scours the cottage to find Palmer in the den, watching *Ted Lasso*.

"Needing a dose of radical optimism?" she asks, plopping herself and her wine down on the couch next to Palmer. "I could use one."

"Trying to channel a goldfish," Palmer responds. She stares somewhat bewildered at the TV, finally hits mute, and turns to look at her. "Jesus, Meaghan. What happened to you?"

Her mascara is running down her face in black streaks. "I ugly cried my face right off."

"Yes, you did. What's going on?"

Meaghan devours the wine in her glass in two gulps and pours herself another. "The entire world thinks I'm a criminal."

Palmer exhales. She gives her a sympathetic smile. "Yes, they do. I wasn't sure you knew. What happened to make you realize it?"

"Some woman went off on me at Ashley's. Palmer, I've worked a lifetime to keep everyone in love with me. The roles I've chosen. The clothes I wear. The foundations I donate to. The Instagram posts. Hell, even the man I married. All in hopes that adoring fans everywhere will stay in love with me. That they won't leave me." Four fast glasses of Cabernet in, Meaghan tears up again. "Now, because of Sinful Admissions, everyone absolutely hates me. I've become the villain of my own story." Another gulp.

Palmer puts a hand on her wine glass and slowly lowers it toward the coffee table. She wrinkles her nose at Palmer and picks the glass back up.

"*I* don't hate you. I could never hate you," Palmer says reassuringly.

"Oh yes you could. If you only knew, you would definitely hate me for never telling you," she blurts out. Her words are slurred.

"What?" Palmer asks. "If I only knew what?"

Meaghan leans forward to whisper in Palmer's ear, as if doing so means she won't really hear her. "About your mom." She leans backwards again, resting into the couch and closing her eyes. "I never told you. I couldn't do it. So, I left."

Meaghan has drunk so much Cabernet so quickly she passes out on the couch, washing the entire day's horrid events from her mind.

❧

AROUND SIX O'CLOCK THE NEXT MORNING, PALMER watches her friend struggle into her reality of a massive hangover. *Why does age make hangovers feel so much worse?* "Headache?" she asks, feigning concern.

"Massive," Meaghan confirms. "If that is even possible." Meaghan attempts to bat her eyes open. They are sealed together with gelled remnants of black mascara, almost like tar. She finally succeeds. *Ted Lasso* flickers silently on the TV, an unwanted background to tension in the air.

"What did you never tell me about my mother?" Her words demand attention.

An awkward silence engulfs the room, thick enough to drown in. Palmer has been up all night. Pacing in the hallway. Pacing in the kitchen. Finally, warming milk to settle her stomach. Is it the guilt? Is it the uneasiness about whatever Meaghan has been hiding? Is it the baby? All options create a swirling storm inside her.

Meaghan brings her hands to her forehead. She knows Meaghan's world must be spinning and last night's events may be ambiguous, at best. She doesn't care.

"Is this why you left? Last night you said, 'I couldn't tell you, so I left.'" She can't take her eyes off Meaghan. Meaghan can't meet her gaze. "It's the only thing between us that I have never understood. Why you left Cottonwood Falls right before we were supposed to graduate without even telling me you were leaving. Without a goodbye! You simply vanished overnight." She waves her hand in the air motioning an eraser.

"Victoria told me you'd left town when I knocked on your door the next day after you never showed at school. I was worried sick about you. It took you a whole week to call me. You'd made it to California. You told me you 'couldn't wait any longer' and 'the screen was calling you.' That was all a lie, wasn't it? Your story didn't fit. It didn't fit … us."

She's wanted to confront Meaghan for years. She's wanted to know the real reason Meaghan walked out on their friendship but has always worried she might have done something to make Meaghan leave. "Is this thing about my mom why you took off?"

Meaghan pulls her legs up underneath her chin and stares at her toes. "Yes."

"Well, it must be pretty bad."

"It is." Meaghan pauses, then looks at her. "I did want to pursue acting, of course you know that. Being someone else has always felt more natural than playing myself. But I could have waited. I ran to California because I didn't know how to tell you what I knew. I've never known how to tell you. I don't want to hurt you and I couldn't risk losing you, too."

"Whatever it is you've been keeping from me all this time, you need to tell me now." A long pause sits in the air between them. "I promise I'll forgive you. Just tell me."

The bold guarantee works. Meaghan sits up on the couch and puts her feet on the floor, clasping her hands together as her elbows rest on her knees and she leans toward her.

"It's about how your mom died."

What? Meaghan never knew Palmer's mother. The two girls became best friends after Palmer's mother died. They shared the unbearable heartbreak brought on by losing a parent—Meaghan's dad walked out on her and Victoria three years earlier. It bonded them for life.

"What are you talking about?" she asks. "My mother died from breast cancer."

"Yes, but there's more." Meaghan takes a deep breath and begins to slowly unfold the secret she's kept so tightly wrapped. "My mom was the nurse on her floor the day Linda died. Your mother had been in and out of our little hospital in Cottonwood Falls for months."

"I remember."

The pain would start in her mom's leg bones and move up through her pelvis and back. It would become so great that it would make her vomit. So they would take her to the hospital and give her a steroid shot in the spine. The pain would ease for a while, and she'd come home. But then it would return in a week or so. Back she'd go to the hospital for a shot and the cycle would repeat. Until the last time, when she went into the hospital and never came home again.

Palmer breathes deeply and closes her eyes, snippets of images running through her mind.

"I remember helping her get into the car that last evening. I can picture her siting in the passenger seat as I swung her legs around onto the car's front seat floor from the driveway. As I shut the passenger car door, she begged my father to make sure he brought her home again." A lump builds up in her throat. She fights back tears. "He never did."

Meaghan rubs her hand on Palmer's leg. "When they arrived at the hospital that last time, she was there a couple weeks before she died. The first week, she was fully conscious. My mother worked evening shifts on her floor. Your dad spent the night at home with you and your sister, so our moms talked a lot, I guess. Your mom was in full command of her mental faculties that first week. She knew exactly where she was and what was happening. She wanted to go home and kept saying your father had promised he'd take her back. But her pain was so great, she knew she wouldn't be going back."

Tears pour down Palmer's cheeks.

How could her mother not have known? Palmer contemplated the very same thoughts not infrequently during her own treatment, and for years afterward.

"She knew," Palmer said. "But the rest of us couldn't even begin to think of that possibility. We couldn't fathom a single day without her. We were all living in denial." *Like Aiden is, right now.*

She looks up at Meaghan again. "What else did your mom tell you?"

"Your mom was scared, but more than that, she was in unbearable pain. At the beginning of her second week at the hospital, Pastor Mosby came to visit her, and they spent quite a while together. When my mother checked on her after he left, your mother pleaded with my mom to help her … to help her die."

Palmer gasps, her hands cover her mouth. That possibility never once entered her mind in all these years. Even during her own treatment. The weight of her mother's wishes is so heavy, she feels like she is drowning, barely able to breathe.

"My mother was completely stunned. She had heard stories of patients asking for assistance, but no one had ever asked her. She didn't know what to do. She didn't want to see your mom suffer, but she also couldn't fathom violating her nurse's oath. Plus, there were possibly criminal consequences."

"What did she do?"

"My mom never said anything to anyone about your mother's request. She was off for the next several days. By the time she went back to work, your mother was in and out of a coma. She'd only wake up from excruciating pain." Meaghan runs her hands on her thighs.

"They didn't know if she would ever come back to full consciousness, or when the end might come."

"I remember sleeping on the couch in the hospital lobby some of those nights."

"Yes. My mom said your dad stayed at the hospital in a chair at her bedside, taking turns with her parents throughout the night, as they watched her labored breathing, awaking only to hear her painful screams. They weren't sure what to do. But finally, my mother was."

Meaghan grabs her hands. "She told your dad and her parents about your mother's request. That your mother had asked her for help to die, to help end her pain. Your family was shocked and angry, so my mother said nothing else. But that afternoon your uncle took you, your sister, and your cousins to the arcade. As you left, everyone overheard you telling your mother that it was okay for her to go. Do you remember that?"

"Of course I do." Tears fall down her cheeks. "We were putting our coats on. Everyone was heading to the elevators. I slipped into Mom's room. I hugged her and said, 'You can go, Mom. Dad will take care of us, you can go if you need to.' I'll never forget giving her permission ..." She wipes her tears with the blanket. "...Because she took it."

"Your words gave everyone permission," Meaghan explains. "Somehow, you knew that the end had arrived. My mom told me that overhearing you flipped a switch for your entire family. After you and your sister left for the arcade with your cousins, my mother went into her room, where your entire family was keeping watch. She asked everyone to leave so she could assess Linda's vitals and do an examination. They did."

She shivers and Meaghan wraps an arm around her.

"When they went back into the room, my mother had left an extra vial of morphine on the nightstand by her IV with a strong enough dose to stop her heart and send her off peacefully. No more suffering. Your family called Pastor Moby. They prayed over her. They cried and held each other and held her too. And then they watched her peacefully slip away."

Palmer's eyebrows furrow with misunderstanding, "What are you saying?"

"My mother found the empty morphine syringe in the trash can. No one ever said a thing. She never asked."

Palmer pieces things together. She pulls away from Meaghan, standing up and looking down on Meaghan still unable to move from the couch, "You're suggesting that my dad and my mom's parents overdosed her? Because of what I said?" Her voice grows louder.

"They helped her die peacefully. You helped her die peacefully."

"My father would never have done that. To her or to us!" She raises her voice. Meaghan sits silently. "Besides, there would have been a vial of missing morphine that the doctors would have been looking for."

Meaghan's eyes stay glued to the floor. "My mother logged all shipments into the drug locker. She simply erased that vial from existence. She waited for someone to come and ask her about it. She worried for years about criminal charges. But she never heard a thing."

Palmer's rage and confusion balloon as she realizes her role in how her mother died. "It's not true. What you're saying can't be true!"

"It's true," Meaghan says. "I think my mother's own worry is partly why she told me. She watched you grow up know-ing what really happened that day. She told me once, in the weeks before our graduation, and never mentioned it again. Once she told me, I couldn't face you with what I knew. How could I tell my best friend what really happened to her mother? What my mother did? What your family did? I couldn't risk losing you forever."

Meaghan stands up and reaches out for her again, but she instinctively pulls away.

"So, I left, instead. By the next time we saw each other, when you came to L.A. that summer after graduation to visit me, I had a new life. I moved on and tried to forget about it. But it has haunted me ever since."

Palmer processes the real implication of the story. "If what your mom told you is true, then I'm responsible for my mother's death." *And I'm responsible for Miles's too.* Her guilt flares up into anger. She searches for a place it can land.

"And you've known and hidden it from me for years! Abandoning your best friend. Lying to her. All so you could keep at least one person in your life who actually loves you. You are so selfish!"

Meaghan stands up. "Palmer, you're not responsible for …"

She snaps. Betrayal surges through her veins like fire. "You hid this from me, and that's why you left! Always running." She points to the door, "Let me help you. Get out."

"What? You said you'd forgive me if I told you the truth. Now you're forcing me out?"

"You heard me. I want you to leave." She glares deep into Meaghan's eyes, hoping it wounds far worse than any other glare Meaghan's endured since Sinful Admissions. If Meaghan was too afraid to tell Palmer for fear she'd lose her, then lose her she will. "I can't be with you anymore."

Palmer folds the blanket on the couch into a neat square, deliberately contemplating her next move as she pins each edge together. Then it comes to her.

"Honestly, Meaghan, if you have been keeping this from me, I can only imagine what else you're lying about. Are you sure you weren't in on Duncan's plan? Should you be in jail too? Maybe Bella is right!" She hits Meaghan where it will hurt her most.

Meaghan recoils and rubs her temples. Palmer's anger becomes relentless; betrayal has that effect. She inches toward Meaghan pushing her toward the door. "Get. Out."

Meaghan teeters backwards. Her face twists and her eyes well with tears. "Where am I supposed to go?"

Chapter 7

FORTY-FIVE MINUTES LATER, MEAGHAN PARKS HER JEEP Wrangler in front of The Oyster House. Bradley's steel-gray Mercedes G-Wagon is parked in the spot beside her. Two weeks have passed since they went out on Serenity. She sits in the car for twenty minutes before mustering the courage to enter.

Meaghan knocks on the front door of the restaurant, which remains locked until lunch opening. She peers through the glass and sees no one. She knocks louder and louder, until her knocking channels Agent Hendrix's, the thought of which makes Meaghan immediately pull her fist away from the door. At that same moment, Bradley walks from the back of the restaurant toward the front door wearing a scowl. When he sees the rude culprit is Meaghan, his scowl transforms into an ear-to-ear grin.

"Well, this is unexpected," Bradley says, opening the door and kissing Meaghan on the cheek. The kiss sends an unmistakable and surprising spark through her entire body. She flashes back to the first night they met on The Hyacinth's beach almost two decades ago. The single kiss they shared that night lit off fireworks inside her; it was magnetic and un-forgettable. She's never felt such passion kissing anyone else. *Never, not even Dunc.*

"I was in the neighborhood," she offers lamely, instantly realizing how absurd she sounds. "Okay, Palmer kicked me out," she admits, throwing her hands in the air, still in disbelief.

"What?" he asks. "Why?"

"That's a bit of a story."

"Come in." Bradley gestures for her to enter. "We're having our family meal in back." Her confusion must show on her face, because he explains, "The chefs and servers eat together before we open. Are you hungry?"

"Always. Plus I'm nursing a serious hangover."

"Okay, let's get you something to eat."

She nods and points to the booth farthest from the door, tucked away behind the waiters' station. She goes over and sits down. Bradley fixes them both a plate of today's lunch special, seafood spaghetti: plump crab, shrimp, calamari, and mussels in a fresh tomato basil sauce and topped with Pecorino Romano. He places a breadbasket on the table filled with warm rosemary rolls.

She tears the roll in two, smears a large dollop of butter on one half, and pops the bread into her mouth. *Heaven.*

As she eats, Meaghan recounts the events of the last twenty-four hours. She feels as though she's playing a seriously flawed protagonist giving her monologue: the spotlight is on, and Bradley listens attentively. He gives her the space to find her words—another habit she remembers from their brief time together. He never rushes her thoughts, even when the silence lingers.

Eventually, a few patrons drift in from the beach.

"My life is a complete train wreck," she concludes. "My husband is a criminal. My daughter refuses to have anything to do with me because she thinks I'm a criminal, too." *And maybe I am.* "The tabloids feast on every bit of it. All of which is successfully ruining my career and my business. And now my very best friend hates me, too!"

Meaghan stuffs the last shrimp into her mouth. She intentionally leaves out that she's facing another deposition after which the FBI likely will indict her on charges of money laundering, landing her in the slammer alongside Dunc.

"I'm not sure I'll get her back."

"You'll get Palmer back. She loves you. You're like sisters. Sometimes sisters fight," Bradley assures her. He disappears to the kitchen and returns with two mugs of freshly perked black coffee and a slice of peach pie with two forks.

"Made this morning with Georgia peaches picked yesterday." He looks to see if she's impressed. She is.

He sets the pie down and his hand grazes hers. Her cheeks turn pink.

"Do you think I'm the worst person you've ever met?" she asks.

"No. I think you're human. In fact, you're still one of the best humans I know." He looks softly in her eyes. "You're salt of the earth. Unfiltered. Quick with your tongue. Quick with your wit. So smart. Brilliant, really. And you've never become Hollywood. You may dress Hollywood and play the part as needed, but out here at least, you're just a crazy Midwestern girl. One of the best humans I know."

Meaghan drops her gaze to the table, feeling somewhat embarrassed, but mostly ... cherished. She remembers this is how it feels to be with Bradley. It feels good.

"Look, you didn't want to hurt Palmer. You were afraid. I get it. Palmer will, too. It may take a little time. She's been through a lot."

Bradley makes her feel … normal. It's wonderful.

"So, what are you going to do now?" he asks.

"I don't want to go back to L.A.," Meaghan confesses. She simply can't handle returning to the scene of the crime. "I love it here. I want to stay the summer as planned. Plus, I can't just leave with Palmer so angry. I left her once before, and look where it got us now. I'm staying."

"Well, then you're staying with me," Bradley says. "For now, at least. You can bunk in the guest room until either Palmer lets you back into The Hyacinth or you find somewhere better"—he winks at her—"which is unlikely."

"That's very generous, but I can't just crash on your doorstep." When she arrived at the restaurant, Meaghan thought Bradley might know someone local who was out of town and had a spot where she could spend a few days until things blow over. However, Bradley's idea entices her. The paparazzi won't know she's there.

"Of course you can," he says.

Butterflies flutter in her stomach. This man is gorgeous, inside and out. Deep tan and tousled blond hair combined with a heart of gold. He's offering to rescue her, something that would never even occur to Duncan.

"Why hasn't someone scooped you up?" Meaghan asks him out of nowhere. The question surprises even her.

"Oh, they've tried," he admits. "I guess after all these years, I still haven't found the right girl." He looks her right in the eyes.

Meaghan feels the weight of everything they aren't saying pressing against her chest. Time hasn't diminished their ability to communicate in careful omissions. "Bradley," she begins, then stops, suddenly uncertain how to bridge the careful distance they maintained for two decades.

His eyes meet hers directly, the practiced facade of casual acquaintance momentarily set aside. "Why are you here, Meaghan?"

The question is simple, delivered without accusation—but it strips away her pretenses, leaving her nowhere to hide. The restaurant continues its gentle hum around them, oblivious to the history suspended between two people at a back booth.

The entire table begins to shake, grabbing her attention, as Bradley's cell vibrates. "Sophia" flashes across the screen. Meaghan diverts her gaze. Her heart sinks a little.

Bradley grabs the phone to answer. "Just a second," he tells her and excuses himself to the kitchen.

A few minutes later, he returns. "Sorry about that."

"No problem," Meaghan assures him.

"You are welcome to my guest room," Bradley offers a second time.

"What a bitch." A loud voice at the bar interrupts the entire restaurant, now beginning to hum with couples and families fresh off the beach, ordering their lunches. Everyone turns to look. Three forty-something couples sit on bar stools eating lunch. Flashy diamond rings and watches, Prada bags and Gucci sunglasses in full show. They all appear to be on their third round of martinis. Each one staring her down.

"Hollywood royalty, my ass," one of the men says.

Bradley motions to the bartender to cut them off. He gets up. She tries to stop him, but Bradley is unstoppable. He walks right over to them.

The first guy, smirking, looks Bradley up and down. "What do you want?"

"I'd like you to leave," he says, surprising them all.

"We aren't leaving," the second guy says.

"We weren't talking to you," the woman next to him chimes in.

"Just that bitch you're with," the first guy says.

Bradley grabs him by the collar and drags him toward the door. "That's it. All of you out."

The women begin to gather their things, but the second guy says, "Whoa, dude. Who do you think you are?"

He comes up and taps Bradley on the shoulder. Bradley turns around, and the guy punches him right on the nose.

Blood spurts everywhere. Everyone in the restaurant gasps. Bradley grabs a cloth napkin from a table and presses it to his face. The women stand clutching their bags to their chests. Meaghan sits frozen, not knowing what to do next.

Bradley extends his free hand to the guy who punched him. "I'm Bradley. I own this joint. And you are never eating here again."

Their faces go blank. The Oyster House is the hottest dining spot in town.

Bradley opens the door and throws the first guy to the curb. "You'd better leave. If you don't, I'm calling Chief Lawhorn." The others follow without hesitation. "Don't ever come back. Got it?"

The guy dusts himself off and the six of them walk back toward the beach. "No problem. Wouldn't want to."

"Perfect," Bradley says. He closes the door, turns around, and takes a bow. "Show's over, folks. Enjoy the rest of your lunch." Bradley makes his way back to her at the back booth.

"Are you okay?" She stands to get a look at his face. "Is it broken?"

Half of Bradley's napkin is red. He pulls it from his nose; the bleeding has stopped. "Possibly broken. Not the first time. I'll be fine. What a bunch of jerks. Are you okay?"

Bradley sits back down across from her. "Yes. Definitely jerks, but not the first time either." She sighs. "Thank you. You can't change their minds, but I appreciate your valor on my behalf." She's humiliated by their name calling. At the same time, she's impressed by the fact that someone stood up for her. *I'm not sure that's ever happened before.* "Sure you still want me to bunk with you?" she asks with a small laugh.

"Absolutely." He grabs her hand, squeezes it, and gives her a wink.

Fireworks, again.

Chapter 8

BY NOON, THE HYACINTH'S FRONT LAWN SWARMS WITH paparazzi. The salon incident sent shockwaves through the Village. The first ripple spreads the news that Meaghan Jones is spending the summer on the Cape. The second, that she's come unglued at Beach Waves. Palmer honestly can't believe she's dealing with more of Meaghan's messes; she's still processing this morning's revelations.

She peers through the window, watching the Chief of Police, Scott Lawhorn, who she called an hour earlier, address the crowd. Chief Lawhorn and his wife, Goldie, are longtime friends of Miles and Palmer, by way of Bradley.

After effectively disbanding the press with his reminder of local ordinance rules that require jailing for loitering on private property, Chief Lawhorn gently knocks on The Hyacinth's door, opens it, and enters the foyer, meeting Palmer as she rushes in from the kitchen.

"Thank you," she says when she lays eyes on him. "Coffee? I've pulled out a hot apple pie from the oven that I can't eat myself." She means it; her nausea persists. Knowing the Chief cannot resist her apple pie, she began making one the minute she called him about the paparazzi. The entire pie is meant for the Chief.

"Maybe a small slice," he says.

"Great. I'll wrap up the rest and send it home for you and Goldie to finish."

"I can't say no to that," the Chief says. They settle at the kitchen table. Palmer last saw Chief Lawhorn and Goldie at Miles's memorial service. They'd driven down from the Cape with Bradley. "How are you doing, Palmer?" The Chief wastes no one's time. It's part of his job to get straight to the point.

Palmer holds a fresh glass of ginger tea in her hands. In her mind, she shouts her guilty confessions to the highest law man in town. *I killed Miles! I killed my mother! I kissed another man!*

Instead, she divulges another piece of shocking news. "Well, I'm pregnant."

She needs to tell someone. She planned to tell Meaghan last night, but first Meaghan was too upset, then Meaghan was too drunk, and finally Meaghan dropped too large a bomb right on their friendship, blowing up their last thirty years. So the first person she tells is the Chief.

"The only other person who knows is Dr. Harlow. And now you." The Chief has heard a lot of true confessions in his day, but his jaw on the floor suggests this one is entirely unexpected.

"All right then," he says and nods his approval. "Thank you for telling me. I promise I won't tell a soul. Not even Goldie. As Chief, there are a lot of things I keep to myself."

"I can imagine," she says. "I'm not sure how I'm feeling really. I've lost Miles. After next year, both boys will be off to college and I'm"—her stomach swirls as she says it—"going to be a single mother?" She's accomplished a lot over the years,

but she's unsure how successful she might be at single parenting a newborn in her forties. Raising another child for the
next eighteen years isn't the life she envisioned for herself only
weeks before. She could see a life with herself at the center; a
life that looked pretty damn amazing, even if it felt extremely
selfish. But poof! That life is gone. And, even worse, the pregnancy itself comes with risks. Dr. Harlow informed her that
her age and her previous breast cancer put her pregnancy in
the "high risk" category, which means she will be receiving
weekly ultrasounds and blood checks to ensure the baby, and
she, remain healthy.

"On the other hand, you're having Miles's baby." His eyebrows furrow as he speaks, and he coughs to clear his throat.
"I assume it's Miles's baby?"

"Oh Scott! Of course it's Miles's baby." But the Chief's
question immediately causes Palmer to wonder if Miles told
the Chief they had been having difficulties. Surely, Miles
wouldn't tell anyone.

"I'm a cop. I assume all possibilities are on the table until
I learn otherwise," he says.

"That makes sense." Her cell begins to ring across the
kitchen. She stands up to see who's calling.

"I'll let you go and see myself out. I've got to be at the
station anyway. I'm interviewing another possible replacement
for Madison." The Chief shoves the final bite of pie into his
mouth. Madison King, the Chief's assistant for fifteen years
who keeps the department organized and running like clock-
work, retired last fall. Palmer points to the foil-wrapped apple
pie. She had to channel all that anger somewhere. "Thanks."
He grabs it. "Oh, I'm sending a patrol car around every hour
to keep the press off your lawn."

"Great. Thank you!" She makes her way across the kitchen toward her ringing phone.

"Call me if you need anything. And, Palmer ..." The Chief pauses. "Congratulations."

"Thanks, Scott." She smiles and watches the Chief disappear out the kitchen. She picks up her phone and presses the green button. "Hello?"

"Hi. Palmer? It's Frances."

The only other time Frances called her in the middle of the day was when Miles dropped dead several weeks earlier. So this call sends her heart racing.

"Everything's fine. There's nothing wrong," Frances quickly adds.

"Oh. Good." She rests her hand on her chest as she exhales a sigh of relief. "How are things ... at the office?"

"We are all doing okay here. Except, of course, we miss Miles desperately," Frances says.

"Of course you do. We all do." *And you can blame me for that.* She decides to change the subject. "How is Liam? What's he up to this summer?"

"He's really great," Frances says. "Swim teaming through early August. He's got his eye set on making regionals in the 50M Fly. But we'll see."

"That's awesome!" Regionals are a big deal, not many swimmers qualify each summer. "He's so talented, I'm sure he'll make it."

"Liam told me Quinn is having a great summer too ... all things considered." A pause lingers for a moment in the air. "Have you met his new girlfriend?"

Girlfriend?

She talks with Quinn once a week on Sunday morning at 8 a.m. because that's the turnover day at Camp Horizons. The campers from the week before all leave by Saturday evening and the new campers don't show up until 10 a.m. on Sunday. Her window to catch Quinn during some downtime is narrow, so she always makes a point to call. He hasn't once mentioned a girlfriend.

"No, I haven't met her yet. He's been at Camp Horizons for weeks now."

"Yes, I know, silly! His girlfriend is a counselor there too, right? Liam said they met after Quinn jumped into the lake to save a drowning girl. He's become quite the hero! What girl wouldn't be smitten!" Frances tells Palmer more about her son's life than her son has told her in weeks.

"Quinn is quite the catch," she admits, but she's unwilling to admit she knows nothing else about her son's life right now.

"Listen, I'm actually calling for two reasons," Frances continues. "First, we started a story wall in the office lobby with all the condolence letters we've received. More than three hundred cards! Almost everyone includes family pictures in front of the home Miles designed and built for them. Some new selfies they've taken and others old holiday photo cards. There's hardly a spot left and still the notes pour into our mailbox every day."

"That's amazing," Meaghan says. "Text me a photo of the wall, will you? I'll want to read every one of their notes when I get back to Alexandria after the summer. I am still getting about twenty cards a day forwarded to The Hyacinth, as well." Palmer neglects to mention that each one leaves her in a puddle, even the ones that simultaneously make her laugh.

"Absolutely. I'll text you right after we hang up," Frances says. "People are also donating to Miles's scholarship fund. The Miles Harding Scholarship Fund for Architectural Study will provide the means for talented architecture students to attend the college of their choice. Four years. All tuition paid." Palmer started the fund with a personal donation of one hundred thousand dollars, which will pay for two students next year.

"The donations have been piling up," Frances says. "Honestly, I can't even believe it. Palmer, we already have five hundred thousand dollars beyond your initial endowment, including fifty thousand dollars from Mr. Duvall."

She collapses onto the kitchen bar stool. "Whoa. That's unexpected." Her adrenaline starts pumping. She feels a hint of the rush she gets when taking the stand or helping to cross-examine another witness.

I've got to get this fund off the ground. How many students could they help in this year alone? Could she make the scholarship process fully operational by the year's end? While having a baby?

"When I return, I will need to get a board together, select an executive director to oversee corporate fundraising and scholarship applications. Any chance you'd help me put a short list together of individuals we know who might be a good fit for an ED?"

"I've already started a list," Frances says. "I'll finish compiling mine in the next few weeks and email it over to you."

"Perfect. Thank you, Frances." Palmer gazes out the large glass kitchen doors as the tide rushes the sand below. "What was the other thing? You said you called for two reasons."

"Oh, right. We finished going through Miles's office, organizing his current projects and assigning them to other architects on the staff. While we were at it, we gathered his personal papers. I assume you'd like them at some point. Should I store them here at the office until you're back?"

The thought of discovering never seen belongings of Miles makes her feel like a pirate opening a treasure chest. Gold must be inside. "I would love them," she says. "Could you deliver everything to The Hyacinth?"

"Well, there's ten boxes full of his personal effects. Are you sure you want them all at the beach this summer?"

Palmer grins. Ten treasure chests to be opened seaside at the beach. What could be more perfect? "I'm sure. Send them all," Palmer says. She thinks about sharing her baby news with Frances but, before she tells anyone else, she needs to tell the boys.

"I'll have them sent out today," Frances says. "Take care of yourself, Palmer, and enjoy your beach time with Meaghan!"

Frances hangs up. Beach time with Meaghan? The lying, selfish Hollywood criminal? No, thank you, Palmer thinks. And then she feels bad for thinking it.

A minute later she receives a text from Frances. The picture is of Miles's office lobby. The entire wall papered with photos and cards from floor to ceiling. She taps on the photo. She zooms in on the image to read the notes and see the images. There are so many faces. So many families, she thinks. Hundreds for whom Miles created the perfect place to build their lives together.

Something catches Palmer's eye right in the middle. She zooms in closer.

Sanford and Cinnamon sit on the steps of their three-million-dollar estate in Great Falls, smiling and each holding one of their two Samoyed puppies. The picture was taken five years ago, after Miles redesigned the entire estate. It's now the property of Cinnamon and her landscaper. Or, quite possibly, Igor Overlauder.

"Damn you, Sanford," Palmer says out loud.

He called her two more times since yesterday morning's missed call at Dr. Harlow's office—once last night and again this morning. Each time his name flashes across her phone's home screen, she feels like she's swimming in the middle of a dead zone, a spot so deep in the ocean there's zero oxygen. She chokes.

She wants to never hear from Sanford again. It doesn't matter that they were close friends and colleagues, the equivalent of professional BFFs. They crossed a line. They can't go back. Why doesn't Sanford know this? Palmer clicks her screen black.

MEAGHAN PARKS HER JEEP WRANGLER IN THE DRIVEWAY of Bradley's townhouse, finds the key in the flower planters on his back porch where he said they'd be, and lets herself in. He's working till close tonight, after a quick trip to the ER, where the doctor confirms his nose is not broken. She hauls her suitcases up to the third-floor guest room and sets them beside the king bed. She walks one floor up and pokes her head out onto the rooftop, where a lavish pool, outdoor kitchen, and firepit overlook the ocean. "Gorgeous," she says out loud.

She spends the afternoon poolside scrolling through Instagram and X, assessing the online damage from yesterday's salon debacle. The headlines are insufferable. "Meaghan Jones' Massive Tantrum." The stories feature eyewitness accounts.

"Meaghan appears to be in complete shambles and absolute denial about her actions. She really should be in jail," claimed one local witness. *There was zero tantrum*, she thinks. *I apologized!* But apologies don't sell papers. She wonders exactly how much Darby has been stirring the gossip pot at Powdered Temptation.

As the sun dips below the horizon over the water's edge, she retreats to the main floor, grabs a bottle of wine from the fridge, and settles down on the couch in the great room. *Hair of the dog.*

She looks around. The townhome is decorated in deep, rich colors that let you know it's a man's home. Both the walls and ceilings of the living room are painted a deep navy, dark leather-tufted couches and club chairs fill the living room, old world rugs adorned with swirls of deep burgundy and creams cover the hardwood floors, and expensive art hangs on the walls. For a bachelor, Bradley has exquisite taste, exception to the 1970s recliner she spotted in his private office. She spies the kitchen sink full of dirty dishes from at least the last week. *What is it with men being unable to do their dishes?*

A baby grand piano sits in the corner of the room. She forgot that Bradley loves to play. Sitting on top of the piano are at least ten different picture frames, snapshots from the best of his life. A wedding photo of Bradley's mother and father who died several years ago in a freak automobile crash on the Rue de Rivoli in Paris. A photo of their entire family when the kids were young, including his five older siblings, all sisters. Individual photos of each sister's family now all grown and living across the globe like a giant family paint splatter. Several photos of deep-sea fishing trips taken to Europe, South America, and one in Cape Town with a five-foot tuna in hand.

Celebrity photos at The Oyster House. Centered in the front middle, among all the other glimpses into Bradley's life, is a photo of Bradley and Miles on the beach at The Hyacinth, smoking cigars and drinking bourbon.

She remembers Bella took that picture while playing around with the camera settings on her new iPhone. It was just an ordinary evening in the Harding household, everyone gathered around the fire and goofing around. Remembering the magic of that simple evening makes her heart ache. She steals the photo from the piano and collapses onto the couch.

As she nods off to sleep on the couch, she wonders if she and Palmer will ever laugh like that together again.

At one in the morning, the door to the townhouse opens and then closes gently, waking her. She hears Bradley slip his shoes off at the door, lay his keys and wallet on the kitchen island, and walk down the long hallway to the living room.

"You're awake," he says when he discovers her under a blanket on his tufted leather sectional, an empty wine bottle on the table and a half-full wine glass beside her on the floor.

"I was asleep," she murmurs, her pulse quickening as he sits beside her.

"Sorry. I thought you'd be in the guest room." He picks the wine glass up off the floor, sets it on the coffee table by the bottle that once held it, and sits down on the couch at Meaghan's side. "I'm glad you're not." He rests one hand on the back of the couch over her and runs the other along the golden skin of her arm.

His touch is magnetic. "Me too." She sits gazing into his eyes, knowing what she wants but knowing she shouldn't have it. All these years she's denied, hell, she's avoided the possibility that anything could still exist between them. But now, Dunc has crossed the line so many times and in so many ways. *Does that mean I can?*

Bradley takes her hand, his thumb tracing circles on her palm. "Meaghan," he starts, his voice filled with emotion. "We've both made mistakes. We've both had our share of regrets. But maybe this is our second chance." He kisses her fingertips.

She swallows hard, her heart pounding. Warmth spreads between her thighs. "Bradley, we can't ..." she begins, but her protest is weak, half-hearted.

"We already have," he reminds her gently, his eyes never leaving hers. "And I've never forgotten. Have you?

"No," she whispers. Her breath hitches, "But I wasn't married, then."

Bradley gently leans down and kisses her, deeply and with invitation.

Lust blindsides her. She cannot resist him. She pulls Bradley to her. "Okay."

She slowly undresses him, first unbuttoning his shirt and then releasing his belt buckle. Still kissing her, Bradley stands enough to kneel back down onto the couch now between her legs. His hands travel everywhere with wild tenderness, but their mouths stay locked together. Desire radiates between them. She sits up and he gently lifts her French terry sweatshirt over her head to reveal her bare breasts.

He sits back and drinks her in as the moonlight streams through the windows. "God, you've never been more beautiful," Bradley tells her. He caresses her nipples with his tongue and kisses her breasts. She shudders. Her back arches. *Heaven. I'm in heaven.*

Every inch of her craves him. Her passion becomes raw and hungry. Bradley stands up, dropping his pants to the floor around his ankles. She pulls him back onto the couch in a seated position with both of his feet on the floor. She finishes undressing herself and climbs on top of him. Her legs part. He enters her.

"You know how I like it," she tells him. He obeys.

Bradley moves his hips slowly at first. He kisses her neck all the way up to her ear and back down to her breast. "Meaghan …" he groans. His breath warms her nipples.

They rise and fall together, thrusting in full embrace, breath after breath, until she climaxes, and he follows, a release of emotions. She collapses on top of him. They cling to each other, completely consumed. She kisses Bradley. She could kiss him forever.

MEAGHAN WAKES UP AGAIN ON THE COUCH THE NEXT morning, naked with only the blanket covering her. Bradley brings her a large mug of steaming coffee. He sits in his boxer briefs on the coffee table beside her where he started last night. "It's surreal I'm seeing you naked right now."

She laughs. "Most of America has seen me naked. Well, at least they think they have. Usually, it's my double." She takes a sip. "Thank you for the coffee … and for last night."

Bradley kisses her. "You're welcome." Her heart races.

She gets up from the couch, grabs Bradley's white button-down oxford off the floor, and slips it on. "I'm cooking you breakfast."

"You can do that?"

Meaghan crosses her arms and marches toward the kitchen. "Nope, but I'm going to try." She pillages Bradley's refrigerator, which is shockingly bare for a guy who owns a restaurant. She pulls out eggs. Twenty minutes later, she presents Bradley with a pile of wet, mushy eggs topped with a spoonful of salsa and a side of burnt toast. They move to Bradley's dining table.

"This is actually good," Bradley says, choking his words out and making a face like he's dying.

"I know. You'd be amazed to discover I have more talents than acting," she says sarcastically as she puts her feet up on the table and crosses her legs.

"I already know that. But I would like to investigate every one of them." Bradley runs his hand down her thigh.

A knock at the door interrupts them.

"Maybe it's Palmer?" she proclaims enthusiastically.

"No, it's Scottie, dropping off today's menu." Bradley stands up from the table and kisses the top of her head, "Can you grab it while I grab my shirt."

"Sure."

Bradley runs back to the living room and grabs the T-shirt he wore yesterday to work under his oxford. She makes her way from the kitchen table to the front door. She swings the door open and Bradley catches it, standing behind her.

Flashes go off one after another. Microphones are shoved in their faces. Twenty people yell their questions.

One guy shouts, "Nice Jeep Wrangler, Meaghan! Tell Holly well done!"

Another yells, "More Sinful Admissions, right Meaghan?"

She slams the door shut and screams, "Not Scottie!"

She spins around. Her wide eyes look at Bradley, immediately realizing she's dressed in his half-buttoned white oxford and he's still in his boxers and that T-shirt. She gasps, both hands cover her mouth. Tears of anger and defeat slide down her cheeks.

"Just when I thought people couldn't hate me more! They found me. Naked and cheating on my husband." Fear hits her like icy water, "Oh my God, Bella!"

The Perfect Boating Lunch

Roasted Chicken Salad

Ingredients

- 1 rotisserie chicken
- 2 tablespoons dijon mustard
- 3 tablespoons mayo
- 2 cucumbers, diced
- 1 tablespoon fresh thyme, minced
- 1 tablespoon fresh chives, minced
- 1 tablespoon fresh tarragon, minced
- salt & pepper to taste
- basil, arugula, and/or watercress
- Havarti cheese
- French baguette

Chop the rotisserie chicken into bite size chunks.

In a bowl, combine all ingredients through salt and pepper.

Slice the ends off the French baguette. Slice in half. Slice each half in half, until you have 4 equal pieces. For each, slice one side open, being sure not to cut through to the other side.

Open the baguettes and place basil, arugula and/or watercress as desired. Layer with Havarti cheese. Scoop chicken salad on top. Drizzle with olive oil if desired and a fresh sprinkle of salt and pepper.

Penne & Roasted Veggies

Ingredients

- 1 box penne pasta
- 1 zucchini
- 1 yellow squash
- 10 cherry tomatoes
- 2 cloves garlic
- 2 tablespoons olive oil
- Kalamata olives
- 1 cup fresh basil
- Italian herb seasoning

Cook the penne pasta according to box directions, adding salt boiling water. Once done, drizzle with olive oil so pasta does not stick.

Slice zucchini and squash into bit size pieces. Halve the cherry tomatoes. Cut the garlic into quarters. Place all on a baking sheet. Drizzle with olive oil, salt and pepper. Roast for 40 minutes on 400 degrees. Let cool.

Slice the Kalamata olives in half. Julienne the basil. Mix olives, basil, the cooled vegetables and pasta together. Drizzle with olive oil. Mix. Add salt and pepper to taste.

Palmer's Secret Brownies

Ingredients

- 2 boxes Betty Crocker Supreme Original Brownie Mix
- ½cup Hershey's chocolate syrup

Combine 2 boxes of brownie mix into a single bowl. Follow the directions on each box. Add in the additional Hershey's chocolate syrup. Place in a buttered, deep pyrex dish. Bake 45 minutes until toothpick comes out clean.

Additional Notes

Encourages inhalation of salt air, swimming in the middle of the ocean, and day cruising along the coast. Perfect for forgetting all your troubles.

July

Chapter 9

IT'S THAT SWEET WEEK OF SUMMER WHEN JUNE SURPRIS-ingly ends and everyone in town eagerly anticipates the July Fourth holiday. Around Cape Henlopen, a weeklong celebration ensues and festivities kick off with the annual Rehoboth Village Art Show. Fireworks will be held nightly across different beaches in the area, and finally Rehoboth, where the annual July Fourth Boat Parade will precede the sparkly show that evening. Outrageously themed boats decorated with streamers, balloons, and so much more will vie for the title of the Village's annual July Fourth Boat Parade winner. Meaghan wishes she could enjoy any of it.

The morning after her night with Bradley still haunts her. Despite the comfort of his arms, the rightness of their connection, she knew it couldn't last. "We can't do this," she told him while waiting for the Chief to rescue her from the mob on Bradley's doorstep. "It was a mistake." The hurt in his eyes had matched the pain in her heart, but she couldn't drag him into her mess.

When she refused the Chief's suggestion that she go to the airport, he returned her to The Hyacinth, where plush streets trimmed with fragrant jasmine bushes afford enough space to accommodate all the attention. Since then, even more paparazzi have flooded into town, camping out across the street from The Hyacinth.

Palmer reluctantly agrees to be sequestered with her at The Hyacinth. What could Palmer say when the Chief showed up with her on the private back deck making the request other than her usual refrains, *Of course*, and *It's fine*.

They don't speak to each other for the first three days. For the first time in her life, she doesn't know how to act because acting isn't an option. She goes down to the pool, stretches in the chaise, and lies in the warmth of the sun. Twenty minutes have passed when Palmer appears at the chaise beside her, sets her phone on the table between them, and offers a faint smile. A peace offering that makes Meaghan swoon.

The phone between them flashes with a text from Bella. They both see it and Palmer immediately opens her phone. It's not a text to Palmer from Bella, but a screenshot from Aiden. Palmer reads the text, hearts the screenshot to Aiden, and hands her the phone.

Bella's words pierce her heart. "Everything feels fake now. The admission, my achievements, even my parents' marriage." Aiden's response makes her eyes well. "Nothing about you is fake, Bells. Your talent, your drive, your heart - that's all real. Trust me, I do get what it's like when your whole world shifts. At least your dad is still alive. Different kind of loss, but I get it. Remember all those summers we spent learning to surf? You were always better than me, and that had nothing to do with anyone but you."

"If anyone might be able to understand what Bella's going through, it's Aiden. Maybe he's not in as much denial as

I thought. He's processing with Bella. He lost his father to death, while Bella lost hers to betrayal," Palmer says. "Shared grief is the foundation for real connection." Palmer doesn't make eye contact, but puts her hand on Meaghan's.

She knows that Palmer means their shared grief. Their shared loss. What once connected two little girls and still does. She breaks wide open. She spills her tears and her guts. "I should have known something was wrong," she confesses to Palmer. "I saw a text from this guy Thorne to Duncan about 'arrangements being made.' I wrote that check from Awaken's account anyway. I never asked questions because I didn't want to know the answers." She unearths every possible detail about Sinful Admissions.

"Mack says they may indict me for money laundering. I could go to jail, like Dunc. My career is ruined. Awaken sales are in the toilet because no one wants to buy anything with my name on it. Everyone knows I cheated on my husband!"

Palmer listens with little reaction, seeming to simply take it all in. "Was the check you wrote off Awaken a bribe or a donation?" Palmer asks bluntly, good practice for her because the FBI and their team of prosecutors will be asking her that same question by Zoom this afternoon during her second deposition.

"A donation!" she answers. But she senses Palmer still wonders what role Meaghan played in the scandal. Meaghan still wonders too. *Can you really know the answer to something if you never ask the question?* She hadn't pressed Dunc too hard about the specifics of that donation. And she'd never told him she'd written the check from her business account.

"It's hard to stay mad at you when you're a complete mess," Palmer says reluctantly. Meaghan reaches for Palmer, wraps both her arms around her, and holds her in a tight embrace. Palmer sits, unmoved and not reciprocating. "You lied to me. For years. You should have told me what you knew about my mom."

"I know," Meaghan says, nodding her head and closing her eyes in agreement.

For now, Meaghan relishes that they are together again. *Will Bradley be right? Will Palmer eventually forgive me?* She will do anything to make it happen.

THE BABY-TO-BE CONTINUES TO SURPRISE PALMER. SHE finds herself passing in front of mirrors throughout The Hyacinth, turning to the side, running her hand over her stomach to see what she feels and smiling every time. It boggles her mind how a little life could emerge from such a tangled mess. She and Miles unsuccessfully tried to get pregnant with each of the boys the old-fashioned way, to the point of exhaustion. In those days, Palmer's OB-GYN recommended Clomid, a fertility drug that magically produced two thriving baby boys. So, when Dr. Harlow told her she's having another baby, she was dumfounded. The only fertility drug this baby needed to be conceived was mind-blowing make-up sex.

"I'm going down to the office," Meaghan yells from The Hyacinth's deck, where the paparazzi can't find her. Palmer turns around to see Meaghan dressed in a Balenciaga power suit. She isn't quite ready to wipe the slate clean and entirely forgive Meaghan—even though forgiveness and apologies are her thing. So, when Meaghan asked her about her appointment with Dr. Harlow, she deflected with vague responses.

Keeping secrets feels like her only defense right now. *The boys deserve to know first.* Palmer knows the Chief will never say a word.

She gives Meaghan a thumbs-up, careful not to alert the press, whose numbers had shrunk by half last night. Perhaps they're moving on because there has been no confirmed sighting of Meaghan at The Hyacinth. Meaghan gets the hint to be quieter and gestures back a thumbs-up to which she raises both hands fingers crossed, wishing Meaghan good luck. Her second deposition starts in an hour by video. Meaghan turns around and heads back inside, right as her phone rings.

"Hi, Aiden!" Palmer says. "What's up, honey? How's The Ivy?"

"Hi, Mom," Aiden replies. "The Ivy is good. Everything's good. Crew practice is super intense. A lot of wall sits and erg workouts plus three hours on the water each day."

"Wow, that is intense." Palmer's mind races, caught in the swirl of wanting to share her news and the harsh reality of their father's absence. *Should I tell them now?* She wants to tell Aiden and Quinn together, but she can't wait until they arrive in August. The bump beneath her blouse feels like a ticking clock. "I got your text, honey. It is so wonderful of you to be there for Bella."

"Well, I read the headlines, Mom. They're pretty unavoidable."

Crap. Her heart sinks. The moment she dreaded has arrived. "Right. I should've called to warn you. I'm sorry, honey."

"Bradley and Auntie Meaghan? It's a little weird, Mom. And by that, I mean it's a lot weird," Aiden says. "Bella is really upset. First her parents bribe her way into college, get thrown in jail, and now Auntie Meaghan is having an affair with Bradley? Bella said Meaghan left five voicemails and twenty missed calls in the past week. Bella does not want to hear from her. Like possibly ever again."

"Yes, I understand how upset Bella must be," she says, her voice wavering slightly. "Remember, though, Duncan isn't exactly innocent in all this." Rumors have circulated about Dunc's actresses for years. *And that time before their wedding.*

"Well, I'm going out to California to see Bella over the Fourth," Aiden announces. "I have a break from crew practice, and someone is covering my shifts at The Ivy."

"Oh." She hesitates, stunned. The Fourth of July has always been a Harding family holiday spent together on the shores of The Hyacinth. This will be the first one they've spent apart. More than that, Aiden has never visited Bella by himself. "That sounds like exactly what the two of you need. Good friends and a lot of fun!"

"Is everything okay?" Aiden's tone shifts, worry creeping in.

"Yes, everything is fine. I have a little bit of news to share and I wanted to talk to you together, that's all."

Aiden hesitates. "I can add him." His voice sounds guarded.

"Right. Okay, sure. Can you make us into a FaceTime call?" Palmer asks.

"Yep." Aiden switches their call to FaceTime and then invites Quinn to join. Quinn picks up Aiden's call on the second ring. Palmer's hands become slippery with sweat.

Quinn is seated next to the most adorable girl with a freckled face and a dark-haired pixie cut.

His new girlfriend?

"What's up, dude. I'm in the middle of meatloaf," he says, shoving a fork in his mouth before he looks at the phone. "Oh hey, Mom." He sets his fork down and readjusts the phone's camera to ensure Pixie Cut is out of the frame.

"Hi, Quinnie." *Oops.* She shouldn't have called him that in front of the girl. She contemplates asking him about the girl Frances mentioned but knows she can't at the moment. *Too many other kids around.*

Aiden says, "So, what's up, Mom? What did you want to talk to us about?"

"Well, um Quinn, could you maybe go outside or find somewhere alone for a few minutes?" Palmer asks.

"Yeah." Quinn gets up from the table. "I'll be right back," he says to Pixie Cut.

Her boys look so grown up. They've lost their father, right as they're coming of age. "I need to tell you guys something. I don't really want to tell you this over FaceTime, but since I won't get to see you for another five weeks, I feel like you need to know."

"What's the matter? Is it something else about Dad?" Quinn asks.

"No, nothing about Dad." She looks upward and bobbles her head back and forth. "Well, actually, it is a little." Aiden's face goes white as a sheet. "Not in a bad way." She's making a mess of the situation. "Oh fine, I'm just going to say it." Palmer inhales a deep breath. "You're going to have another sibling. I'm pregnant!"

"What?" Aiden exclaims.

Quinn scrunches his face in confusion. "Seriously. Repeat, please."

She feels the weight of her words settle like a storm. She repeats herself more slowly. "A baby. I'm going to have a baby."

Both boys cringe.

"Oh no. Please no. You've gotta be kidding me! Like this is an actual joke, right? You're playing some sort of prank on us?" Quinn adds. "You're going to tell us you're getting a dog, right?"

She crumbles inside. "We are not getting a dog. It's not a prank or a joke. I'm going to have a baby," she says.

Quinn shakes his head. "Is it … Dad's?"

"Of course the baby is Dad's! What are you thinking, Quinn?"

Aiden starts crying. He turns into a sobbing puddle right there on the phone.

Her heart wrenches. "Oh God. Aiden, please don't cry, honey. Your father … would be happy. I know it is so unfathomably hard because he's not here. But we have another little piece of him with us now. One we never could have expected. Honestly, that part is a miracle."

She tries to console him, but her words only exacerbate his tears. All at once, it occurs to Palmer that by telling Aiden she is pregnant with his father's baby, she is forcing him into a reality that he has been, at worst, completely avoiding and, at best since reading his text with Bella, only recently begun to admit. The reality in which his father is never coming back.

"I definitely was not expecting this kind of news. Like nowhere in the realm of possibilities," Aiden says still crying.

"I know it's a lot. I get it. I really do …" She wishes she could hug him and rock him back and forth.

Quinn cannot even look at Palmer. "Are you really sure the baby is Dad's? Because we all know you two were arguing for a month before he died. Dad told me you wouldn't even be in the same room with him. I mean that's pretty hard to have a baby then."

"Quinn Harding!" Palmer screams his name like he's a two-year-old she found coloring the entire wall in red and blue Sharpie. Her heart races, equal parts outraged and appalled. The boys know about her argument with Miles. *Do they know about Sanford too?*

"Are you really sure it's Dad's baby?" Quinn repeats his question, his gaze hardening into skepticism.

"Quinn. I am certain this baby is your father's. Yes, we argued. The biggest argument we ever had. And then we made up. Because we couldn't live without each other. Even though I am trying to do that very thing right now—live without your father. We love ... loved each other." Sorrow closes her throat. Her emotion spills over as tears stream down her face. "We made up the night before he died. This baby was conceived that evening. There's no one else for me. There never has been, and I seriously doubt there ever will be again. So you can take your accusations and stick them where the sun doesn't shine. You will never speak that way to me again, Quinn Harding. Are we clear?"

Quinn shakes his head. "This is disgusting! It's embarrassing! Aren't you too old to have a baby? Dad is gone! You're going to be a single mother at your age!" Quinn keeps pushing. He's mortified. But he pushes Palmer to an edge she didn't know existed within herself until this very moment. "Can you get rid of it or something?"

Blank. Aiden's face goes blank.

She feels anger rise, conflicting with her grief. Palmer hangs up.

Chapter 10

THE HEADLINES GROW FROM INSUFFERABLE TO VICIOUS. "Cheating Meaghan Caught in More Sinful Admissions" and "Meaghan Cheats Again! Colleges & Dunc Betrayed" scroll across every newsfeed on X, Threads, Facebook, and Instagram. The paparazzi stalk Bradley at his door and run a nasty headline insinuating his parents' car crash may not have been an accident, citing their inheritance money as motive. Holly sends Meaghan links to the top ten new articles daily, each one worse than the previous. This morning, when Holly calls, she informs Meaghan that she's lost the role playing Belle Dixon in *Moonlight Magnolias*.

"It's so unfair," she says. "Why is it that Dunc's betrayals slip away unnoticed like sand through fingers, while I stand here bared to the world? I can't count on two hands the actresses Dunc has been rumored to have slept with over the years. Do they number fifteen or twenty? Not a single picture ever attempted. Not a single rumor ever written."

"That's Hollywood," Holly laments. "Bad boys get away with whatever because they're bad boys. You're America's sweetheart."

She clarifies. "I was America's sweetheart."

"Well, does Bradley want you to be his sweetheart?" Holly asks.

"Oh Holly, I can't even think about that. Every time I do, the storm clouds gather. I've got to focus. It's a big day."

They hang up. *Does Bradley want to be sweethearts?* Meaghan avoids contemplating that possibility. Her life is a disaster; she can't bring him into the storm. The thought stabs at her; he's too good for this chaos. He's too good for that. *He'll end up hating me, too.*

He tries calling her daily. Yesterday, she finally answered, swiftly telling him that she needs time to figure things in her life out. While Bradley agreed to give her the time she needs, the federal prosecutors are done waiting. Today is deposition day. The tension wraps around her like a tight corset, leaving her almost breathless. Meaghan sits at the grand desk in The Hyacinth's office with her laptop logged into Zoom, waiting to join the meeting. *It's so unfair.* She thinks about all that Duncan has done. Her mind wanders back to the first time she learned about Dunc's philandering ... on their wedding day.

DUNC WANTED A SHOWY HOLLYWOOD WEDDING AT-tended by hundreds of A-listers to properly announce to the world that she now belonged to him. She wanted an intimate wedding in Cottonwood Falls that Bella, already two years old, could be a part of without being overwhelmed by flashing cameras and people she did not know. Their wedding was the one thing she would not compromise on; it was the last. The day she had longed for morphed into an elaborate masquerade.

Around five in the morning, her high school sweetheart, Drew Cunningham, threw rock after rock at her window until she opened it, climbed down onto the roof below, slid down the front banister, and met him on Victoria's front porch swing. It wasn't her first time. She had been sneaking out that window since she was thirteen.

"Well now this is something I wasn't expecting," she told Drew as she kissed him on the cheek. "Coming to sweep me off my feet?"

He laughed. "As if I ever could," he said sitting down on the swing to join her. "No, I overheard something last night and I couldn't not tell you. You need to have all the information. Before … today."

"Okay?" she said. "Not much can shock me these days. I mean, I live in Hollywood."

"I get that, but still …" He paused.

"What did you overhear, Drew?"

"I was at the One Horse Bar last night, where Miles threw Duncan's bachelor party."

"Yes." She wasn't sure Miles threw Dunc the party as much as Dunc had demanded it. "Go on."

"Everyone in town was there, and Duncan got totally hammered. I overheard him describe in detail to Miles two other women he slept with last year on a location shoot in Australia. Like … a lot of detail."

Her heart plummeted, each beat a sickening reminder of her unyielding love and the crushing betrayal. Suspicions confirmed. She realized she'd never be enough for Duncan, but that didn't matter.

"Names?"

"No names."

"Did anyone else overhear? Any reporters lurking?" She had seen a few adventurous paparazzi lurking around the land of Oz to get a photo of her in her wedding dress, but nowhere near the number who would have stalked a Hollywood wedding.

"No one else was even remotely near us."

"Are you sure?"

"I'm sure. Miles and Duncan were seated across the table from each other in one of the bar booths. I was in the booth behind Duncan. I was alone."

"Good," she said. "Thank you for telling me. You're a good friend, Drew. You always have been." She stopped swinging and stood up. "Now, it's my wedding day. There's a lot to do."

His mouth opened, "You're sure?"

"Have you met my beautiful daughter?" she asked him.

Later that morning in the bride's room, she waited for Palmer to tell her the same story Drew shared. Most certainly, Miles told Palmer and Palmer would tell Meaghan. How could she not?

But Palmer said nothing. Meaghan felt a hollowness inside, knowing how difficult it is to find the words that can break a person you love. She hadn't been able to find them herself. So she explained why she was marrying Dunc, even though Palmer hadn't asked. "Bella needs her father. More than anything in this world, I want Bella to feel loved in a way I never did."

LOOK AT WHERE WE'VE ENDED UP! NOW, BELLA HATES them both.

AT NOON, MACK, JP DONAHUE, AND A LINEUP OF ASSO-ciate lawyers attend the Zoom deposition from their L.A. of-fices. Meaghan's stomach does Olympic Gold–worthy flips as they all wait for the prosecutors to join. She slides her fingers through her blond hair, over and over, until Mack coughs, look-ing straight at Meaghan and raising one eyebrow. Instinctively, she rests her hands in her lap. She's an actress; she can take a cue.

The prosecutors spend their first hour asking Meaghan questions she already answered in her first deposition.

Then they turn to the check she wrote for SCC Farms. "Did you know that the charity was a front for funneling money to Chip Sullivan?"

"I did not know." Meaghan's eyes dart between Cybil and Mack.

"When did you find out?" Cybil asks.

"When my lawyer told me a few weeks ago."

Cybil points again at the check. "Can you read what is written in the memo line of the check?"

Meaghan focuses on the memo line and freezes.

"Please read what's written on the memo line aloud for the transcript."

Meaghan looks at Cybil. "It appears to be the initials BJ." Meaghan looks at Mack. "I did not write those letters." She feels the weight of judgment creeping in. She adjusts herself in her seat, channeling the resolve of a lead character in a thrill-ing drama. "I did not write that."

Cybil ignores Meaghan and continues. "What do you think BJ stands for?"

"Look, I know where you think you're headed with this, but I never write anything in the memo line of Awaken checks. It's too damn short!" Meaghan blurts out.

"Only answer the question, Meaghan. It's okay if you don't know the answer," Mack reminds her.

Cybil repeats. "What do you think BJ stands for?"

Mack interrupts. "Objection. You are asking the witness to speculate. She has been asked once and answered. My client should not be pressed to guess at the meaning of the letters if she does not actually know the meaning."

Cybil pushes. She will get her point on record. "The initials 'BJ' as they are written together could stand for Bella Jones, right?"

"They could be, I suppose," Meaghan responds, feeling the encroaching tide of panic wash over her.

Mack glares at Meaghan. "Enough! Objection. Meaghan, do not answer."

Meaghan ignores Mack. "They could also denote a blow job, right?" She grows angry. The words escape her lips as she attempts to reclaim power in the deposition. She isn't sure whom she is angry at. The prosecutor for finding the check and asking the question? Duncan for committing fraud and knowingly putting her in this position? Or herself for ending up right here in this very moment? But her anger is her shield.

"Have you ever donated to a college association before or any youth mentoring programs?" Cybil asks.

Her eyes widen. She sees Thorne. Two years ago at a school charity event. His seemingly innocent inquiry about her connection to youth organizations now leaves a sour taste in her mouth—had he been fishing for information? Had he been lingering too close? The notion of someone she barely knew becoming a threat feels absurd, yet the world of Hollywood has taught her that appearances can be dangerously deceiving.

"No."

"Do you have any personal connection to the sport of equestrian riding?"

"No."

"Why did Awaken donate these funds instead of you personally?"

She pauses to think. "The business would get a tax write-off and create a connection with the college demographic."

"And also because Chip Sullivan needed to have it laundered from a clean source?"

"Enough! Do not answer, Meaghan." Mack clears his throat. "You are presenting us with new evidence that we have not yet been able to review, as we received it just this morning from the prosecution. This appears to be a recurring theme with the prosecution. So I am requesting the judge grant us a one-week extension to review the new evidence the prosecution offers as exhibits to Mrs. Jones's testimony." The court adjudicator present for the deposition phones the presiding judge, who reluctantly grants another week's extension. "Any other surprises today?" Mack asks Cybil with a smirk.

"Not today." Cybil ends the Zoom.

Meaghan sits in The Hyacinth's office chair completely floored. "I'm going to jail," she says out loud in deep despair. "I am going to be indicted and I am definitely going to jail."

Mack rings her. "You are not going to jail," he says when she hits the green button.

"Not even a hello?"

"I know exactly what you're thinking. I'm not letting you go to jail. Our investigative team will spend the next week tracing back the check. They will figure out who had it, when they had it, how long they had it. We will uncover all the stops the check made along its way into Chip Sullivan's fake charity account."

"I love you for trying. Keep me updated if you find anything. And Mack ... not a word to Bella."

"Understood. Bye, Meaghan."

She sits back in the leather tufted rolled-arm desk chair. She taps her fingers on the desk, her mind swirling. She ponders her next move. Even if she's not heading to jail, how can she get the world to ever love her again? How can she get Bella to love her again?

Am I unlovable?

She winces at her deepest fear. She's determined not to give into it. She swings the chair around and stares out the window. The tide inches closer with each wave, creeping toward her as if wanting to pull her under. All at once, Meaghan stands up and pushes the swivel chair back. She knows exactly what to do next.

PALMER SITS SLUMPED OVER AT THE KITCHEN BANQUETTE, her head resting heavily on the table. Sunlight streams through the window, highlighting the tear streaks on her face, her phone still gripped tightly in her hand.

Meaghan enters the kitchen, briskly, lips pursed, on a mission. She stops short when she lays eyes on Palmer. The weight of unresolved conflict hangs thick in the air. "Palmer," she says gently, scooting Palmer over and sitting down right beside her.

She lifts her head, anger simmering beneath her vulnerability. "Quinn asked me to get an abortion!"

Meaghan's eyes fly open, shock blooming across her face. "Excuse me?"

Her lips quiver and her voice trembles. She stops sobbing momentarily. "I'm pregnant. I don't have cancer. I'm having a baby."

The news jolts Meaghan upright.

"And I told the boys this afternoon on FaceTime. Aiden broke down crying! Quinn became so enraged and …" She shakes her head. "Disgusted by me—his words—that he asked me if I could consider getting rid of it."

Meaghan's brows furrow in concern. "That's a lot of information all at once." As Meaghan processes Palmer's confession, her expression lightens, a smile creeps across her face. "Let's circle back to you're pregnant?"

She hesitates, saying nothing, consumed with emotion. Meaghan hugs her tight, but the hug feels heavy with unspoken truths. Then Meaghan pulls back and points her finger right at her. "I told you there was no cancer!"

She rolls her eyes at Meaghan. How is Meaghan always right? "This is astonishingly amazing news," Meaghan says. "The best news I've heard in a very long time!"

"I agree," she whispers, consoled by Meaghan's excitement. "But the boys don't. Quinn also asked me if the baby was Miles's. Can you believe that?"

Meaghan collapses back into the banquette. "What a little jerk. I mean that in the nicest way possible, you know how much I love my godsons. But still, what a little jerk."

"Total jerk. Although he had a reason, I guess."

"I can't think of a single one," Meaghan says. "Not even having lost his father recently. He can't talk to you that way, Palmer. You are his mother."

Her chin trembles. "It gets worse. Quinn and Aiden knew that Miles and I were having the fight of our married lives. The entire month before his stroke."

Meaghan sits back. "You two were fighting? You and Miles are the happiest couple I know. You never fight."

"I know. It was awful. For an entire month, we didn't speak."

"That sounds more like my marriage," Meaghan admits. "Why? What was going on between you?"

Palmer fills her friend in on the fight. With each word, heat creeps into her cheeks. As she recounts their final weeks, the words twist in her throat like barbed wire. "What if that stress of our argument spiked his blood pressure? What if my mistakes—" A sob forces its way out, and she buries her face in her hands, the weight of guilt crashing down. *Did Miles somehow know about Sanford? Did he suspect?* She can't tell Meaghan the truth, not now. The fear of judgment, of exposure, clings heavily to her chest.

"Palmer." Meaghan rests her forehead in her hand, keeping one arm around Palmer. "That is absolutely not true. You can't blame yourself for Miles's death. Life is hard. Sometimes bad things happen to good people. Why didn't you say anything?"

"I couldn't admit it to anyone! I can barely admit it to myself! I didn't think the boys had any idea we were even arguing and I would have gone to my grave keeping it from them. But they know now. Apparently, Miles told Quinn. I'm not even sure how Aiden found out. Why didn't I protect them better?" She folds her hands into her lap. "I've spent my whole life giving those boys everything. Working tirelessly to create a perfect happy life for them. It's all I wanted. I've made their happiness my happiness. Isn't that what mothers do? And now look where we are! They are both livid with me."

"You can't control everything, Palmer. You can't control their happiness forever." Meaghan pats her hand, which feels both comforting and stinging, a reminder of her inability to protect those she loves.

"Oh please," Palmer scoffs. "This coming from the most renowned Hollywood bossy pants ever rumored." She smirks. "Yes, if there's anything these past months have proven, it's that not everything is in our power. But finding a way to keep the boys thriving? That's my role. I owe it to Miles."

"Miles ..." A warm smile comes over Meaghan. "God, I really miss him."

"Me too." She nods, the lump in her throat tightening. Memories flood back—the laughter, the love, the weeks they fought, the night they made up. The shadows of her betrayal loom large in her heart. *What would Miles think of me now?*

Meaghan nudges her. "You're having a baby."

"A baby," she whispers. A little bit of joy bubbles up inside her.

Chapter 11

MEAGHAN'S PHONE VIBRATES ON THE NIGHTSTAND NEXT to her jolting her awake. An unknown number flashes across the screen. She rolls over and glares at her bedroom's Alexa, which dimly displays the time. Midnight. Only 9 p.m. in California, she thinks. Perhaps Bella has a new phone. Perhaps Bella finally decided to return her daily voicemails and texts. She anxiously picks up her phone, hits the green "Accept" button, and puts the caller on speaker as she lies face down on her pillow. "Hello?"

"Meggie?" a voice asks quietly on the other end. Her heart sinks. Not Bella. "Meggie," the voice repeats. There is only one person in the world who calls her Meggie. "It's me. It's Dunc."

She rolls onto her back and places her forearm over her eyes. "Yes, Dunc. I know. I know because I have spent the entirety of my adult life listening to you on the other end of this phone." Silence. "What do you want? Why are you calling?"

"I saw the pictures, Meggie. All over the news. The pictures of you naked with that guy ... Miles's friend, right? The guy you used to write to. Looks like you're doing more than writing now." Her skin crawls realizing that Duncan remembers

Bradley. "I'm calling to tell you that even though I'm sitting in jail, I know about your cheating, Meggie, like everyone does ... and, well, I forgive you."

She sits straight up in bed. The room is still dark. "You ... forgive me?" She laughs out loud. "That's rich. Really rich." She can't stop laughing. "You're forgetting how many women over the last eighteen years ... your 'actresses' ... have made their way into your bed! You think that just because those affairs aren't splashed across every newsfeed in America, people don't know? That I don't know? Give me a break. Plus, there's the little fact that you're currently sitting in jail! You have destroyed my entire life. And you're calling to tell me that *you* forgive *me*?"

"I'm just saying, I saw the headlines, I know what's going on, and I'm not going to leave you or do anything drastic. I forgive you."

"I don't care if you forgive me! I don't forgive you! You have ruined everything! You ruined my acting career. I can't land a single role. You've ruined a business I created entirely on my own. Stores won't even pick up my fall line. No one wants to buy *anything* with my name on it."

She takes a breath and forges on. "But, honestly, the one thing I absolutely will never be able to forgive, is that you have ruined my relationship with our beautiful daughter. You have driven her completely away. She won't take my calls! She won't text me back! You made everyone in the world hate me! It's unbearable." Her face grows red, and her hands shake.

"I didn't think it would turn out like this, Meggie." Duncan breathes heavily into the phone on the other end. "I didn't think we'd get caught."

"Why did you do it? At least tell me that much."

Dunc sighs. "I want the very best for Bella? You know how competitive Hollywood is. Thorne Cassidy approached me with this idea ... this 'opportunity.' He promised it would secure Bella's future, make her stand out among the elites. He said everyone was doing it."

"Thorne Cassidy?" Meaghan's voice sharpens. "So you're saying Thorne set us up?"

"He didn't exactly set us up. He opened the door, and I walked right through without hesitation. I never considered the potential fallout. My focus was on the prestige Bella's acceptance to SCC would bring her and us, elevating our status to Hollywood royalty. Don't you want that?

"We were already Hollywood royalty!" She becomes confident that she's made the right decision. She knows what needs to be done; there's no doubting it's her only option. "What you want—what you've always wanted—is the very best for *you*. What you never realize is that you already have it. Nothing is ever enough for you. Not our sprawling estate in the Bel Air Hills. Not the three Lamborghinis or the two Ferraris sitting in your garage. Not all the accolades that go with an award-winning career as a movie director. Not being married to me, until recently the most sought-after actress in Hollywood. And not Bella, your own flesh and blood! You needed to be sure Bella's accomplishments made *you* look good. You never realized they already did."

"You're right," Duncan submits. It's a first.

"What were you thinking creating a fake CV for Bella?"

"I didn't create the CV. I didn't even know about the CV. But Waverly says it doesn't matter who created the fake, because we paid for it."

Mack told her the same thing. Still, Meaghan gasps. "*You* paid for it."

"Look, the prosecutors interviewed me again last week," Duncan tells her. "I told them everything. I told them you offered to make a donation."

"Did they ask you about the initials on the check?"

"What initials?"

Should I tell him? "Jesus, Mack is going to kill me for telling you this. The prosecutors may try to say we are coordinating our stories." Despite these possible consequences, Meaghan can't wait. She needs to know Dunc's answer whatever the price. "On the memo line of the check I wrote, someone else wrote Bella's initials."

"I don't know anything about Bella's initials. The prosecutors didn't ask me. They didn't show me the check or mention it."

"Mack says they are going to bring money laundering charges against both of us unless we can prove someone else wrote those initials. It will extend your jail time." She feels a slight pleasure in delivering this little death nail.

"Christ, Meggie!"

"You need to think really hard about who could have written those initials. It's the only chance we've got right now. Mack is working on it too."

"Okay. But honestly, I have no idea who wrote Bella's initials except that it wasn't me."

She sighs. If there's one thing she can count on with Dunc, it's that he's either consistently unhelpful or flat out lying.

"One last thing." She readies herself for the final blow. She wasn't expecting to hear from Duncan, but since he called to offer her his forgiveness … now seems like the perfect time. "I'm filing for divorce."

More silence. "Meggie … don't do that. I don't think you want to do that." A not-so-thinly-veiled threat.

"Don't even think about trying to turn this around on me, given the latest headlines. I'm sure I can find plenty of witnesses who will attest to your philandering ways."

"I don't think so," Duncan warns. "You know there's not a single person in Hollywood who would dare cross me."

"I think you'll find you've lost your Hollywood power, Dunc. Remember where you're sitting. Besides that, I know I can find at least one. Remember Drew Cunningham?"

"No." Dunc snorts. "Who the hell is Drew Cunningham?"

"My high school boyfriend. Junior year. He overheard you the night before our wedding at the bachelor party. You admitted you were sleeping around then. We weren't married, but we were living together. Bella was a toddler, and we were exclusive, raising her together. I'm pretty sure Drew would be willing to tell a judge what he overheard." She pulls out a phrase she's learned from listening to Palmer over the years. "It establishes a clear pattern. Affairs with multiple women while we were in an exclusive relationship."

She imagines everything coming into focus for Duncan on the other end, as he sits on the phone in jail. "You have taken enough from me, Dunc. You've taken everything." She feels warm tears roll down her cheeks, part rage and part mourning. "If you ever loved me, do this one last thing. Set me free."

Several silent moments pass. "Okay," Dunc says. "Okay."

Every muscle in Meaghan's body releases. Divorcing Dunc is the only chance she has to get the world to fall in love with her again.

"Thank you. Mack will draw up the papers and deliver copies to you and Waverly tomorrow. Once you sign, we can file in court. Shouldn't take long." Meaghan dictates the sequence of events that will legally end her marriage, although divorcing Duncan feels less like an ending and more like a fresh beginning. "All of our interests are already separate except the Bel Air house. I want it."

There's a long pause on the other end of the phone. "Okay, Meggie. You can have the Bel Air house, but I'm keeping the cars. Send the papers over. I'll let Waverly know to expect them." Duncan makes one last plea, "We can still talk though, right?"

Meaghan scoffs. "We've barely talked in years. Why start when we're divorced?"

"Right," Duncan admits. "Bye, Meggie."

"Goodbye, Dunc," Meaghan says. And she means it.

PALMER MEETS THE UPS DELIVERY GUY AT HER SCHEDULED pick-up time on the steps of The Hyacinth's front porch. She waves at the last two remaining paparazzi across the street who wait, desperate for any picture of a disheveled, cheating Meaghan, possibly with her new man. What they don't know is that Meaghan hasn't seen Bradley since the day the paparazzi caught her on his door. The *People* and *Us Weekly* reporters wave back to her.

The UPS guy turns around to witness the friendly banter as he climbs the last stair. "You've got quite the crowd," he says.

"Much smaller in recent days!" *Although wait till the divorce news leaks*, she thinks while smiling at the UPS guy. Meaghan told her this morning over breakfast that she asked Dunc for a divorce late last night. She has expected, and privately hoped, that this day might come since their wedding.

"Looks like I'm picking up," he says.

"Yes, I have two boxes that are going." She reaches inside the front door to grab them.

"Let me help you with that." The UPS guy scoots her to the side, stacking the boxes one on top of each other.

She pats the top of the boxes in his arms. "Thank you," she says gratefully, because she remains reluctant to lift anything heavy during her first trimester. Things are risky at the moment, which Dr. Harlow reminds her of each week at her sonogram. "I've spent the past three days preparing those boxes. One for each of my boys—surprise summer care packages. One is at camp and the other college."

After recovering from the shock of their reactions to the baby news, Palmer feels bad about hanging up on Aiden and Quinn. She shouldn't have acted that way; she's their mother. So, in an attempt to apologize and smooth things over from a distance, Palmer has been cooking and hunting down their favorite summer treats to deliver the ultimate care package to their doorsteps. Homemade caramel apples with chopped nuts and chocolate sprinkled on top, Fisher's popcorn flavored with Old Bay from the beach stand, gummy sharks from Candy Kitchen on Main Street, new sweatshirts from Rehoboth Breeze and, of course, a preloaded Visa card with two hundred dollars to spend on something fun.

Some might call the care package a bribe. She sees it as a heart-felt gesture, hoping it will bridge the growing gap between her and her sons. More like, apology in a box. She hopes the boxes will win them over, because she can't stand for them to be so upset and unhappy with her.

"Lucky kids!" the UPS guy says. "All I ever got at camp or college was an envelope full of stamps and a plea to write home. Which, of course, I never did." He checks his electronic pad. "Looks like I'm picking up these two boxes, but a bunch of boxes came in for you last night and they're on my truck. Where would you like me to put them all?"

"Oh, they're here! I've been waiting for those. If you don't mind, could you stack them in the office? It's down the hall a bit." Her anticipation buzzes; she believes these boxes may hold pieces of her past that could help shape her future. She has been tracking the UPS code for days now, watching the boxes navigate their way across Eastern Virginia and Maryland, over the Chesapeake Bay Bridge where they unavoidably got stuck in hours of traffic, and finally on to the Delaware coast.

Twenty minutes later, the delivery driver departs and Palmer winds her way through her office amid a sea of boxes. She sits down in the middle of the floor, her heart pounding with a mix of excitement and anxiety, and spends the entire afternoon going through each one. In the process, she discovers Miles's original pencil sketch of The Hyacinth's renovation, which she's never seen before. Joy lights her face; she makes a mental note to frame it and hang it in the great room, feeling a sense of connection to Miles.

One box contains twenty volumes of Miles's old agendas. They read like the Cliff's Notes version of their lives together. Client meetings that she recalls turned into beautiful renovations. Quinn's baseball games, Aiden's regattas. Gift ideas scribbled next to her birthday, some given, others forgone. Family vacations. Summer poker nights with Bradley, Scott, and other friends at Rehoboth's Elks Lodge. Alexandria's annual turkey trots on Thanksgiving mornings.

So many memories. Like a floodgate opening, they wash over her.

Hours later, she pulls the lid off the last box to find a file full of old family photos and a leather-bound journal. The earliest photo captures her cradling Aiden, still in the hospital when he was only a day old. Another depicts Miles and then three-year-old Aiden holding just-born Quinn, arm in arm, at the same time. She clasps the photos to her chest. They transport her back to a wonderful and dreadful time.

Those early days tortured her. She recalls the conflicting desires of work and motherhood. When she was at work, she wanted to be at home with her babies, missing them terribly and wondering what new thing they'd done that day. When she was at home, she wanted to be at work. Her phone was constantly pinging with questions from clients and the associates who worked for her. It was too much, but it didn't matter. She had to please everyone—her clients and her family.

The outside world admired and consistently praised her triumphant balancing act. At baseball fields and school events, other parents were always saying, *You make it look so easy* and, *I don't know how you do it all.* But on the inside, she felt like she was doing a hundred million things and not even one of them very well.

The memories overwhelm her and she rubs her face. A new resolve builds within her. She won't allow the past to define her future. She can't feel that way again. She can't live like that again! How can she raise a baby alone while working, when she could barely raise her boys with Miles? Not knowing the answer, she shoves the pictures back into the box.

Determined to face her fears, she stands up, intent on finding Meaghan to discuss exactly how she will manage single parenting a newborn at her age while continuing to flourish in her career. As she tosses the photos back into the box, Palmer sees the leather journal. She opens it and flips to the back because she always reads the last page first. There's an entry in Miles's handwriting. The last line reads, *It's his choice. It's his life.*

Palmer finds the beginning of the entry several pages beforehand. It's dated a week before his stroke. She inhales sharply, heart racing while desperately yearning for more insight into Miles's thoughts.

How did he truly feel about their recent conflicts? Might he have suspected about Sanford? The guilt and fear make her heart race. She fumbles the pages, longing for clarity but feeling only more confusion.

Then she freezes, staring at the entry above Miles's last one. A single line reads: "March 4. Dunc. WTF. See file folder: DJ."

Duncan? Mystery ignites within her. What was Miles doing with Duncan in March?

She reads the note again. She's been through every box and there is no file folder marked "DJ." Did she miss it? She rifles through each box again, with no success.

Finally, Palmer dials Frances, who picks up after the first ring. Frances spends the next five minutes uninterruptedly telling her about the excitement in town for Miles's new scholarship fund.

"I have four potential board members lined up who seem like the perfect candidates. Three live locally. The fourth was raised here and now is a senior advisor at Goldman Sachs in New York. And we haven't even begun promoting the opportunity and I already have a list of twenty high school seniors on the East Coast, who want to know how to apply for next year. They heard about it through word of mouth and decided to reach out!"

"This is wonderful, Frances," she interjects. "We'll want to expand applications to come from kids across the entire country. But the reason I'm calling is that I'm looking for one of Miles's folders marked 'DJ.' I don't see the folder in the boxes you sent. Could it still be at the office?"

"If it wasn't a current project, I boxed it up and sent it to you," Frances confirms. "We went through everything. Hold on. Let me pull up and search the active file directory to make certain." She hears clicking on a keyboard accompanied by a lingering silence as her anticipation grows. "No, there's nothing active or archived with those initials."

"Frances, can you think of anywhere else that Miles might keep files?"

There's audible fingernail tapping on the other end as Frances exhausts all possibilities before blurting out, "What about his computer?"

"His MacBook!" she exclaims, suddenly remembering its existence after the past few months. "Where is it? Still at the office?"

"Nope. I sent it with boxes to The Hyacinth," Frances says. "You should have it."

Excitement surges through her; hope flickers like a beacon. She remembers a smaller rectangular box that the UPS guy left on the table in the foyer. "Thanks, Frances."

"Good luck! Talk soon, sweetie."

Palmer throws her cell on the couch and jogs to the foyer. She tugs at the little tab and rips open the last box, pulling out Miles's MacBook. Then she rushes back to her office, sets the laptop on the desk, plugs in the cord, and pushes the power button. The laptop comes to life. Her heart pounds, eager for whatever lies within. She reviews Miles's second to last entry in the journal once more: "March 4. Dunc. WTF. See file folder: DJ."

She thinks as she clicks on the file folder icon. *If I were Miles, where would I keep a file about Dunc?* She finds a folder marked "Personal" and scrolls through. Nothing. Another folder is marked "Clients." Miles redesigned the private wing of Duncan and Meaghan's home several years ago; Miles could have tucked something from the fall in there. *Ah-ha!* There it is—a file that says "Duncan Jones."

She clicks it and then opens each document one by one. Drawings. Estimates. Receipts. Nothing out of the ordinary. Hmmm. Well, it did say the file was named *DJ*, not *Duncan Jones*.

She scrolls through the folders again and finds one at the very bottom, labeled Z. She clicks. At least fifty other subfolders greet her.

Another hour passes as she opens each one to study its contents. Darkness floods the room and the window now frames a full moon. Halfway through the subfolders, she clicks open a folder titled, *Private*. Inside sits one other folder. *DJ*.

"Gotcha," she says. A thrill of anticipation rushes through her. A light in her complicated world finally turns on.

MEAGHAN HEARS PALMER SCREAM.

She looks up from her phone to realize it's dark outside her window. The entire day is gone. She's spent hours on calls, first with Mack to get the divorce papers drawn up, then strategizing how to address the divorce in the press with Holly, and finally receiving a bleak Awaken sales update. Now she jumps off her bed, which has become her command station, and flies down the stairs. Along the way, she opens doors, searching for Palmer, and closes them just as quickly when she doesn't find her.

"Palmer! Where are you?"

"Meaghan! Meeaagghhaaaaan!" Palmer's screaming echoes through The Hyacinth as if bouncing off the ocean's waves beyond its walls. She follows the trail to Palmer's office and throws the door wide open.

"Are you okay?" She rushes toward Palmer, who's seated at her desk, MacBook perched in front of her.

"Yeah. I'm fine."

"Christ! You gave me a heart attack. I thought something was wrong with the baby!"

"Nope, we're good," Palmer assures her. "But you've got to hear this."

She unclenches her jaw. "Hear what?" Palmer grabs her wrist and pulls her behind the desk, a conspiratorial gleam in her eyes, so she can see the computer too.

Palmer has a FaceTime audio file open on the computer screen. "Listen." Palmer hits play.

"Can't take it anymore." The recording begins mid-conversation.

"Dunc, you're not making sense. Take a breath and tell me what's going on." Miles's voice plays over the laptop speakers.

"It's bad ... I mean really bad ... I don't know how we got here." Duncan's voice trembles and he's audibly winded. Meaghan can picture him pacing nonstop around a hotel room somewhere, probably Morocco.

"How you got where? Where are you?" Miles asks.

"I screwed up. I really screwed up. And now I think we are going to be in so much trouble. Real trouble. Life-changing trouble."

"What did you do, Duncan?"

"I want Bella to have the best. That's why I did it."

She says, "That's always his line." Palmer nods. They continue listening.

"Of course you do. I know that. Tell me what happened. Why are you calling me?" The tension in her chest tightens as she wonders how often these conversations between Miles and Duncan occurred. She looks at Palmer, who holds up her index finger, silently telling her to wait.

"There was a guy, a dad of one of Bella's friends. We started chatting at a school charity event a couple years ago. I took a real liking to the guy. He thought my work was brilliant," Duncan says. "Anyway, he said his daughter was definitely getting into SCC. I mean, she hadn't even applied yet. He told me he 'made sure of it.' Then he offered to hook me up with the person who 'made sure' the kid got in."

"He has to mean Thorne Cassidy," Meaghan interjects.

The recording continues. "I was so nervous for Bella. I said sure. I mean, I thought, what could a little reassurance hurt? So, I connected with the guy and one thing led to another and I kinda 'made sure' Bella would get in, too."

"What are you talking about? How did you 'make sure' Bella got into SCC?"

"I paid someone. To take the SAT and put her name on it. So she'd have a really good score."

"Jesus, Dunc."

"I know. It was wrong. But I am not the only one. Everyone is doing it." The sound of shoe tapping rapidly fills the recording, then abruptly stops. "That's the problem, though. Some parents are saying the FBI has been wiretapping our calls for months now." Miles exhales frustration on the other end.

Duncan continues, "It's a little worse than that ..."

"Christ almighty, Dunc. How could it be worse than that?"

"Meaghan's in on it. Except she doesn't really know."

"Explain," Miles demands.

"I asked Meggie to donate to the college. We agreed that it couldn't hurt. Lots of people do that. See, 'the guy' told me to disguise the bribe as a donation to his charity. It has some college name. He said it would be less obvious if Meaghan did it, that I should have her write the check. So I did. And she did."

"And now the Feds know everything," Miles says.

"I don't know what they know."

"Let's assume they know everything. How did you communicate with 'this guy'?"

"We talked and texted. He gave me some burner phone," Duncan explains. "But I deleted all the texts. You know, so there's no trail or evidence. But the wiretapping means they might have listened in on the conversations, right?"

"I'm guessing. Do you still have the burner phone?"

"Yeah, but there's nothing on it. It's irrelevant," Duncan says.

"Send it to me."

"Why? I told you, dude, I deleted everything."

"Just do it," Miles says, annoyed. "Listen, you have to tell Meaghan and Bella. They need to know what's coming. It will be worse for everyone if they're surprised by all this." A long pause passes between the two men on the phone. "And then find yourself a damn good attorney. You're going to need one."

"Okay, I can tell Meaghan," Duncan says. "You think we'll be okay?"

"I don't know, man. I don't know."

"Me neither. I gotta go, Miles. You're not going to tell anyone, right?"

"No. Don't forget, send me the phone."

"I'll do it right now. Honestly, I don't want to keep the damn thing." They say their goodbyes.

Right as the recording appears to end, Miles comes back on. "Note to files. I have just recorded a phone call I accepted over FaceTime on my laptop. It's a conversation between myself, Miles Harding, and Duncan Jones. March fourth." A single click ends the recording.

"I can't believe it." She shakes her head. "This totally exonerates me. Right now, the FBI and their team of prosecutors have decided I'm definitely in on this whole scheme because Bella's initials are written on the check that I wrote. On the memo line."

"What?" Palmer asks.

"I didn't mention it the other day. I didn't want to upset you or add more stress. But turns out that's why they deposed me again. They think I wrote Bella's initials on the check, and, because of that, I knew the check was a bribe. But Miles's recording tells the exact opposite story in Duncan's own words!"

She grins widely and claps her hands as if the horror show has finally ended. "I'm not going to jail, Palmer! The world will love me again! Bella will come home to me!"

Palmer looks up at her, an expression of cautious hope spreading across her face. "What if this is just the beginning, Meaghan? You might finally have the chance to rebuild your life—and with someone who truly loves you."

Meaghan's pulse quickens—the thought of rekindling something deeper with Bradley, who has always been there, tantalizes her. But could she truly allow herself to embrace love again, after all the chaos?

"Why would Duncan call Miles? Of all people? They weren't close. We all know Miles tolerated Dunc because he loved you," Palmer says.

She contemplates the question. "I don't know for sure, but my guess is that even though Miles didn't love Duncan, Miles was the only person outside of Hollywood Duncan could talk to. Dunc literally has no other"—she raises her hands in air quotes—"'friends' outside of L.A. He certainly could not trust anyone in town with this kind of confession. It would be leaked to the press immediately. And while the press appear disgustingly content to ignore his cheating habits, this would be all over the papers. Dunc's admitting his guilt before ever being accused."

Palmer considers this possibility. "The morning after we made up, I felt like Miles was still keeping something from me. Something pivotal. I swear he started to tell me and then Quinn walked into the kitchen. We started talking baseball practice and school, and then it was getting late and Miles left for work. Maybe this was what he was going to tell me about. On March fourth, we were in the middle of not speaking to each other."

"I'm sure he didn't want to involve you in anything related to Sinful Admissions. He was protecting you, like he always did." She pauses and wonders aloud about the possibility of Bradley needing protecting too, and whether she betrayed him simply by being near him.

She circles back. "Why would Miles think to record the conversation? He seems to start the recording as soon as he realizes something is wrong. But what would prompt him to think about recording the call at all?"

Palmer starts to nod her head. "He knows I wouldn't believe him otherwise."

Meaghan grimaces, "What?"

"Dunc confided in Miles years ago—the night before your wedding at his bachelor party. Duncan told Miles about two other actresses he'd slept with while you two were living together and raising Bella, right before he asked you to marry him. When Miles told me the next morning, I didn't believe him. I couldn't fathom anyone cheating on you. Why would they? I mean, look at you. You're amazing. I figured Miles got drunk and heard wrong, or misconstrued what Dunc told him—not purposefully, only that Miles misunderstood."

A light goes off in her eyes. With only a few words, years of wondering cease. The connections become clear. "That's why you never told me. You didn't think it was true." Meaghan crouches down so that she's eye level with Palmer, still sitting in her desk chair. "I waited for you to tell me about those women that morning in the bride's room of the church when we were alone, together. But you never did. I figured you didn't want to hurt me, which I understood. Because I was not telling you about your mother for the very same reason."

"You knew about the women? You knew Dunc's story was true."

"Yes. Drew overheard Miles and Dunc talking at the bachelor party. He came to the house and told me that morning before I left for the church. I'd heard rumblings before about Duncan's actresses, but when Drew told me what Dunc said, I knew all of it was true," she explains. "I knew who Dunc was when I married him. But I wanted Bella to have a father; I wanted her to have a real family."

"And now—it's your turn. You can carve out a new life for yourself, Meaghan. But first, you've got to call Mack," Palmer urges her. "Like, right now."

"You're right, this is precisely the evidence he's been searching for. And you found it!" She squeezes Palmer's hands. The moment feels electric, and for the first time in a long while, she thinks about what it would be like to let someone back in. She stands up, runs back to her command station upstairs, grabs her phone, and returns to Palmer's office, pulse racing as hope swells within her.

She can't stop smiling. She clicks Mack's contact photo and her phone starts to ring. She puts the call on speaker.

It rings five times before Mack answers in a whisper, "Hey, Meaghan."

"Mack. I'm here with Palmer. We have something you need to hear," she says.

"Well, I can't really talk right now. I'm at the prison with the divorce papers you had me prepare, and I'm with Dunc and Waverly. I stepped outside the holding room to take your call."

"No, you need to hear this right now," she says.

Palmer interrupts, "It's a recording Miles made of a conversation with Dunc in March."

"Hi, Palmer," Mack says.

"He confesses to Sinful Admissions and says he asked me to write the donation check. It's all right here!" Meaghan can taste sweet vindication.

Mack's intrigued. "Okay. Play it."

As the recording plays, the air around them seems to shimmer with possibilities. When it ends, the line is silent and she imagines Mack's brain clicking away, analyzing what he's heard. "Wow," Mack says. "Miles recorded Dunc's confession and an explanation of your innocence *before* he was arrested and pled guilty."

"I know!" she says. "This is the evidence we've been trying to find."

Mack hesitates. "Yes, but it's not that simple. I'm sorry."

"What do you mean?"

"First, the confession is muddy. It isn't clear that you didn't know what he meant by donation. Dunc knew, right? Second, the prosecutors will say that the recording is still only his word. There's no hard evidence." Another pause. She can hear Mack thinking. "What we really need are those text messages from Chip Sullivan directing Dunc to ask you to write the check as a cover up. Those would substantiate that you thought the check was a donation only and that the person who had the relationship with Sullivan was Dunc, not you. They would distance you from the crime."

"Not exactly the get-out-of-jail-free card I was hoping to hear, Mack," she says, her optimism wavering.

"Not yet. Look, we have a couple things going for us. First, we're working on the handwriting analysis of Bella's initials. We have enough documents collected that I'm pretty sure we can match the handwriting to someone else other than you. Second, I'm here with Dunc, right now. I'll ask him what he did with that phone. Dunc thinks he deleted those messages, and he did, but it's quite possible they aren't really deleted. Is anything ever these days?"

"Okay, let me know what he says. And when those papers are signed."

"You got it. Good work, ladies. Good work." Mack hangs up. Ten minutes later, Duncan confirms to Mack that he sent the burner phone to Miles.

"Dropped it in the UPS that afternoon. Haven't thought of it since. Those messages are gone for sure. There's nothing on that phone," Duncan swears.

What Dunc doesn't realize is that Mack employs a team of twenty-something computer wizards who might be able to get those text messages back. So Mack asks Meaghan and Palmer to search high and low until they find that phone. The next morning, Palmer asks Frances to go back through Miles's things left at his office, this time with a focus on looking for a phone. She provides no reason for her request and Frances doesn't ask for one. Instead, sensing the urgency, Frances also offers to scour the Hardings' home in Alexandria. Palmer accepts.

At The Hyacinth, Meaghan helps Palmer go through every place the phone might be and dig through the boxes one more time. She does all the reaching and bending so Palmer doesn't put the baby at any unnecessarily greater risk.

The three women find nothing.

Chapter 12

THE FOURTH OF JULY ROLLS INTO THE VILLAGE AMID haughty rumors. While locals and vacationers alike wander in from the beach to grab lunch and watch kids play championship rounds of cornhole in the Village square, one topic crosses each of their lips—who will win this evening's Christmas in July boat parade? At Palmer's spirited suggestion, Bradley agrees to let the Chief decorate and enter Serenity, rekindling an old tradition that sparks nostalgia. The Chief, determined to fulfill a promise to his wife, Goldie, to compete in the parade, has longed for this moment, especially with their twenty-fifth wedding anniversary approaching. Palmer, ever the romantic, delights in orchestrating their participation; she dreams of seeing town gossip Darby Shaw, who wins every year with her husband, Jonathan, dressed up as Santa, experience the thrill of defeat.

With a tinge of excitement, Bradley calls her to "check in on the baby." His enthusiasm is palpable, and he's been especially attentive since she told him she's expecting, about a hundred times more so than he ever was with Aiden or Quinn. She surmises that Bradley's standing in for Miles, which she finds lovely and best-friend appropriate. Yet, despite her gratitude, she senses a dual motivation behind his calls; "checking in on the baby" can be translated as checking in on Meaghan. Her suspicion is confirmed when he offers a meticulously considered Fourth of July plan.

"Why don't you both join me on the Fourth to watch the parade? I can offer the rooftop overlooking the ocean parade route and not a single person to bother us, escaping the prying eyes of the town. Chef Antonio asked me to let him run The Oyster House for the holiday, hoping to impress me enough that I'll consider leaving him in charge for good. It will be a perfect day."

"Chef Antonio always delivers, so that sounds fantastic. It's great you're giving him some rope. And, yes, watching the parade at your place sounds like a much-needed invitation. These walls sure seem to be closing in. It will be like old times," she blurts out. Memories of previous Fourth of Julys when the Harding clan swam in Bradley's rooftop pool flash through her head. "Except not at all like old times."

"Not at all," Bradley admits. "You'll bring Meaghan?"

"That depends. Are you two even speaking?"

"Well, not really," he admits. "But I'm tired of that. I think it's time we face our history and start over."

"Bradley, she told you the evening you spent together was a mistake."

"She did. But not having her as a friend is an unacceptable option. So I'd like us to get back to being friends. And friends spend the Fourth of July together. Bring Meaghan."

"I'll try," Palmer gives a supportive nod.

It doesn't take much coaxing. Meaghan agrees.

PALMER SPENDS THE JULY FOURTH MORNING IN THE kitchen while Meaghan walks their private beach. She prepares a fresh potato salad as a side dish to Bradley's grilled steak and lobster tails. She kneads together a fresh loaf of homemade focaccia bread and tops it with sautéed onions and fresh tomatoes, placing the bread on the counter to rise, when she hears a knock at the front door.

Palmer always avoids answering a knock at the front door, because who comes to your front door these days unannounced? The knock grows louder instead of going away, luring her reluctantly into the foyer. She peaks her head to the side window and sees the Chief standing on her front porch.

"Scott, what are you doing here?" She opens the French doors. "Shouldn't you be helping Goldie with Serenity? The launch is in a few hours."

"Good morning. Yes, I should be with Goldie, but I tried to reach you on your cell … I've been calling and texting you all morning. When I couldn't get an answer, I grew worried and wanted to make sure you … and the baby are okay."

"I'm so sorry! I have no idea where I set my phone down." She looks around the foyer, checking under yesterday's mail on the foyer table. "I've been in the kitchen all morning. I didn't hear it ring." She tosses the mail to the side, unsuccessful in her search, places her hands on her hips, and comes face to face with the Chief. "You came all this way. I feel awful. I've ruined your morning."

"Not at all. I'm glad you're all right," the Chief tells her with a smile. *Another friend of Miles's going out of his way to keep an eye on me.* "Listen, I was trying to reach you on the phone because … Paige, you remember my new assistant?"

"Yes," she says.

"Well, Paige has been getting the department back in order from all the chaos that has accumulated these past months since Madison retired. And yesterday, she unearthed an envelope. It was addressed to me, personally, but in my office's disarray, I didn't see it before. I must have set it down and then piled other papers on top of it." The Chief tries to solve every mystery he comes across.

"I can't imagine," she winks. She has seen his office before. "Well, I'm glad Paige is digging you out! What does this envelope have to do with me, Scott?"

"Well, Miles sent me the envelope." She gives the Chief a confused look and then begins to panic for no reason other than her own guilt. "It was marked Private and Confidential."

She rocks back and forth on her heels still standing in the middle of the foyer. "Did you open it?"

"Yep."

She braces for impact. "What was in the envelope, Scott?"

"A note to me from Miles," he says.

Her imagination spins out of control at all the possibilities. *About Sanford? Had he sensed they might be more than friends and wanted him to investigate?* She's not sure what to say next.

"And a cell phone." Her mind pivots and spins in a different direction. "But that's the weird thing. There's nothing on the phone. It's completely wiped. No emails. No text messages. No browser search history. It could be a burner phone, in which case it appears to have burned everything. I just don't know why Miles would have a burner phone, or why he would send it to me. And that's why I'm standing on your front porch." The Chief gives a frustrating grin. "Besides the fact that you didn't answer your phone."

"Right. Sorry about that," she apologizes again. She leans in and asks, "But you still have the phone?"

"Of course."

"Scott, I think that phone might belong to Duncan Jones. He sent the phone he used to communicate with Chip Sullivan—the guy who coordinated the entire Sinful Admissions operation—to Miles. I found a recording on Miles's laptop a few days ago. He recorded a conversation with Dunc and, in that conversation, Miles asked Dunc to send him a phone. Dunc said he deleted everything on that phone—texts and more—so it makes sense there's nothing left. We've looked everywhere for the phone and turned up nothing so far."

"Well, I'll be," the Chief says. "That's a pretty impressive cell phone then. And you're in luck. If anyone can recover 'deleted' text messages, it's Tommy, my computer guy in the lab."

"Scott, this could vindicate Meaghan completely. It is literally the only lead we've got. We need those text messages."

"If they exist, we'll find them," the Chief assures her. "I've got to get back to Goldie. I'll call the department on my way and get that phone into Tommy's hands. Shall I call Mack too? We can coordinate and be sure to exhaust all possibilities."

"Yes. I'll have Meaghan give him a heads up to expect your call," she says as the Chief walks toward his car. "And, Palmer, find your own damn phone, please. I'd like to be able to reach you ... without driving out to the Cape." He gives her a knowing glance.

"I will. Tell Goldie good luck! We'll be watching and rooting for Serenity!"

She closes the front door behind her and pauses, reflecting. With the pregnancy and now this news, there's a hope beginning to flicker like the fireworks that will light up the Cape tonight.

She scours her office, the master suite, and the kitchen for her cell, but turns up nothing. Exhausted, she heads out onto The Hyacinth's deck and collapses into an ocean-facing chaise lounge. On the table next to her, Palmer discovers her cell, face down, so as not to overheat from the warm sun.

"No wonder I didn't hear you." She picks up her phone and sees four missed calls and a text message. All from Sanford.

"Palmer, pls call. We've got a problem. A big problem. -S"

Crap, she thinks. The big litigation he was working on must be in hot water. She desperately wants to avoid speaking with Sanford, something she's successfully done since the day of Miles's stroke. She scrolls through her phone; she deletes Sanford's text and, without listening to them, all his voicemails. She decides for the moment to focus on the immediate joy.

ONE HUNDRED AND FIFTY SPARKLING BOATS SAIL FROM Lewes Beach to Rehoboth Village. The clear night sky shows off its brilliant stars even before the sun dips below the water's crest. A breeze cools onlookers who line the beaches and boardwalks up and down the coast. Bradley places fresh lobsters flown in from Maine that morning into a boiling pot on the outdoor stove top and sears filets in butter, garlic, and rosemary, before throwing everything onto the grill to finish them off. Meaghan sits next to Palmer on the outdoor couch beside the pool, anticipating Serenity's oceanic runway debut. She tries to stop thinking about the last time she was here. But flashes of the things she and Bradley did together pop into her mind, leaving her a little breathless.

"So, you're saying the Chief might have discovered the only evidence to clear you?" Bradley asks after she and Palmer fill him in on all the details. "Who would have thought things would shake out this way?"

"Miles," Palmer says, unequivocally.

She nods and sips her champagne. "It's a plot twist so twisted not even the *Law & Order* writing team could dream it up." She flashes her hand across the air announcing the headline, "Dead man solves unsolvable FBI case. Local lawman assists. Puts Hollywood royalty back on throne." She looks up at Bradley. His smile warms her, making her blush unexpectedly. *God, he's gorgeous.* Was she ever this attracted to Dunc? Never. Not even in the beginning. The feeling is exhilarating. One she realizes she's kept buried for so many years. It scares the bejesus out of her.

"Okay, Princess," Palmer says, patting her hand as she stands up, then grabbing the binoculars. Palmer stands next to Bradley at the grill. He hands Palmer the tongs, leaving his hands free to reach for his champagne flute. She notices Palmer's small baby bump rubs up against the grill controls. Thirteen weeks along; Palmer radiates a gentle glow. "What do I do now?"

"Leave everything on that side for a few more minutes, then we'll turn them over," Bradley says.

"No," Palmer replies, watching the boats pass in the distance. "I mean what do I do now?" Her eyes well up. "Miles should be here tonight. How do I ever get past the feeling that he should be here?"

Bradley puts his arm around Palmer. Meaghan walks over and group hugs them both. "He should be here. It's unfair and it's wrong. But you must keep moving forward, putting one foot in front of the other. That's what you're doing here tonight. That's what we're all doing here tonight." She looks at Bradley. "Miles would want all of us to be here tonight, together."

"He would," Bradley says, gently smiling at her.

"I know. Sometimes the moment gets me, though. It becomes too much." Palmer hands the tongs back to Bradley, grabs a napkin, and blows her nose very loudly.

"Whoa," Bradley says raising a hand between her and the grill. "It happens to all of us. It's like he's running late and then you remember he's not showing up, ever again. I broke down at the Elks Lodge last weekend in the middle of poker. No joke."

Palmer's eyes widen. "Now that's embarrassing." They all laugh. "Did they let you stay?"

"It was embarrassing. And they did let me stay. But only once; next time I'm out," Bradley says.

Palmer raises the binoculars to her face again. "Look! It's Serenity!" Palmer hands the binoculars to Bradley, pointing to the line of boats approaching. Meaghan jumps up and stands between them, searching for Serenity, who easily stands out among the competition.

Serenity is festooned in American flags placed all around her taffrail. The white stars on each flag are accented by tiny white lights that flicker more brightly as the sun falls. Four self-feeding water cannons that resemble individual fountains dance in her corners like the ocean's own brand of fireworks. A Statue of Liberty, adorned in sparkling deep navy that looks like galaxy glitter, centers the ship's stern and towers almost fifteen feet high. Sparklers flicker continuously in a circle around Lady Liberty. Katy Perry's hit song "Firework" booms from Serenity's belly. The crowd cheers wildly in succession as she passes like they're doing the wave in a baseball stadium. Serenity is magnificent.

"She looks … remarkable," Bradley says, unexpectedly impressed. "The Chief and Goldie did an amazing job decorating her."

"I think she could win!" Meaghan suggests. "She's a total knockout!"

"Absolutely gorgeous," Palmer chimes in.

"I agree … she could win," Bradley says, and Meaghan catches his eyes lingering on her face longer than necessary.

"It's time for Darby and Jonathan Shaw to go down! Mr. and Mrs. Claus must lose this year!" She relishes the thought of Darby being put in her place. "You know she's the one who fed the paparazzi extra details about the salon story debacle earlier this summer." Darby is an uncontrollable gossip who constantly feeds the rumor mill.

"Meaghan," Palmer scolds.

"You think the same thing," she responds. "I'm just willing to say it out loud."

"I do!" Palmer laughs. "I really do. They'll announce the winner soon enough." Five unidentified local reviewers judge each boat on criteria established decades ago, inspecting each vessel up close before the parade launches and then during the parade, piloting their course. The master of ceremonies announces the winner later tonight immediately before the Village's fireworks show.

Bradley places the steaks, lobster tails, Palmer's potato salad, and focaccia on the teak dining table. "It's a shame, really. We'll undress her tomorrow. I need Serenity back to a basic watercraft next week."

Palmer pulls up a seat. "Why?"

"I'm taking her to Cape May for a few days. I can't take her dressed like Lady Liberty."

"What are you doing in Cape May?" she asks, trying to seem uninterested but suddenly feeling disappointed he's leaving town. She sits down beside Palmer and hands her plate to Bradley to fill.

"Scouting a location for a new restaurant." Bradley places one of everything on her plate and hands it back. Their fingers brush, sending electricity through her body. The familiar spark reminds her of those stolen moments from their youth—before Hollywood, before Duncan, before everything got complicated. She and Bradley lock eyes. *He feels it too.* She can't drag him into her mess. She might be indicted soon. Plus ... *Bella.*

She picks up her fork and regains her composure. "I didn't know you were thinking of opening a second location."

"He's not," Palmer chimes in.

"The restaurant will be a totally new concept," Bradley says. "I've been testing the concept with potential investors for the past year and there's been a lot of interest. All the food will be sourced with local farmers and fisheries. Our menu will change daily, inspired by what's available at that moment. I envision long tables with guests seated side by side, getting to know each other for the first time. A restaurant and an experience, both centered around community. A place anyone can come to. Good food, good people, reasonable prices."

"Spectacular," she tells him. "People will fall in love not only with the food, but with each other."

"Hopefully," Bradley says and takes the last bite of his steak. He sits back and watches the last of the parade boats, pouring himself another glass of Cabernet. "People need to reconnect with each other again. We spend too much time yelling at one another over the internet. In my experience, the best way to reconnect starts with sharing a meal. It's an equalizer, levels the playing field so people can sit and talk. People rarely disagree about good food."

"I love it," Palmer tells him.

She wipes her mouth with her napkin. "So, you're looking for partners?" Bradley's eyebrows furrow. Meaghan meets his gaze.

"Like I said, I've been testing the idea with a few investors. They are always a good sounding board. I'm still on the fence as to if I might bring someone in."

She sips her wine. "I failed once in the restaurant business in L.A. It was a terrible experience." She shivers unexpectedly. "A private equity group approached me with the idea of a celebrity restaurant. I envisioned hospitality that delivered far beyond expectations. But what they pitched me and the reality that unfolded were quite different. The food was average and the service spotty. I was embarrassed the restaurant bore my name. I didn't know how to fix the problems, so I walked away." She sits back in her chair. "But you know all those things I don't." She looks at Bradley. "And I'm looking to reinvent myself. I need to pivot, and that pivot needs to be big, bold. A restaurant that brings people together could be the right next step. A first do-over if you will." *I need people to fall in love with me again.* "So, if you're looking for a partner or investors, maybe consider me?"

Bradley shoots Palmer a curious glance.

"She's getting a divorce," Palmer blurts out.

She whips her head around to glare at Palmer.

Palmer throws both hands into the air. "What? He's going to find out soon anyway … along with the rest of America."

She looks right at Bradley, "Yes, I'm getting a divorce. I need America to understand that Duncan's actions aren't mine." She takes a bite of steak. "Honestly, the divorce is a long time coming."

"Interesting," Bradley says with a smile and wide eyes. His cell vibrates on the table beside him, catching everyone's attention. "Bridgette" flashes across the screen. Bradley picks up the phone and pushes the silent button, sending Bridgette to voicemail.

Bridgette? Sophia a few days ago? Meaghan's jaw clenches. She exhales deeply, swallowing her bitterness. "You sure get a lot of phone calls." She stares at Bradley, who nods with hesitation. She forges onward. "In addition to separating myself from Dunc, I'm thinking through what other changes make sense to get my life back on track. I need America to see that I'm a giver and not a taker. A creator and not a destroyer." She thinks back to the salon. "This restaurant concept seems like what I hoped mine would be but wasn't."

"Supporting community and building community," Palmer says.

"Exactly," Meaghan and Bradley say at the same time. Everyone laughs. Her edge softens again.

"You two appear in sync," Palmer says, raising both palms in the air as if surrendering. "I'm only saying."

Are Bridgette and Sophia in sync with Bradley too?

"Why don't you come with me to Cape May," he offers.

Her heart flutters. She is terrified and excited by Bradley's invitation. *What will Bella think?* Terror takes over, "I can't ... I ..."

Without warning, Meaghan is interrupted by her cell phone ringing. She digs out the phone still buried in her purse, which sits on the edge of Bradley's plush outdoor couch. "It's Mack. I need to take this."

"Please do. Let's hear Mack's update," Palmer says as she and Bradley begin to clear the dishes from the dinner table.

"Hey, Mack. Happy Fourth!" Meaghan answers.

"Happy Fourth to you! I hope you're out enjoying the holiday."

"I am." Bradley pulls a berry trifle with layers of custard and whipped cream from the refrigerator beside the grill. She turns around and takes a seat on the couch. "Any news?"

"Yes, actually. JP called me earlier. Do you have a few minutes?"

"I'm all ears."

"Well, first, the defense team used forensic accounting to trace the check you wrote, in addition to a handwriting analysis. Chip Sullivan wrote Bella's initials. Apparently, another kid involved in the scandal is named Henry Jones, and Chip wrote both kids' initials on each of their checks to keep the Joneses straight. We secured sworn affidavits from both a forensic accounting expert and a handwriting expert to prove this in court."

"Wonderful!" Meaghan says. "I couldn't have asked for better news!"

Palmer's eyebrows go up. She mouths "What?"

She puts one hand over her phone and whispers back, "Check initials confirmed to be written by Chip Sullivan."

Palmer gives her two thumbs up. Bradley claps silently as he sets out three small plates on the table.

She returns to listening. "This definitely puts a dent in their case," Mack says, "but it's not enough to uncouple you from Duncan. We need those text messages."

"I get it. We need hard evidence that demonstrates I wrote a donation check, not a bribe." *Yes, that's what I did,* Meaghan tells herself.

"Exactly. So I'm working with the Chief there to sort through Duncan's phone. It may take a little time."

"Noted," she says. "Any other news?"

"Yes, I met with Bella to tell her about the divorce, like you asked. We had dinner at KoKo's in Pasadena."

"Smart," she confirms. "Very out of the way. A good safety."

"Yes. So, I'm sitting at the table, having a drink and waiting. Guess who Bella walks in with?"

Meaghan's head spins like a rolodex. Who might be willing to still hang with Bella these days given all that has transpired? "Lassie Cassidy?"

"Who?" Mack asks.

"Lassie Cassidy. Thorne Cassidy's daughter," she reminds him.

"Ah, yes. No, Lassie left town for the summer, although apparently, Thorne wasn't involved in the scandal."

"Okay. But Duncan said it was Thorne who told him about the scandal and that he'd already secured Lassie's enrollment."

"I don't know what to tell you, except that Duncan is wrong. Thorne is not indicted, he's not listed as an un-indicted conspirator, he's nowhere in this case."

She's confused but lets it go because Mac is always right. "Well, who did Bella bring, then?"

"Aiden."

She clutches her chest, absorbing the impact of Mack's words. She waves Palmer over. "I'm putting you on speaker. Palmer's right here. If you set up a dinner with Bella, why did she show up with Aiden?"

"Well, he's visiting her," Palmer explains.

Mack says, "It's more than that. They walked in holding hands. They were ... together, you guys." Palmer and

Meaghan's eyes widen. "When I told Bella about the divorce, I expected her to go a little crazy. Break down crying, get angry. Something. Instead, she looked at Aiden, who took her hand and said, 'Maybe it's for the best.' And Bella agreed."

"That's it? That was her reaction?" she asks, shaking her head. "Unbelievable."

"Maybe she knew already? Maybe Dunc called her?" Palmer asks.

"If Bella won't talk to me, she definitely won't talk to Dunc."

"Agreed," Mack says, tapping his pen on his desk. He's in the office even on July Fourth.

Palmer chimes in. "Maybe Bella already considered the likelihood of a divorce herself. I mean, it's not that unexpected. She hears things, even if they aren't published in *People* or *Us Weekly*."

"That's possible. Either way, I'm glad she took the news okay," she says.

"I told Bella that you wanted to be the one to break the news, but her blocking all contact with you didn't make that feasible. I encouraged her to reach out to you. Then the three of us had a phenomenal meal. They both seemed good, guys. Really good. Surprisingly good, given everything they've been through recently."

I want to have dinner with Bella! Her heart melts. She's grateful for Mack, but would do anything to switch places and share a meal with her daughter.

Bradley comes over and sits across from Palmer and Meaghan. "Personally, I think Aiden and Bella could be perfect for each other."

Mack stops tapping his pen. "Um, who's that?"

"Bradley, Bradley Heartfield. Sorry, Mack, I was listening in."

"Oh …" Mack says with a curious tone. "Not at all. I didn't realize the three of you were together."

"Thanks for telling Bella, Mack. While I wish I could have told her, you telling her might have been an even better choice. Really, I owe you," she says.

"The list is long, Meaghan," Mack says with a wink that she can see even through the telephone.

"Anything else to report? Otherwise I'll let you go watch fireworks," she says.

"One other thing. Can you take me off speaker?" Mack asks.

"Sure." She punches the button and brings the phone to her ear.

"Wanted you to know the divorce papers are now signed by you both. I'll file them in L.A. County court after the holiday."

"Got it. Holly and I prepared the PR strategy, so please coordinate with her on the filing date. We'll go from there. Talk soon," she says and hangs up.

"Aiden and Bella?" Bradley teases their mothers. "I don't think I would have put those two together on my own before current circumstances, but, like I said, they could be quite the match." His phone whistles. "It's the Chief. They're nearing the end of the route. Wanna go over and welcome Serenity into port?" he asks.

"I think I'm going to call it a night. You two go," Palmer says.

"This has been a wonderful evening, but I'm exhausted as well," she says. "I'll go back to The Hyacinth with Palmer."

"You two sure? It's the last time to see Serenity as Lady Liberty," Bradley asks.

"That's right," Palmer says and points to Meaghan. "You should go to Cape May. The restaurant could be an amazing opportunity. I can't think of a better team than you two."

Meaghan looks at Bradley. The opportunity to reinvent herself beckons, but not without reservation. Can she risk being seen with Bradley this week in public?

"Honestly, it's too risky. The week my divorce papers will be filed. Those front door headlines aren't that old." She shakes her head. "I don't think so."

"You won't be seen together!" Palmer says. "You'll take Serenity over. There will be zero press looking for you in Cape May."

"I have a house on the beach rented for the week. I'm not sure how quickly negotiations might go, so I decided to stay a few days. The house is completely secluded. Sits on five acres of beach-front solitude," Bradley says.

Was he hoping Bridgette might stay over? Or Sophia?

Meaghan feels the urgency to lay claim ... something she's never experienced. *Competition.* "You're sure no one will see us?"

"I don't see how they'd find us."

St. Thomas flashes through her memory. Those stolen moments along the shoreline, ocean waves thundering nearby while they shared secrets beneath a canopy of stars. Her pulse quickens. Cape May threatens to recreate St. Thomas entirely, a prospect she cannot afford in her current circumstances. She issues her final stipulation. "Separate bedrooms. Business only." She jabs her finger toward Bradley. She counters her jealousy with the pragmatic need to preserve her standing. She locks away her longing and discards any chance of retrieving it.

"Only business," he confirms. "We are clear on that."

She can't help but smile. "All right, I'll go."

Chapter 13

THREE DAYS LATER, PALMER AND MEAGHAN PULL INTO THE Rehoboth Village marina to find Bradley removing the last few flags around Serenity's taffrail.

Bradley runs up the dock to greet them, not even a little out of breath. "I still can't believe it." Bradley embraces Palmer and Meaghan. "Scott and Goldie transformed Serenity into a true beauty! I'll never forget the stunned look on Darby's face when the judges announced her the winner … Talk about fireworks. Darby looked like she might explode herself!"

"Priceless," Meaghan chimes in. "I would have loved to see that."

Bradley grabs Meaghan's bags and she closes the liftgate. "Let's take our champ out on the water. Shall we?" he asks Meaghan.

She looks at Serenity docked at the pier. "I have to admit, I'm a little jealous not to be going," she tells them.

"Why didn't you say so? You should come with us!" Meaghan offers.

"No thanks," she says, surprising herself with how firm her voice sounds. "The baby and I need some quiet time." She rubs her middle. "I'm going to relax. Cook a bunch of meals so that they're ready in the freezer when the boys arrive in a couple weeks for August. Buy too many insanely cute baby clothes and too much techy baby gear that I'll never be able to figure out how to use. All from the comfort of my couch. And I've decided to start working on Miles's scholarship fund. There's a lot to do if we want to make the program a success, starting this fall."

"I want you to rest and relax," Meaghan pleads. "Do nothing. I called Garner's Farm and they're delivering your dinner the next two nights."

"Meaghan! You shouldn't have done that."

"It's what I do. I can't make you dinner, but I can make sure you're eating dinner. And thank God you're eating again!" Meaghan hugs her and kisses her forehead.

"Call us if you need anything at all," Bradley says. He turns toward Meaghan. "You ready?"

Meaghan gives her another goodbye hug. "Have a good week, Mama." Meaghan faces Bradley. "Ready." As the two walk down the pier toward Serenity's dock, Meaghan's blond hair blows in the breeze. Her giant Prada sunglasses hide her brilliant blue, smiling eyes. Bradley carries her bags in one hand and lightly touches her back shoulder with the other. They are mid-conversation. She has no idea what they're discussing. *But they look like they belong together.*

She climbs back into her Volvo and steers toward The Hyacinth. As she drives up the coast, her boss, Harold, calls. Her stomach tightens with the old familiar anxiety, but she takes a deep breath. *This can't be good.* Maybe Sanford's litigation problem has now reached Harold. She considers letting it go to voicemail, then decides to face whatever's coming. Her palms grow sweaty as she presses the answer button on her steering wheel.

"Hello? Harold?"

"Palmer, hi. It's Calinda." Calinda Tate is the savviest Vice President at the firm. Harvard undergrad and Yale Ph.D. in economics. She's fluent in Mandarin, Russian, and Spanish and ran two marathons last year. If Palmer wasn't Calinda's boss, she would feel severely threatened by her brilliance. But she is Calinda's boss, which is why she put her in charge of her largest client, SuperSonic, while she's away for the summer.

"Hi, Calinda. How are you?"

"I'm okay, thanks for asking. But I'm calling with some not great news about SuperSonic."

SuperSonic holds hundreds of patents on 5G cellular technology that keeps cell phones secure. Last year, WavePro, their direct competitor, sued SuperSonic for stealing the technology from their labs, claiming WavePro invented it first.

She braces for the news, her hands surprisingly steady on the wheel. "What's up?"

"The judge found SuperSonic liable. Ordered them to pay the billion-dollar fine. We lost, Palmer. Badly. SuperSonic says they're going to shop for new economic experts."

She pulls her Volvo into the circle drive. She stares out the car window at the tall grasses waving in the driveway's center around a towering, white-bloomed crepe myrtle. A few months ago, losing her biggest client would have sent her into a tailspin, the kind she imagines everyone else at Mintz, Krowl & Harding is currently experiencing. She would have shouldered this failure as her personal burden, spending sleepless nights trying to fix it. But the news doesn't faze her. It's a blip on life's radar, she now understands. Insignificant.

"I'm sorry," she says. "I know how hard you've been working on this one."

"It's a huge loss. Needless to say, everyone's pretty upset here." Calinda exhales. "We can do a full debrief when you're back, but I thought you'd want to hear the news right away."

"Thanks for letting me know, Calinda. You handled everything exactly as I would have." She hangs up and sits in her Volvo contemplating her next move. The urge to fix everything tugs at her. She should work the phones, soothe everyone's worries, and reassure them all there's a path forward to renewed success.

But she can't bring herself to make the calls. The calls are exhausting. They are inconsequential. For the first time, she recognizes this urge for what it truly is: is an impossible task she's always set for herself. She can't make them all happy. She can't control everything. She powers off her cell and walks into The Hyacinth.

PALMER SPENDS THE ENTIRE WEEK IN INSOLATION. IT'S the first time in nearly twenty years she finds herself entirely alone. No kid duties. No work obligations. No social commitments. It's heaven. She loses herself in the kitchen, preparing her favorite summer foods and planning the dinner menu for the last Sunday in August, when they will spread Miles's ashes on The Hyacinth's beach.

Afterwards, she turns her focus on Miles's scholarship fund, and after reviewing Frances's detailed emails, she calls Frances a few days later.

"Hey there, how are you doing?" Frances asks. She instinctually thinks to reply with a baby update, but she has not yet told Frances about the baby. Frances will have a million questions and she will have zero answers. However, Quinn may have told Liam about the baby, and Liam may have told Frances. So she steers the conversation delicately.

"I'm fine, considering everything." She knows it leaves much open for interpretation.

"Glad to hear it. Liam told me"—*here we go*, Palmer thinks—"about Quinn! You must be so proud of him. It's only his first summer as a counselor at Camp Horizons!"

She slumps back in her tufted leather office chair. She feels a wave of bitterness wash over her. It's true; Quinn's having the summer of his life, and she hasn't heard so much as a peep since she told the boys about the baby. No thank you for the summer care package she sent. Only silence. She can't express that to Frances, though.

"I am very proud of Quinn," she manages to say, forcing sincerity into her voice.

"To be voted best camp counselor three weeks in a row! A feat never achieved before! An honor, clearly. Liam says everyone greets him with a bow now, like he's the king or something." Frances giggles, her enthusiasm palpable, but it only deepens the pit in Palmer's stomach. In this one instance, she feels grateful that Frances has the gift of gab, making her almost impossible to interrupt. "I guess jumping in and saving that little girl has made him a regular hero. Liam said all the kids sign up for the adventures Quinn leads, and all the other counselors' adventures attract no one. Those little kids *adore* him! I hear his girlfriend feels the same, too."

Palmer's head drops into her hands. She's elated for Quinn, but the credit feels like a punch to the gut. She yearns for him to share what's going on in his life with her, but instead the distance echoes.

"I am so happy good things are happening in his life." This, she means wholeheartedly. "Quinn does love little kids," she adds begrudgingly.

"Did you ever find the phone you were looking for?" Frances changes the subject.

"Yes! Yes, we did, and it is in the right hands now. Thank you for turning things upside down there to help us search."

"Oh that's great news. And you got my emails on potential board members for Miles's scholarship fund?"

"I did. There are several bios that look promising."

"I agree." Frances bounces a pen on her desk and Palmer feels her check the clock on the other end. "Anything good in Miles's boxes?"

Frances's question sets a lightbulb off in her head. "Some wonderful things. I've been through all of them." But she hasn't read the entire journal yet. She pauses, recalling Miles's memories waiting within—untold stories and insight into his feelings. "I found Miles's original hand drawing of The Hyacinth. One I'd never seen before. I'm framing it and hanging it in the foyer here."

"Wonderful! All right, well I'm late for a meeting here. Let me know if you need anything else on the foundation front, or otherwise. And hug the boys for me when you see them!"

"Will do. Take care, Frances."

Palmer hangs up, but the phone feels heavy. She opens her top right desk drawer and pulls out Miles's leather journal. In all the commotion of searching for Dunc's phone, she'd forgotten about it. She walks over to the white slipcovered couch in her office, pulls a soft, fuzzy blanket on top of her, and curls up with Miles's secrets.

CAPE MAY CAPTIVATES MEAGHAN WITH IDYLLIC CHARM and quaint offerings. Enchanting Victorian houses, picturesque restaurants, and small boutique shops line Washington Street and welcome her into town. Bradley docks Serenity at the Boathouse Marina and switches them into a white Land Rover that he has waiting. They navigate around the Cape toward the secluded beach house Bradley's rented. The Cape May light house, which can be seen from any point on the peninsula, serves as their landmark. Paved roads turn to gravel, gravel roads turn to dirt. Finally, they arrive at a two-story sky-blue beach cottage with deep-blue shake shingles, a bright-red door, and fragrant white and blue hydrangeas lining its perimeter. The back of the house is swathed with native vegetation, tall grasses, marshes, and dunes with a wooden walkway that leads to a two-hundred-foot dock and their own sand beach.

She takes one look around. "Bradley, it's fantastic."

"Just wait." Bradley grabs their bags and unlocks the keypad with the realtor's code. A wall of glass at the back of the house welcomes them with a sprawling panorama of the Delaware Bay as it pours into the Atlantic Ocean.

Joy fills her like sunshine. "Wow."

"I love this house," he says. "I always rent this place when I'm on Cape May. There's no place more quiet and serene." Bradley sets Meaghan's bag in the master suite. "Why don't you settle in for the week. Unpack, relax, head down to the beach if you'd like. I have a few calls to make and then I'll cook us dinner."

"With what?" Meaghan asks. "We only got here a few minutes ago. You've already been to the grocery store?"

"I had a friend do some shopping ahead of our arrival." Bradley opens the sixty-four-inch stainless steel refrigerator in the middle of the kitchen. Shrimp, rockfish, clams, oysters, an abundance of fresh produce, and several bottles of Veuve Clicquot fill three shelves. Two crusty baguettes sit on the eight-burner stove.

Sophia?

"You sure did." Meaghan smiles, peeking in the refrigerator doors that Bradley has opened. "Make your calls. I'll see you at dinner."

She slips into her bikini and wanders down to the beach. She lays her towel in the warm sand, sits on top, and peers out into the deep blue. Her heart aches for Bella. She wants to gossip with her over coffee and pecan sweet rolls from Tartine Sycamore, get pedicures at the Nail Garden, and shop all day on Rodeo Drive. She wants to listen to Bella divulge every detail of her life, including everything she's feeling about Aiden. She remembers the last time they laughed together, and how much the light has dimmed between them since.

She opens her Instagram and taps on Bella's profile. Still blocked. She can't see any of Bella's posts, or anyone else's posts she might be tagged in, although that seems unlikely. Meaghan begins to scroll through her own feed. The red dot on her Instagram inbox shows 303 notifications since that morning. *What?*

She clicks the inbox arrow. Mentions are everywhere. ExpressNews. CelebrityProfile. TMZ. *Entertainment Weekly.*

Hell, even CNN in Español. Every news outlet, national and international, tags her in their story. Her chest tightens as the reality sinks in. The world knows Meaghan Jones is divorced.

Her heart pounds. *All those years with Duncan.* The right decision. The necessary decision. *But another failure.* Will it save her?

After a dip in the ocean and a hot shower, Meaghan dresses in Awaken's white linen pants paired with a simple navy halter tank and goes downstairs for dinner.

"Come on," he tells her. They head down to the beach, where Bradley has moved the dining table, along with two chairs and candles.

"Bradley," Meaghan says, "this is not supposed to be a romantic dinner." She shakes her head.

"It isn't, I promise. This …"—he waves his hand between the two of them—"is only business."

She meets his gaze, old emotions stirring inside her. "I'm impressed by how dedicated you are to your work."

"It's all I think about," he winks and pulls the chair out for her.

She feels the heat between them. It's undeniable, despite her brazen attempt to deny all her feelings for Bradley.

"Speaking of business …" she takes a seat at the table. "You know, I officially got divorced … today." Her pulse quickens, wanting his validation for this pivotal moment. Bradley's eyes widen and he nods. "That's officially a wrap on my marriage."

"I heard that news this afternoon, actually. Twitter. Or do we call it X, now?" He shrugs his shoulders. "I'm not taking advantage of your divorce, but a nice dinner seems appropriate. At the very least, an acknowledgement of new beginnings?"

He takes his seat across from her. A spark of understanding passes between them, magnified by the setting sun casting golden hues around them. The evening sunlight sparkles on the waves before them, creating millions of tiny rainbows in their spray.

"So, how does it feel?" he asks. "To be official?"

"Wonderful. And petrifying. I feel like I'm all at sea." She waves her hand in the direction of the water. "Unable to find the horizon. Unsure which direction leads me home." She exposes herself to him.

"You'll find your way. I'm certain of that. And no one will find you here for a few days, so you can pause for a moment. Get your bearings." Bradley smiles. He stands up and ladles cioppino, an Italian seafood stew, into two deep ceramic bowls. Then he pulls two warmed baguettes from a basket to soak up the stew's fennel- and garlic-laced broth and pours her a glass of crisp Sauvignon Blanc.

Dinner is perfection. Bradley is perfection. As he serves her, she dreams of standing up beside him, ripping his clothes off, and having wild, passionate sex with him on the beach. She yearns to feel him inside her again. She wants to be utterly consumed by Bradley. But she can't. *Bella could find out. What would one more thing do to our relationship?* She can't imagine. So instead, Meaghan devours the meal he's prepared and two glasses of wine.

"Can I get seconds?" she asks. "You've got to feed a divorce."

Bradley obliges. They fill their dinner conversation with restaurant details and scenarios. Bradley shares the names of chefs he's considering, menu ideas to draw from based on the seasons and local farms he's been cultivating relationships with for years.

"You've been planning this for a while now, haven't you?"

"For many years. Just never found the right spot to do it. But I think what we're seeing tomorrow could be it." He wipes his mouth with his napkin. "What would you want from this restaurant … *if* we were to go in together?"

To be with you. She clears her throat and her mind. "What I want and, quite frankly what I bring to the table that no one else you're talking to can, is my unique sense of style, hospitality, and celebrity. I realize the celebrity part needs work at the moment, but I can make this restaurant an inviting place people want to be. That's what I did before in L.A. My restaurant failed because I didn't have the right partners who knew the business side. You do." She leans forward and puts both elbows on the table. "Besides that, I can meet your capital requirement. Not many individual investors can."

"Your signature style would be a dramatic touch."

"If we do this, I'm going to want complete design authority," she tells him.

"How about final approval if we disagree on a design concept?"

"How is that not the same thing?"

"I guess it is," he laughs. As his laughter fades, silence hangs between them. Each weighing the opportunities and the risks involved.

"You're not asking the obvious question."

"What's that?"

"'Might I be a liability?' Rather than bringing people in, I might turn people off. At least right now … at least for the moment." Her voice catches slightly, a break in her confident facade.

"I think you bring more to the table than your celebrity. I've always thought that." He smiles at her. "But the point you make … it's a fair one."

She leans into him and quietly asks, "What if my situation gets worse? What if they indict me?" She can't stand contemplating the worst too loud. "I don't think you'd want to be business partners."

He looks toward the sea, reflectively. "How about a silent partner in that instance? I would always value your style. Your design capabilities. Your insights on creating hospitality. Maybe we'd avoid publicizing our partnership until we were certain it would be a boon for the restaurant."

"I could live with that." *Finally a door that stays open.*

Two hours later the sun has fallen and the tide laps at their toes, but their conversation hangs between them like a thread. "Time to retire for the evening," he says. Meaghan helps Bradley carry the dishes and candles back to the house. "We'll leave the table and chairs; they aren't going anywhere."

Back at the house, she offers to clean up the kitchen. "You cooked. I'll clean." Bradley remains noticeably careful to respect her wishes. He tidies the countertops, wipes down the stove, and leaves the rest for her.

As she stands at the sink, she feels the warmth of his gaze on her, and the air feels charged with unspoken emotion.

"We're meeting the realtor at 11 a.m., tomorrow morning. We'll leave here at 10. You'll be ready?" he asks.

"I'll be ready," she says. "Have you told the realtor that I'm coming?"

"You mean, that … Meaghan Jones is coming?"

"I mean, divorced-today, paparazzi-magnet-tomorrow, Meaghan Jones is coming," she clarifies.

"I have not. Why alert anyone ahead of time? It's only more opportunity for something to go wrong."

"Maybe I shouldn't go. I mean, how do you trust this realtor to keep my presence secret once they see me, if you don't trust them ahead of time?"

"I trust them ahead of time, I only want to minimize all risks for you. You've been through enough. The realtor is the listing agent as well as the selling agent; that means a two-million-dollar commission if I buy. No one will risk that kind of cash by leaking your whereabouts for a lesser amount of cash. You're coming." Bradley snaps Meaghan with a towel, then hands it to her to finish the dishes.

Warmth spreads through her. Their eyes lock.

He breaks her gaze, turns around, and heads out of the kitchen. "Goodnight, Meaghan Jones!"

"Goodnight, Bradley Heartfield!" She turns around to face the sink and melts a little. His noble resisting of their obvious attraction makes him that much harder to resist. She finishes cleaning up the kitchen and goes to bed.

Chapter 14

PRECISELY AT ELEVEN THE NEXT MORNING, BRADLEY AND Meaghan wind down hilly roads, lush with green grasses, over-looking the sea in the distance, a mix of excitement and dread bubbling inside her. They turn onto a long cobblestone drive, lined by what Meaghan imagines are one-hundred-year-old oak trees, bending toward the center of the drive and creat-ing a luxurious canopy. As they approach the drive's end, a two-story country farmhouse reveals itself and, directly be-yond it, the ocean. The setting is quaint and grand. Intimate and majestic. Utterly breathtaking.

Bradley parks the Land Rover, gets out, and opens her door for her.

"Gorgeous," she says, staring through the house's wide front windows at the sparkling sea behind her.

"Bradley! Braaaadddlleey!"

Her heart skips a beat as she turns around at the pierc-ing, shrill voice. An overexcited bleach-blonde woman wear-ing a deeply V-cut blouse that instantly announces her breasts bounces right toward them. The woman opens her arms to greet Bradley and kisses him, once on each cheek.

"How are you, darling?" the woman gushes, a bit too intimately for Meaghan's liking, as she breezes right past Meaghan, leading Bradley to the front walkway at the bottom of the stairs. "Isn't this entrance to the property striking! It's exactly what you've been looking for, right?" The woman clings to his arm as they take in the view together.

Meaghan crosses her arms tightly. Why is this woman lingering so close to Bradley? Jealousy roils within her. She can't help but notice the easy chemistry between them.

"Truly breathtaking. Exquisite find," he responds, slipping from her grasp, a glimmer of discomfort flashing across his face. "I'd like to introduce you to my ..." He searches for the right word, "business partner."

She turns around, "Okay."

"Bridgette, this is Meaghan. Meaghan, this is Bridgette Babson, my realtor. She sells more real estate on Cape May than any other broker. She's been looking for the perfect property for my restaurant concept for almost five years, along with her partner Sophia. They're the dynamic duo of real estate over here."

Bridgette and Sophia. The names that are always showing up on his cell phone.

"That's right. We go way back," Bridgette says and tosses her hair behind her shoulder. "And you're *the* Meaghan. Meaghan Jones, right?"

"The one and only." She's considered changing back to her maiden name since the divorce, but the world knows her as Meaghan Jones. Plus, she shares the name with Bella.

"Which I know you'll keep to yourself, right, Bridge?" Bradley asks.

Bridgette winks. "You bet, sweetie."

"All right then, let's see this place," Bradley says.

"Let's go in!" Bridgette wraps her arm around Bradley's waist and he opens the front doors.

Meaghan's jaw clenches.

They enter the foyer, which is accented by oak-paneled walls and a double high ceiling.

"This would be an outstanding spot to greet guests in the winter," Bradley says. "In the summer we could greet everyone on the grand porch outside."

"Brilliant," Bridgette placates.

Meaghan feels her muscles tighten. The way they speak to each other—the familiarity—it fills her with dread. She walks past Bridgette to Bradley, and her muscles relax slightly. "We could fit several plush settees in both places."

"When guests arrive, they can sit and enjoy cocktails, taking in the views," Bradley says. "Afterwards, they'd be seated as an entire table, together." Bradley's smile widens, the ease in his voice provoking an ache inside her.

"Marvelous." Bridgette hangs on Bradley's every word. Once they are done with the foyer, she grabs him by the hand and leads him through each room in the grand farmhouse. As Bridgette gives them the tour, she speaks almost exclusively to Bradley, occasionally allowing Meaghan into their conversation. Bridgette explains the property's history, previous owners, square footages, possible kitchen layouts, and seemingly hundreds of intricate details, from who carved the spiral staircases to the excavation depths and construction of the wine cellar beneath them.

She's exceptional at her job. Meaghan knows that a smart and beautiful woman can win a man's heart every time. *Has Bridgette ever won Bradley's?* She tries not to let it, but the thought sends her fuming.

Two hours pass, and she tries to engage in the tour, but all she can focus on is Bridgette, who adheres herself to Bradley like a second skin.

Bridgette announces she has another appointment back in the town center—a couple in from New York City decided the Hamptons are too much for them.

"I'm happy to show you any other properties you'd like to see this week, Bradley," Bridgette says a bit suggestively.

What else has Bridgette shown Bradley? "Do we really need to see anything else?" Meaghan interrupts.

Bradley nods in agreement. "Thanks for the offer, Bridgette," he says. "But I am really feeling this one."

"This place won't be on the market long, that's for sure. Think about it," Bridgette responds. "Call me tomorrow? I'm available."

Meaghan's eyes roll.

"We'll definitely talk tomorrow."

Bridgette embraces him, kissing him goodbye on both cheeks, and then reaches her hand out to shake Meaghan's. "Pleasure."

Reluctantly, Meaghan shakes her hand in return. "All mine."

Bridgette crosses to the front of the property, gets in her BMW, and heads down the drive.

Meaghan clenches her fists, forcing herself to take a calming breath.

Bradley turns to her. "So, what do you think? Incredible, right?" He smiles at her, but she can't bring herself to smile back. "What?"

"What exactly is your relationship with Bridgette?" The words fly out of her mouth before she can reign them in. She has no claim over him, but an urgency pushes her forward. Why does this bother her so much? It's a feeling she's never experienced before.

"Just my realtor," Bradley replies, his brow furrowed. "She looks for properties. Sends me a list of options. I tell her if I want to see any." He walks right up to Meaghan. He places his hands on her shoulders. "Meaghan, what is wrong with you?"

"She is falling all over you!" She takes a step back out of his grasp. The next question pops out of her mouth before she can close it. "Have you slept with her?" She covers her mouth with her hand. *Agh! None of my business!* She can't help herself. She needs to know.

His eyes turn dark, and she feels the heat of his gaze piercing her. "Whoa. Have I slept with her? No, I have not slept with her, Meaghan. I'm insulted you would even ask me that." He turns away from her and begins to walk back toward the house. Then he then turns around again and walks back to her. "But what if I were sleeping with her, why would you care?"

She swallows hard. He's right. Why does she care? Standing speechless in the sand, her heart races. The ocean waves crash behind her, accentuating the wild storm brewing inside.

He continues, "Our connection goes way back, despite your attempt to avoid it for almost two decades. The other night—that was one of the best nights of my life. And I'm sorry it ended so poorly for you. But that wasn't my fault. I won't remember what we shared as anything other than euphoric. But you've deemed that evening a complete mistake. You have made it very clear that you are only here for business. So, if I am sleeping with Bridgette, again I ask, why do you care?" He indulges those last words.

"Because she is throwing herself at you!" The words escape again. Jealousy courses through her veins. But is she really ready to confront everything they once were?

"You're jealous. Meaghan Jones is jealous," he concedes, a slow grin thawing the heat of the moment.

His accusation snaps her out of her rage. She pulls herself together. "You're right. I shouldn't have asked. It's none of my business." Her fingers twirl through her hair as she looks away from him, afraid of the truth hiding in her eyes.

"Let's tour the house one more time ourselves before we leave. Without Bridgette," she says, attempting to regain control as she walks back toward the house.

Bradley steps forward, closing the distance between them. He reaches for her shoulder, pulling her gently toward him, and as he does, a tender ache of familiarity consumes her.

"Meaghan ..." He pauses, looking deep into her eyes. Their breath mingles in the salty air. She scans his face and sees everything they've shared.

"Are you ready to let me back in?" His question hangs in the air like an unspoken promise, one that may change everything.

She opens her mouth to respond, but the words fail her. Instead, she feels the weight of their situation pressing down— or maybe lifting her up. A part of her wants to dive in. Yet fear constrains her.

In an instant, a wave crashes against the shore nearby, breaking the moment. Her heart pounds as confusion clouds her mind. What decision should she make? Can she step back into his world, knowing the risks?

The air hangs heavy with uncertainty; the stakes have never been higher.

PALMER REMEMBERS TO CALL MEAGHAN BEFORE DELVING into the leather journal. She's sent confirmatory proof-of-life texts that all is well at The Hyacinth, but she promised she'd call Meaghan this afternoon after they toured the property. Plus, she really wants to know if Meaghan and Bradley might have gotten beyond only business.

"Hi," she says when Meaghan picks up. "Where are you?"

"I'm sitting on the sand with my toes in the water. It's so warm here today. We got back about an hour ago. Where are you?"

"I'm lying down on the couch in my office with the air-conditioning on high," she tells Meaghan. "So? What's the verdict? Do we love the property?"

"Oh ... we love the property." Meaghan indulges her in a ten-minute verbal tour of the seaside farmhouse complete with descriptions of how each space could be utilized for the restaurant. "I'll text you some pics when we hang up."

"Sounds exquisite," she says.

"More than exquisite. If I had to dream up a different and better property for this concept, I couldn't. It's absolutely perfect. The long tree-lined drive, the layout of the house, the sprawling beach and ocean out back; the potential is nearly unlimited. We need a few days to flush out the details to see if we can make everything work."

"I can't wait to see it," she admits and then fills Meaghan in on SuperSonic. "They lost their case, and the judge took the other side's damages number, not mine," she says. "So now our client has to pay a billion dollars, which means they don't want to pay us anymore."

"Yikes," Meaghan says. "You'll find a new client."

"Maybe, but the odd thing is ... I don't care. Normally I would be extremely upset. So upset I'd manifest a physical reaction to news like this. Nervous energy. Endorphins kicking me into how-to-solve-this-problem mode. I've got nothing." She wipes her hand in front of her face. "I'm completely devoid of feeling anything."

Meaghan takes a deep breath. She lies back onto the sand and watches a cloud move across the face of the sun as if in slow motion. "What if the things that we've wanted for so long, the things we've spent our entire lives chasing, in the end aren't the things we really want at all?"

Palmer stares up at the ceiling. The sun's shadows transform as the clouds pass by on her side of the Cape. "Maybe," she says, rubbing her hand across her stomach. She's pretty certain that endless hours at the office with Calinda aren't among the things she wants anymore. "Send me the pics."

"I'll do it right now," Meaghan tells her, sitting up again.

Palmer hangs up. She pulls the blanket to her chin and opens Miles's journal. She flips right to the last entry. How mad was he all those weeks he avoided her? What did he know? She bites her fingernails and begins to read.

The last weeks of their life together spill out on the pages. She's forced to relive the details of their argument. His frustration and disappointment repeat. She can't hold back her tears. The words cut like a knife, sharp and swift. Miles can't believe what he's hearing. He's betrayed. He's abandoned. Anger, anger, and more anger rage through his pages. All of it, with himself.

She stops reading. She stares at their silver-framed wedding picture sitting on the bookshelf behind her desk. Two young kids, naïve and desperately in love, about to embark on the greatest journey of their lives.

"You couldn't speak to me because you were embarrassed. Embarrassed by your own reaction." The realization hits her as she says the words out loud. "You got over being mad at us. You were mad at yourself." She wipes her cheeks dry. The next two pages of his final entry read like a love letter. A love letter to Aiden. On those pages, he worked through his feelings of losing his first-born son as he grows up and grows into his own life. *It's his choice. It's his life.*

"Damn it, Miles," she says, closing the journal and grasping it to her chest. "Letting go is excruciating. But you already knew that." How excited would he have been to become a father once again?

She rolls onto her back and opens the journal at the beginning. She rereads Miles's first entry on the day of her diagnosis. *We can do this.* And they had.

The next entry is dated four weeks later. The day of Palmer's first surgery—a lumpectomy to remove the tumor in her breast. Weeks later, when the pathology would come back with unclean margins, the surgeon would end up removing more cancerous tissue, requiring a second surgery.

She's in there. There is not a single thing I can do. I'm out here. I held her hand as the drugs helped her drift off. She slurred her numbers like a three-year-old, trying to count backwards. Then they took her away. I am helpless. I'm so scared I'll lose her. I cannot lose her.

Palmer's jaw drops. Miles had been an echo-chamber of cheerleading during her treatment, resilient in his belief that all would be well and she would be healed. Making sure his belief became hers. Not once did he utter a word of doubt or worry out loud. *Instead, he kept those worries right here.* His journal chronicles her cancer battle, every setback and every victory. His entries are regular while he sorts through his own fear and uncertainties, his own private battle. She feels sorry that he couldn't share his feelings with her; sorry he couldn't be completely vulnerable. At the same time, she's grateful. He kept her going. She reads every word with renewed understanding and appreciation for her husband.

Until she finds it.

Hidden among the other entries. Perfectly disguised.

APRIL 17TH. SHE SLEEPS NOW. THE DOCTORS SAY HER *white blood cell count is dangerously low. I've never felt more helpless in my life. Four nights now I've sat in this same chair, watching her chest rise and fall, terrified each time there's a longer pause between breaths.*

Nurse Lauren came in tonight. She's been working the night shift all week. Tall, graceful in her movements. She brings a calm to the chaos that surrounds us here. I was in the corner chair again, trying to muffle my sobs. Palmer doesn't need to wake to my fear.

Lauren knelt beside me. Not with coffee or pastries like previous nights. Just herself. "Talk to me," she said.

And I did. God help me, I told her everything I can't burden Palmer with. How some mornings I wake up convinced this is the day I'll lose her. How the boys ask me if Mommy is coming home, and I lie with such conviction that I almost believe it myself. How I'm drowning in medical bills but can't let Palmer know because she'd insist on working remotely, and she needs to focus on healing.

"I haven't slept more than three hours at a stretch in months," I admitted. "Sometimes I sit in my car in the hospital parking garage and scream until my throat hurts just to release some pressure."

Lauren listened, no judgment. She held my hand as I confessed my darkest thought: that sometimes I imagine what life would be like afterward—as a widower, a single father—and the mere fact that my mind goes there makes me feel like I'm betraying Palmer, like I'm giving up on her.

"That's not betrayal," Lauren whispered. "That's the brain's way of preparing for the worst while you fight for the best."

When her shift ended, she pressed a piece of paper into my palm. Her phone number. "For the 3 AM moments when you need someone who understands but isn't inside the storm with you," she said. "Sometimes you need to speak your fears aloud to someone who isn't afraid of them."

I should have torn it up. Instead, I tucked it into my wallet. Not because I want anything from her—God, no—but because for the first time in months, someone saw me. Not Palmer's husband or the boys' father or the strong one holding everything together. Just Miles. Afraid. Exhausted. Human.

I don't know if keeping this number makes me unfaithful. I don't plan to use it. But knowing it's there feels like a lifeline when I'm drowning.

Palmer, I love you more than life. Every ounce of strength I have is yours. But tonight, I needed to be weak for a moment.

PALMER STARES AT THE JOURNAL ENTRY, HER FINGERS tracing the edges of the page where Miles's handwriting grows more cramped toward the bottom, as if he'd been rushing to capture every thought before they escaped him.

She closes her eyes, imagining how it all transpired. Miles hunched in that uncomfortable hospital chair all day and night. She lay unconscious, tubes snaking from her arms, monitors beeping in the background. She'd been so sick. Weak from chemo. Bald. Breastless. Too many drugs and a dangerously low white blood cell count. It was the lowest of their low points. The night nurse—Lauren, apparently—offering Miles a kind of comfort she couldn't.

A knot forms in her throat. Not quite anger, not quite hurt. Something more complex.

"You never told me," she whispers. "About the bills. The sleepless nights. Screaming in the parking garage."

She tries to remember Lauren. Tall, Miles had written. Graceful. She vaguely recalls a woman with dark hair checking her vitals, speaking in soothing tones. Had Lauren known, even then, that she'd formed a connection with Miles? Had she looked at Palmer differently, knowing the private fears her husband had shared? Did all husbands in the oncology unit share them with her?

Her eyes fall on the line about the phone number. She wonders if he ever called. Part of her wants to be angry that he kept another woman's number, that he created an emotional bond outside their marriage during their darkest hour. But another part understands the desperate need for someone to see you drowning when everyone around you expects you to swim.

"You were drowning too," she says, running her fingers over his handwriting. "I never saw it because you never showed me."

She sets the journal in her lap, feeling the weight of it—the weight of all that Miles carried alone. How many other burdens did he shoulder in silence, presenting only strength and optimism to her while confessing his fears to paper? And at least once, to a stranger.

She picks up their wedding photo again, studying his face. The young man who promised to share everything with her. She wonders now how much of their life together was filtered through his desire to protect her, to be the strong one, to carry what he thought she couldn't bear.

"We could have carried it together," she tells his smiling image. But even as she says it, she knows she might have done the same in his position. Love makes us shield each other, sometimes when we shouldn't.

Her breath catches as her mind lands on the more recent month when they barely spoke, after Aiden's announcement. That night at the office, working late with Sanford. Both of them frustrated with a case, exhausted from the tensions at home. Sanford had brought her a drink, sat too close, touched her arm with understanding fingers. He leaned in, she leaned in too, needing connection, needing to feel something other than the emptiness between her and Miles.

The kiss had been brief, electric with wrongness. She pulled away almost immediately, the taste of someone else on her lips like a shock of cold water. She remembers standing abruptly, gathering her files, mumbling excuses.

"I'm sorry," she'd told Sanford. "I can't."

She drove home through tears, walked into their silent house. Miles had been reading in his office, not looking up when she entered. She wanted to confess, to break their silence with her new guilt, but instead she showered for nearly an hour, letting hot water wash away the evidence of her weakness.

She never told Miles, burying it deep as if doing so would erase her mistake. But standing in their bathroom with shame burning her skin more than the scalding water, she'd known with absolute certainty: Miles was the only one she wanted, the only one she'd ever wanted. Their silence had created a void she'd briefly, foolishly tried to fill elsewhere, only to discover the void itself was preferable to a connection with anyone other than Miles.

"We both had our moments of weakness," she whispers to the journal. "And we both came back to each other."

She clutches the journal to her chest, feeling strangely lighter. Their marriage hadn't been perfect—what marriage is?—but it had been real. Complete with fears unspoken, moments of weakness overcome, and a love that pulled them back to center every time.

She closes the journal and lets it fall to floor.

MEAGHAN STUDIES THE RESTAURANT PROJECTIONS WITH the same intensity she once reserved for scripts. Her producer's eye catches details others might miss—traffic flow patterns, sight lines, atmospheric lighting. She and Bradley spend every day at the farmhouse loaded with laptops, Excel sheets, drawing papers, measuring tapes, and the entire Benjamin Moore paint wheel. Together, they draft a strategic plan for the new restaurant, from construction and layout, design concepts and colors, to how many nightly guests at each long table they'd need to turn profit the first year. Every hour immersed in planning is an hour she doesn't spend thinking about the three scripts Holly pulled from her consideration this morning at the request of the films' producers.

On Friday, late in the afternoon, they return to the secluded beach rental from the farmhouse to finalize the details on their end before Bridgette submits their offer to the seller. She checks her phone—still no messages from Bella, but another notification about a tabloid story discussing her missing in action this week as yet another step along her fall from grace. When Mack calls, she forces herself to focus.

"We've set up a company owned and funded by you and Bradley. Bradley owns 70 percent and you 30. Correct?"

"Correct," she confirms, watching Bradley review their business plan with an intensity that exudes sexy businessman, making her heart flutter. There's something undeniably attractive about his focus—his brilliant mind completely absorbed in their shared vision.

"The business will own the property. Correct?"

"Yes."

"Our new paralegal, James, is sending you both the paperwork now via DocuSign."

"Great," she says. Bradley stands, meanders to the kitchen, and begins to pop open one of the bottles of Veuve Clicquot, setting out two flutes. Despite everything falling apart in Hollywood, this moment feels grounded. After a week of hard work, tonight they will celebrate.

"Meaghan, there's one other thing." Mack sounds strange. Mack never sounds strange.

"What is it?"

"I spoke with Scott Lawhorn about an hour ago. He finished running the final queries on Duncan's phone." She stops still. *Sinful Admissions could end right now.* A glimmer of hope sparks inside her. Maybe she could salvage what's left of her career, repair her relationship with Bella, stop being America's favorite cautionary tale.

"And?"

"Dunc was right. There was nothing left on that phone. We didn't find a single thing, not even on its cloud backup. I'm sorry, Meaghan."

She sits down on the couch. She rubs her forehead with her fingers. "Now what?"

"We keep looking."

"I know that, but now what happens to me?"

"Hold on a second, Meaghan. I'll be right back." Her knee bounces up and down like a pogo stick. She avoids meeting the eyes of Bradley, who is watching her from across the room. He moves toward her, his presence both comforting and complicated.

Mack comes back on. "I've got you on speaker in my office, Meaghan."

"Meaghan, this is JP Donahue." JP helped Mack discern what in the hell was happening the day that the FBI knocked on her front door and arrested Duncan, and he attended her deposition.

"Hey, JP."

"Look here, darlin'," JP's Texas drawl thickens his words. "The FBI needs their pound of flesh. They're looking to make examples of high-profile parents like yourself. Three other 'celebrity' parents have already taken plea deals. The fact remains that you wrote the bribe check from Awaken and have admitted to doing as much. What Duncan said on that recorded conversation doesn't stand a chance in court. The evidence points to your involvement in bribery and laundering money through Chip Sullivan's non-profit."

"They're determined to show that even America's sweetheart isn't above the law," Mack tries to soften JP's blow. "In the end, it simply doesn't matter that it was Chip Sullivan who wrote those initials; you wrote the check. Meaghan, at this point, they will indict you. I'm sorry."

She slumps back into the couch. Her carefully constructed world—the roles, the awards, the adoring fans—are all crumbling because of Duncan's schemes. Divorcing him won't matter ... even if the divorce feels like the best decision she's made in a while.

"When?" she asks. "When will they indict me?"

JP says, "We aren't sure. They were waiting until the forensics on the phone came back. Now that they have, could be any time. Hell, could be tomorrow."

"Hold on there," Mack interrupts. "That's unlikely. I'm pretty sure I can get the judge to agree to giving us a few more weeks to finalize our evidentiary search. I can probably stave off their attempts until the end of August when you return to L.A. You are returning, right?"

"Do I have a choice?"

"No. You don't," JP says flatly.

"End of August?" Meaghan asks. She glances at Bradley, their plans for the restaurant suddenly feeling like a lifeline to normalcy. Or, quite possibly the stupidest decision Bradley might ever make. Can she ask him to?

"End of August," Mack confirms.

"How long could I be in jail?"

Bradley spins around in the kitchen to stare at her, his face a mixture of concern and determination.

"Best case scenario, three months. Worst case scenario, six months," JB says.

"Three to six months." The words taste bitter. "Long enough for the industry to forget me completely." She nods, reassuring herself. "Okay, I can do that if necessary. I'd prefer it isn't necessary."

JP snaps his fingers. "The prosecution's building a narrative—privileged Hollywood elite thinking they're untouchable. They want headlines, possibly more than justice." He pauses. "We need to examine the evidence in the other cases, too. How many parents were arrested in this little conspiracy?"

"Twenty-three," she says with a shiver. Her mind races back to Thorne Cassidy's face. She pictures him standing behind the Paramount Pictures VP the night of Bella's birthday party, which now seems a lifetime ago. His warning—"We are screwed"—takes on new meaning. Was he trying to warn her, or setting her up? Agent Hendrix and his team must have concluded he wasn't involved, otherwise he'd be sharing a jail cell with Dunc right now. *So then why the warning?*

"That's a great idea," Mack says. "Looking through the other cases might reveal some connections we haven't considered."

"Exactly," JP agrees. "All right, we've got work to do. I'm heading out to meet the Missus for dinner. Bye, Meaghan."

"Thanks, JP," she says. Mack takes Meaghan off speaker phone.

She looks up at Bradley, who stands in front of her holding out a glass of champagne. The gesture is sweet and painful—here he stands, still believing in her when the rest of the world has turned away. She puts the phone on mute. "You don't have to stay involved in this," she tells him softly. "The restaurant—it's all too risky with my legal troubles."

He sits beside her, close enough that she can feel the warmth radiating from him. "I'm not going anywhere," he says quietly. "I've spent twenty years watching you from a distance.

I'm done with that." She accepts her glass and mouths thank you.

She unmutes the phone. "We'll get the DocuSign completed and sent back tonight, Mack."

"Meaghan, I have to ask, mainly as your friend, do you really think now is a good time to open a new restaurant? Your name alone could sink the venture before it opens. Aren't you risking Bradley's reputation if thing keep going south?"

"We've already thought of that. Should things get worse instead of better, which appears a real possibility now, I will be a silent partner for the time being. I'll work behind the scenes, using everything I learned building my brand in Hollywood to create something real this time. We will only announce my involvement once I'm back in the public's good graces. Which must happen, eventually, right?"

There's a pause on the other end. "Glad you've thought that through." Mack avoids answering. "My only other question is whether you've considered, beyond the potential reputational consequences for Bradley, whether now is a good time for you to launch an entirely new project?"

"Now is exactly the time," she responds, conviction replacing her earlier uncertainty. "The restaurant will be my first move in a different and better direction. It's an opportunity for me to create something that builds community and unites people ... unites them around something besides Meaghan Jones, herself. I spent years being whatever Hollywood wanted. Maybe it's time to just be me."

Mack relents. "All right, then. The restaurant is a carefully considered next step. I'm on board. Sign the papers."

"Will do. James will have them in his inbox shortly. We'll talk soon." She tosses her phone onto the coffee table. Beyond it, the sea gently ebbs across the horizon, dark black with the moon shining overhead.

"Not great news?" Bradley asks.

"No text messages on the burner phone," she says, staring blankly at the ocean. "I think I'm going to jail."

"I've always wanted to start a restaurant with a hardened criminal. One who is a complete control freak, known to be a bit hot-headed, and I've recently discovered is the jealous type. Honestly, you're making all my dreams come true." Bradley smirks and she purses her lips and shakes her head at him. He sips his champagne.

"You're still sure about this?" she asks. "Your reputation is spotless. Mine is radioactive. I'm giving you a chance to opt out completely guilt-free. We don't have to sign these papers tonight or at all. You can take some more time to weigh all your options."

Bradley leans toward her. "The work we've done together this week to plan out this venture has never come so easy. You see things I miss, think of angles I'd never consider. Maybe because you spent years studying how to connect with audiences. Your creativity is inspiring. You bring ideas I'd never come up with on my own or with anyone else. I've never been surer," he tells her. His blue eyes twinkling in the moonlight. She breathes deep and steadies herself. He raises his glass to hers. "To the start of a magnificent partnership." The moment their glasses touch, she shivers. They spend the evening emptying the bottle of Veuve Clicquot, a roaring fire before them and the dark waves lapping the shore at their backs.

Chapter 15

SATURDAY MORNING'S BRILLIANT SUNNY GLOW SHIM-
mers between the sailboats dotting the harbor as Palmer steers
her Volvo back toward the marina. Her doctor's warning
echoes in her mind: "Stress isn't good for the baby." But how
can she avoid stress when Meaghan requires a discrete rescue
upon her arrival from Cape May back to The Hyacinth, her
sons barely speak to her, and Miles's journal threatens to unravel everything she thought she knew about their marriage?

In an attempt to unwind, she decides to spend a little time
in the Village before meeting Meaghan and Bradley at the
Marina. A Saturday browsing Main Street shops and enjoying
lunch outdoors is a treat she and Miles always enjoyed together. Going it alone feels awkward.

After visiting Browseabout Books, she walks down Main
Street, stopping in the Tideline Gallery and Coral Cove, before winding up on Penny Lane at Powdered Temptation.
Queasiness settles in her stomach, forcing her to acknowledge
that she hasn't been eating well lately. A meal will help.

Mindy, according to her nametag, greets her at the counter, full
of bubbly energy and words. Mindy tells her that she's the president

of her sorority, Alpha Delta Pi, at James Madison University and proceeds to spew a detailed list of her responsibilities at the sorority house, while Palmer scans the menu feigning listening.

Palmer watches Mindy chattering about her sorority life, remembering her own carefree summers before responsibilities and secrets weighted her down. Before cancer. Before Miles's death. Before this unexpected pregnancy complicated everything. A twinge of jealousy creeps up inside her, a longing for carefree youth.

Mindy rings up the cash register, "A bunch of us rented a big blue house with a funky pink roof for the summer down on Bethany beach. Some working as lifeguards, some boutique clerks, two working at Fun Land. You can make so much more money during the summer at the beach. Everyone pays top dollar here."

"Sounds like the perfect summer adventure for you girls," she says. "I'll have the ham and Swiss crepe with a spring salad on the side. Oh, and a chocolate chip cookie for dessert."

"You've got it."

"Is Darby around?"

"She ran out to pick up the milk order for the week. She'll be back." Mindy blabs on, sharing tidbits about Darby's latest town encounters, appearing herself to relish in the local gossip Darby supplies. Palmer notices how Mindy's eyes gleam with the excitement of small-town drama; everyone always has something to discuss. The realization stirs her unease. Mindy takes her cash and returns her change. "Go ahead and find a seat on the patio. I'll bring your order out."

She sits at the black iron bistro table for two on the front patio. She can't stop thinking about Miles's journal, which may be the source of her new, frequent headaches. For days now, Miles's description of his connection with Lauren has circulated in her mind. She's been sobbing in the shower with the water beating down on her. She breaks down in the kitchen while putting on the coffee. Her headaches get so bad her vision becomes blurry at times. She goes through all the emotions. Behind them all, her own guilt softens. She and Miles are the same. In the face of losing the other, both faltered, if only for a moment. Then both made their way back to the other. Two flawed humans who love each other deeply. It's heartbreaking and comforting at the same time.

"Ham and Swiss crepe, spring salad, and a chocolate chip cookie." Mindy sets her order on the table, interrupting her people watching.

"Thank you. This looks delicious."

"Oh, and Darby called. I told her you'd ordered lunch. She said she had one other quick stop to make and then she'd be back."

Her phone buzzes with another missed call from Sanford. Fifteen in total now. Each one a reminder of that night at the office, of choices made in moments of desperation. She switches off her phone, but the guilt remains powered on, running in the background of every thought.

That's when she spots him through the window of Penny Lane Wine & Spirits. Her heart skips a beat. She squints. *Sanford.*

He turns around as if summoned by her staring eyes and meets her gaze. Then he exits the shop and strides over to her table.

"Palmer?" He smiles. "I was just texting you. How are you?"

She hates that question. "Hello, Sanford."

He pulls out the chair across the table from her and takes a seat.

She leans across and whispers, "What are you doing here?" Her words insinuate that he shouldn't be here at all. But she knows that Sanford and Cinnamon, like most who work in D.C., spend many summer weekends relaxing along the Cape.

"That's kind of a long story," he says. "Do you have a few minutes?"

She checks her watch. Meaghan and Bradley will be docking in half an hour. "I've got ten."

"I've been trying to reach you."

"I know. I haven't been ready to talk."

"I get that. I do." Sanford's eyes gaze up and down Penny Lane. "Look, first I want to apologize. For kissing you."

"Shhh!" She looks around to make sure Darby hasn't returned. "Keep your voice down." The crepe grows cold on her plate as Sanford talks, the smell suddenly nauseating. A seagull lands nearby, watching them with judging eyes. She feels exposed, as if every patron on the patio can read her secrets written across her face.

"Okay!" Sanford looks around as well and confirms there's no one within earshot. "Anyway, I'm sorry. I shouldn't have done that."

"No, you shouldn't have!"

"I was in a bad spot with all the Cinnamon stuff. Feeling like no one wanted me. And, well, you've always been there for me, Palmer. I mean you're one of my best friends. Hell, probably my very best friend. I can't imagine my life without you."

Her stomach churns—morning sickness or guilt, she can't tell anymore. She remembers Miles writing about his moment of weakness. Had he felt the same sick mixture of justification and shame?

Sanford pours on, uninterrupted. "Listen, I took a step I shouldn't have because I was feeling weak and deflated. It's not something I'm proud of—risking our friendship to make myself feel better. So, I apologize. I am truly, deeply sorry."

"Thank you." Her shoulders relax, but remnants of unease linger as she rests back in her chair. "I've been waiting for that, I guess."

"And then when Miles had his stroke, I didn't know what to say to you. I couldn't be there for you—be the good friend I know you needed—because I'd screwed up so badly."

"It's okay," Palmer says. She realizes Sanford needs her forgiveness perhaps as much as she needs to forgive them both. Her partner in work-crime all these years. She's missed him.

"The boys and I, we're getting through." She puts her hand on her stomach. "They've been gone all summer. Quinn's at Camp Horizon and Aiden's in Charlottesville. They're coming to spend August." She looks around. Still no sign of Darby.

Sanford exhales. "There's another reason I've been trying to reach you. It's Cinnamon."

She picks up her water glass. "I saw her on Instagram a few weeks ago dancing and drinking at the Hamilton with Igor Overlauder. And Darby mentioned last week that Jonathan— do you know Jonathan? Darby's husband?"

"Never met him."

"Well, Darby said Jonathan saw Cinnamon at Big Fish Market last Thursday," Palmer says. "Said she looked different. Happier."

"Different how?" Sanford's brow furrows.

"Like she'd found her summer groove, according to Jonathan." Palmer shrugs, noting how Sanford seems oblivious to the undercurrent in her words.

Sanford nods and offers an uneven smile. "The Instagram post didn't go unnoticed."

"Nothing screams *I'm trying to make my ex jealous* like an evening with Igor all over the internet. The landscaper's out of the picture?"

"Seems to be, yes," Sanford says.

"What about Cinnamon did you need to tell me?"

"She knows."

Palmer sits back up to the table and leans in. "She knows what?"

Sanford shakes his head. "She knows about us making out that night in your office." The weight of his confession lands heavily between them, the implications stretching beyond just his failed marriage.

Mindy looks up from the cash register and smiles at Palmer, who forces herself to smile back. Mindy goes back to cleaning the register countertop.

She whispers, "We were *not* making out." Sanford raises both of his hands, as if Palmer holds him at gunpoint. "How does she know?!"

"Someone saw us that night and told her."

Palmer's eyes widen. "Who? Everyone had gone home. And who told her?"

"Stuart."

"Your associate!" A couple walking by looks at her.

"Yes, my associate, who is no longer my associate," Sanford confirms in a stern whisper. "Remember, that evening, I asked him to bring over all the previous litigation rulings to your office. Except we forgot I asked him. He told me that he walked onto the floor and saw us in your office. The shades weren't drawn."

"Shit," she says. "I have told no one about that night. Not even Meaghan."

Sanford shakes his head. "He's always wanted to one-up me. Find a fast track to partnership. So, he told Cinnamon, thinking he could blackmail me into making him partner. Instead, Cinnamon is blackmailing me. She's threatening to tell the entire world about what Stuart saw if I don't stop the divorce proceedings. Apparently, Cinnamon would like to stay married to my money." Sanford sits up and looks her square on. "I can't stop the divorce proceedings, Palmer. I can't stay married to Cinnamon."

Oh, no. No, no, no. "Sanford, no one can find out about this. My kids would never speak to me again! No one ever will after discovering I cheated on my husband right before he had a stroke and died!" The weight of her words plunges into her gut, adding to her discomfort.

Her hands begin to shake. A sudden rush of pain grips her side, forcing her breath shallow. The faint whisper of panic threads through her. "I need to leave. I can't be here with you. I can't talk about this anymore."

She scoots her chair back and stands up. She takes one step and immediately doubles over. The pain shoots through her side like lightning, different from anything she's felt before. Not like the morning sickness, not like stress. This feels wrong. Her hand instinctively protects her belly, the secret she's carried alone since Miles's death. The last piece of him she has left.

Sanford reaches for her, catching her before she lands. "Palmer, what's going on? Are you okay?"

"Do I seem okay?" The pain stabs her repeatedly, she can't stand up straight. All at once, Darby appears.

"What is going on!" Darby bends over to meet her, putting her arm around her. "Palmer, what's happening?"

"It's my stomach and my head. I'm so dizzy. I can't see straight." She is flanked by Darby on one side and Sanford on the other. "I'm pregnant," she blurts out.

"What?" Darby and Sanford exclaim in unison.

"Mindy!" Darby screams. "Mindy! Grab my cell phone. Call 9-1-1!"

Darby and Sanford bring her into Powdered Temptation and lay her down on a bench, where she curls up on her side until the ambulance arrives. The pain radiates and intensifies, leaving her breathless, and she can't help but recount the consequences of her hidden truths. What will this mean for the boys? What will it mean if they find out about Sanford?

A few minutes later, three beefy emergency rescue paramedics lift her onto the stretcher. She catches Darby on her phone, already spreading the news. The town gossip machine churns to life, and she realizes her carefully constructed world of secrets is about to unravel. The pregnancy, Sanford—how long before it all comes crashing down?

Sanford reaches for the handle and starts to climb in with her. "No," she says putting her hand up to him. The pain subsides momentarily, allowing a frightening clarity. She's done exactly what Miles did—sought comfort in a moment of weakness. But unlike Miles, her indiscretion might cost her everything: her reputation, her children's respect, and now possibly this baby. The irony threatens to suffocate her.

Sanford gently grabs her hand, folds her fingers over, and brings her hand to her side. "Yes," he tells her and climbs in.

As the ambulance doors close, she hears Darby's voice carrying across the parking lot: "Jonathan, you'll never believe what just happened ..." The words fade as consciousness slips away, leaving her wondering which of her secrets will surface first.

THE LATE AFTERNOON SUN BURNS ACROSS THE MARINA as Meaghan's phone explodes with notifications. Her stomach lurches at the headline splashed across her screen—the same headline lighting up every gossip site and news feed in the country. It has taken less than twenty-four hours for a canary at the FBI to leak Meaghan's impending indictment to the highest-paying tabloid, *The National Inquirer*. Has Meaghan actually been indicted on money laundering charges? Not yet. Does it matter? Not at all. The mere possibility of Meaghan Jones being indicted sends the internet into a raging tailspin. In the entertainment world, accusations carry the same weight as convictions.

"You are not going to believe this," she joins Bradley on the navigation deck.

"Pretty sure nothing could surprise me at this point," Bradley says.

She shows him the story on her phone. The headlines read, "Meaghan Jones to be Indicted."

"I was right." He smiles at her. "What do you do now?"

"A few months ago, this kind of thing would send me into crisis mode. Three assistants, two PR firms, and a war room of lawyers all scrambling to protect my image."

Bradley steers Serenity through the channel, his hands steady on the wheel. "And now?"

"Now I'm wondering if I even care anymore." She runs her fingers through her salt-tangled hair. "The old Meaghan would be calling every contact in her phone. This Meaghan just feels … tired."

"Growth looks good on you," Bradley says softly.

"Though I have to admit," she says, "watching some desperate FBI desk jockey cash in on my misery still stings." She scrolls down, then freezes. "Wait a minute."

She zooms in on the small follow-up story right below. Her heart clenches. "Look at the storyline that follows." She sticks her phone in front of Bradley's face again. The next headline reads, "What will poor Bella do? Take comfort in her newest love?" Right below it is a photo of Bella and Aiden surfing together at Black's Beach in California. The two of them stand dripping wet, walking out of the surf, carrying surfboards, and holding hands. Bella looks back at Aiden, both smiling ear to ear.

"My God," she whispers. "I've dragged them both into this circus. Palmer will never forgive me for exposing Aiden to this."

Bradley navigates around a moored sailboat, his jaw tight. "This is going to torture them! Aiden has no idea what he's in for."

Holly's name flashes across the screen, interrupting Meaghan's spiral of guilt. She answers.

"Did you see it?" Holly asks.

"Which disaster? The indictment leak or my daughter's love life being splashed across the tabloids? Yes, I saw it. That didn't take long," she says.

"Never does. I'm drafting a statement. I'll send it over before we push it out."

"Holly," her voice cracks. "I have to talk to Bella. She needs to hear this from me, not the internet."

"Honey, I don't think the impending indictment will make Bella want to talk with you. If anything, today's news only reinforces her belief that she's right about you ... that you were involved."

"You don't understand." She paces the deck. "Every time I tried to protect her, I only made things worse. I can't keep failing her."

"Meaghan ... you've already lost her."

Holly's words sting so badly she feels like a thousand bees are attacking her at once. She sinks onto the cushioned bench, her mother's voice echoing in her head: *Everyone leaves you eventually.* The familiar old panic rises—the need to chase, to fix, to make everyone love her again.

"No," she whispers, more to herself than to Holly. "I won't chase her this time. She needs to find her own way back."

A commotion on the pier draws her attention. A woman stands at the top of the pier waving her hands above her head. No one else is on the pier; most boats are out of their slip, sailing the day away.

"I've gotta go, Holly. Call me later." She hangs up and asks Bradley, "Who is that?"

Bradley secures the last knot, tying Serenity in place, and turns around. The woman comes running down the pier, crying and frantic.

"Darby?" Bradley asks as she reaches them. "What's wrong?"

Meaghan tenses. *Darby Shaw. Town Gossip. Salon story spreader. The last person we need right now.*

"Palmer collapsed. Just a few minutes ago. They've taken her to the hospital." Darby barely gets the words out, she's so out of breath. Her eyes are red from crying. "She's pregnant! There's a man with her!"

The world tilts beneath Meaghan's feet. Her own problems evaporate in an instant. She exchanges an alarmed look with Bradley. Everyone in town will know about the baby within the hour if they don't already. "What man? Who's with Palmer?" Darby shakes her head and throws her hands into the air. "I don't know!"

For once, she thinks, *Darby Shaw has nothing to say. And for once, I choose someone else's crisis over my own.* She's already dialing the Chief's number as she runs toward her car.

Gorgeous & Simple Beach House Dinner

Cioppino

Ingredients

- 1 bulb fennel, thinly sliced
- 1 yellow onion, minced
- 2 shallots, minced
- 3 cloves garlic, minced
- 1½ tsp salt
- 2 tablespoons olive oil
- dash of crushed red pepper
- 2 large bay leaves
- 2 28 oz can peeled tomatoes
- 2 cups dry white wine
- 1 pound baby neck clams, scrubbed, unopened
- 1 pound mussels, scrubbed, unopened
- 1 pound raw extra large shrimp, peeled and deveined
- 1 pound rockfish or other meaty white fish, like halibut or cod

Over a medium high stove, saute fennel, onion, shallots, garlic, salt, olive oil, crushed red pepper and bay leaves for 3 - 4 minutes until the onion is translucent.

Stri in the tomato paste to create a roux.

Open the cans of peeled tomatoes. Squeeze each peeled tomato by hand into the pot, adding the remaining juices last. Next stir in the crushed tomatoes. Let simmer for three minutes, until bubbly.

Add the wine. Pour yourself a glass and sip. Cover the pot for 30 minutes and simmer, allowing the flavors to combine into a gorgeous stew base.

At this point, you may turn off the burner and let the stew sit until you are almost ready to serve. The stew base could be made as early as the morning and reheated to this point when ready.

About twenty minutes before serving, add the clams and mussels to the warm stew base, cooking until they begin to open, usually about five minutes. Next stir in the shrimp and fish. Simmer another five minutes, until the shrimp are pink, the fish white and the clams and mussels all open. Season with additional salt and pepper to taste.

Ladle into bowls. Serve with a side of warm bread to soak up broth.

Additional Notes

Gorgeous enough to be served by candlelight. Makes a perfectly disguised romantic dinner.

August

Chapter 16

AIDEN AND QUINN DON'T COME. A WEEK IN THE CRITI-
cal care wing of the maternity ward of Bayview Hospital does
nothing to lure Palmer's sons to her side. Her worst fear is
coming true; she is losing her children. Quite possibly all three
of them.

She stares at her phone, the headlines blurring together
in an endless scroll of speculation. *Star's Daughter and Dead
Architect's Son: What did they know?* A different picture of Bella
and Aiden taken the July Fourth weekend, this time hiking
Runyon Canyon Park, holding hands, is featured underneath
the headline. Another smaller photo inset from two summers
ago, laughing on the beach, back when life made sense. When
Miles was alive and her sons came home.

Her hands cradle her growing belly, a reminder of both
miracle and scandal. Darby's whispers echo through town—
Sanford Banks's baby, they say. Poor Miles hadn't been gone
two months before she ...

She clicks off her phone, unable to bear another Sinful
Admissions headline, continued speculation about Aiden's
knowledge of Bella's admission to SCC. The morning sun

streams through The Hyacinth's master bedroom windows, but she remains shackled to her king bed by Dr. Harlow's orders and Meaghan's watchful eye.

Advanced preeclampsia. The diagnosis rings in her ears like a death knell. "Advanced preeclampsia can come on suddenly, sometimes in a matter of hours," Dr. Harlow had explained. "The protein in your urine indicates your kidneys and liver are severely stressed, which explains the piercing pain in your side. We will run more tests to see if we can determine why your placenta is not working correctly. All we know for certain is that the baby is at risk. You are at risk." She'd never seen Dr. Harlow so concerned.

"At risk … for what?" Palmer mustered.

Dr. Harlow grabbed her hand. "At risk of not making it, honey. Eclampsia can result in premature birth, pregnancy loss, failure of your organs like kidneys and liver, and even a stroke." Her head snapped at the mention of "stroke." The Harding family could not suffer another stroke. "But none of those things will happen because we will take all the necessary steps to ensure you deliver a healthy baby in January."

One of those steps? Bed rest, indefinitely.

Meaghan keeps insisting the boys are coming. "They're just delayed," she says every morning, along with Palmer's protein test and blood pressure check. But delayed has stretched into a week, then two. It's the second week of August, a full week after their originally scheduled arrival for their summer vacations.

The Life Rolls On surfing contest begins in only three days—the boys haven't missed it since they were old enough to stand on a surf board. It's the largest fundraiser supporting individuals with spinal cord injuries in the country. The contest attracts surfers from around the globe in three cate-gories—disabled surfers, amateur surfers, and pros with cor-porate sponsors who bring big money into town. Last year, Quinn placed fifth in the amateur division and Aiden thir-teenth. They donated half their winnings to the foundation without Palmer or Miles even suggesting the gesture. She can't imagine them missing this week.

Quinn's texts grow more distant. *Wrapping up a few loose ends here, Mom. Planning to drive out in a day or two, Mom.* But a day or two turns into three or four and three or four turn into more. He's a no-show.

Aiden won't even promise an arrival date anymore. Too many shift changes at The Ivy. *They need me*, he claims.

I need you, she wants to scream. But she can't risk pushing them further away. She can't bear considering they may know about her moment of weakness with Sanford. Or worse, that they've heard the rumors spreading through town like wildfire about the baby's paternity.

The Atlantic Coast Kite Festival flags should be going up now, their bright colors marking the height of August cele-brations. But she only watches the ceiling, counting the hours between blood pressure readings and trying not to think about Miles's ashes, still waiting to be scattered on their beach the last Sunday of August. *Sunday evenings at The Hyacinth were Miles's favorite.*

A light knock interrupts her spiral. She unglues her eyes from the ceiling and rolls gently onto her side, resting her hand underneath herself for support and curling her knees to-ward her chest. "Come in."

The door opens a crack. Meaghan peeks her head in. "Hey, you. Wasn't sure if you were resting your eyes." Meaghan sets a wicker tray on the bedside table. "I brought lunch." Meaghan makes her way to the other side of the king-sized bed, pulls the covers back, and crawls in beside her. Her forehead rests against Palmer's back, her hand making soothing circles on her arm.

"Not asleep," she says.

"Well, I'm here for your entertainment, then," Meaghan replies.

"If by entertainment you mean you're here to test my urine and take my weight again, I'm going to give you a nasty review." The joke falls flat, reminding them both of Meaghan's own media troubles.

Meaghan rolls onto her back and stares at the ceiling, crossing one foot over the other. "Please, I'm used to really bad reviews now. Have you not been watching TMZ lately? I'm a cheating, recently divorced, soon-to be-jailed, complete-ly unemployable ex–Hollywood star whose business empire is collapsing, all because apparently I've stolen the futures of hundreds of college-bound teenagers across the country."

"I haven't turned on TMZ. I've been lying here thinking about the boys." Her voice cracks.

"You saw the latest about Aiden and Bella?" Meaghan asks, her voice careful.

Palmer's throat tightens. "The Runyon Canyon photos? They're everywhere."

"They look happy together." Meaghan pauses.

"Happy? They're being hunted by paparazzi, their private moments splashed across every tabloid in the country." Her fingers return to worrying the comforter's fringe. "The media's trying to connect Aiden to the scandal, suggesting he must have known about Bella's admission."

"He didn't know anything." Meaghan's voice carries an edge of desperation. "None of the kids knew."

"Of course he didn't. But try telling that to the internet." She closes her eyes against a wave of nausea. She stays on her side, unable to look Meaghan in the eyes. Since the indictment leaked, doubt gnaws at her. How could her best friend face charges if she wasn't involved? What had Meaghan done? Or, perhaps worse, what had Meaghan known, and done nothing to stop? Either way, she can't shake the thought, and thinking it feels like a betrayal.

Finally, she turns over and faces Meaghan. "Surely, they won't want to miss Life Rolls On. All their friends come. We host a party on our beach the last night." Her fingers find the fringe at the edge of the comforter, smoothing it obsessively. "And we're supposed to spread Miles's ashes. We agreed to it before they left for the summer. Sunday evenings at The Hyacinth were Miles's favorite."

"They're coming," Meaghan reassures her.

"They aren't delayed!" A single tear falls across her nose and into the corner of her other eye. "They don't want anything to do with me. I'm their mother. I only want them to be happy. And now I've made them so unhappy. I've made them so angry and disgusted; they won't come home." Her voice grows louder. "Not when I'm sick and in the hospital. Not when they already planned to be here for the whole month. Not even when they're supposed to be surfing with their buddies for a week. They are too ashamed and embarrassed of me." She catches herself shouting and covers her mouth, the truth burning in her throat. "They're not coming!"

Meaghan leans over and wipes a tear from her eye. "They'll come. I promise. They'll come."

Once again, she doesn't quite believe Meaghan. The weight of secrets—hers and Meaghan's both—settles heavy in the air between them.

THE INDICTMENT FRENZY STALLS WHEN NEW YORK CE-lebrity couple Jenna and Luke Abbott announce the surprise arrival of twins—a baby boy and a baby girl—at Lenox Hill Hospital on Manhattan's Upper East Side. The celebrations light up Instagram. Congratulations pour in over TikTok. It's like internet whiplash. The news cycles spin away from her disgrace, proving once again how fickle fame can be. One day you're America's sweetheart, the next you're trending as #CollegeCheatingMom, and then—poof—you disappear behind someone else's joy.

Meaghan is so grateful for the media distraction, she orders the largest floral bouquet available from Rachel Cho's on 54th Street, trimmed with sweets plus one blue and one pink teddy bear, and sends the gift that afternoon to Jenna and Luke's delivery suite. She also hopes the gesture reminds people of her kindness.

She walks into The Hyacinth's office for a series of late-afternoon Zoom business meetings while Palmer rests. The magazine rack beside the desk is stacked with covers from Awaken's launch five years ago. The memories flood back—the excitement in the conference room as she unveiled her vision for a brand that would empower women to embrace their authentic selves. "We're not just selling clothes," she had declared. "We're creating a community where every woman feels worthy." The irony of those words hits her now.

She considers trying Aiden. She's called Aiden and Quinn every day since Palmer collapsed, giving them all the updates and inquiring about their arrivals. But the last two days, neither has answered, something she can't tell Palmer.

Before she can dial Aiden, a calendar reminder lights up her screen. *Completely lost track of time!* She opens it, clicks the link on her calendar invite, and immediately finds herself in the middle of the Awaken conference room in their New York City headquarters, where her CEO, Claire Perkins, and the rest of the Awaken C-suite wait.

Claire's smile doesn't quite reach her eyes. It's the same expression she's seen on countless faces lately—people trying to balance loyalty with disappointment. "Meaghan! Great to see you!" Three years ago, Meaghan stole Claire from Athleta by offering her something irresistible—5 percent of Awaken. "Because I believe in building women up," Meaghan said. Now she wonders if Claire regrets hitching her star to a falling celebrity.

"Hi, Claire! Hey, team!" She scans the familiar faces, noting the subtle shifts in their expressions. The way they lean slightly back from their screens, creating distance. Only Elizabeth Stowe has officially quit—her husband heads admissions at Boston University—but she feels the others pulling away, protecting their own reputations.

"Before we start," Claire says, "I want you to know we still believe in Awaken's mission. This isn't just about numbers."

Her throat tightens. "But there are numbers?"

"Listen, Meaghan, we've cut the numbers every way we know how, and we end up at the same answer. Since the college admissions scandal broke in February, Awaken sales continue to plummet."

"Not a total surprise." The words catch in her throat.

"We haven't seen the floor yet, and we are down 45 percent compared to last year. The decline is across the board. In every single category. Across all demographics."

"Our core demographic," Claire adds softly, "they feel personally betrayed. These are women who bought into our message of authenticity and empowerment. Mothers who wanted to teach their daughters about working hard and believing in themselves."

Her chest constricts as Claire's words mirror her own daughter's accusations. She remembers the woman at the salon: *You're not Hollywood royalty. You're Hollywood trash.* The same fury she'd heard in Bella's voice.

"I built Awaken because I wanted to create something real," she whispers. "Something that wasn't about the facade of Hollywood."

"We know," Claire says. "That's what makes this so hard. Meaghan, I've made the decision to cancel Awaken's runway show at New York City's Fall Fashion Week."

The irony crashes over her—she's always insisted their models represent real women, not just celebrities. Now she's toxic to her own brand. She's tried to control every aspect of Awaken's image, like she's tried to control Bella's future. And both are slipping through her fingers.

Claire and the CFO, Ramon Simmons, lay out their plan to keep Awaken on life support. It's economical and necessary, and completely unsexy. The exact opposite of Meaghan Jones. It's everything she's fought against when building the brand. But maybe that's what authenticity truly looks like—facing reality instead of manufacturing the perfect image.

"These steps should keep us afloat hopefully long enough until things blow over," Ramon tells her.

How long will that be? "I'll do whatever you think we need to do to keep us going." For once, she thinks, she'll let go of control. Trust others to help save what she built.

"I'm sorry, Meaghan," Claire says.

"No, *I'm* sorry." She means it in ways she never has before. "Thank you all for your hard work and continued dedication. It has not gone unnoticed. I want ..." Her cell abruptly interrupts their Zoom meeting. Holly's name flashes across the screen. "Um, I need to grab this call. Are we good here?"

Claire nods. "Yes, I'll let you know when we've pulled out of the NYC show on the official. We'll be in touch."

She hits the large red "Leave Meeting" button and simultaneously hits the green answer button on her cell screen. "Hi, Holly."

"Hey there. Sorry to interrupt. Your schedule says you're in an Awaken team meeting." Holly maintains unlimited access to her schedule because she's usually the one setting up her appointments. When things get to be too much, Holly always adds in a two-hour Meaghan time block. "But ..." Holly pauses. "Did you see it?"

"Oh God, what now?"

"The Abbotts' twins are old news already. *Entertainment Weekly* just dubbed Bella and Aiden *'Hollywood's Star-Crossed Lovers.'* They're calling it a modern Romeo and Juliet—childhood friends reunited by scandal."

Meaghan's eyes shut. Her forehead collapses into her cupped hand perfectly perched with her elbow on the walnut desk in front of her. Her daughter's pain has become tabloid fodder, and it's all her fault. "What did she say?"

"They ambushed them outside a coffee shop near UVA's architecture building. Apparently, she's with him in Virginia now. Bella and Aiden were holding hands—the photos are everywhere. He tried to shield her, but ..." Holly pauses. "She wanted to speak."

"And ..." she interjects.

"She looked right into the camera, Meaghan. Like she was speaking directly to you. She said, and I'll quote here, 'It turns out there's evidence that proves my mom is a lying bitch and a criminal who doesn't believe in her daughter's ability to succeed in life on her own.' And then the guy asked, 'Have *you* seen that evidence, Bella?' Then Bella poured her orange juice on the guy and walked off."

Her hand trembles as she opens her laptop, finding the video instantly. There's her daughter, beautiful and fierce, gripping Aiden's hand like an anchor. The way she used to grip Meaghan's hand when she was little. Now that strength is turned against her.

"Meaghan, I don't have to tell you how bad this is. Bella has gone rogue. She's publicly turned on you. Your own daughter. Sure, she has refused to speak with you for months, but the public hasn't known that. Now, she's confirming there's evidence of your supposed crime."

"At least she has Aiden," Meaghan whispers, surprising herself with the thought. "He'll protect her the way I should have."

"You know what you need to do," Holly says. "You've put up with this long enough. You need to tell the world your daughter is a liar."

"No." The word comes out sharp and clear. "I won't destroy her to save myself. Not again."

"I'll call you later," she says, and ends the call.

She watches and rewatches the video of Bella's exchange with the reporter. Three times. Four times. Five times. Each viewing reveals something new—the protective way Aiden steps closer to Bella, how her daughter's voice shakes beneath its anger, the flash of pain in her eyes that mirrors Meaghan's own. With every viewing, more tears fall down her cheeks as she tries to remember how she got here. Duncan, she recalls, Duncan is how she got here. But is everything all Dunc's fault? Not everything.

Her phone buzzes in her hand. She picks up FaceTime. "Hi, Mack."

"Has Bella seen any evidence of your crimes?" He comes across as accusatory and undiscriminating, his lawyering on full display.

"What crimes!" She wipes her nose with her sleeve. "I haven't committed any crimes!"

"I don't have to tell you the fact that your daughter has now publicly called you a criminal doesn't bode well for a jury trial and pretty much condemns you in the court of public opinion. Forever."

She sobs. "I've been telling myself since the indictment leaked that maybe, just maybe, I can handle America not loving me. That part *might* be tolerable, but only if I could get Bella back." She sniffs, "But now ..." she finds a Kleenex in the bottom desk drawer and blows her nose. "She loathes me."

"The timing is suspicious," Mack says. "Bella makes this statement just as we're closing in on something about Thorne Cassidy."

Meaghan straightens. "What do you mean?"

"Do you remember how everyone thought Thorne Cassidy was involved in Sinful Admissions? His name was circling around town when the arrests were made. Everywhere you turned, you ran into it."

"At Bella's party," Meaghan says slowly, the memory sharpening. "He didn't just walk by and whisper, 'We are screwed.' He was wearing a new watch—chunky, ugly thing. Kept fiddling with it."

"A recording device?" Mack suggests.

"And Lassie," Meaghan continues, the pieces falling into place. "She latched onto Bella immediately after the arrests. Always asking questions about Duncan, about our finances ..."

"Right, yes," Mack confirms. "I remember Bella telling me Thorne's daughter Lassie attended the party and after the arrests became very chummy—like she knew how Bella felt because they were in the same boat. Then Lassie conveniently disappears to Toronto right when the FBI would have been wrapping up their investigation. Almost like her father's work was done."

"Okay," she says, following along. "What's missing?"

"Well, if the FBI thought he was involved, you'd think that somewhere in all the evidence across all the cases—papers, transcripts, wire taps, hard drives, cell phones—his name would show up. Someone would mention him. Or he'd show up himself in a conversation. Or his computer would be logged into evidence. There had to have been something to make the FBI think he was involved. Something to investigate. Even if that investigation led to determining his innocence. But there's nothing."

"And that strikes you as odd?" Meaghan asks.

"It did at first. But now, no actually. Because what if they already had their informant? Thorne flipped early. Wore a wire. Recorded everything. And in exchange, his name stays clean. His daughter stays out of it. And you and Duncan take the fall." Mack's voice hardens. "I've got to go find JP. We might have just found our angle." Mack hangs up.

She rocks back and forth in the leather office chair, staring out The Hyacinth's office window, as golden hour christens the sky. The sun makes everything look like it's been dipped in honey. In the still quiet, Meaghan thinks of Bella.

The irony strikes her—how many times had she sat in this same chair, thinking of how to protect Bella's future? Every calculated move, every controlled decision, had pushed her daughter further away. Just like with Awaken, her need to manufacture the perfect outcome, so that everyone would love her, had destroyed something genuine.

She glances at her phone, thumb hovering over Bella's number. What would happen if she simply told the truth? Not through lawyers or publicists or carefully crafted statements. A mother telling her daughter: I was wrong. I was scared. I love you.

Her little girl who sat on her hip during rehearsals, refusing to be set down. Her little girl who hid behind her pant legs during auditions. Her little girl who insisted on sitting on her lap during hair and makeup. Her little girl who refused to leave her side and now can't get far enough away. How can she call her baby girl a liar? Her little girl who now stands strong beside Aiden, no longer needing her mother's protection—or her interference.

The realization hits her like a wave: Maybe letting go isn't losing. Maybe it's the first step toward winning back what matters.

In the kitchen, a plate breaks. The crash so loud, she can almost feel porcelain shatter into what must be a million tiny shards spilling across the wood floor. She immediately jumps out of her chair. Worried that Palmer may have gotten out of bed, she runs down the hall, through the great room.

Her mind eases slightly when she remembers Bradley is bringing them dinner before heading to The Oyster House for the evening rush. Maybe he snuck into the kitchen from the upper back deck so as not to disturb her calls. Her heart beats in her chest, worry unexpectedly replaced by thrill at the thought of seeing Bradley. Nearly out of breath, she rounds the corner into the kitchen. She gasps when she sees what's before her. Both hands cover her mouth.

"Quinnie!" Meaghan opens her arms and pulls her godson into her. Quinn is home.

"Aunt Meaghan," Quinn mumbles into her shoulder, holding two large pieces of a shattered plate, one in each hand. She feels his tears dampen her shirt. When he pulls back, his eyes—so like Miles's—meet hers with understanding.

She nods, thinking of Bella and Aiden, of broken plates and broken facades, of truth that cuts but also heals. "Your mom's upstairs," she tells him, but she holds onto his arm for one more moment. "Quinn? Thank you for coming home."

She watches him bound up the stairs to Palmer. She pulls out her phone one more time, opens a new message to Bella, and types: "I saw you with Aiden today. You looked strong. You looked free. I'm sorry if I ever made you doubt yourself. When you're ready—if you're ever ready—I'll tell you everything. No more lies. I love you."

She hits send before she can second-guess herself. Then she begins picking up the broken pieces of the plate, knowing some things need to shatter so they can be rebuilt.

WHEN AIDEN CALLS TWO DAYS AFTER QUINN ARRIVED AT The Hyacinth, Palmer thinks all her prayers are answered.

Then Aiden asks her to lie.

"Bella and I are coming to the Cape together," Aiden says, his voice carrying an unfamiliar warmth laced with a hint of excitement that catches her off guard. It's the first time since Miles's funeral she's heard anything but grief and denial in her son's tone. Mack was right. She hasn't heard Aiden so elated in months. "I'm wrapping up summer crew tomorrow. My last shift at The Ivy is the day after. I think the time on the Cape will help me ... you know, process everything with Dad."

Her throat tightens. "Of course, honey. How are you doing with all that? I know it's unspeakably hard."

"Some days are better," Aiden says after a pause. "Bella gets it, you know? With everything happening with her dad ... she understands. We talk about it a lot."

A memory surfaces—Bella and Aiden at fourteen, sprawled on The Hyacinth's deck chairs, sharing earbuds and whispers while the sunset painted the sky pink. Now they share deeper hurts and losses.

"We'll be there in time for the Kite Festival and Life Rolls On." Aiden's voice brightens again, reminding Palmer of Miles's ability to push through pain with optimism. "Mom, we cannot wait to spend the last few weeks of summer on the Cape!"

"This is such great news, Aiden!" His enthusiasm is contagious. Like an elixir that makes her forget she's sitting shackled to her king bed with a belly the size of a small beach ball. "You and Bella will both be here soon. And Quinn is home. Meaghan will be unbelievably happy. Being together is exactly what we all need."

"Mom ..." Aiden's tone shifts. "We can't stay at The Hyacinth. The paparazzi ambushed us outside of We Pour Gold yesterday. They kept shouting questions about the scandal, about Meaghan. We barely made it to the car."

She closes her eyes, the headlines flashing in her mind: *"Bella Jones Denounces Hollywood Mother: 'She Stole My Future.'"* "What? Where on earth are you going to stay?"

"You know my buddy Jasper on crew?"

"Sure, we took him to lunch last spring after your first Regatta of the season." *The last time Miles watched Aiden row.*

"Right. Well, his girlfriend is lifeguarding on Dewey for the summer. He's heading up for the last few weeks of summer, too. He says we can crash with them."

She can't believe what she's hearing. Another piece of her family sliding away. "Aiden, you have your own room here. You have an entire house here that's yours. Bella too; she always stays in the coral bedroom. Please come stay at home. Your father would want us to be together, especially now."

"Dad would want me to protect the people I care about, like he always did," Aiden says softly. "Right now, Bella needs protection. From the media, from the scandal … from all of it."

Aiden speaks about Bella with the same tenderness Miles used to speak to Palmer. Their son is falling in love.

His voice carries the quiet authority Miles used when making difficult decisions. "I didn't have to tell you, but I know we can trust you to not say anything." This guilt trip is apparently a round trip, it's come back to her. "And Mom … being at The Hyacinth might be too hard. Dad built the house. I'm afraid everything will remind me of him all the time."

Palmer swallows the lump in her throat. "I know, sweetheart. I expect to see him in his office, around every corner, really. But eventually, you will need to come home. To see how life can be without him. He would want you to keep living."

"I'll find a way to come see you when Meaghan isn't around." He pauses. "How are you feeling?"

She glances at her belly, the unexpected piece of Miles she carries. "I'm okay. A little tired. This kid is quite active."

"Like Quinn was," Aiden says. She swears she hears him smile. "Dad always told that story about Quinn kicking his hand so hard during one of your checkups that he spilled coffee all over the doctor."

She shakes her head, tears threatening. "I can't. This is crazy. You two can't stay somewhere else. You belong here."

"Mom, please … for Bella. The tabloids are brutal. She's trying to prove herself on her own merit. Every time she's connected to Meaghan, it falls apart."

The weight of secrets—Sinful Admissions, Sanford's kiss, Miles's journal—presses down on her. Sympathy and an overpowering desire for her son to love her again cause her surrender. "All right, I won't say anything. I won't like it, though. Please tell Bella that I want her to think about how she can see Meaghan while she's here. I'll leave that to her to figure out."

She touches her wedding ring, twisting it gently. "Your father would be proud of you, Aiden. The way you're looking out for Bella ... that's pure Miles Harding."

"I miss him," Aiden whispers, his voice cracking. "Every day, I miss him."

"Me too, sweetheart. Me too."

"I'll call you when we get to town," he says composing himself.

Three days later, he does.

Chapter 17

DR. HARLOW ARRIVES FOR HER EVERY-OTHER-DAY HOUSE call, giving Meaghan a chance to slip out for an hour. She grabs a large golf umbrella and Palmer's black Patagonia rain slicker from the foyer closet. Why doesn't Palmer own Awaken's bestselling Drip Drop Jacket? She makes a mental note to call Claire and ask her to send one. She slides behind the wheel of Palmer's Volvo. Earlier this morning, Quinn left to spend the day surfing at Dewey Beach, home to the greatest swells on the Cape, preparing for Life Rolls On, which kicks off tomorrow.

She drives along the coast and down into the Village, where she's meeting Bradley at The Oyster House. The sun hasn't appeared for the last two days. Instead, the skies hang dark, ominous, and laden with heavy clouds. A storm lurks somewhere out at sea. The weatherman on the radio predicts the tempest will make landfall today, but he's predicted that for the past three days in a row and still no storm.

When she parks the Volvo in front of the restaurant, the Cape May ferry sits docked on the other side of the boardwalk. The seas must be too choppy for its regular trip. As she exits the car, a gust of wind nearly knocks her over. She catches herself on the parking meter in front of the restaurant. She grabs hold of The Oyster House's door, opens it slightly, and squeezes into the restaurant while patting her hair back into place.

"Hey," Bradley calls out from the kitchen without his usual warmth. He makes his way toward the front, greeting her with a perfunctory nod rather than his customary hug. "Quite a storm brewing out there."

"Brewing, yes. Arriving, no," she says, slipping her coat off. "How come the weather guy here never gets the weather right?"

Bradley takes her jacket, hanging it in the coat closet with mechanical precision. "The Cape defies prediction." He pokes his head to look out the front door and down the street at the beach. "The waves are halfway up the bulkheads on the boardwalk already." He motions to her without meeting her eyes. "We're over here. The notary is waiting."

She notices a slight tension in his shoulders as he leads her through the restaurant. "Everything okay? You seem … distant."

He stops, turning to face her. He whispers, "I've been trying to talk to you about something important for days, Meaghan. But you've been wrapped up in your legal issues and avoiding anything resembling a real conversation."

"That's not fair. I've been dealing with—"

"I know what you've been dealing with. We all know." Bradley sighs. "The Reinhardt Group called yesterday. They're reconsidering their investment in the Cape May property."

"Because of me," she says, not a question. Mack filed the new corporation papers last week, which could have made her silent partner status less silent, if people were looking.

"They mentioned 'brand association concerns.' Their words, not mine."

The sting of his words hits her square in the chest. "Bradley—"

"We have paperwork to sign." He turns away, continuing toward the corner booth.

A tall, olive-skinned woman with long black hair stands up from her seat and extends her hand. "Ms. Jones, I'm Jewels King. It's truly an honor to meet you."

She grabs Jewels's hand with both of hers, grateful for the warm reception. "The pleasure's mine. Thank you for helping us out this morning. And … for keeping this quiet." She winks at Jewels and takes a seat in the booth across the table.

"Absolutely. I've known Bradley, Palmer, and Miles since they moved to Cape Henlopen. I helped Bradley purchase this gem right here. And I helped Palmer and Miles purchase The Hyacinth property before they redeveloped the entire thing." Jewels shakes her head. "I can't believe Miles is gone. Everyone misses him. How's Palmer doing?"

She slides into the booth. "She's pretty remarkable, given everything that's happened."

"Losing Miles must be so difficult, but I can't imagine Palmer handling that loss any other way. She's a fortress. And she's expecting, I hear! What wonderful news," Jewels says.

Meaghan rolls her eyes. "Let me guess, Darby?" She hates a gossip.

"Darby," Jewels confirms.

"Half the Cape probably thinks Sanford is the father," Bradley says, his tone edged with something she can't quite place.

"Sanford Banks?" Jewels asks. "I've heard some rumors. "

Rumors indeed. "Sanford is a family friend. He was in town recently having lunch with Palmer when she had some complications with the baby. He went with her to the hospital. Anyway, shall we sign these?" she asks, eager to change the subject.

"Of course." Jewels hands her a stack of papers flagged with bright-yellow arrows that read "Sign Here."

As she signs the first document, Bradley watches her pen move across the paper. "Do you actually believe what you've said? That you didn't know what that check was for?"

The question hangs between them as she looks up, startled. Jewels shifts uncomfortably in her seat.

"This isn't the time or place, Bradley."

"I need to know what I'm getting into here, Meaghan. Not just with the restaurant." His eyes remain fixed on hers, searching.

She passes the paper to him without answering. He signs and returns the document to Jewels, who excuses herself to the ladies room. Rain begins to tap on the windows as they continue through the stack in tense silence.

"You know what kills me?" Bradley says quietly as they near the last document. "I've spent twenty years thinking I knew exactly who you were. That night on the beach, in St. Thomas—I thought I saw the real Meaghan Jones. But maybe that was just another role you were playing."

The words strike like a punch in the gut. "That's not fair."

"Isn't it?"

The lights in the restaurant flicker as they sign the final document. At the precise moment the last document returns fully executed to Jewels's hands, Chef Antonio emerges from the kitchen with a bottle of Krug Brut Rose Champagne in one hand and a giant grin on his face. He's practiced running The Oyster House himself; those signed papers mean he soon will.

"Is time for celebration. Is official, no?" he asks, oblivious to the tension.

"It's official!" Bradley confirms, his enthusiasm muted. The lights flicker again.

"Whoa," she says. "Do you usually lose power in the rain?"

Bradley stands up and makes his way to the window. "Not in the rain, but occasionally in a big storm when the wind gusts." The lights flicker again, shutting off. Everyone looks at each other but no one speaks. A few seconds pass until the lights flicker back on.

Bradley hesitates before raising his glass. "To new beginnings," he says, his eyes searching hers as if looking for something he's not sure is there anymore.

Meaghan stands up from the booth. "Chef Antonio, I adore your enthusiasm, but I think we need to postpone our celebration. I should get back to The Hyacinth." She can't leave Palmer alone in a storm, and Dr. Harlow will be heading back to the hospital soon.

"You take her something to eat?" Chef Antonio asks.

"She'd love that. Thank you!" Chef Antonio returns to the kitchen.

"Where's Quinn?" Bradley asks, his tone shifting slightly.

"He went to Dewey for the day to surf. I'll text him. Maybe he's already home given the rain." She sits back down and pulls her cell out.

"I should get going, too," Jewels says. "Looks like the weather gods have turned against us quickly this morning." She packs up her papers in her briefcase, stands up, and shakes their hands. "It's been a pleasure. Congratulations, you two!

When that restaurant opens, I better be on the first night's guest list."

"We've got your reservation and will add a plus one!" she says with forced brightness. "Thank you for all your help."

Bradley opens the door for Jewels, who pops her navy-and-white polka-dot umbrella open and runs down the street toward her office, water splashing over her heels.

Meaghan glances at her phone again. "Quinn isn't responding. I should get back to Palmer before it gets worse out there." Chef Antonio pops out of the kitchen and hands her a paper bag full of takeaway containers. "Thank you. She will love this." Chef Antonio nods and disappears, again.

Bradley helps her put on her slicker, then spins her around, his hands lingering on the jacket's collar. He gazes so deeply into her eyes; she wonders if he can see her truth. The choice she made was wrong, she knows this, now. But she can't go back.

"How are you feeling … about Bella?" he asks. "I saw her press statement."

She places her hands on top of his. "It's as if someone is ripping my heart out, over and over." Her gaze drops to the floor. "I lost her trust so easily when this scandal broke. I suppose that's because she's beyond humiliated before the entire world. I ache for that trust again." She lifts her head again. "I ache for her."

"I can only imagine," he offers. His hands slip out from underneath hers and make their way to her shoulders. "Time. Everyone needs time."

Outside, the lightning flashes and the sky cracks open. The rain begins to lash.

Bradley releases her. "You better hurry."

They walk to the front door and he props it open with his knee, struggling to keep the door steady against the wind. As they stand under the awning together, he says, "Please be careful driving. Text me when you get to The Hyacinth."

She fights with the wind to open her umbrella, preparing her sprint toward the Volvo. Despite everything crashing down around her, despite his doubts and frustrations, he still cares for her. The contradiction makes her heart ache. Bradley is unconditional.

The umbrella pops open. She attempts to shield their faces from the rain but fails. Within seconds, they are soaked. Rain drips from their wet noses. Her heart pounds in her chest. Her adrenaline races. She lingers.

Then she leans in and kisses him. Their lips meet in the deluge, and for a moment, he responds with the same intensity she remembers from their night together. But then he pulls back, his hands gently pushing against her shoulders.

"I can't do this, Meaghan. Not until I know which version of you I'm falling for this time."

The rain beats down harder between them. She steps back, readjusting her umbrella, his words cutting deeper than the cold rain.

"I'll call you ..." she says quietly. "... when I get there."

She makes a mad dash for the Volvo. Thunder cracks overhead as Bradley watches her drive away. The rain begins to blur her taillights—much like the blurry boundaries of their relationship over decades, full of almost and might-have-beens.

DR. HARLOW'S PORTABLE SONOGRAM DEVICE FILLS Palmer's bedroom with the whirring echo of her baby's heartbeat.

"Amazing." She grins ear to ear. Dr. Harlow pats her arm reassuringly, smiling back.

"Getting to hear that sound every other day, keeps me going. And by going, I mean sitting right here and moving absolutely nowhere else." Rain starts to dance against Palmer's windows, growing heavier by the minute.

"Good girl!" Dr. Harlow tells her. "The baby appears to be doing well considering your preeclampsia diagnosis. As hard as it is to stay put, you're doing a great job."

Dr. Harlow moves her magic wand around Palmer's belly. The screen lights up. She can make out fingers and toes, but nothing else. Even after two other pregnancies, she has a hard time deciphering the images on that little screen.

"Everything looks on track," Dr. Harlow says, setting her wand down. "Your urine and bloodwork show the preeclampsia is stable."

"Does that mean I can get out of this bed now?" she asks eagerly.

Dr. Harlow studies her. "I'll grant you thirty minutes of standing time a day. Not all at once. I don't want you walking around at all. I want you mostly in bed still. Let's try that for the next two days until I return and we can evaluate."

She beams and decides not to mention her headache. "Yes! I'll take it. I'll be very careful. Thank you!" She claps her hands together. Dr. Harlow goes to unplug the sonogram device, but before she can, the power goes out.

"Hmmm," Dr. Harlow says, moving toward the windows to assess the situation. "The waves are enormous. The storm has moved in."

"You should get back to the hospital. I appreciate your house calls so much, but I wouldn't want you to be stranded here. I know your other patients need you," she says.

Dr. Harlow attempts to peer further out at sea, as if she could even see through the sheets of rain that appear over the water. "I'm not sure I should leave you with the power out and the storm coming."

"Meaghan will be back any moment. She texted fifteen minutes ago and said she's on her way. I'll be fine. You should go before any roads begin to flood."

"All right," Dr. Harlow agrees after a few moments of consideration. "I still need to round at the hospital, assuming they have power." Dr. Harlow gathers her equipment and heads toward the door.

"Thank you. Travel safe. I'll see you the day after tomorrow." She watches Dr. Harlow disappear from her bedroom doorway. She listens to the front door open, the wind catching it momentarily, and close again. She's alone and in the dark. The light coming in from outside is gray and shadowy, making the whole house feel spooky.

The storm intensifies, rattling the windows with each gust. She shifts in bed, uncomfortable with the emptiness of the house around her. She hears the waves crash against the shore with mounting fury, their rhythm matching her unease.

She turns again and all at once, a sharp pain shoots through her abdomen. She gasps, clutching at her belly. Her headache intensifies slightly and dizziness follows. The room spins in nauseating circles around her. Panic rises in her chest as she fumbles for her phone.

"This isn't right," she whispers, dialing Dr. Harlow's number with trembling fingers, hoping she hasn't gotten too far down Cape Drive. The call fails to connect. She tries again. Nothing. The screen displays "No Service" where signal bars should be.

"No, no, no," Palmer murmurs, fighting against the sudden dizziness. The storm must have knocked out the cell towers. She's completely cut off.

Where are the boys right now? Surely, Quinn can't still be at Dewey. Since he arrived at The Hyacinth, Quinn has remained distant from her. He speaks to her in short sentences and appears tense when they're together, which isn't often, since being together requires that Quinn come to her room.

She wants to reach Quinn and Aiden, but she can't.

As another wave of pain rises and subsides, Palmer notices Miles's journal on her nightstand. She reaches for it, needing something—anything—to distract her from the fear gripping her heart. The leather-bound book feels solid in her hands, a tangible connection to her husband.

She flips through the pages, landing on an entry dated the night before his stroke. Her breath steadies as she reads his words:

"We made up today. I wish she could see that I'm not trying to control his future—I only want what's best for him. Sometimes I wonder if we're growing apart, these small fractures widening between us. But tonight, I remembered why I fell in love with her. How she fights for what she believes in. How she never gives up. Tomorrow, we'll try again. I'll listen better. Because no matter our mistakes, we always find our way back to each other."

Tears blur her vision. All this time, she's carried guilt about their final arguments, but Miles had understood. They both made mistakes, but their love had remained the constant that guided them home to each other. The realization washes over her like a balm, easing the tightness in her chest.

Another pain grips her, sharper than before. Palmer breathes through it, one hand pressed protectively over her belly. "Please be okay," she whispers. "Please hold on."

TWENTY MINUTES PASS UNTIL SHE HEARS THE FRONT door swing open and close again, followed by the click of heels on hardwoods. "Hello? Palmer, you all right?" Meaghan climbs the stairs toward the master suite. "No power?"

"No power!" She quickly wipes her tears and closes Miles's journal. Her voice strains with worry and her head throbs. "I'm having some pains—bad ones."

"What kind of pains?" Meaghan rushes into the master suite, completely drenched. Her feet bare and wet, her hair dripping.

"Sharp, here," she guides Meaghan's hand to the side of her abdomen, "and a throbbing headache now. I tried calling Dr. Harlow but the phones are down."

"How long has this been happening?" Meaghan asks, already reaching for her own phone.

"For about half an hour." She winces as another wave hits her.

"I'm calling an ambulance," Meaghan says firmly, then stares at her phone. "I don't have service, either," she mutters.

"No cell service. No power," Palmer says, fear evident in her voice.

"We're going to figure this out. The baby will be fine—you'll both be fine. I promise." Meaghan squeezes her hand, determination replacing panic in her eyes.

"Dr. Harlow mentioned this might happen with pre-eclampsia," Palmer says through gritted teeth. "The pain comes in waves. The headache is the worst part—like my skull might crack open."

Meaghan arranges pillows behind Palmer's back and lights candles on the nightstands. "We need to keep you calm. Your blood pressure—"

"I know," Palmer interrupts, breathing slowly through another wave of pain. "Stress makes it worse."

Meaghan stands beside the large bedroom windows, watching the waves swell and crash, inching closer and closer as the beach disappears before her eyes. Palmer sits perched on her king bed. Candles flicker on the nightstands.

"The tide is creeping up. There's not much sand left out there," Meaghan says.

"We've never flooded. Miles made sure there's enough beach between the house and the ocean to avoid the worst hurricane. Not once have we taken on water. We'll be fine."

A gust of powerful wind slams the window. Meaghan instinctively jumps back, as if slapped across the face. The Hyacinth shakes. Meaghan audibly winces.

She grimaces, pressing her finger harder against her temple. The time between shooting pains grows longer, and she relaxes a bit. "We will be fine," she repeats though her voice lacks conviction.

The air between them feels as heavy as the clouds outside. It's laden with her secrets and suspicions.

"I tried reaching Quinn," Meaghan says, continuing to watch the waves below her. "Earlier, before I left the restaurant. He didn't answer me either."

"He would have never done this before," she says. "Not let me know he's okay." She shakes her head and rests it back into her pillow. "He's angry still." She doesn't mention her concern for Aiden and Bella, who are on the Cape, somewhere in the middle of this raging storm.

"Everyone is angry with us, Palmer. Haven't you noticed?"

A light bulb goes off in her mind. Their circumstances may be different, but the people they love most don't want much to do with either one of them.

"Everyone *is* angry with us." She immediately feels lighter, as if suddenly sharing her burden with Meaghan is a remedy she didn't know she needed. "It's exhausting, right?"

Outside, the thunder cracks and lightning rips through the sky, illuminating a blazoned trail to where the horizon meets the ocean below.

Meaghan collapses backwards onto the bed. "So. Exhausting." She turns onto her side and props her head on her elbow. "I don't think I can keep doing it."

Palmer musters a sympathetic laugh. "Well, you can't simply make other people stop hating you, Meaghan. You can't control them. Remember?"

"Exactly. The only thing we can control is ourselves, and maybe that's the answer." Meaghan rolls onto her stomach. Her legs bend at her knees and flop above her. The scene is as familiar as high school.

"What are you talking about?" she asks. "We already control ourselves. So far, that hasn't helped. You're talking nonsense."

"No, I'm not. Listen, what I did with Sinful Admissions was reprehensible, I admit it. Right here, right now. I shouldn't have done it."

Is Meaghan finally going to confess what she's been contemplating since the indictment leaked? Meaghan pops up from lying on her belly, her legs fly under her, and she lands crisscross applesauce in front of Palmer on the bed.

"What did you do?" she asks.

"What did I do? I wanted to keep winning. It consumed me at any cost. Getting the right roles, lobbying for the Oscars, throwing unrivaled parties, hell, even marrying Dunc. All of it, I did to win. The more I won, the more people loved me. And their love is like oxygen. I couldn't live without it. And then, in a single moment, I helped Duncan smooth Bella's way into college, which turned that love for me into pure loathing. It's like being smothered with a pillow; I can't breathe." Meaghan's eyes fill with tears. She blinks and one slides down her cheek.

"I've spent my life being afraid I'm unlovable," Meaghan continues, her voice barely audible above the storm. "That's why I did what I did. Not just with Bella's admission, but everything. The parties, the marriages, the desperate need for acclaim." She reaches for Palmer's hand. "My father walked out, and I've spent every day since trying to make sure no one else would. That's why I helped Duncan bribe SCC. I was terrified Bella would leave me too if I didn't."

Palmer squeezes Meaghan's fingers, wincing as another wave of pain washes over her.

"You think you're unlovable?" Palmer asks in disbelief. *I've loved you my whole life.*

"If I was loveable, wouldn't my father have stayed? That's the question I've been quietly asking myself for years. It's landed me right here, in a heap of a mess. But this morning, at the restaurant, I had an epiphany. Bradley doesn't let people's perception of me define how he feels about me."

She smiles at the realization that Meaghan might finally be catching on. "He sure doesn't," she says. "He never has. No matter how many Oscars or how many years in jail."

"Exactly. He's unfazed by my accomplishments, and he's equally unfazed by my failures. It finally sunk in this morning, signing those papers with him. That feeling is completely freeing, and it made me wonder, if Bradley's caring can be unconditional, why can't my own?"

"What do you mean?"

"I mean ..." Meaghan looks around the room, searching for the right words. "I mean, I love me. And that's enough. I have spent years seeking everyone else's love, living in fear of not having it and being destroyed when they leave. I should have been living my life making sure I love myself—that the choices I make and the people I surround myself with nurture my own self-love. Because that's a love that no one else can take away."

"Oh, Meaghan." She leans over and wipes the tears from Meaghan's cheek. She is stunned by the confession Meaghan has now made about helping Duncan. But she's spent a lifetime watching Meaghan play other people, hoping the masses will love her. Sitting here now, watching Meaghan discover that playing herself will give her the greatest love of all, overwhelms everything else.

"Same goes for you," Meaghan says, poking her finger into her leg. "You spend your entire life focused on making everyone else happy. When we were little, I watched you tirelessly attempt to make your father and sister happy after your mom died. For years, your happiness has come from making Miles, Aiden, Quinn, and everyone at your office happy. When they're angry, you're completely miserable. What if you made yourself happy?"

She flinches. "I can't make myself happy," Palmer says.

"Why not?"

Her cheeks burn. "Because I'm a terrible, horrible person."

"What?" Meaghan asks. "What are you talking about? You're amazingly perfect."

"No, I did something so awful."

Meaghan waits.

"I cheated on Miles," she blurts out and buries her head in her hands.

Meaghan sits up straight.

"The night before he died," she says. "With Sanford."

"The guy from work. Who was in the ambulance with you?"

"Yes! And … someone saw us and told Sanford's soon-to-be ex-wife. She's threatening to tell everyone if he doesn't agree to her terms in the divorce."

"Jesus, Palmer." Meaghan shakes her head. "Where did they see you?"

"He kissed me in my office."

"Kissed you? As in one kiss. Not … you know, sleeping together."

"Nooooo." She waves her hands in the air. "I didn't sleep with Sanford. But that doesn't matter. I cheated on Miles. I am a terrible, horrible person. I'm living in constant fear that the boys either already know and that's why they're so mad, or they're going to find out and hate me even more."

"Did Miles know?" Meaghan asks.

She shakes her head, considering the possibility. "I don't think so. The timing wouldn't have allowed for it, I'm pretty sure." She leans in toward Meaghan. "Even if he did, he had his own moment of weakness once."

Meaghan slumps over in disbelief. "Miles? What are you talking about?"

"When I was the sickest and in the hospital. There was this nurse, Lauren. He wrote about that night in the journal we found." Meaghan knows the leather journal because it's where Miles kept the things he couldn't tell anyone else. It's where he kept his conversation with Dunc.

"He was terrified of losing me. One night, he broke down completely. She comforted him, gave him her number. He wrote how he felt drawn to her—how for a brief moment, she really saw the true him." Palmer's voice softens. "I wonder if he ever called her."

Meaghan takes a deep breath and raises both of her hands to Palmer. "Okay, I'm a little pissed you've been keeping this to yourself, but I'm not going to make this about me." Meaghan clears her throat. "You kissed someone when you thought you were losing Miles, and Miles kissed someone when he thought he was losing you. That might make you feel like your love for each other was fragile. Or it could demonstrate just how strong your love was. When tested, you both found your way back to the other one. You chose each other. Palmer, you and Miles are the greatest love story I know. And I know a lot of love stories."

She smirks, considering the possibility. A few seconds pass. She nods in agreement. "It's a pretty damn good love story."

Another wave of pain courses through her body. She clutches her belly, breathing hard.

"But if the boys find out about Sanford, they'll never forgive me." Her voice breaks. She places a protective hand over her belly as another wave of pain makes her wince.

The house groans against the force of the wind outside.

"What if I can't do this alone, Meaghan?" The words tumble out, raw and unfiltered. "What if I'm not enough for this baby? Miles should be here. We were supposed to do this together."

Meaghan moves closer, taking Palmer's trembling hand. "You're not alone."

"Everyone's leaving. The boys hate me. Miles is gone." Her eyes fill with tears. "What kind of mother will I be when I couldn't even keep my marriage vows?"

The rain whips the trees outside the window. They lash and thrash. Meaghan stands back up to reevaluate the beach, now entirely submerged. Water slaps the walls of the deck, up and over.

"We need to move away from these windows," Meaghan says, urgency in her voice. "They might not be safe."

Palmer tries to stand but clutches her belly, doubling over. "I can't—"

A deafening crack splits the air. Downstairs, the sound of glass shattering fills the house as the ocean breaches the living room's glass wall. Water rushes in with a roar.

The unspoiled panoramic views of ocean sunrises and dolphin-watching sunsets collapse under the weight of the waves. "Meaghan!" she cries out as the storm breaches The Hyacinth, and the floodgates open.

MEAGHAN ANSWERS ON THE FIRST RING WHEN BRADLEY calls, cell service restored. "There's water everywhere."

In the great room of The Hyacinth, it's halfway up her calves. Wall paintings swing from nails like marionettes. Family photos are strewn around the room. Water inches up the legs of the baby grand. The wind screams and the water thrashes inside now, too.

"Go upstairs with Palmer," he instructs her. "I'll call the Chief. We'll get someone over there as soon as possible. The main roads are flooded and the power is out in the Village. It may take a little time for them to reach you, but they'll be on their way." His voice is calm and reassuring. "Palmer's all right? You're all right? No one's hurt?"

"Ask the Chief to send a paramedic as well. Palmer's had abdominal pains—they're subsiding, but she needs to be checked again. We can wait upstairs safely. But the great room is destroyed." *Miles's great room.* She looks around her, although it's difficult to see with the storm still raging. She heads up the stairs, leaping over every other one until reaching safety. "Bradley, we haven't heard from Quinn."

"He's all right. He's here, at The Oyster House." His voice cracks. "He was at Dewey ... with friends when the waves began to turn violent. They packed up and began to drive toward the Village. By the time they got to town, the water was over the bulkhead and the streets were flooding. So they parked the Jeep in the street and walked three blocks to the restaurant. Quinn texted Palmer, I made sure of it. The signal is so bad in town right now, it must not have gone through."

"Oh, what a relief to hear. I'm so glad they made it to you."

"And in good form. They haven't stopped eating since they walked in." He clears his throat.

He pauses. "Hey, Meaghan?" Her heart flutters.

"Yes?" She wonders if Bradley will bring up how she kissed him before running out into the storm hours earlier.

"The friends that Quinn came in with." He stalls.

"Yes? They're friends from school in Alexandria. The ones here for Life Rolls On."

"Yep. Nick and Alexander. They come every year with their families."

"I remember Nick. Black wavy hair ... fully Italian."

"Oh yeah, that's Nick." Bradley hesitates. "Quinn showed up with two others."

"Well, I'm sure that's fine. You don't mind keeping everyone there until the storm ends?"

"I don't mind at all. But ... the other kids Quinn showed up with are Aiden and Bella." Silence floods the line.

"Bella is with you?" A million emotions engulf her.

"Yes. Bella is right here."

Is she ... is she okay?" Meaghan's voice trembles.

"She's physically fine," Bradley lowers his voice, "but shaken from the storm." *So many storms.*

He sighs with a weary relief that Meaghan senses. "We'll stay here until the storm passes. Take care of Palmer and yourself in the meantime. We will get through this together."

"We will," she nods even though he can't see her. "Thank you, Bradley. Truly." She hangs up, a strange mixture of fear, relief, and determination settling within her. No matter what storms they face, they aren't alone.

Chapter 18

EARLY THE NEXT MORNING, WHILE THE STORM SLOWS, everything happens quickly. The Chief sends two fire trucks to The Hyacinth. By the time they navigate North Shore Drive and arrive at the house, the storm moves out completely. Palmer stands for the first time in weeks, though Meaghan catches the way her friend sways slightly. A rush of anxiousness floods through her.

"Palmer, are you sure?" she asks, eyeing the basement steps. If standing doesn't go well, a large firetruck is right outside, ready to whisk Palmer to the hospital. Still, the worry gnaws at Meaghan's stomach. Together, they gingerly maneuver down the stairs into the great room, where Palmer witnesses the devastation firsthand.

"My God," Palmer whispers in disbelief, her pale face turning paler. The room is ravaged. A half inch of water still sits on the floor. The backside of the room where the glass wall stood is now completely open to the beach, which is littered with seaweed, rocks, and large branches. The two chaise lounge chairs that sat on the deck float along the shoreline, swaying in and out with the tide. Palmer steps into the room and she pulls her back against the wall for support.

"I don't think so. There's too much debris, and the water makes the floor slippery. You stay right here." Nurse Meaghan returns, a hint of command in her voice, hiding her growing dread.

"That was some storm," one of the firemen says to her as he passes by with giant sheets of plywood. "Cell lines are spotty and power is mostly down across the Cape. Looks like it will be a couple days before things are back up to running."

"Well, that explains why we haven't been able to reach Bradley or the kids for the past several hours," Palmer says.

Dr. Harlow arrives moments later, concern etched across her face as she quickly assesses Palmer. Meaghan's heart races. "Palmer, how are you feeling?" the doctor asks.

"I'm fine," Palmer insists, though her pale complexion looks anything but fine.

Dr. Harlow raises an eyebrow. "Your blood pressure spiked during the storm. We can't ignore that. Let's monitor it closely."

Her stomach twists at the sight of Dr. Harlow's serious expression. "Come on, Palmer. I'm putting you back in bed," Meaghan commands. "I can oversee this crew and we'll get things cleaned up. You two need to keep resting." She pats Palmer's baby bump, hiding her anxiety.

"Great idea," Dr. Harlow agrees. "I'll call this evening and check on you."

Palmer doesn't disagree with either of them. For the next several hours, Palmer listens to the sounds of wet vacs sucking up water, glass and debris sweeping across the floor, and hammers pounding boards into place for makeshift walls, as three beefy firemen rescue them. Meaghan pushes through her fear and dives into the cleanup effort, gathering broken picture frames, soaked books, and knickknacks. Steeling herself against worry, she focuses on the task at hand, even as the image of Palmer's pallor looms in her mind.

Around noon, the front door of The Hyacinth swings wide open.

"Mom! Mom!" Quinn rushes into the foyer, dark-brown curls flopping over his hazel eyes, his sneakers squeaking against the wet floor, and stops abruptly when he witnesses the destruction. Bradley trails behind him carrying three large white pastry boxes.

She wraps her arms around Quinn, who stands shell-shocked peering into the great room. "Your mom's upstairs, Quinnie." Quinn turns and races up the stairs to Palmer.

Bradley looks at Meaghan and the men behind her pounding the last few boards together. He smiles, but the warmth doesn't quite reach her. "Hello."

"Hello." She smiles back, trying to mask the storm of emotions swirling inside her.

"Should we discuss what happened in the rain?" he asks, his tone shifting to something more serious.

"We should. But not right now." She has a million questions for Bradley, and all of them are about Bella. Before she can ask even one, Bradley moves into the great room to assess the damage.

"Whoa," he says. "This room will need to be gutted. I'll call the contractor Miles used originally. I'm sure he'll help." Bradley turns back around to her. "Let's check on Palmer," he says and they head up the stairs.

"How was Bella?" she asks, trying to contain her excitement.

"She was a little dodgy at first. I suppose uncomfortable with me since the whole incident where her mother was photographed half naked on my doorstep. I can't blame her. But after a little pizza and hot chocolate, she warmed up. Honestly, she seemed great. She and Aiden have clearly clicked. Like Mack said, they're *together* together." Bradley raps on Palmer's bedroom door in time to catch Quinn racing to her side and throwing his arms around her.

"You're okay?" Quinn asks. He hugs Palmer and doesn't let go.

Palmer melts in his embrace. "Oh Quinn, yes, I'm okay." She cradles her son's face in both her hands. He smells of salt-water and pizza. "Are you okay?"

"The great room is destroyed," Quinn says. "All Dad's work is gone. He's not here to put it together again."

"We'll put it together again. And wherever Dad is, he'll see it. I promise," Palmer reassures him. "You survived the storm all right? It was scary."

"Yep, Bradley let us stay at the restaurant the entire time. We ate a lot of food and played cards and charades all night long. But the Village is wrecked. The sandbags along the boardwalk couldn't stop the water. Almost every street flood-ed. That's what took us so long to get here."

"Is Aiden with you?" Palmer asks. "Bella?"

Quinn shakes his head. "They went back to their friends' house in Dewey, where they're staying. Aiden said they need-ed to see if there was any damage there." Quinn looks at her. "Bella won't come here; she just won't. I asked her so many times, but she refuses. I'm sorry, Auntie M."

She walks over to the bed and places her hand on Quinn's back. "You don't need to be sorry, Quinn. It's not your fault."

"Listen, I've got some pretty amazing food here." Bradley hoists the white box above his head. "Figured the guys down-stairs and you ladies could use something to eat."

"Warm chocolate croissants. We made them this morning," Quinn says.

"You made them?" Palmer asks, surprised. "Yep. Me and Bradley. The others were still sleeping. But they woke up when they smelled the croissants."

"Who wouldn't! Let's eat them," Palmer says, holding onto Quinn and rocking with him back and forth. "I'm starving."

"You are eating for two," Quinn says and offers the slightest grin to Palmer.

"I am." Palmer nods and smiles.

In the kitchen, Bradley brews a large pot of fresh coffee and loads two platters with the fresh croissants. Meaghan sets out plates and fills glasses with ice and orange juice. The three firefighters slip off their wet coats and gather in the breakfast nook. They inhale their breakfast in ten minutes before announcing they're heading back into the Village to help clear the streets. After they leave, Meaghan grabs one of the platters and Bradley grabs four mugs and a warm carafe filled with deep roasted coffee. They head back up to the master suite to devour the croissants. They head back up to the master suite to indulge in the croissants, but her mind keeps racing back to Palmer's precarious health.

"So how did you make it to The Henlopen Oyster House?" Palmer asks Quinn.

"Well, I picked up Aiden and Bella because we were going to spend the day at Dewey practicing for Life Rolls On. OMG, the contest is supposed to start today."

"Darby already texted me. They're postponing three days to get the Cape cleaned up and power and cell lines all working again. It will start on Friday," Palmer explains. "Continue."

"Well, I picked up Aiden and Bella and we hit The Bakers Dozen for donuts. We lingered a little too long because by the time we got to Dewey the waves were already super intense."

"Why did you stay then?" Palmer asks.

"We tried to wait it out. But the longer we stayed, the darker the water and sky got. So we decided to leave. But we couldn't drive the Jeep because the wind was so bad we couldn't see, so we pulled over and left her on the side of the road."

"Oh my God. I hate thinking of you all out there alone," she murmurs, anxiety tightening her throat as images of the storm flash through her mind.

"Yeah, it was pretty scary. We started walking and I realized we were near The Oyster House."

"Wait a minute," she interrupts, looking up from her phone. "You know where Aiden and Bella are staying?"

"Yep," Quinn answers, looking at Palmer.

She stands up. "Take me there right now." She's used to other people doing exactly what she says. "Please, Quinn. Take me there."

Palmer says, "She doesn't want to see you. If you don't respect her wishes, you risk pushing her further away."

She shakes her head. "I don't care! Last night, I found out that my daughter who I haven't seen or spoken with in months is staying only miles away from me. This morning, I found out my godson knows exactly where she is. I have to see her."

"Mom knows too," Quinn blurts out. Palmer glares at Quinn.

"What?" She inches closer to Palmer. "You know where Bella is staying?"

"Yes. I know."

"How long have you known?"

269

"A few weeks."

"How could you not tell me? All that talk last night between us, and you didn't mention my estranged daughter is minutes away? My heart has been literally ripped out of my chest for months now, and you just forget to tell me? At the very moment I'm baring my soul to you?" She raises both arms in the air above her head, shaking her closed fists. "What kind of friend are you?"

Bradley moves toward her and pulls her arms down to her side, "Maybe we should calm down a second here." She rips her arms away from him.

"Bella is my goddaughter. I love her. And I love you. She simply isn't ready to see you. If I had told you where she is, you'd have done exactly this—blown up, gone over there, and forced yourself on her. Then she would hate you even more! And she'd hate me, too. This right here," Palmer says as she swirls her hand in the air between them, "this is exactly why I didn't tell you."

"I don't care. I'm going over there." She sets her plate on the coffee table, croissant half eaten.

"Why don't we all go?" Bradley offers, attempting to defuse the situation, the tension crackling in the air. Then he looks at Palmer. "Oh, you can't go."

"I can go. Dr. Harlow approved me standing a few minutes each day," Palmer insists.

"No way," Meaghan blurts out. "You spent last night with a massive headache and pain shooting across your abdomen."

"I was very stressed. Dr. Harlow said as much. I'm better this morning. She's going to check on me this evening. And I'll come straight back to bed," Palmer says.

"You shouldn't go. It's too much," Meaghan says, balancing her desire to finally be reunited with Bella and Palmer's health.

"I'm trying to help you, Meaghan, because I love you, contrary to how you might feel at this moment. And I love Bella. If we all go, there's a chance she will feel it's more like a reunion, after a very scary storm, than a confrontation."

"Okay." She throws her hands in the air, frustration bubbling beneath the surface but knowing Palmer means well.

"I'll pull the G-Wagon around," Bradley says, and they all rush to follow him downstairs. As she glances back at Palmer, unease washes over her. She knows this confrontation with Bella could change everything, but she can't escape the fear of losing her daughter forever. Hope and trepidation stir within her. She breathes deeply, having just survived a giant storm that left a massive wreckage in its wake, and readies herself to face an even bigger storm—one with the potential to destroy her entire family. She grabs Palmer's hand as they leave The Hyacinth. Surely, they can weather this too.

THIRTY MINUTES LATER, BRADLEY PARKS THE G-WAGON on Stockley Street in front of a bright turquoise A-frame with a hot-pink roof. The house looks like the cotton candy ice cream cone from Coastal Creamery. It's also far enough inland to have avoided any storm damage. Bradley helps Palmer out of the car. Quinn gets out too. Meaghan plans to stay in the G-Wagon until Bella and Aiden come out of the house to meet her. If Bella sees Meaghan first, she might not come out at all.

The plan works. As Palmer, Bradley, and Quinn meander up the walkway, Aiden and Bella come flying out of the ice cream cone, followed by Jasper.

"Mom!" Aiden says. She hasn't seen him since the week after Miles's memorial service when he returned to UVA.

Bella rushes to hug her first and pats her midsection, "I can't believe we're having a baby!"

"Bella." She pulls Bella back by the shoulders and inspects her. "My beautiful goddaughter. You're all right?" Bella nods.

"You look like you swallowed one of those personal-sized watermelons!" Aiden jokes. He's not angry or disgusted. Maybe Bella's influence has changed Aiden's attitude toward his new sibling.

She smirks. She opens her arms and hugs her son. "Hi, sweetheart." Aiden looks different too. More grown up. He looks … like Miles. "I needed to come see for myself that you two are okay. That was some storm."

"Good morning, Mrs. Harding," Jasper says.

"Hi, Jasper. Thanks for taking these kids in." She remembers Jasper being able to devour two double cheeseburgers, a large French fry, and an Oreo shake at the Frosty Shack in Charlottesville. Now she owes him more than lunch after a regatta.

Aiden runs his hands through his hair, "We survived all right, Mom. Bradley took us in." Aiden gives Bradley a fist bump. Followed by one for Quinn.

Meaghan emerges from the G-Wagon.

"Mom? What are you doing here?" Bella turns to Palmer, her lips pursed.

Meaghan walks toward Bella with her arms open. "Bella."

Bella steps backwards distancing herself from Meaghan, as if Meaghan's open arms are oppositely charged magnets pushing Bella away.

"Stay away from me," Bella pleads but Meaghan pushes toward her. "Mom, stay away! I don't want to be with you!"

Meaghan stops in her tracks. "You've humiliated me and left me with zero friends. You're a criminal. The FBI is sending you to jail. Jail, Mom! And the icing on the cake, you're caught committing adultery in your underwear with this guy." Bella points to Bradley. "Soooo embarrassing! I have absolutely zero respect for you. Please don't come near me." Tears pour and, in her rage, she struggles to catch her breath.

Aiden rushes to her side and turns to her. "Mom, you promised."

She feels awful. She shouldn't have brought Meaghan here. "I know I promised, I ..." Before she can begin to explain herself, three girls with long blond hair pop out of the ice cream cone house like a triple dip of sweet cream.

"What's going on out here?" asks the first one. The second rushes toward Jasper and grabs his hand. The third walks right up to her. She looks oddly familiar.

"Hi, Mrs. Harding. How are you?" She can't place her. "Darby said you are doing much better. I was so worried when you collapsed that day." She tries to put a name to the girl's face.

"You were with my mom when she collapsed?" Aiden asks the girl.

"Yeah, at Powdered Temptation. Your dad announced to everyone at the restaurant that some woman saw the two of them making out one night in your mom's office and ..."—the girl puts her hand on her wrist as if recounting a funny story—"your mom was so embarrassed, she collapsed right there. We had to call an ambulance."

"My ... dad?" Aiden asks. Everyone looks on in confusion, as things slowly come into focus for Palmer.

Shit!

"Yeah, your dad … Sanford," the girl says as she bounces her right index finger in the air. "Sanford Harding, right?"

Meaghan closes her eyes, as though trying to unsee it. Aiden's jaw drops. Bella reaches for his arm now, returning his gesture from only moments before. Quinn's narrow eyes land on her.

Her heart hammers against her ribs. The world narrows to Aiden's devastated face, his features twisting from confusion to betrayal in real time.

"You couldn't even wait until Dad was gone, could you?" Aiden's voice breaks, each word like a physical blow.

The accusation steals her breath. "Aiden, no—that's not—"

She recoils and then turns to the girl. "Mindy?" Alpha Delta Pi. James Madison University. College friends renting a house together at the beach for the summer. "You're Mindy, right?"

"That's me!" Mindy says.

Bradley walks right up to her like he's perfected his missile lock. "You made out with Sanford in your office?"

"Bradley!" Meaghan reprimands.

Palmer pauses. She leans into Bradley and whispers, "Yes."

Mindy scans the party on her front lawn that's now come to a screeching halt. "What's wrong?" Mindy asks.

Aiden looks at Mindy. "Sanford is not my dad."

"Why don't we head back inside. Give everyone a chance to talk," Jasper says to Mindy and the other two girls, who quickly turn around and head inside.

She turns to Quinn and Aiden. "It isn't what you think."

"How is it not what we think? You were making out with Sanford in your office," Aiden exclaims.

"Sanford kissed me. Once. In my office. He was in the middle of divorcing Cinnamon, feeling so low, and there I was. Your father and I had been arguing for weeks." She can't help but glance at Aiden, who immediately drops his eyes. "I let Sanford kiss me. It shouldn't have happened. It was a mistake. Sanford has apologized for crossing the line."

She wants to scream, *Your father took my nurse's phone number! God only knows what he might have done!* But that's a secret she will take to her grave. Tarnishing Miles's memory for her children is not an option.

"Did Dad know? Is that what caused his stroke?" Aiden asks.

"No! He couldn't have known. It happened only two nights before his stroke. It's what made me realize that I couldn't go on arguing with your father. That he's all I ever wanted. Your father was the greatest love of my life. He always will be."

Aiden and Quinn stare blank faced. Bella puts her arm around Aiden. Meaghan reaches for Quinn, who buries his head in her chest.

"I'm so sorry," she tells them.

She reaches for Aiden. He flinches and pulls away from her. She reaches for Quinn. "I'm so sorry," she repeats. But he turns his shoulder away from her, too.

"Oh God damn it!" she screams. Her voice rips from somewhere primal, startling even Palmer. Blood rushes to her face as months of grief, guilt, and hormones explode. "You know what? I am not sorry. I didn't do anything wrong. Sanford kissed me! In that kiss I found the answer to the question I had been wondering for weeks—did I still want to be with your father? The answer was yes! We made up the next day. We apologized to each other. We found our way back to each other. And in doing so, we created a whole new life together! It's a freaking miracle! So, God damn it, I am not going to be sorry for it!"

Everyone looks stunned. Except Bradley.

Bradley glowers at her, freezing her stiff. She doesn't move. "If Sanford kissed you only that one time, how did he end up in the ambulance with you that day? Did he come stay with you while Meaghan and I were in Cape May?

"No!" she exclaims. "I ran into him, and he apologized to me because I hadn't spoken to him since."

"I've seen Sanford in the Village since then. A few times. And he's come into The Oyster Bar for lunch at least once," Bradley contends.

She cannot believe Bradley's accusatory tone, especially in front of the kids. "Well, I haven't seen him. As you might notice, I've been shackled to my bed until recently."

"Speaking of that," Meaghan says, "we need to get you back. This is too much. You've been standing here too long."

She nods her head in agreement; she feels weaker, but she can't distinguish if that's from her standing, her screaming, or the emotional beating she's taken. She clasps her hands together.

"You guys should go," Quinn says.

"Aren't you coming?" she asks him. Her voice sounds small, foreign to her own ears.

"I don't think so. I'm going to stay right here." Aiden throws his arm around Quinn's neck and pulls him onto the sidewalk. Bella grabs Aiden's other hand.

Palmer takes a step toward them, but the world tilts. Her knees buckle, and she pitches forward. Bradley catches her before she hits the ground.

"Palmer!" Meaghan rushes to her side.

"I'm fine," she waves them off, though her face has drained of color. "I stood too long." But the terror in Meaghan's eyes tells her it's more than that.

On the corner of the street, a single photographer captures the scene. Tonight's TikTok; tomorrow's headline. Together, Aiden, Bella, and Quinn disappear into the cotton candy ice cream cone house.

MEAGHAN PACES THE BEDROOM, CAREFUL TO KEEP HER footsteps light so Palmer can rest. The evening sun streams through the windows, casting long shadows across the hardwood floor. She pauses to check her phone again—no missed calls from Bella, just three texts from Mack that make her stomach twist into knots.

Palmer stirs on the bed, her face drawn with exhaustion. The dark circles under her eyes have deepened since yesterday, and Dr. Harlow's return visit only brought more concerning news: higher blood pressure readings than this morning, increased protein in her urine, and strict orders for complete bed rest.

"Water?" she asks Palmer, already pouring from the pitcher on the nightstand.

Palmer nods weakly. "Any word from the boys?"

She hands her the glass, forcing a smile that doesn't reach her eyes. "Not yet. I'm sure they'll call soon."

The lie tastes bitter on her tongue. She's left messages for both Aiden and Quinn—casual, upbeat voicemails that betray none of the desperation she feels. They need to come home. Palmer needs them here.

Her phone buzzes in her pocket. Mack's name flashes on the screen, and she steps into the hallway to take the call.

"Tell me something good," she says quietly, leaning against the wall.

"I wish I could." Mack's voice is grave. "The prosecutor just called. The indictment is coming down in forty-eight hours."

Meaghan closes her eyes, her free hand instinctively twisting a strand of hair. "Money laundering?"

"Yes. They're moving forward with the full charges." There's a pause. "I'm sorry, Meaghan. Without those text messages, we don't have enough to stop it."

"I understand." She keeps her voice steady despite the panic rising in her chest. "Thanks for letting me know."

She ends the call and takes a moment to compose herself before returning to Palmer's room. The walls of The Hyacinth suddenly feel like they're closing in around her. In forty-eight hours, her name will be formally connected to a crime she didn't knowingly commit. The world that once adored her will have one more reason to despise her.

When she re-enters the bedroom, Palmer is watching her with knowing eyes. "Bad news?"

She sinks into the chair beside the bed. "Mack called. The indictment is coming in forty-eight hours."

Palmer reaches for her hand. "There has to be something else we can do."

"There isn't. Not without those text messages." Her fingers tremble in Palmer's grasp. "I've run out of time."

The sound of the front door opening downstairs interrupts them. Heavy footsteps cross the foyer, followed by Bradley's voice calling up.

"In here," she calls back, quickly wiping her eyes and straightening her posture. The last thing she needs is for Bradley to see her falling apart.

Bradley appears in the doorway, his face weathered by more than just the summer sun. He carries a small bag from the pharmacy, which he places on the dresser before turning to face them.

"How's our patient?" he asks, but his eyes don't quite meet Palmer's.

"I've been better," Palmer says. "But I'd be a lot better if my sons would answer my calls."

Bradley shifts his weight, glancing at Meaghan before clearing his throat. "That's actually why I stopped by. I just got off the phone with Aiden."

She watches Palmer's face light with hope. But her own heart sinks knowing what's coming.

"They're not coming, Palmer." Bradley's voice is gentle but firm. "I tried everything I could think of. Aiden says he can't face being at The Hyacinth right now, and Quinn is following his lead."

"But it's almost time to spread Miles's ashes," Palmer whispers, her voice barely audible. "We agreed—the last Sunday in August. We all promised."

"I know." Bradley runs a hand through his hair. "Aiden said maybe later in the fall, when things have ... settled."

"Settled?" Palmer's voice rises. "What exactly needs to settle? Their father is gone. I'm pregnant with his child. I'm confined to this bed with preeclampsia that could kill me or this baby. And my sons can't even bother to come home because they're— what? Embarrassed? Angry? Too busy with their summer fun?"

"Palmer, your blood pressure," Meaghan warns, reaching for her wrist. She straps on the bedside monitor Dr. Harlow dropped off this morning.

Palmer pulls away. "My blood pressure is the least of my worries right now." Tears well in her eyes, spilling over before she can stop them. "I've lost everything that matters. Miles is gone. My boys hate me. My career is slipping away. And this baby—" Her hand moves protectively to her stomach. "This baby might never know any of them."

The room falls silent except for Palmer's ragged breathing and the distant sound of waves crashing on the shore below. Meaghan feels the weight of her friend's pain alongside her own, and something inside her breaks.

"I understand," she says finally, her voice barely above a whisper. "I've lost everything that matters too."

Palmer turns to look at her, really seeing her for the first time in days.

"In forty-eight hours, I'll be indicted," she continues. "My daughter won't speak to me. My career is in ruins. My marriage is over. The world that once adored me now despises me." She gives a hollow laugh. "And the man I've secretly loved for twenty years can barely look at me."

She doesn't dare glance at Bradley, but she feels his presence shift by the door.

"We're quite the pair, aren't we?" Palmer says, reaching for her hand again. "Two women who had it all, now watching it slip through our fingers like sand."

She squeezes Palmer's hand. "Maybe that's the problem. Maybe we never really had it all. We just thought we did."

"What do you mean?"

"I mean, maybe we've been chasing the wrong things. Making everyone else happy. Living up to expectations. Trying to be perfect." Her eyes meet Palmer's. "And in the process, we lost ourselves."

As Palmer appears to consider this, Meaghan witnesses the tension in her face softening slightly. "So what do we do now?" Palmer asks.

"I don't know," she admits. "But I think it starts with accepting that we can't control everything—or everyone. Not your boys. Not my daughter. Not even our own futures."

The setting sun casts the room in golden light, illuminating the tears on both women's faces. Outside, the ocean continues its eternal rhythm—waves rising, crashing, receding, only to rise again.

"The tide always turns," Bradley says softly from the doorway. "Miles used to say that, remember? No matter how bad the storm, the tide always turns."

Palmer nods, wiping her tears with the back of her hand. "He did say that."

"Maybe it's time we stop fighting the current," she suggests, "and learn to swim with it instead."

As if in answer, Palmer gasps softly, placing a hand on her belly. Palmer reaches for Meaghan's hand and places it over the spot where the baby is kicking. She feels the flutter beneath her palm—tiny but persistent, a reminder that even in darkness, new life continues. "Maybe you're right," Palmer whispers. "Maybe it's time to let go."

She nods, feeling something shift inside her. She's spent her entire life trying to make people love her, terrified of being abandoned. But maybe true strength isn't in holding on tighter—it's in having the courage to open your hands and trust that what's meant to stay will remain.

Chapter 19

MEAGHAN STANDS BEFORE THE PRESS, HEART POUND-
ing, finally ready to tell her truth. No more sabotaging herself. No more running from reality. When Mack called late
last night with the news—her indictment is coming in two
days—rather than wait for the FBI to parade her in handcuffs,
she decided to face the world on her own terms. She wants to
come clean. She needs to be honest with herself, the world,
and especially with Bella. The mere thought of it makes her
feel lighter.

At 10 a.m., the morning that the Life Rolls On surf contest finally begins, thirty news crews show up at the police
department to hear what she needs to say. She stands next to
the Chief, his now not-so-new assistant Paige Barrette, and
two other local officers. No one else attends. She has to do
this on her own; not that anyone offered to be at her side. No
Palmer. No Bradley. None of the kids. They haven't spoken
since the catastrophic morning after the storm on the front
lawn of the ice cream cone house. A scene she tries to wipe
from her mind nearly every minute of every day. Their absence
brings her clarity.

At the station, cameras flash, microphones pop, and all eyes study her. Will Meaghan Jones turn herself in? Has the Chief coordinated with the FBI for her arrest right here, right now? Or will Meaghan Jones tell the world her daughter is a liar, like Holly suggested and the media has since posited? *They have no idea what's coming.*

The Chief taps the microphone at the podium. "Good morning. I'm playing the role of traffic director, today. Please stay inside the taped area. Don't spill out onto the side lawn. When you leave in your vehicles, alternate with beachgoers when accessing the main road to avoid a logjam as happened earlier this summer. The roads are clear of debris and all water has receded since the storm, so all else is back to normal in the Village." Everyone nods. "Mrs. Jones, the podium is yours."

Her breathing steadies as she steps forward, shoulders squared, the trembling in her hands suddenly gone. "Good morning. Thank you for coming. For months, you have speculated about my guilt in association with the Sinful Admissions scandal and the arrest of my husband." She clears her throat and corrects her errors. "My ex-husband, Duncan Jones. In doing so, you've pursued people I love, often making them a story when they simply are not. You've camped out at my best friend's home for weeks when she's grieving the sudden loss of her husband. You've followed my daughter across the country, invading her private moments, repeatedly. You've tracked down a dear friend's personal family tragedy, suggested foul play, and laid it out for the world to devour. Your job is to pursue me; my job is to let you. This is how fame works. I've always known that and tried to play the game graciously. But pursuing the people I love most in this world goes too far. So, today, I'm here to end the need for your intrusions. I'm putting the speculation to bed; I'm here to tell you the truth."

Necks stretch for better views. Camera lenses focus. Microphones shoot higher into the air, as if that were even possible. Meaghan looks out into the crowd. "I'm guilty."

Jaws drop. Audible gasps echo across the lawn. Paige's hand clasps her mouth. The Chief's eyes widen and then drop to the ground. Meaghan looks behind her at him. She imagines the betrayal he must inevitably feel, having spent hours and department resources pouring through Duncan's burner phone looking for evidence of her innocence. Yet here she stands, professing her guilt.

As she speaks, she realizes this confession is for herself, not simply for the press. The words liberate her.

She turns back to address the crowd. "I wrote the check that bribed Chip Sullivan and secured my daughter Bella's admission into SCC. I wrote the check as a business donation from Awaken. For those of you who don't know, Awaken is my women's clothing company. This check with my signature is the evidence the FBI has against me." Hands fly up, waving incessantly in the air. *Just wait.* She ignores them.

"When I wrote this check, my understanding from my then husband was that I was donating to the Southern California College. Charitable donations are not illegal. I did not believe I was doing anything criminal. However, I ignored the hints around me that something nefarious might be going on; ones that should have caused me to question. After much reflection, I know that my actions were very wrong. I willfully turned a blind eye to the warning signs flashing before me, choosing comfortable ignorance while something sinister flourished in the shadows that I refused to examine. I am guilty of creating favor to help my daughter attend SCC. Whether that guilt rises to the level of criminal action, I will let the FBI decide. And they will decide soon. I've been informed that I can expect to be indicted within two days. Rather than hide, I am here to own my part in this."

Waving hands settle as she continues. "My daughter, Bella Jones, is the most capable young woman I know. Intelligent, down to earth in a world that is anything but, and giving of her time and her heart. But the college application world is beyond competitive and highly unpredictable. Even the best students often don't get in to their desired schools these days. So I put my thumb on the scale. Duncan put his whole hand and then some. Regardless, I shouldn't have." She looks directly at the camera. "Bella, I apologize for interfering in a path that was yours to own. But that was never about you. It was about my fears and need for approval. My intentions were honest and good, but their results were not. You are of me, you are not mine, and I am deeply sorry.

"To the woman in the salon, this is for you. So many lives have been impacted, ruined if you will, by my actions and the actions of every guilty party involved in Sinful Admissions. The scandal is criminal. But even the ability to make a legal, charitable donation that may be looked on favorably by a college acceptance board, skews opportunities and disadvantages deserving students. We need to change that." *I need to change that.*

"In an effort to do so, I am launching the Awaken Foundation. The foundation will work to ensure an equal and transparent admissions process to a basic college education for our young adults. First, we will establish an annual scholarship fund to support those who seek a college education but cannot easily access admissions due to their circumstances. I am funding the foundation with an initial endowment of fifty million dollars." The reporters inhale collectively. "And I'll be asking other major organizations to work with us to grow this fund."

"Second, in addition to scholarships, the Awaken Foundation will work with colleges from across the country to develop and implement standards that provide complete transparency in the college admissions process. To date, thirty colleges have already signed on, including several Ivies. We expect to garner the support of at least five hundred, setting basic transparency standards for admissions across our country. My agent, Holly Fisher, will be releasing a detailed statement this evening, the first from the Awaken Foundation."

"One final note. This is about more than just making amends. My need for approval has shaped my entire life—my career choices, my marriage, even how I parent. Today marks the beginning of a different path."

Hands fly up and resume waving.

She takes questions until there are none left. Will she go to jail? Probably, yes. How long? That's for the lawyers to decide. Is she speaking to Bella? Not at the moment. Has she spoken to Dunc since the divorce papers were filed? No. Will the FBI arrest her here? She doesn't know. She's returning to California at the end of the month, regardless. The questions bounce off her as if she's wearing Cleopatra's armor. She places both hands on the sides of the podium, staring out into the brilliant morning sun as she spews answers like arrows. Behind the reporters, she watches three seagulls flying overhead. She hears the boats in the harbor, some ready to ferry passengers once more, others setting sail for an afternoon of fishing. She feels calm and content; a peace she's spent years trying to find.

For the first time in her life, she isn't performing. The truth has set her free.

Once all questions are exhausted, the crowd disperses, exactly as the Chief asked. All at once, a black G-Wagon whips into the gravel parking lot and slides right up along the sidewalk curb, catching everyone's attention. Bradley gets out, leaving the motor running, and slams his door. She walks toward him, and he approaches her like he's on fire.

"I was at the restaurant, listening to your presser. My car just kind of steered its way over here." She reaches out to embrace Bradley. He steps backwards, distancing himself from her. "You did it? You knew."

She sees he's surprised. "Yes. I mean I tried to use my position to help Bella get into school. I don't believe what I did was criminal, although the FBI disagrees, but it wasn't right. I saw text messages on Dunc's phone. I didn't question them. I'm going to have to pay for that. I know that."

"I didn't think you did it. I didn't think you were the kind of person who expects she can buy her way into whatever she wants or needs, legal or not legal. I thought you were level-headed, down to earth. A simple Kansas girl. I thought you were the same Meaghan Jones I fell in love with in St. Thomas twenty years ago. I thought Hollywood couldn't change you."

"I am that same person," Meaghan reassures him.

Bradley's disappointment cuts deeper than his anger would. "That Meaghan wouldn't bribe college officials. That person would respect other people's needs and desires because she feels for them. Understands them. Not cheats and manipulates them."

Meaghan grabs his arm. "Bradley, I've made some mistakes, but that person you're describing, she's right here."

Bradley shakes his head. "I don't think so. After all these years. I've never found anyone else who could make me feel how you did. I've walked away from girlfriends who wanted nothing but to marry me. Amazing women who could have given me a beautiful family. All because I had this flawless picture of you in my head that no one else could ever come close to portraying. I fell in love with you in St. Thomas, you know that. You were unassuming … unpretentious. Quick-witted and humble. Beautiful inside and out. That's the Meaghan Jones I knew. Turns out, after all these years, it was simply my imagination."

"Bradley, please. I'm not perfect—I never was. That flawless picture you've carried isn't real. But the woman standing here, owning her mistakes, trying to make things right—she's real. And she's worth knowing," she pleads with him. Bradley shakes his head and begins to walk backwards, toward the G-Wagon. She walks toward him. Bradley abruptly raises both hands motioning her to stop. "Please!" she screams.

Bradley reaches the driver's side of the G-Wagon, slides in, and pulls away. Dust spews into the air, still so wet after being submerged in flood waters that each tiny particle catches the sunlight and shimmers. She sees only a swirl of stars around her.

As she watches him drive away, she stands taller. She's no longer defined by who loves her or who doesn't. The woman who needed everyone's approval is gone, replaced by a woman who knows her own worth. In two days, they'll come for her with handcuffs and cameras, but they won't find the Meaghan who's been running. They'll find a woman who finally stopped.

THE SUN FEELS AMAZING. ITS WARMTH KISSES EVERY inch of her skin. Palmer sits, feet up, on the chaise lounge now returned to its usual spot on the deck overlooking The Hyacinth's beach. Mandatory bed rest in the sun. Meaghan stares at her laptop on the outdoor dining table, legs extended on the bench seat, scrolling Instagram and X to assess this morning's announcement. Two sailboats glide along the horizon. Although they are not visible, they listen to the faint murmurings of the Life Rolls On announcers, each time followed by loud cheering and drums banging. Somewhere down the beach, Quinn and Aiden are surfing with their buddies while Bella applauds from the shore.

She leans her head back onto her chaise. The sun's warmth can't dissipate the heaviness in her heart. Memories of little Quinn and Aiden sliding onto the sand on their surfboards flood her mind. Miles jumping into the waves, high-fiving them, cheering their ability to remain standing till the end. The announcer interrupts. She sits up and glances at Meaghan face down in her screen. "What's the verdict on this morning on social?"

"So far a mixed bag," Meaghan replies, a hint of frustration in her tone.

"An improvement from the past weeks, then." As she watched Meaghan this morning, she felt a surge of relief. All summer she's wondered what Meaghan had really done and really known. The depths to which Meaghan might have gone, alongside Duncan, to feel loved by all. But this morning, she was elated to watch Meaghan confront the situation head-on. "You did the right thing. Like I said, I thought it went well."

"Except for the part where Bradley told me he hates me?"

"Except for that." She sips her lemonade. "He didn't exactly say he hates you. In fact, you told the press off on his behalf. You instructed them to leave him alone. One might say you fell on your sword for Bradley. And Bella. And me. Thank you."

Meaghan stretches her arms and legs forward, basking in the brilliant sparkling sun. "You're correct. Bradley did not explicitly say he hates me. Instead, he said I'm not the woman he thought I was; that woman captured his heart and he put her on a pedestal because she's so categorically wonderful. That woman he kissed by the beach bonfire the first evening we shared right out there." Meaghan points to the beach before them. "That woman he invited to St. Thomas weeks later, stealing her away to a secluded paradise for five days of laughter, food, and drink, a gazillion rounds of Rummy, and hands-down the hottest sex of my life, falling madly in love." Meaghan throws her head back into the air. "Oh my God, the sex!"

Meaghan's aviators reflect her gaping jaw.

St. Thomas! The past twenty years slowly come into focus for her. "Hold the phone. You went to St. Thomas with *Bradley?*"

"Yep."

"I thought you went to St. Thomas with Dunc!"

"Nope."

"Meaghan, on your wedding day, we were alone in the bridesmaid room, and you told me that when you came back from St. Thomas, you knew exactly what you wanted."

"Oh, I knew exactly what I wanted. What I wanted was Bradley Heartfield," Meaghan says.

She blinks. The layers of Meaghan's emotional turmoil rush to the surface. *She's always loved him, too.*

"After we got back, I started filming *Desperate Nights*. Do you remember Dunc directed that movie? The first and last film we made together. Anyway, Bradley and I had made plans for him to get a house in L.A. and for me to announce our relationship. But I spent all day and most nights with Duncan on set. I quickly became the next thing Dunc needed to conquer. The press began to talk about us as a couple, even though we weren't one yet. They loved the idea of us. I've often wondered if Dunc paid off some paparazzi to get the story started." Meaghan shrugs her shoulders. "I told Bradley I needed some time to deal with the headlines; I needed to get through the movie filming and let the rumors cool down. The last thing I wanted was to subject Bradley to the Hollywood media. He's too good for them."

She can't believe her ears. "Meaghan, I'm your best friend and you never told me any of this."

"You caught us kissing that first night beside the bonfire. After St. Thomas, Bradley and I didn't want to tell anyone, not even you and Miles. We agreed on that. We needed time to figure out if what we had was real, true, and good, on our own first. By the time the *Desperate Nights* filming wrapped, Hollywood had made Duncan and me their new king and queen. The world seemed to think that Dunc and I could accomplish anything we wanted in Hollywood. I wanted everything. And Duncan was charming … in the beginning. Before I knew it, I was pregnant with Bella. Bradley and I emailed for a while until Dunc found them." Meaghan stares into the sky, searching for clouds where there are none. "It was so long ago."

"I can't believe we never knew about St. Thomas. I mean, the fire between you two has been smoldering this entire time. That is obvious. Miles and I used to talk about what an amazing couple you'd make, despite the different worlds you live in. We could see it so clearly," she tells Meaghan. *You couldn't.*

"Fast-forward twenty years and the man hates me. He can't believe the horrible human I've become." Meaghan's shoulders slump, exhaustion coloring her voice.

"Can I get a sidebar?" She scoots to the end of the chaise closer to Meaghan. "Bradley does not hate you. Everything you've told me only proves that point more. He's shocked, Meaghan. You made a mistake, not one you thought was criminal … though in two days, the world may have more to say. You're not alone in this. Everyone makes mistakes."

She raises her hand and says, "Prime example right here. This town is buzzing with rumors that Sanford Banks has fathered my dead husband's baby!"

Meaghan huffs a laugh. "I'll see your small-town rumor and raise you international ruin of name, career, and reputation, which will be mine in less than forty-eight hours."

"We are a pair," she offers compassionately. "Give Bradley some time to come to his senses."

"Everyone keeps saying that. Time. Time. Time. Well, I wish time would hurry up!" Meaghan's head collapses into her hands. "Do you think Bradley will pull out of the Cape May restaurant?"

"Uh, no. I think once Bradley digests all that's happened, he will want to spend all his time with you."

"Maybe." Meaghan refreshes her browser. "The world is confused after this morning. No one loves me, and they all agree I should be in jail. But they respect that I've come clean."

"It's a start."

"It's exhausting. I've said my piece. I've done what I needed to do to be happy with who I am and what I did. Moving on!"

Palmer absorbs the reality of her own situation, "Moving on." She picks up her recently arrived fall edition of *Magnolia Journal* and starts thumbing, searching for solace in something familiar. "I called Frances this morning. She will be reaching out directly to Mack so that we can make the necessary legal changes to run Miles's scholarship fund through the Awaken Foundation. She also couldn't stop asking me baby questions."

"Did you tell her?" Meaghan asks.

"Not yet. I need to tell Harold first. If I'm leaving a career I've spent decades building at a firm with my name on it and his, I owe him the courtesy."

"Will he see it coming?" Meaghan asks.

"I doubt it. Men are blind. But once I tell him I'm co-founding a new foundation to support our youth, I bet I can squeeze a generous donation out of him. I'm leaving behind the workaholic mindset I've always clung to." *A new start.*

Meaghan wipes her palms against her legs, nodding. "You deserve this chance."

"I couldn't think of anyone else I'd rather do this with." She pats her stomach. "I'm excited to build something new. Something completely different than I've done before. The opportunity to be at home is invaluable. I'm not squandering the year I have left with Quinn before he leaves for college. Assuming the kid comes to his senses and comes back home soon. I can't keep worrying about them."

"Nope. They've gotta figure some things out on their own."

The doorbell rings.

Meaghan pops up off the bench. "I'll get it!"

"I think that's obvious."

"I'm expecting something. Or it could be the contractor!" Meaghan navigates through the kitchen doors.

She settles into her thoughts; the anticipation of the moment knots her stomach. What more could happen? The door swings open, and Meaghan returns with an overnight FedEx box and presents the package to Palmer on the palm of her hand, curtseying as if she is the queen. She is the queen. "For you, my lady."

"Always playing a role."

"Not anymore. From here on out, I'm playing myself." Meaghan grins at her. "Open it!"

"What are you expecting? What is this?" Palmer asks.

"I noticed you are missing our fabulous Drip Drop jacket, so I had Claire overnight two—a large size in black to wear while you're pregnant and a small in bright yellow for when you're back to your usual size. See what you think!" Meaghan says.

She eagerly rips open the outside packaging and sets it aside. She reveals a perfectly wrapped silver box with a white velvet ribbon. "I don't think this is an Awaken raincoat. Or two!" She turns the box over in her hand inspecting all sides. She gasps. Her hand flies to her heart, a second time. "It's from Carlucci's."

"Where Miles bought your engagement ring."

"Yes. Carlucci's is a gem."

Meaghan picks up the FedEx box. "There's a note." Meaghan hands her a white-sealed envelope with her name on it. She opens the envelope and reads the card inside to herself. "What does it say?"

She chokes back her tears and reads the card out loud. "Palmer, some time ago, Miles asked me to send this to him on this date at this address. He's not with us, so I'm sending it to you. We miss him dearly. Miles was one of the good ones. He loved you like no one else I've ever seen. Over the years, I've seen a lot. Our hearts are with you and the boys. Come visit us when you're in town next time. Much love, Sil Carlucci."

Meaghan sits down on the chaise beside her. She pulls the ribbon and opens the silver box. From inside it, she pulls out a smaller navy-blue velvet ring box and a tiny notecard. Taking the card from its snug envelope, she can see it's in Miles's handwriting. "He wrote this note himself."

"Palmer, my love. Twenty years ago, today, I made the best decision of my life. Even though you leave the lights on in every room of the house and often work too late." The two women laugh through their tears. "You make every day worth living. You are my everything. I'll love you for eternity. Yours forever, Miles." She sets the card down and flips open the velvet box. An emerald-cut diamond eternity band catches the sunlight—a symbol of their undying bond.

She pulls it out and places it on her finger, marveling at its beauty. "Twenty years next week. Seems like yesterday."

Meaghan turns to her, "Damn. Miles was the absolute best."

"The absolute best." Her chest tightens with memories, but within her, resilience rises. She contemplates the paths before her—grief, hope, and an uncertain future. At her side, Meaghan anchors her, both women ready for the storm ahead.

Chapter 20

THE LATE-AUGUST SUN PAINTS THE CAPE HENLOPEN beach in amber. After tucking Palmer in for an afternoon nap, her condition stabilized but still high risk, Meaghan paces along the shoreline, picking up smooth stones and skipping them into the surf, gazing into the depths beyond her.

"Mom." The sound is so faint, she wonders if she's dreaming. "Mom."

She turns around. Bella appears over the dunes, Aiden beside her. Her heart clenches. Her daughter's hair whips in the breeze—so like her own, yet somehow wilder, freer. Aiden squeezes Bella's hand, whispers something in her ear, then retreats back toward The Hyacinth. It's like seeing her daughter for the first time. *She looks like a grown woman.*

"Bella." Bella wraps her arms underneath Meaghan's and latches on. "Oh Bella," Meaghan says, squeezing her daughter as tight as she can.

Bella begins to sob. "I've lost everything, Mom. Everything." Bella breaks open like a fire hydrant in the city on a hot summer day, tears gushing everywhere. Meaghan holds on tight. "I've lost Dad. I've lost all my friends. I've lost my school—everyone glares at me on campus, I hate going there. And now you're going to jail, too."

"Oh sweetheart, I'm so sorry. I screwed up. Dad screwed up. And you're paying the price." She strokes Bella's hair. "I know you feel like you've lost everything, but you haven't. Trust me that you haven't." She lifts Bella's face and looks her daughter in the eyes.

"Want to walk?"

Bella nods, falling into step beside her. The waves crash against their silence. No cameras, no lawyers, no handlers. Just mother and daughter.

"I used to carry you on my hip during every audition," she finally says. "Did you know that? You'd wrap your little arms around my neck so tight, like you were trying to give me strength. But really, you were the strong one. You always have been."

"Mom—"

"Please. Let me get this out." Meaghan stops, turning to face her daughter. "I promised you everything, and here it is: Your father orchestrated the whole thing. The bribes, all of it. But that's not the real truth you need to hear."

She takes a shaky breath. "The real truth is that I failed you. Not because I signed those papers—though God knows that was wrong—but because I didn't trust you. I was so scared of you feeling unworthy, unloved, the way I always have, that I tried to buy you success instead of letting you earn it. I tried to control your future instead of letting you build it."

"Like with Awaken," Bella says quietly. "Creating this perfect image."

"Exactly like that. Everything in my life has been about maintaining the facade. Perfect actress, perfect mother, perfect brand." Her laugh transforms into a sob. "I was so busy trying to make you feel worthy, because I didn't, that I never saw how worthy you already were. Grandma Blessing told you that my father died."

Bella nods and her phone buzzes in her pocket, but she silences it without looking. "When you were a little girl. I know it was awful, Mom."

She exhales deeply, searching for the words. *No more lies.* She takes Bella's hands in her own. "It's not true. I've never known how to tell you what really happened, so I said nothing. I let you believe Grandma Blessing."

"What happened?"

"He left us. He went to work one morning and never came back. I never heard from him again. I have no idea where he is or if he's even alive. And I don't care to know. He chose to leave us."

"Why did Grandma lie?"

"Embarrassed, I'd guess. Denial, maybe? It was awful. I felt rejected, deserted. I can only imagine how she felt. I've been trying to fill the hole he left ever since. I've spent a lifetime seeking other people's love to try to make up for losing my father's, slipping into so many roles so I didn't have to play my own. I realize that now. And when your dad and I had you, I tried with all my might to make sure you had your father's love. I want you to know that you do. Your dad has made some pretty big mistakes, but he loves you, very much." Tears fall down Bella's cheeks.

"Dad said you knew everything. About the bribes, about Chip Sullivan—"

"I didn't. But I should have asked questions. Should have looked closer when Duncan had me sign those checks to SCC

Farms. Should have wondered why Thorne Cassidy was suddenly so interested in our finances."

Bella's head snaps up. "Lassie's dad?" Her cell buzzes again.

"Mack thinks he might have been wearing a wire at your birthday party. The FBI flipped him early, had him gather evidence against all of us. That's the working theory anyway." Meaghan wipes her eyes. "But that's simply more Hollywood drama. The real story—the one that matters—is how I lost sight of what was real. Of who you are."

"And who am I?" Bella's voice wavers.

"You're the girl who taught herself calculus when your tutor said you couldn't handle it. Who spent three summers interning at homeless shelters instead of taking the acting jobs I pushed at you. Who stood up in front of cameras and chose truth over protection." She reaches for her daughter's hand. "You're braver than I ever have been."

"I was so angry," Bella whispers. "Not just about SCC. About everything. I look back on all my achievements and I wonder if they were real or if you and Dad had bought it for me."

"I know. And I'm so sorry, baby. You deserve to know that everything you've achieved—your grades, your volunteer work, your strength—that's all you. No checks, no bribes, no Hollywood magic. Just my amazing daughter."

Bella's fingers tighten around hers. "I saw what happened with Awaken. The sales, the cancelled show."

"Turns out you can't build a brand on authenticity while living a lie." She smiles sadly. "But maybe that's the lesson I needed. Sometimes everything has to fall apart before you can build something real."

"Like me and Aiden?" Suddenly, Bella glows.

"Like you and Aiden. When I saw you defending him from those reporters, saw how he protected you ... that's when I knew. You don't need my protection anymore. You need my trust."

The sun dips lower, turning the ocean to fire. Bella steps closer, resting her head on Meaghan's shoulder.

"I'm not ready to forgive everything," Bella says softly. "But I'm ready to try."

She wraps her arm around her daughter, feeling the strength in her. "That's more than I deserve. And it's everything I need."

They stand together as the light fades, two women finding their way back to truth, back to each other.

Bella's cell rings a third time. "Someone really wants to talk to you." Bella pulls her cell out of her jacket pocket. Her head tilts. Bella turns the phone around and shows her the screen. Lassie Cassidy's face and name flash across the screen.

"Answer it," Meaghan says.

LASSIE DIVES STRAIGHT INTO OBNOXIOUS BEST FRIEND mode. "Hey, B. I'm back in Cali for a few weeks." She sits kicking her legs in the cool pool water of her family's L.A. home. Her FaceTime filter makes the world around her appear in vivid golden hues.

Meaghan watches through Bella's screen, assessing Lassie's ever-flashing smile. Excitement mixes with caution in her gut. Bella grudgingly plays along. "Oh. Shoot, I can't get together," Bella says before Lassie can even ask.

"Pourquoi pas?" Lassie smiles and shimmies her shoulders. "That means, why not? I'm learning French. I'm applying to universities in Quebec province. Toronto is getting old, already."

"Cool. French-speaking Quebec? Very idyllic." Bella fake swoons, but Meaghan can see a hint of unease flit across Bella's face, a mask they both wear too well. "Anyway, sorry I can't hang. I'm on the East Coast."

"Yeah, I totally saw that whole thing." Lassie splashes her feet ferociously, as if her splash was a drum roll. "Not why I was calling. I've been at home going through stuff to take with me back to Canada 'cause I'm gonna be there a while. I found something I think your mom might want."

Meaghan's hands fly into the air behind Bella's screen. Why in the world would she want anything from Lassie? Bella reads her hand language. "Oh, that's sweet of you to think of my mom. But I'm sure whatever it is you can give to someone else. I appreciate you thinking of her, though."

"I think she will want this." Lassie sips Coke out of a can from a straw. "It's a phone."

Meaghan's eyes nearly pop out of her head. So many questions swirl—what phone, where did Lassie find it, and why is she offering it now?

Bella pauses, contemplating what to say next. "Why would my mom want a phone that you found?"

"Because I looked through it. There's a lot of stuff on there. Text messages between my dad and Chip Sullivan. They mention your mom." Lassie stops her splashing, the gravity of the revelation sinking in. "Look, I don't know what all went down. But from what I can tell, I think this could help your mom out."

"What do the text messages say?" Bella's voice carries a mix of curiosity and wariness.

"A lot," Lassie says. "Too much for me to comprehend everything, but I can tell enough to know this phone will benefit your mom." Lassie looks down at her Coke. She slurps the last of it loudly. "I always loved her, ya know? She made me feel … welcomed." Lassie sets her empty Coke can down on the pool deck, sincerity glimmering in her eyes. "I haven't told my dad. Can't seem to reach him. He's traveling in Europe. Oh well." Lassie shrugs her shoulders. "How can I get this to you?"

Meaghan senses that, much like her own daughter, Lassie has had enough of being underestimated.

She pivots her focus to Bella, sensing the tension in the air. She knows they must decide quickly—evaluate whether to trust Lassie and her intentions.

Bella mutes the FaceTime and glances at her. "I think we should listen to her."

"Are you sure?" Meaghan's heart beats faster, recognizing the weight of Bella's choice to trust not only Lassie, but her mother too.

"Yeah," Bella replies, her voice firming. "We need evidence to confirm Mack's suspicions, right? And we don't have much time. Maybe this is it?"

A smile breaks through her apprehension. They step into a new chapter, together.

Chapter 21

THERE'S A KNOCK ON PALMER'S BEDROOM DOOR. HER eyes fly open. Sunlight pours through the window, splintering into a rainbow across the floor.

"Come in," she says not wasting precious standing time on crossing the room to open the door. Bradley quietly swings the door open and enters.

"Hello," he says.

"Bradley," she responds, surprised. "I wasn't expecting you."

"Me neither," he says, stepping into the light. "I hope it's okay I'm here?"

"Of course it's okay. You're family." She remembers her first morning this summer on the Cape when she ran into Bradley at Big Fish Market, their shared grief so raw and on display. He was exactly who she needed to see at that very moment. But the last time she saw him, the morning after the storm swept across the Cape and they went to the ice cream cone house, he was incensed with her because of Sanford. Openly accusatory and in front of the kids. It's been a week since Meaghan's press conference and neither of them have seen or spoken to him.

He walks over to the bed and stands beside her, "May I?" She nods and slides over. He sits down on the bed beside her. He looks like he hasn't slept in a million years. Bags bulge under his eyes, and his hair is uncombed like a stack of hay. He wears a face full of stubble, scruffy and ragged, like their turmoil. "I owe you an apology."

"Wow!" She turns her chin. "Not what I was expecting."

"I ran into Sanford last night at Foretelina."

"Ah." She nods. "Everyone's late-night go-to."

"It wasn't a pretty scene. I ripped into Sanford at the bar. I shouldn't have, but … Miles was my best friend. He isn't here and, whether right or not, I feel like it's my job to take up his arms."

"I've kind of noticed," she tells him. "You've been so attentive with me, especially since finding out about this one." Palmer places her hand on her stomach. Her pregnancy and emotions weigh heavier than ever. "I've been silently grateful. But your condemnation the other morning … in front of the boys." She scolds him with her tone and shakes her head. "What happened with Sanford?"

"I punched him. Without saying a word. I punched him."

"Jesus, Bradley. He doesn't deserve that."

"He does, but I apologized afterwards. Then he told me everything."

"What did he say?"

"That he kissed you and he shouldn't have. That he was in the middle of this whole Cinnamon thing, feeling like no one wanted him. That you're his best friend." Bradley stares at her.

"We're work besties, you know that. Miles knew that. He also knew that only he could be my truest, best friend."

"I know," Bradley says, his expression softening. "Sanford told me he was so down on himself that he took advantage of your friendship when he knew better."

She looks down and pulls at the edge of her comforter. "I did kiss him back." She breathes deeply and closes her eyes, remembering. "But the minute my lips touched his, I knew. Miles is the only one for me."

"You two had been arguing," he interjects.

Palmer perceives that Bradley knows pretty much everything. But does he know everything? "Yes," she says, her voice tighter. "We had been arguing. It was bad."

"Miles mentioned it, but only once. Said it was driving him crazy. That he knew he was to blame for being so damn foolish about Aiden, but that he couldn't help how he felt. Said it wasn't your fault, it wasn't Aiden's fault; he was the only one to blame for weeks of silence and he knew it. He told me he felt lost without you, Palmer. When you called him and invited him home for lunch, as soon as you asked, poof ... his foolishness about Aiden vanished."

"Miles told you that?"

"Yes. We spoke the morning he had his stroke. I called to line up our June tee times at the club. He was giddy with love for you, Palmer. He told me what had happened and how he wished he could erase the past month but that it didn't even matter because he loved Aiden no matter what he chose to do with his life. He said you two were finally back to being as in love as ever. He said, 'The Hardings are back.'" Sanford makes air quotes with his hands. "You guys have always been the perfect couple. Even when you're arguing."

She grins a bittersweet smile and shakes her head. "Why on God's green earth did you wait all summer to tell me this?"

"You two made up. I didn't see the point in bringing up your argument. But when you admitted to kissing Sanford before that evening, my mind was blown. I didn't understand how that could happen. Until I talked to Sanford."

"You mean punched him?"

"Punched and then talked." Bradley looks out the window. Sunlight bathes the room in a golden hue. Late afternoon dawns, and the deep-blue ocean dances in its light. She notices Bradley appears uncomfortable all at once. "There's one other thing Miles told me a long time ago. I think given all that's transpired, he would have told you himself."

She stares at Bradley. He can't look her in the eyes. She can't stop looking at his. *He knows.* She takes her hand still folded in his and puts hers on top. She pats his. "The nurse?" she asks.

Bradley's head snaps to attention. He looks at Palmer, eyes wide. "You know?"

"I know," she says. "I found a journal he kept. Did you know about the journal?" Bradley shakes his head. "Me neither. He kept it at the office. Everything Miles couldn't say to me, he wrote in that journal." She raises an eyebrow. "Or confided in you, it seems."

Bradley smiles, "He was my very best friend."

She nods. "Anyway, he journaled that night in the hospital, and I read it."

"Okay," Bradley says digesting her words.

"I went through all the emotions—anger, hate, betrayal, sadness, and ... understanding. Marriages are tested. People are not perfect. In the end, they learn what they mean to one another. Perhaps the glimpse of something else was all it took to drive us right back into each other's arms. That's what matters." Palmer looks out the window. She watches the waves go in and out. She tilts her head and looks at Bradley, "Why is Sanford in town … again?"

"I asked the same question. Although I asked because I accused him of hanging around you all summer, angling for a widow's vulnerability."

"Bradley!" she says emphatically.

He shrugs. "This is where it gets interesting. Sanford told me that once Cinnamon tried to blackmail him, he hired his own private investigator. So far the PI has discovered that Cinnamon has had three affairs."

Palmer's mouth hangs open. "The longest one, which appears to have been going on for at least a few years, is with someone who lives on the Cape."

Palmer covers her eyes with her hands, "No!"

"Apparently the PI has narrowed the options down to a few unlucky guys. Sanford said that he keeps coming out here to meet with the PI … and do a little digging himself."

"Who could it be?" Palmer asks.

"Zero idea. And also I don't care."

"Thank you for being Miles's best friend."

"God, I miss him," Bradley says earnestly.

"Me too."

A pulse of longing fills the space momentarily as they both become lost in memories.

Bradley stands up. He presses the creases from his Bermuda shorts. "I have another surprise for you."

"Who else did you punch?"

Bradley smirks. "Your children are downstairs."

"What?" Palmer radiates joy. "How did you get them to come here?"

"I told them what Sanford told me."

Her palms touch and she brings her hands to her chest. "Thank you," she whispers.

"We had quite the chat over three giant root beer floats. You realize all this time, up until learning about your kiss with Sanford, Aiden has blamed himself for Miles's stroke?"

"I suspected that, yes. I haven't been sure what to do about it. Until recently, he didn't appear to even acknowledge that he'd lost his father."

"Well, like I told you, I also told Aiden exactly what Miles told me that morning. That he knew his response to Aiden's opportunity with that professor was nothing but his own pure jealousy. How very proud of Aiden he was. Quinn too for that matter."

"Miles told you how proud he was of the boys that very morning?"

"Yeppers. And I made sure the boys will never forget." He exhales. "I think a burden has lifted off Aiden's shoulders. He was light as a feather afterwards."

"Thank you." She offers Bradley a Namaste gesture, expressing her deep gratitude. "One thing, you didn't tell the boys about the nurse, did you?"

"Never. That one's between me and you."

"Perfect. I can't believe they're downstairs!"

"Doesn't hurt that I paid them each a hundred bucks to get in the car and didn't tell them where I was going. So, good luck!" She rolls her eyes at Bradley, who chuckles. "Only kidding. I think you'll find Aiden and Quinn a little more forgiving. They love you, Palmer." She melts into the pillow behind her. "You're their mother. And you're an amazing mother. Miles always said so." He bends down and hugs her.

"I am so grateful to you," she whispers.

"I'll send them up?"

Palmer sits up straight in bed. Her adrenaline surges. She smooths her hair into place. "Right away."

After a few moments, the boys enter the master suite wearing mixed expressions, hesitation and hope. They startle slightly finding her in bed, medicine bottles on her nightstand.

"Mom," Aiden says first, the tension palpable in the air.

"Hey, honey ..." Palmer starts, but before she can finish, Quinn steps forward, his voice slightly shaky.

"Is it true? About you and Sanford?"

She swallows hard and nods, bracing herself for their reactions. "It is. We shared one kiss, when your father and I were arguing, and I immediately knew how very much I loved your father. But it shouldn't have happened, and I am so sorry for how it must have made both of you feel. I lost myself with everything happening. But I want to be honest about it, and I want us to move forward together."

Aiden looks down, his shoulders tense. "The whole thing is my fault. If I hadn't ..."

"No!" she interrupts, her voice filled with urgency. "You need to hear me clearly right now: You are not responsible for what happened. Your father's choices are not your fault. You did nothing wrong."

Quinn nods, but Aiden looks torn. "If I had handled things differently, if I hadn't grown distant, it could have been different."

"We're all figuring this out as we go," she tells him, reaching for his hand. "I was lost too. We won't be perfect, but we have a chance to come back to each other. I need you both to know how much I love you."

Tears fill Aiden's eyes as he finally meets Palmer's gaze. "I just miss Dad so much. And I didn't want to lose you too."

"I miss him too," she admits, an ache rolling through her voice. "Every single day. I can't erase the past, but I promise to be here for both of you. We will create new memories together as a family."

"Together," Quinn repeats, his voice steady. "We still have each other. No matter what."

Aiden nods vigorously. The dam has broken, releasing the pent-up grief and love around them.

She pulls them both into a hug. "We can walk this path together," she whispers against their shoulders. "No more secrets. Only love and honesty, wherever that leads us."

MEAGHAN WATCHES BELLA, AIDEN, AND QUINN SIT ON the freshly recarpeted floor of the great room, scrolling through their phones. Bella's head rests on Aiden's shoulder. Quinn sits across from them, at times playing footsies to annoy them both. Palmer ordered two new sofas to replace the ones wrecked by wind and rain in the storm, but they're backordered and won't arrive until October. No one cares. The vast glass walls in the great room, restored by George DaSilva, once again frame breathtaking views of the cresting sea, reflecting Meaghan's internal shift.

As Meaghan leans against the wall, Miles's original hand sketch of The Hyacinth hangs proudly above her. She sips a Coke Zero and wonders whether Lassie Cassidy might set her free today. But underneath her hopeful facade, a gnawing dread lingers—the indictment is expected anytime now and this phone might be her only shot at salvation.

Her phone rings, breaking the nail-biting silence. She hesitates. Bella looks up at her. She shakes her head. "Holly." The kids return to their phones.

"Hey, Holls," she says, meandering into the kitchen and settling into the island barstool. "Anything?" Both she and Holly have been anxiously awaiting even the smallest interest in a script for her since the presser.

"Nothing," Holly replies, the disappointment palpable. "I'm sorry."

"It's okay," she says waving her hand through the air. "I didn't really expect a role, only hoped."

"Me too," Holly admits. "I've been thinking … it's time for a change. Would you be open to me approaching your career outside of the Hollywood Box? I've got a few ideas and some contacts I can reach out to."

"Like what? Commercials?"

"Oh no, not commercials. You're America's sweetheart. We can't have you selling insurance. Think bigger—opportunities for different roles. Not on the big screen."

"Work your magic, Holly," she says, "The only thing is, obviously, I can't start a new project until I'm released from jail. Do you think I'll have a career after I get out of jail?"

"Martha Stewart sure the hell does," Holly remarks.

"She sure does," Meaghan says slowly as the idea hits her like a jack-in-the-box, both exhilarating and terrifying. Her call waiting goes off. She pulls her cell from her ear and looks at it to see who is calling.

"I've got to take this," she says and then adds, "Martha Stewart the hell out of my options, Holls."

"Will do."

She taps the green "Hold and Accept" button and screams Bella's name while walking back into the great room.

"Hi, Meaghan!" Mack's voice rings through the speaker. Bella crawls on her knees from Aiden to her as she crouches on the floor by the wall.

"Hi. I've got Bella here on speaker. And, for that matter, Aiden and Quinn, too."

"Hey, everybody. I've got JP Donahue at my side as well." Mack's tone radiates urgency. "We've got some news. Magnificent news!" Bella's smile radiates hope. "Thorne's phone is legit. It's never been erased. It holds conversations dating back several years."

JP Donahue chimes in, "Meaghan, that phone is your get-out-of-jail-free card."

She gasps loudly. The palm of her hand meets her forehead. "Really?"

"Yes, ma'am."

"What's on it?"

Mack takes back the conversational reins. "There are a whole lot of pretty damn important conversations recorded on this baby. But the one that's your ticket is between Thorne and Chip Sullivan, a month before the FBI arrests."

"Okay," she says, coaxing Mack along as if he needs to be.

"Sullivan tells Thorne he thinks the Feds are on to him—which is ironic, because at this point Thorne is working with the Feds, recording this very conversation. Sullivan explains that he's devised a brilliant, fool-proof plan to evade the Feds … along with Duncan Jones."

"Oh God," she says and turns to Bella. "Bella, maybe I should hear this alone first."

Bella snaps her fingers at her. "Uh-uh. Nope. Let's hear it, Mack." Bella grabs her free hand and one of Aiden's. She nods at Bella. *My baby is all grown up and in control of her own life now.*

"Sullivan tells Thorne that Duncan has agreed to pin the entire thing on you, Meaghan. That Dunc duped you into writing the check. Sullivan says, and I quote, 'Duncan asked Meaghan to donate to the college. She gladly did. She had no idea it was really a bribe. She's committed a felony and didn't even realize. If we get busted, she gets busted. That's the beauty. The Feds will never send Meaghan Jones to jail, she's untouchable. She's America's sweetheart. Having her in on the scheme will protect our asses.'"

Mack translates. "They thought involving you would get them off the hook. It's kind of like the opposite of guilty by association."

"What a bunch of dipshits," JP adds bitterly. "Instead, the FBI did the exact opposite. They made an example out of you. And used Thorne to do it."

"Until now," Mack says. "We've done a little more digging on Thorne. Did you know Thorne is a rowing coach at Beverly Hills High?"

"I knew he was a coach somewhere, but I never paid much attention," she says.

"Same," Bella says. "Why would we? Since elementary school, Mr. Cassidy has always just been Lassie's dad. Drives you to the mall when needed."

"Well, three years ago, Coach Thorne became aware of the scam Sullivan was selling through his coaching position," Mack explains. "He wanted in on it. That's when he wrote the check, securing a spot for Lassie in the scheme."

"Think of it as a pre-paid discount," JP says.

Mack continues. "The FBI was already on to Sullivan. They needed to build a case, though. So they flipped Thorne. He wrote your fake resume, Bella. Everyone thought it was Sullivan, but the FBI screwed up the handwriting analysis, perhaps intentionally. It was Thorne. He admits to doing so to keep everything in play and help draw Duncan in further."

"Oh my God," Bella says, the realization dawning on her.

Meaghan turns to Bella. "Well, that explains your mysterious equestrian career." She pauses for a moment. "But if Thorne was working for the FBI, why would he whisper to me that 'we're screwed' the night before the FBI arrests?"

"He didn't want to blow his cover. Sullivan already knew the FBI was coming for him. People were talking, they were worried. By being worried too, Thorne kept himself disguised," JP explains. "And that's why the FBI never arrested him."

She sees the story fall into place, but there's something still off. "Why did the FBI never have his phone?"

"Bureaucratic failure. The FBI never came looking for it. So Thorne tossed it in the family junk drawer," Mack explains.

"I don't know what he did to piss off his daughter, Lassie, but it must have been pretty bad for her to find this phone and turn it over to you," JP blurts out.

Bella looks at her. "It was." Meaghan wraps her arm around Bella's shoulder, sensing the unity between them.

"What do we now?" she asks, leaning forward, her voice barely above a whisper.

"We're submitting the phone and all its data into the court record this afternoon," JP declares confidently. "We've got an appointment with the prosecutor's office in three hours. We expect them to drop all possible charges."

This is it. A wave of disbelief washes over her.

"I'll let you know when everything's settled," Mack reassures her. "Congrats, Meaghan."

"I'm speechless," she replies. "But what if it is not enough?"

"It's enough," JP confirms. "We'll be in touch." The line drops.

Meaghan's arms fall to her sides. She wants to jump for joy, but instead feels like she could collapse. The weight lifted from her was heavier than she knew. She's exhausted and exhilarated.

Bella throws her arms around her like she's a little girl home from sleepaway camp, squeezing tighter and tighter. Aiden follows, wrapping his arms around both her and Bella. Quinn stands up and embraces all three of them. Tears fill her eyes. She's vindicated. But, more than anything, she's steeped in love. It surrounds her edges and bubbles up from within.

Chapter 22

EVERYONE'S HOME. ONLY THREE DAYS OF SUMMER RE-main before everyone goes their separate ways for the fall. Palmer wakes up at three o'clock in the afternoon to a wild rumpus echoing through the house. It begins in the hallway outside her bedroom door, spills down the stairs, into the kitchen, and out onto the beach. Their voices float up. Aiden's. Quinn's. Meaghan's. Bella's. Are the boys tossing a football?

The sweet smell of simmering garlic and fennel catches Palmer's nose. Is Bradley cooking? Are Bella and Meaghan with him in the kitchen? When she hears the word "bonfire," she remembers. It's the last Sunday in August. In a few hours, they will spread Miles's ashes along The Hyacinth's shore followed by a beach bonfire dinner, because that was always his favorite thing to do on a Sunday summer evening.

She gets out of bed and walks into her closet off the master bath, gently cradling her belly. Dr. Harlow now permits her slow, brief movement from one spot to another within the house. She grabs a step stool, and the sunlight pouring in through the window turns her eternity ring into a disco ball as she reaches for the breadbox.

What remains of Miles fits in a box. The husband who was her rock through all the hard times, promising their perseverance while battling his innermost fears quietly by himself. The father who showed up at every practice, coached every game, steered their boys into young manhood, and struggled desperately to let them go. He was perfect, and he was flawed. Every beautiful thing he was, is now reduced to bits and silt that fit into a bread box. It is unfair. It is wrong. And yet right beside this box is a new life that he created. They're all still here, every one of their lives touched and shaped by him.

The only way to keep Miles alive is for us to keep on living.

She returns to bed. Her phone buzzes beside her. It's the call she's been dreading. She picks up the phone and answers, "Hi, Harold."

"Palmer! How's the baby?" She feels guilty for not having told Harold she's expecting before her ride in the ambulance with Sanford, after which word quickly traveled across Delaware and Virginia, into the heart of the D.C. legal circuit. Harold doesn't seem dismayed.

"We're good, thank you for asking," she responds. "How's everything with you?"

"All good here. Made it back to the office for a few quiet days in August before the return of every vacationer on the East Coast. It's peaceful. Needless to say, the missus ain't too happy I'm here. I've left her with seven grandkids on Nantucket."

She imagines Harold sitting back in his large leather desk chair looking out his window down Constitution Avenue at the Capitol. The sweltering summer sun and unbearable humidity roasting tourists as they walk along the Mall. "We've sure been missing you this summer. Can't wait to see ya back in the office."

"About that, Harold."

"Mmmhmmm."

"Harold, this baby and Miles's stroke, it all really changes the calculus for me." She takes a deep breath.

"What do you mean, changes the calculus?"

"I'm not coming back, Harold." As soon as the words come out, she feels a weight lift. "I'm a single parent now. I have a senior in high school and a new baby. I can't be running to the office all the time, dealing with demanding clients at their every whim and ever-changing court calendars. It will be too much."

"Listen, Palmer, I get it. I really do. You know how many babies the missus and I have raised? It's a hell of a commitment, especially on your own. But we're here to support you. We'll make it work. I may be old, but I can be flexible. Don't walk away from a career you've spent decades building. You're at the top of your game now, honey. Despite the kerfuffle with SuperSonic. We want you back."

She presses her lips together, half-smiling and shaking her head. "The thing is … I don't want to come back."

"What do you mean you don't want to come back?" Harold sounds perplexed. "You can have it all, Palmer. We can help you."

"No, Harold, I can't have it all. I've realized this summer that it is impossible for anyone to have it all. Something is always sacrificed. I've spent a lifetime pulled in a million different directions, always achieving and always working to make sure others are happy—clients and colleagues, the boys, Miles—without making sure I truly am."

"You haven't been happy?"

It's a question she's been contemplating all summer. "I've been happy. I could be happier. Look, I love Mintz, Krowl & Harding. I love my career!"

"I don't get it," Harold interrupts, confused. "If you love your career, why are you leaving it?"

"It turns out, I love me more."

Silence permeates the line. "Okay," he says finally, retreating. "I love you like my own daughter, Palmer. You'll always have a place here if you change your mind."

"I know, Harold. I love you too."

"Enjoy your last days of summer, and we'll work out the details when you're back in the city."

"Thank you," she whispers.

She can hear Harold stand up and walk over to his windows. She imagines him teetering back and forth on his loafers. "Hey, one last thing, have you heard from Sanford?" he asks.

She isn't sure what to say. Does Harold think Sanford is the baby's father like everyone on Cape Henlopen? Surely not, but it's a possibility. Gossip doesn't understand territorial boundaries. "No, I haven't spoken with Sanford in many weeks, now."

"I heard from a very discrete source that Cinnamon has been partaking of several side dishes over the years. I always suspected; she's a bit of a floozy, Palmer. She once hit on me at the D.C. Bar Association Christmas Party at the Hay-Adams Hotel Bar. Imagine, hitting on me! I'm a geezer. Anyway, I heard the longest fling has been with someone on the Cape, which of course made me think of you."

Palmer's ears perk up. "Really?"

"Hand to Jesus. Everyone at my poker game last week was talking about Cinnamon. One fella kept referring to Cinnamon's fling as Santa Claus? I have no idea why, but he must be one jolly guy." Palmer freezes. "The guys said Mrs. Claus, I presume his wife, caught them together in June. Anyway, that little rumor hasn't caught fire here, and we all promised to keep a lid on it, for Sanford's sake. But I thought you might want to know."

"I won't say word," Palmer tells him.

"Goodbye, Palmer," Harold says and hangs up.

She can't believe her ears. Her mind goes wild connecting the dots. There's only one man who plays Santa Claus. Locals line up to visit him at Christmas Towne each December in the Rehoboth Village square. And, along with summer vacationers, they watch him navigate his until-this-year-award-winning entry in the July Fourth Boat Parade.

She sets the phone on the table beside her. Miles's ashes are still on her lap. "Oh!" she hollers loudly, causing Meaghan to fly through the kitchen, up the stairs, and burst into her room. Bradley follows behind her.

"What's wrong?" Meaghan asks. "Are you okay?"

"Oh! I can't believe it!" she shouts.

"What?" Meaghan begs.

"Harold just told me … in not so many words," she shakes her index finger in the air. "I think Cinnamon is having an affair with Jonathan Shaw! Apparently, it's been going on for years."

A slow smirk appears on Meaghan's face as the implications sink in.

"Why are you smiling? It's awful! Poor Sanford."

Bradley throws Meaghan a surprised look. Meaghan stops smiling. "Okay, yes, it is. You're right. But … the gossip that will ensue will give Darby a little taste of her own medicine."

She considers the notion. "Or not," Palmer says. "I'm calling Darby right now. Someone should check in on her." She winks.

She presses Darby's contact. When Darby picks up, Palmer tells her the gossip she's heard about Cinnamon and Santa. Darby denies hearing anything of the sort. "That's good, because that kind of untrue gossip can be so hurtful," she says, and Darby vehemently agrees.

Next, she asks Darby if she can help end the nasty, untrue rumor that Sanford is her baby's father. "I'm having Miles's baby, Darby. Those rumors need to end."

And just like that, they do.

THE EVENING SKY BLAZES WITH ORANGES AND PINKS AS the sun slowly descends. Meaghan watches Bradley on the beach, carefully arranging driftwood for the bonfire, while Aiden and Quinn toss a football nearby. They've been awkwardly polite around each other since that morning in the police department parking lot when he made it clear he wanted nothing to do with her.

Inside, she helps Bella stack graham crackers, Hershey's chocolate bars, and giant, oversized marshmallows onto a melamine platter. They're having Miles's favorite meal for a Sunday evening supper—steamed mussels in a garlic-and-sausage broth and grilled flank steak on baby bib lettuces with blue cheese, and s'mores roasted on the bonfire.

"I'm going to take the platter out to the Yeti so the chocolate won't melt," Bella says.

"Why don't you let me," she offers, grabbing the platter from her hands. She needs this moment.

The sea breeze catches her hair, sending strands dancing across her face. She tucks them behind her ear and takes a deep breath of salt air, gathering her courage. As she approaches, Bradley looks up. Their eyes meet across the sand, and for a moment, everything else falls away—the boys playing, the crackling fire, the gentle rhythm of waves—leaving only the two of them in a world that suddenly feels achingly familiar. This is where it all began, on a summer night much like this one, when they were younger and unbound by the future.

"Hi," she says, her voice nearly lost in the sound of the surf.

"Hello," Bradley replies. There's caution in his eyes, but also a small glimmer. Her heartbeat quickens.

She sets the platter down on a nearby blanket. "I was hoping we could talk." She realizes that they're alone for the first time since she kissed him in front of the restaurant in the rain. Her palms grow sweaty. She wonders if enough time has passed, like Palmer suggested, for Bradley to come to his senses and if the recent discoveries might have helped. She clears her throat. "I need to say a few things to you."

"Okay," he says. They move away from the others, their feet sinking into the cooling sand. The setting sun casts long shadows ahead of them. They walk in silence until they reach a quiet stretch of beach, the exact spot where they first spoke all those years ago—where he'd first told her she had starlight in her eyes.

"I made a mistake." She stops to face him, looking into his deep-blue eyes. They're the color of the ocean; she desperately wishes she could swim away in them. She takes a breath, refocuses, and attempts to avoid the distraction. "After our week in St. Thomas, I knew the thing I wanted most in this world was to spend my life with you. I felt it with every ounce of my being."

Bradley's face remains devoid of emotion, but he doesn't look away.

"I remember every detail of our week together in St. Thomas," she continues. "The way you traced patterns on my back as we watched the sunrise. How you knew exactly how I liked my coffee without asking. The sound of your laugh echoing across the water when I tried to paddle board." She pauses, swallowing hard. "But I got swept up in Hollywood. You were right about that the other day. And, then, I got pregnant with Bella, and after growing up without my own father, I needed to make sure she had hers. So I married Duncan. And I couldn't let you go, so I quietly kept you near. Our exchanges were what lit me up those years. But when Duncan found them, I couldn't risk breaking up Bella's family."

She buries her toes in the sand, gathering her courage. "So, I let all these years go by. Seeing you over the summers, pretending nothing had happened between us, leaving so many questions and feelings unresolved between us."

The waves crash gently behind them, a steady backdrop to her racing heart. "You said the other day that you didn't marry, didn't start a family, because you had this perfect image in your head of who you wanted to spend your life with—an image of me. I am so sorry for that. I would never want you to miss out on something magical, like having children, Bradley, because of me."

"Thank you." Bradley is distant, as if he's trying to maintain the emotional space between them. He kicks at a small shell near his foot. "The thing is that I made those choices, not you. I can't blame you for decisions I made ..." He hesitates. "Even if

I want to a little bit." He winks. "I waited. Every last weekend of September, I went back to our beach in St. Thomas. I ordered two rum punches. I watched twenty sunsets alone, holding onto the hope that someday you'd come back."

She takes a step closer, her eyes never leaving his face. The fading light catches the flecks of gray in his hair, evidence of the years that have passed between them. "I know you think I'm not the girl you met on that beach out there twenty years ago. In some ways you're right. I lost her in Hollywood. But I found her again this summer."

"And what happens when Hollywood calls again?" Bradley asks, his voice raw. "When the next big role comes along?"

"I don't care about Hollywood anymore," she says fiercely. "I care about being the woman who deserves the kind of love that waits twenty years. The kind of love that orders two drinks for one person, just in case. The kind of love we have."

Bradley's head tilts and his eyes soften. The waves retreat and advance behind them, like the push and pull of their feelings over so many years. He steps forward, closing the distance between them until there's none.

"I chose Duncan for Bella, and admittedly also to feed my actress ego, but my heart's been yours all along, Bradley Heartfield. I was a fool to ever attempt otherwise. I love you, Bradley. I always have."

"Prove it," he whispers, his breath warm against her cheek. "Meet me in St. Thomas. Last weekend of September. Our spot."

"I'll be there," she promises. "I'll be there every September for the rest of our lives."

He reaches out, gently lifting her chin with his fingertips. The heat between them rises, warming her against the evening chill. His lips find her forehead first, then the bridge of her nose, and finally her lips. Her knees weaken at his touch. His lips are soft and warm. He tastes like salt air. He kisses her bottom lip two more times before wrapping his arms around her, drawing her entire being into his embrace. The beach around them—the place where everything began—fades into the background.

"I love you too," he whispers against her hair.

The sun dips below the horizon, setting fire to the clouds above them. Behind them, distant voices call their names, but for this moment, they remain suspended in time—two people who found their way back to each other on the shores of The Hyacinth's beach, exactly where they were always meant to be.

WHILE DINNER FINISHES COOKING, BRADLEY JOINS EV-eryone already gathered on the shore. The sun begins to fall in the sky, the waves lap at their toes, and the bonfire blazes behind them, sending sparks dancing skyward.

Aiden pulls the urn from the bread box. He holds it up to the fiery sunset, takes the lid off, and holds it out to Bradley.

"Are we ready?" Bradley asks.

No, Palmer thinks, seated in an Adirondack chair on the shore. *How can we ever be ready?* She nods at Bradley. "If you feel like it, say a few words and then sprinkle some of the ashes into the sea," she instructs. Meaghan crouches beside her and loops their arms together.

Bradley slides his hand into the urn and brings out a hand-ful of Miles's remains. "Thanks for being the best friend a guy could ever want. Thanks for all the golf games—even when you claimed that impossible shot on the seventh hole, and all the late nights at Foretelina. Thanks for making me family. I love you, brother." He lets the silty silvery ashes slip through his fingers and into the waves, which surge forward as if to claim them.

Meaghan follows. Her fingers tremble as she reaches into the urn. "Thanks for always saving my ass, Miles, and knowing what was best for me even when I didn't." Salt spray mingles with the tears on her cheeks.

Bella dips her hand in and grabs some ashes, standing beside her mother. "We love you, Miles," she says, the breeze lifting her hair as she speaks. "Thank you for all the ice cream at Double Dippers, but most of all for teaching your son how to care for the women in his life." Aiden catches her eye.

Meaghan and Bella let go of their handfuls together.

Still holding the urn, Aiden offers it to Quinn. "I can't! I can't do it!" Quinn says, his voice breaking. He backs away, shoulders hunched, and walks several feet down the beach.

"It's okay, Quinn," Palmer says, standing even though she shouldn't. She rushes to his side. "You don't have to. You really don't. I only want you to be sure you won't regret not saying goodbye here now because we only get to do this once."

Quinn stares at the horizon, jaw clenched, hands balled into fists at his sides. He exhales and gathers himself, shoulders straightening. He walks back to Aiden and grabs a handful of ashes. He stands with his palm closed, "This isn't Dad!"

She joins Quinn and puts her arm around him. "It isn't Dad. It is how we can say goodbye to Dad. Dad will always be with you."

Quinn opens his palm right as a breeze picks up. Ashes swirl into the air, catching the crimson light until the sea reaches up and takes them under. "I love you, Dad."

She watches Aiden stare down at the urn. After Bradley told Aiden the details Miles shared about his internship, their ensuing disagreement, and how foolish he'd felt, she let Aiden read Miles's journal entry. One last conversation with his father rid Aiden of any guilt. Now, she watches Aiden take a handful of Miles's ashes. He walks closer up to waves so that his ankles are submerged. "Thanks for showing me the way, Dad. You're the greatest. I love you." His fingers unfold. "Rest in peace."

Aiden hands her the urn. She takes a handful of ashes, and some splinter across her eternity ring, momentarily obscuring its radiance and coating it in black residue. The grit between her fingers feels nothing like the warmth of Miles's hand.

"Twenty years was too few with you, Miles Harding. I will love you for eternity." She turns to her boys. "From these ashes, we will rise. That's what your father would have wanted." She releases the silty particles into the sea; her eternity ring shines again.

Aiden puts an arm around her, and she rests her head on his shoulder, inhaling the scent of salt and sunscreen that clings to him.

"I remember when you were shorter than me," she tells him, wiping a tear from her cheek. Quinn walks over and does the same. She is flanked by her children once again; she beams.

"Let's eat!" Bradley says, his voice cutting through the emotional haze.

They devour the mussels and steak salad, relaxing in Adirondack chairs and on beach blankets strewn around the bonfire. The food tastes richer somehow, as if grief sharpens their senses. They take turns each telling their favorite Miles story. Hole-in-ones when no one was looking, accidentally falling backwards off the boat with a splash that soaked everyone, hiking the sand dunes and running out of water only to discover the oasis of a convenience store over the next hill.

Afterwards, Bradley pours champagne into five flutes and a sparkling apple cider into hers. The glasses glint in the firelight. Bella breaks out the s'mores platter, busying herself with setting out everyone's plates. Aiden and Quinn race down the beach in search of several long, small sticks perfect for roasting the jumbo-sized marshmallows, their laughter echoing back up the shore.

She catches a glimpse of Meaghan and Bradley sneaking in a kiss, beside the fire, his hand tenderly cupping her face. Moments later, everyone encircles the flames. They raise their glasses.

Bradley cheers, "To Miles!" And everyone repeats together, "To Miles!"

They sip champagne and build triple-stacked smores. She watches everyone, laughing, talking, eating. She recalls what she asked Miles that first evening Meaghan and Bradley met, when she'd caught them kissing in front of the bonfire. *What if we all stayed here, together?*

Post-s'mores with chocolate-stained faces and sticky fingers, the kids dig out several boxes of sparklers from the canvas beach tote Meaghan brought down from the house. They hand them out. Everyone gets three wands, and they light them off each other's. The night air fills with shimmering twinkles of white, blue, and red. Bella dances hers around the fire. The boys write bad jokes in the air. Meaghan and Bradley share a blanket as a cool breeze comes off the ocean, together drawing the outline of their new restaurant in the sky. The sun says its final goodbye for the evening, falling far below the water's edge, leaving behind a dusting of early stars. Palmer watches, admiring her family—broken, healing, growing. She cradles her belly with her hand, letting go of one life and holding onto a new one.

Beach Bonfire Sup(p)er Bites

Open Flame Steamed Mussels

Ingredients

- 4 pounds mussels, scrubbed
- 1 pound mild Italian sausage
- 3 cloves garlic, minced
- 1 shallot, minced
- 2/3 cup olive oil
- 6 tablespoons butter
- 2 cups dry white wine
- 1/4 cup basil
- 1/4 cup pecorino romano cheese, grated
- salt & pepper to taste

Scrub and clean the mussels, set aside.

In a large dutch oven, saute the Italian sausage, crumbled into small pieces. Once browned, put into a bowl and set aside. Toss the garlic, shallot and olive oil into the dutch oven. Saute 2 minutes. Add the butter and simmer 3 more minutes. Deglaze the pan with the white wine, removing from the bottom any brown sausage bits. This can be done ahead of time and stored in the refrigerator until the bonfire is ready.

Reheat the duth oven and broth over the bonfire. Once simmering, add the mussels. Cover and steam until the mussels open. Sprinkle with basil, cheese and salt & pepper. Serve immediately.

Grilled Flank Steak Salad

Ingredients

- 2 lbs flank steak
- 2 heads bib lettuce
- 4 oz blue cheese crumbles
- 1/2 cup buttermilk
- 1/2 cup sour cream
- 1/4 cup mayonnaise
- 2 teaspoons chives
- 2 teaspoons basil
- 1 small garlic clove
- 1 half lemon squeezed

Marinate the flank steak in olive oil, salt and pepper for several hours.

Tear the bib lettuce into salad leaves in a bowl. Prepare a homemade buttermilk dressing by combining the buttermilk, sour cream, mayonnaise, chives, basil, garlic and lemon juice.

Over the open flame, grill the flank steak 4 minutes on each side, up to 7 minutes if you'd like well done. Let set for 5 minutes. Slice the steak against the grain into strips. Top the lettuce with steak, blue cheese and dressing.

Ultimate S'mores

Ingredients

- honey graham crackers
- Hershey's chocolate bars
- Jet-Puffed giant marshmellows

You know what to do. Jet-puffed giant marshmellows are the secret ingredient to make them the ultimate.

Additional Notes

Makes any summer evening unforgettable. Bring your favorite people, a cooler, beach blankets and sparklers. May cause kissing.

The End

Want to Stay in Cape Henlopen a Little Longer?

The charm, secrets, and seaside romance continue—and the holidays are coming!

In *Christmas Confessions*, glittering lights and festive cocktails arrive in Cape Henlopen alongside a dangerously charming investigative journalist asking exactly the wrong questions.

Lila Montgomery's chic coastal inn looks as perfectly curated as her life, but behind the holiday parties and twinkling décor, she's hiding a secret identity that could destroy everything. Dr. Elizabeth "Tibby" Harlow fled Manhattan carrying a devastating secret she's never spoken aloud. Cape Henlopen gave her a second chance at life, but not necessarily at forgiveness.

As Christmas sweeps through town, long-buried truths begin to surface.

Readers love this novel for secret identities, second-chance romance, strong female friendships, and slow-burn love set against a cozy holiday backdrop—plus festive recipes, including the fan-favorite Boozy Christmas Rum Cake.

Many readers start with *Beach House Confessions* and return to Cape Henlopen for the holidays.

🎄 **Continue the Seaside Secrets Beach Read Series with *Christmas Confessions.***

**Three buried secrets. Two best friends.
One dangerously charming journalist determined
to expose them all.**

Secret identities, second-chance romance, and uplifting
women's fiction set in a festive coastal town.
Perfect for fans of Christina Lauren's In a Holidaze
& Elin Hilderbrand's Winter Street Series

Available on Kindle, Audible & Paperback

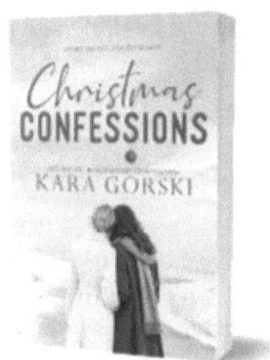

CHRISTMAS
Confessions

CHAPTER 1

The Proposal

December 16

LILA MONTGOMERY NEVER MEANT TO LIVE A DOUBLE LIFE;
somehow it just happened.

She stands in the Salt & Hearth kitchen, pouring two
glasses of Veuve Clicquot for Mr. and Mrs. Jenkins, who are
celebrating their forty-fifth wedding anniversary, when Nate
swoops up behind her, clutching her waist and sweetly inhaling the scent of her hair. Nate's culinary team and the bistro's
waitstaff bounce to Michael Bublé's "White Christmas" as they
prepare, plate, and serve. Nate sways, bringing Lila with him.
Her shoulders soften. *Nate. He feels like home.*

All at once, he spins her into the restaurant freezer, nearly missing the Christmas tree decorated with kitchen utensils standing at the freezer's edge, and closes the door. He traces her neck with kisses and pauses at her ear. "I have something to ask you," he whispers.

Her heart races. "Okay." She tries to catch his gaze, but he traces the other side of her neck. "Ask me."

He stops, shaking his head. "Nope. Tonight!" He winks, kisses her once more on her lips, and disappears back into the rush of his kitchen.

Tonight! Her lips curve upward in anticipation. She brings the Jenkins champagne to Table 15, then makes her way through the cozy bistro to the foyer reception, ready to greet the last guests checking in, glowing with the persistent warmth of Christmas lights left on all night. After five years together—two in New York City and three on Cape Henlopen, working together to transform the crumbling beach house her grandmother left her into a chic coastal retreat called the Sandpiper House—Nate is going to propose.

One Last Confession...

The summer may be over, but not every truth has been told.

As a thank you for reading *Beach House Confessions*, you're invited to download an exclusive deleted scene—the night before Palmer arrived at the beach house.

Once this confession lands in your inbox, you'll also receive The Styled Draft: Insider Edition—where I share behind-the-scenes details, story inspirations, and early news about upcoming books.

You can also find bonus content and series updates at karagorskibooks.com.

Unlock Palmer's confession here →

Thank you for reading — and for spending a scandalous summer at the beach house with me.

Kara Gorski

Here, the next chapter is always waiting.